WHAT LIES IN SHADOW

TINA WAINSCOTT

St. Martin's Paperbacks

This is a work of fiction. All of the characters, organizations, and events portrayed in this novel are either products of the author's imagination or are used fictitiously.

WHAT LIES IN SHADOW

Copyright © 2008 by Tina Wainscott.

ISBN: 0-312-94164-1
EAN: 978-0-312-94164-2

Printed in the United States of America

St. Martin's Paperbacks edition / February 2008

St. Martin's Paperbacks are published by St. Martin's Press, 175 Fifth Avenue, New York, NY 10010.

10 9 8 7 6 5 4 3 2 1

BACK IN BABY'S ARMS

"The whiff of paranormal aspects, the passion, and the assorted conflicts within *Back in Baby's Arms* are what make Ms. Wainscott a favorite with both contemporary and paranormal fans."

—*Rendezvous*

"A story of rebirth and renewal. . . . tightly woven, very readable . . . The suspense . . . makes this book a real page-turner."

—*HeartRate*

A TRICK OF THE LIGHT

"Tina Wainscott is back and in a big way. . . . Suspenseful, poignant, and gripping. A great read."

—*Romantic Times*

"An unusual and satisfying romance with a supernatural twist."

—*Publishers Weekly*

"A five-star reading experience to savor . . . unforgettable!"

—*The Belles and Beaux of Romance*

"Ms. Wainscott has done a great job and has written one for your keeper shelf."

—*Old Book Barn Gazette*

"Fans of paranormal romances will feel they are on the way to heaven reading Tina Wainscott's latest winner."

—*Affaire de Coeur*

"Quintessential romantic suspense. Wainscott, an award-winning author, knows how to keep her story moving and the sexual tension flowing . . . a book that will speak to both the primary fear of all parents and the hearts of all readers."

—*Once a Warrior Review*

"Remarkable . . . one of the most touching love stories I've read in a while . . . this is truly a 5-star!"

—*ADC's Five Star Reads*

St. Martin's Paperbacks Titles by
TINA WAINSCOTT

"Ms. Wainscott does a great job. Lots of tension and you're not sure who the killer is."

—*Old Book Barn Gazette*

"WOW! Ms. Wainscott is a suspense reader's dream author. The plot twist that develops halfway threw me for a loop and I loved every minute of it. More twists and turns kept me turning the pages, cursing myself for not being able to read faster."

—*Rendezvous*

UNFORGIVABLE

"Unforgettable, a rich, dark tapestry of good and evil—and the threads that bind them together. Excellent suspense; it literally kept me up all night reading."

—Kay Hooper, author of *Touching Evil*

"A truly great read! Wainscott creates finely honed tension in a first-rate thriller where no one is who they seem and everyone is someone to fear. Don't miss it!"

—Lisa Gardner, *New York Times* bestselling author of *The Third Victim*

"Tina Wainscott kicks off her foray into the suspense genre in a very big way . . . gripping, gritty, and quite terrifying."

—*Romantic Times* (Top Pick)

"How Mary Higgins Clark used to write . . . I will be keeping a sharp eye on this author!"

—Detra Fitch, *Huntress Reviews*

"Tina Wainscott delivers hard-hitting suspense with a touch of romance."

—Megan Kopp, *Romance Reviews Today*

"Ms. Wainscott shows another side of her true talent as a writer . . . [The] suspense . . . grabs the reader from the very beginning and keeps the reader hooked until the very last page."

—*Interludes Reviews*

This book is dedicated to my uncle, David Copestakes, and to my aunt, Sharon Copestakes. My love to you always . . .

When I started the blog, my best friend, Beth, said, "What can one little secret hurt?" Now I knew. My little secret was about to destroy a friendship, my marriage—and very possibly my life.

—JONNA

In the middle of the road to life, I found myself in a dark wood, having strayed from the straight path.

—DANTE, *THE DIVINE COMEDY, INFERNO*

Montene's Diary
Blog entry: November 1, 11:30 p.m.

Dear blog friends,

Tomorrow I'm having a romantic lunch with a man who is not my husband. And the thing is, I am not a cheat. My mother was a cheat, and I despised her for it. I both pitied my father for not seeing it and resented him for not doing anything about it. Her affair was the dirty secret I felt compelled to adopt as my own.

But here I am. A lonely wife. A desperate housewife, if you will. I badly need a connection with another human being. Okay, a male human being.

Those of you who have been here since the beginning of my blog know that Johnny and I dashed from wild chemistry to marriage in three months. Before we had a chance to catch our breath and get to know each other he plunged into his work and I buried myself in mine. We still have the chemistry, but we only talk about surface things—our work, movies, and books—not our pasts, the scars left from childhood, or our dreams. Many of you suspect that Johnny's long hours at the office, dinner meetings, and the invisible wall between us mean he's probably cheating. That thought was too painful to contemplate. Some of you said I should cheat, too, but that thought was too distasteful to contemplate.

Until I learned something that I cannot tell even you, my blog friends. That was the catalyst for me to accept an invitation from someone I've become fond of through my blog.

You and I know him as Dominic. It's just lunch. People have lunch together all the time and no sex comes of it. Just lunch.

What's the worst that can happen?

—Montene

CHAPTER ONE

Bitter cold wind whipped around my long leather coat as I made my way from the T's Haymarket subway station to the restaurant in the North End of Boston where I was meeting a man I knew only as Dominic. A man who knew me only as Montene. We agreed to keep it that way to protect the . . . well, the not quite exactly innocent.

I started Montene's Diary as a safe way to connect to others, to vent my frustrations and ask questions. I adopted a pseudonym, changed any names I used, and kept personal details vague. I liked the blog concept. It was my diary, yet because it was on the Internet, others could comment. But there weren't just a handful of women eager to share stories and advice; there were hundreds! Men, too, like TonyD, who offered me tips on kinky sex that would "bring my hubby around more," and Studly1 (yes, that's his ID), who posts on every blog entry that he could perform acts upon my person to make me forget my husband altogether. Men have proposed sex and marriage and everything in between. Before the blog, I didn't even know there was so much in between.

Then one of *The Boston Globe*'s columnists picked

up on the blog and the fact that I lived in Boston. I wasn't vague enough, I guess: "Who's Montene? She's you, me, and every woman who's unhappy, unsatisfied, and unsure what to do about it."

If my identity were revealed, I would probably lose some of my few clients. My husband, Rush (aka Johnny), would feel betrayed. I have, after all, revealed more of myself to strangers than I have to him. I shared my deepest desires with people who cannot sate them while I was too afraid to voice them to the one man I wanted to sate them. I knew this was screwed up, but I couldn't seem to force my mouth to ask for what I needed.

So this lunch constituted a test. If I can fall in love with someone else, I can't really love my husband. Right?

My eyes watered and the cold stung my cheeks. In Boston's Little Italy, even the aromas of roasting garlic and tomatoes didn't interest my stomach. I loved this area of the city with its quaint restaurants and coffee shops, all saturated in the culture of Italy. None of that charm registered today.

For better or worse I was walking toward Petries, a cozy, dimly lit restaurant. I wondered how many other men and women were there today for reasons of illicit lust. Such allure words like *illicit* and *lust* and *affair* had. If only I could ignore all the other stuff that went along with them, like *guilt* and *self-recrimination*.

For better or worse. Those words echoed rudely in my mind, poking at my conscience. *Cheat, cheat, cheat,* my inner voice called me with each step. But so was Rush.

No, this was not an act of revenge. I needed to do this for myself, to make me feel better. That I couldn't bring myself to confront him said volumes about my marriage. About myself, too. The sad truth was, I had a better rapport with the man I was about to meet than I did with my own husband of a year and a half. Rush was the gorgeous stranger who shared my bed every night and seduced me regularly and wonderfully. And what would Dominic become? A casual flirtation. A dip of my toe into the waters of infidelity.

Less than a block from Petries I slowed to a stop. The sun was wicked bright, the sky wiped clear by the wind. I juggled the bags I'd accumulated, one filled with exotic fruits and another with silk orchids. I pulled out my Blackberry, tugged off my gloves, and used my thumbs to punch in my best friend's phone number. I was trying not to become a Crackberry—a BlackBerry addict—but the all-purpose device with the QWERTY keyboard was hard to resist. I leaned against the sun-warmed window of a pastry shop.

"Beth, tell me again why I'm doing this." I heard the breathlessness and reticence in my voice.

"Getting cold feet?" she asked with a chuckle.

"Cold feet, cold arms, c-cold everything."

"One word, Jonna: Kirsten."

My nemesis. I'd barely met the woman. What I did know was that she was rich, successful, and beautiful in an exotic Angelina-Jolie-I'll-steal-your-husband way. Far beyond my midwestern, middle-class self. Soon after Rush and I had married, I walked into his office and caught them having a discussion. A deep, personal discussion. I saw the body language of people who had been intimately involved—and maybe still were.

Okay, I overreacted. Blame it on my first boyfriend's betrayal when I walked in on something much more incriminating. Rush admitted he and Kirsten had dated but assured me he'd broken it off when he and I met. He even promised to stop working with her since it made me uncomfortable.

To Beth, I said, "You're sure—"

"They're definitely working together. She's messengered stuff over, and I saw her in the lobby. It's very suspicious that he hasn't told you. And there was the thing in the conference room. Don't forget about that."

My mouth tightened into a frown. How could I?

"Jonna, stop playing ostrich and take control of your life. Doesn't it feel good to do something?"

"To do *something,* yes. But this. . . ."

"Women have affairs all the time, for less reasons than you have." Like my mother. "You keep saying you want to be a little wild and crazy. Well, here's your chance. Don't wimp out now."

I wanted to be more like Beth, uninhibited, adventurous . . . fun.

Beth continued in a huskier voice, "And there's nothing like the feeling of meeting someone new, talking to a man you want to have sex with. Knowing you can have him with a crook of your finger."

That was the part of Beth I didn't want to be like. It bothered me how often she fell into bed with some stranger. Fifty-two of them, she'd recently told me, as though it were equal to reaching a weight-loss goal. She teased me because I'd only had sex with two men. Did her brief marriage to a guy who ended up being a stalker ruin her for love?

"Dom's waiting, princess. Don't be the weak link in your own life."

Weak link, her favorite phrase. I glanced down the block at the sign for Petries. "I won't."

"Call me as soon as you're done!" she chirped, and hung up.

I slipped the BlackBerry into my big leather bag and took another breath before moving forward. I was late. A few minutes later I curled my fingers around the ornate door handle. *When I open this door, I will become one of those women, women who cheat.* I have looked askance at such women, those I spotted indulging in a flirtatious lunch or drink with men I knew not to be their husbands.

I hadn't cheated yet. I wasn't sure I could take this to a physical level. To be honest, I wasn't sure I even wanted to. I just needed to flirt with the idea of being with a man who had fallen in love with my thoughts and desires without ever seeing my face. Or, at least, Montene's thoughts and desires. He'd written the magic words: "How could any man ignore a woman as intellectually beautiful, as funny and special, as you are?"

I pulled the door open.

I barely noticed the man who was asking, "Table for one?" My eyes scanned the elegant, white-draped tables for a man with light brown hair that went down to his collar and a red shirt. As I said, "I'm meeting someone," I spotted him. Blue eyes drank me in as he rose from his chair, revealing that he was very tall and that his shirt was partially unbuttoned. Not a speck of chest hair on his smooth, sun-kissed skin. I started toward the table.

The host said, "Ma'am? Your coat?"

I exchanged it for a ticket and then continued toward the table where Dom stood waiting. He had a gym build, wide at the shoulders and narrow at his hips, with perfectly contoured muscles. Closer, I saw the colored contacts that made his eyes so vivid. His boyish smile put me at ease a little.

"Montene," he said, reaching for my hand. When I set down my bags and extended it for a handshake he kissed the back of it instead, keeping his gaze on me. Soft, warm lips lingered against my cold skin, and I smelled cinnamon and citrus cologne.

"Dom," I said in a croaky voice, and cleared my throat. The moment was surreal. I felt excited and ashamed and guilty and adventurous all at once.

His pleased expression screamed, *Sex me, baby*. His perfectly white teeth made me run my tongue over my two front teeth that overlapped slightly. I smiled with my mouth closed as he presented me with a yellow rose.

" 'Soft and romantic, more subtle than red,' " he quoted from my blog.

"My favorite. Thank you." I sat down while he pushed in my chair—something else I had said I liked.

"You're absolutely beautiful," he whispered in my ear, filling the shell with the heat of his breath and his voice, before taking his chair opposite me.

I was terrible about receiving compliments, but I murmured a thank-you as I noticed a glass of wine already waiting for me.

"Annie's Lane Riesling," he said as he lifted his glass. "Cheers."

I touched my glass to his and took a sip, but it wasn't the wine that was tingling uneasily through my veins. It was the one-sided intimacy. He knew so much about me. I'd never met him, and yet he knew my fears, insecurities, preferences, and dreams. I considered my anonymity a cloak, but I felt as though I were sitting at the table naked.

I tried to reconcile the sexy creature across from me with the sensitive e-mails he'd sent. He cried during sad movies but hid it from his dates. He'd never really been in love but wanted to be. He was close to his mother but scarred by a cold, ineffectual father. He hadn't, in fact, shared so much with any other woman as he had with me. He had come to my blog because of the article, curious about learning firsthand how a woman thought and felt, and he'd fallen in love with me—or my persona, anyway. He'd found it easy to open up to me via our private e-mails, something I could relate to. I knew more about him than I did about Rush.

I secretly associated people with certain foods. I'd pictured him like an onion, strongly flavored, with lots of layers. In person he reminded me of a chili pepper, red and hot and spicy.

I was already wondering what I'd write in my blog entry. It was a habit of mine, mentally writing as I went through my day. That's when it hit me: *he'd* be reading everything I wrote about him. On top of the fact that he had an intimate hold on my psyche, I realized my mistake in choosing to meet someone who was part of Montene's world.

That wouldn't be the biggest mistake I made. Not by a long shot.

CHAPTER TWO

Dominic took her in. Lovely, far different from his usual fare of hot-rod women trying desperately to hold on to their last shreds of youth. At first he wondered if he should be offended that she hadn't put on a lot of makeup and jewelry for him, but he figured that was her style. She was fresh. Unaffected. Just growing into her looks at twenty-six, with a creamy complexion and silky, shoulder-length hair. Her eyes were the same chocolate brown as her tresses. Demure, a little nervous, and probably feeling guilty for this, her first transgression. He would delight in easing her into the valley of sin.

"You're nervous," he said with a smile. "Don't be. We're just having lunch, doll."

She released a quick breath. "Right. Exactly. Just lunch."

He took her hand in his. "For now."

He hid a smile as her throat convulsed at those last two words. He let his gaze soak her in . . . lovingly, tenderly, growing steamier as he let it lower to the slight swell of cleavage the deep red sweater revealed. She wasn't dressed for a torrid lunch date. Too bad. But that would change. The way she was looking at him would change, too. Now she looked shy and unsure, fiddling with her spoon, but soon she would be just as hungry as he.

After they ordered, she placed her hands on the linen tablecloth and studied her short, unpolished nails for a moment. Then she raised her eyes to him and smiled nervously when she saw that he was looking at her.

"So," she said on a breath.

"So," he repeated with a smile.

"Here we are."

"Yes." He took her hand again. "I'm honored to be here."

She glanced away from their loosely linked hands as though she found the sight uncomfortable. "There's something exotic about your looks. What's your heritage?"

"I get my looks from my mother. She was adopted, so she never knew her ethnic background."

She often made up one. Middle Eastern for a while, perhaps related to royalty. Then Italian, if that suited her purposes. She especially liked being Egyptian. She changed her name just as frequently, though she'd legally changed it to Paloma. He had always called her Mamu.

"What do you do? For a living? If you can say," she added with a sheepish smile. After all, she hadn't told him what she did.

He gave her a modest smile. "I got money from an inheritance. For fun I tend bar at a private club." He took her questions as promising, as well as the way she kept looking at his mouth when he spoke.

"Really?" she said with a smile, revealing the imperfection of a small overlap between her two front teeth. "I love creating cocktails. It's my special—I mean, it's fun."

"Your *specialty*?" He cocked an eyebrow. "What do you do, Montene?"

"Let's just say I help organize parties." She gave him

a sweet smile, this time closing her mouth. He wondered why, with her husband's money, she didn't get her flawed teeth fixed.

He knew from her posts that the so-called Johnny was thirty, that he wasn't stingy where she was concerned, and that their sex life wasn't lacking. The deficit was in the sharing of feelings, hopes, and dreams, which was more important to her than the money and sex. That had shaped his strategy when he first approached her.

Their food came, a bowl of minestrone for her, gnocchi for him.

He picked up his fork but paused. "All those women on the blog urging you to have an affair . . . you've been resistant up until now. You going to tell me what changed your mind?"

She took a sip of wine. "Not yet."

He nodded his acceptance of her non-answer.

As they ate and talked, he could tell that she was different from any man-hungry married woman he'd ever met. She wasn't primping or rubbing his leg with her bare toes. She wasn't dropping hints about where they might go after lunch. Montene was genuinely torn about being with him. That would make winning her over more of a challenge. And ultimately more satisfying.

When her BlackBerry rang, she reached for her bag and pulled it out. "Sorry, I'm expecting an important call." She looked at the number on the display and rolled her eyes. "That's not it."

He smiled. "A friend dying to find out how lunch is going?"

Her cheeks pinkened. "Probably."

"Go ahead." He nodded for her to take it privately.

She dropped the phone into her bag. "She can wait."

He liked her honesty. "I'll bet she's hovering nearby, making sure you're all right."

"Right again."

When the BlackBerry rang again, she frowned at the screen. "I have to take this one."

She walked away from the table as she answered. Sweet figure, probably worked out just enough to tone. He imagined her hot and sweaty and breathing hard, but it wasn't an exercise bike she was riding. The call had her marching toward the entrance.

He reached beneath his chair and pulled out a package that he deposited into one of her bags. Her purse was tucked between the bags. She was looking through the glass door, finger clamped between her front teeth. He slid his hand into the depths of her purse and found her wallet. He pulled it onto his lap and opened it. Looked at her driver's license; she was smiling obediently and probably hoping for a decent picture. It was. As he'd learned to do long ago, he deftly pulled several bills from her wallet before he closed it and dropped it back into her purse.

She exchanged the ticket for her coat and wrestled her way into it as she headed over. Her face was flushed. "I have to go. My friend told me my husband is out there."

She started to pull out her wallet, but he stilled her arm.

"It's my pleasure. I hope I'll have it again."

"Thanks." She brushed her hair from her face. "I'm sorry. E-mail me," she said as she grabbed her bags. She was gone without even a backward glance.

But she would be back. He smiled. Yes, Jonna Karakosta would be back. Soon he would have her just where he wanted her.

CHAPTER THREE

My heart kicked into overdrive the moment Beth's urgent voice said, "Rush is outside!"

"You're kidding." But I knew she wouldn't do such a thing. "What is he doing here?"

"No idea."

"Where is he?"

"About four storefronts down, pacing."

"Pacing?" That didn't sound good.

"Possibly talking on his cell phone."

"Okay, gotta go. I'm going to see why he's here."

After saying good-bye to Dom, I stepped outside and took a deep, calming breath. Except that the cold air froze my lungs, so it wasn't calming at all. I coughed as I searched in both directions. When I spotted Rush, I pasted on a happily surprised face and headed over.

He looked even taller than his six-foot-one frame in his long black coat, reminding me of Keanu Reeves in *The Matrix*. I'd watched the movie four times, and Keanu in his coat was the reason. Rush was indeed on his cell phone, pacing on the sunshine edge of the shadow that the building cast on the sidewalk. I needed to know if he'd seen me with Dom and, more precisely, why he was there, which happened to be nowhere near Back

Bay, where his office was. I pulled my cashmere cap over my head, though my hair still whipped crazily about my face.

He watched me approach, a trace of surprise in his expression. Was the hardness in his dark green eyes because of his call? Or seeing Dom and me?

"Set it up," Rush said to someone on the phone. "Okay, get back to me on the time."

Rush was no less gorgeous than Dominic, and even better, his looks weren't polished. His thick eyebrows had a square arch shape instead of Dominic's perfect—and probably trimmed—arch. Rush's dark blond hair had a slight wave to it that he tried to tame by drying straight, but that was as much preening as he did. He once admitted he thought his nose was too small and that he'd asked his brother to break it so it would be more interesting. Fortunately, he'd declined.

"Fancy meeting you here," I said, forcing a smile. My stomach quivered, ready for a confrontation, an accusation. The logical part of my brain knew that Dom and I hadn't looked overtly provocative, but if Rush had watched us for any length of time, he would have figured out it wasn't a business lunch. "What are you doing in this part of town?"

"You remember DEMCO, the company with the shipping comparison software? Sturdivant Technologies is looking at it for a possible acquisition, so they can integrate DEMCO's software with their shipping system. A few of the angels are getting together this afternoon at O'Shea's to bang out strategies with DEMCO'S CEO, Mike Patterson." He nodded toward the cigar shop. "I'm bringing the cigars. Heaven has the best in the city."

"That's wonderful," I said, meaning it. I knew what a possible acquisition meant for everyone involved.

It was odd, telling people that my husband was an angel. I then had to go on to explain that Rush co-owned

AngelForce, a company that organized private investors' funds to grow early-stage technology companies.

Back in college, Rush had put together a company that developed an advanced type of GPS tracking software and discovered how hard it was to get early-stage funding. His roommate, Hadden St. Germain, came from a wealthy Boston family and had a background in venture capitalism. He gave Rush the funding but had no experience to share. Money, it turned out, wasn't enough; he needed guidance, too. Then Rush discovered angel investing, where investors, known as angels, not only injected their pooled money into entrepreneurs' dreams but also mentored them.

After Rush sold his company, he shifted his focus to the investment side and teamed up with Hadden. AngelForce vetted prospective companies and undertook due diligence, where they researched the viability of the company's product or technology. They also provided marketing and accounting services to start-ups. As some angels did, Rush joined DEMCO's board, having already gone through the process of selling his company, so he had a personal stake in its success.

I knew he was pleased, but even so, his smile was forced, too. It occurred to me that maybe he was meeting Kirsten and I'd thrown *him* off. That annoyed and hurt me, though I had no right to feel that way after meeting Dominic.

Rush peered into my shopping bags. "Dinner?"

My bag was bursting with fruit: papayas, with their rich, peachy flesh that would contrast beautifully with the green kiwis and yellow star fruit; rods of raw sugarcane; and the odd fruits that had not only caught my eye but Rush's as well. I pulled the fruits that looked like hairy red balls out of the plastic bag. "Aren't they cool? These are rambutans, from Asia. For the 'Winter in the Tropics' party I'm doing this weekend."

He eyed the fruit as his long fingers grazed the springy "hairs." I love Rush's hands; they're like the rest of him, long and lean and strong. Normally I loved sharing my passion for food with him, but this exchange was killing me. Had he seen me having lunch with Dom? Had he, had he, had he?

"I was meeting a potential client," I said, nodding toward Petries. I hoped Rush didn't notice the absence of my portfolio.

"Get the job?" he asked.

"I . . . don't know. H-he'll let me know." Stuttering, stumbling over my words. I loathed lying. How did my mother handle all of her lies? Did she feel this overwhelming sense of guilt and self-degradation?

As he put the fruit back in my bag, he eyed me with a raised eyebrow. "Do you have to dress up for this party?"

I followed his gaze to a silver bag tucked between the *carambolas* and the yellow mangoes. The red script announced for all to see: "House of Pleasure," the name of a shop that sold racy lingerie, among other things. I felt my face flame and my mouth go dry as my mind scrambled to figure out where the bag had come from. "No, of course not. That's for later. For you," I added too quickly. "I mean, for me to wear, but for you to . . . see. It was supposed to be a surprise."

He took hold of my chin and tilted my face up. I was ready for anything—accusations, questions—but he simply said, "I look forward to seeing it on you tonight." He looked into my eyes as he said it, and I felt my insides quiver. Then he leaned down and kissed me, his gaze on me while he did so.

My legs wobbled when he walked into the cigar shop. He reminded me of a pomegranate: smooth and richly colored on the outside, not so easy to manage on the inside. My BlackBerry rang; I knew who it would be and answered with, "Be right there."

"Must have information!"

I disconnected and headed toward the Java Café. As I passed Petries, I looked in. The table where Dom and I sat was empty now, our dishes still cluttering the table-top. I pushed on, looking around for him or Rush. I saw neither.

The Java Café was decorated in every shade of coffee. The floors were espresso, the walls café au lait. I spotted Beth at the table that was next to the large glass window, the sun lighting up her strawberries-and-cream hair (the only description of her milky red hair she'd accept). She'd probably picked the location for that reason. Sometimes sweet and demure, other times naughty and bawdy, she was a contradiction that made our friendship vibrant. Her sea green eyes, meticulously outlined in gray eyeliner, were as wide as her coffee mug. The natural red stain on her white skin was brighter than normal, flushed with excitement over my drama.

I held up my finger to tell her to wait as I dashed to the counter and ordered a frappe—what they call milk shakes in the Northeast. Yes, the cold kind, and in the winter yet. It was strange, but I craved frappes as soon as it got chilly. Armed with a mocha frappe, I zipped over to the table where Beth's annoyed expression morphed to eagerness again.

"What'd he say? Oh, my *gawd,* I couldn't believe it when I saw him walk past the restaurant! I mean, how wicked crazy is that?"

"He *said* he was getting cigars at Heaven." I took a long pull on my thin, frothy frappe.

"Maybe he was. I've heard they have the best in the city."

I felt a modicum of relief at that. Maybe he was telling the truth. "Did he look inside the restaurant?"

"He paused, like he was reading the menu in the

window. Did he say anything about you and Dom? Do you think he saw you?"

"He didn't mention it, but I diffused the situation by saying I was meeting a prospective client. It wasn't as though Dom and I were groping each other."

"Darn for that, but good thing. Who would have thought, of all people, that Rush would be in the area?"

"Maybe it's a sign. I mean, the first time I've ever done anything like this, and my husband shows up."

"Dumb luck," Beth said, waving it away. "And it's not as though he can really object."

"He didn't ask about my supposed client. If he'd seen me, or suspected anything, he would have, wouldn't he? Trying to trip me up. At the least he might have teased me about having lunch with another man, you know, the sort of fishing type of teasing."

"See, no problem. It was just a freaky coincidence. So, how did it go?"

I relaxed for the first time in over an hour, my fingers tracing the brown mosaic tiles embedded in the tabletop. A smile even crept across my face. "I felt like a naughty girl, which was exciting all by itself. I felt nervous, giddy." My smile faded. "I felt awful. I don't know how people can cheat."

"Remember what Rush is doing. My God, Jonna, he came on to your best friend! What kind of man does that?"

"Well, he didn't exactly *come on* to you."

"No, he's not that stupid. He was feeling me out, figuratively speaking, testing my loyalty to you. Which, of course, is rock solid. He called me in, asked me to sit down next to him, and touched my hand. Like this." She placed her pale hand on mine. I stared at the orange freckles she tried to bleach into oblivion. "But it was the way he was looking at me. Hungrily. Questioningly." She gave me just such a look. "I've seen that look plenty of times; I know it. He asked how I was doing, if I was seeing anyone, making it sound casual. I pulled away, said I had a lot of work to do. What does it sound like to you?"

"Odd," I had to admit. Still, I had trouble imagining Rush being so slimy.

"I subtly let him know I wasn't interested, and he seemed to respect that. Only now it looks like he moved on to someone else."

My stomach clenched painfully and I took a long, cold sip of my frappe. "I appreciate your loyalty."

Beth leaned over and hugged me. She smelled soft and sweet, but her body was all hard angles. Even her breasts were suspiciously firm. "I was afraid to tell you for a while. I thought maybe it was just my imagination or he was having a weird day or something. At thirty he's too young to be having a midlife crisis. Even worse, I was worried you'd think *I* was coming on to *him*. But when Kirsten started coming around again, I had to say something. I love you like a sister, Jonna. I don't want you hurt. Dominic is just what you need right now. Someone to boost your shattered ego and maybe even give you the impetus to leave Rush. I know you crave stability, but needing it is a weak link. It's exciting to have your options open. It's about being spontaneous, free."

Beth and I had met at the hotel where we both worked at the time. We'd been having an after-work drink in the bar when Rush had walked in, so she'd been through the whole relationship with me. Apart from teasing that she'd seen him first, she'd been supportive. She'd been my confidante when I'd worried Rush and I were moving too fast, even though I ignored her advice to slow down.

She was the only person who knew about my blog. Most of the time I was glad she knew. She was my sounding board, and she had fun with it, too. Every now and then, though, I wondered: what would happen if she and I ever had a falling-out?

"It's a good thing I work with Rush," she said. "I can let you know what's going on."

"Doesn't it make you feel funny, being in the middle?"

"I consider my job and our friendship completely separate." She rubbed at her lacquered nail. "You didn't tell Dom why you finally had the guts to see him, did you? I wouldn't want him posting that on the comment board."

"I played coy about it."

Beth had made me promise not to post about Rush's advance and affair.

"Just in case it ever comes out that you're Montene," Beth reminded me. "I don't want to get fired. I love working at AngelForce."

Beth had been miserable at her last job, so when a secretarial opening came up at AngelForce I lobbied for her. She'd long been wanting to work in what she called the Dream Factory. She was secretary to the marketing director and the research assistant. Rush assured me that Beth did a good job, but I could tell he wasn't thrilled about her being there. He'd quasi chided me about having a watchdog looking after him. Now I wondered if he'd changed his mind about her.

I pulled out the silver bag, and Beth's eyes lit up. "Ooh, House of Pleasure! Who is this for? Dom, maybe?" she said, pulling out pink crotchless panties and making them dance.

I wasn't smiling. "Dom must have slipped this into my bag during lunch. Rush saw it when I was showing him my fruit." Beth raised an eyebrow at that, and I tapped my bag with my toe. "I was all nervous, babbling about what I'd bought at the market, and there the bag was. He knew what was in it. He, of course, thought I'd bought it for him."

"Dom, you bad boy, you. How incredibly sexy and roguish!"

I didn't share her enthusiasm. "It's because of the blog. Remember the whole vibrator discussion that turned into the kinky lingerie discussion? I said I'd never wear crotchless panties. There'd be too much . . . air." Beth pulled out a matching shelf bra that left the breasts bared. Delicate lace trimmed the elastic bands. I felt a funny twist in my stomach. "Don't you think it's a little . . . forward? I mean, we only had lunch."

"It was a date. Don't kid yourself."

"But it doesn't jive with the guy I've been corresponding with these last few weeks. He comes across as a respectful, sensitive guy and then brings me this."

She was inspecting the tags. "Just because he's sensitive doesn't mean he can't have a sexy streak. Maybe he's inexperienced and doesn't know what's appropriate. He spent some bucks on you. I know this brand."

"You would," I said, snatching the underwear from her and stuffing it back into the bag. "People are looking."

"Loosen up. Give 'em something to talk about." She flashed a smile at a man sitting nearby, then whispered, "He's been flirting with me ever since I got here."

Everywhere we went someone was flirting with her, or at least that's what she wanted to believe. She seemed to need men's attention and sometimes interpreted innocent gestures as come-ons. Beneath her well-fed ego I caught glimpses of an insecure girl, like the way she criticized beautiful women, claws out and gleaming. Even better than being classically beautiful, she had a unique beauty that she ended up obliterating in her attempts to fit the mold. She wore flats to disguise her height, used a cinnamon lip gloss that burned her lips into plumpness, and used makeup to round out her narrow face.

Her voracious shopping habits also made me wonder. Weekly manicures, creams, and face products were her biggest weaknesses. They worried me more because whenever I brought it up, she brushed the issue aside.

Beth took a bottle out of her purse and rubbed some of that expensive lotion on her hands. The cloying scent of gardenias even overwhelmed the coffee aroma. "So what did you think of Dom? Was he sexy? I glanced in as I walked by, but I couldn't really see him." She took my hand and squirted a blue puddle on my palm.

"He's . . . yes, sexy. Charming. I liked the way he really looked at me when I talked. Like he cared. I felt as though we were communicating." Every time Rush and I started to delve into deeper subjects, our discussion turned to lovemaking.

"So, you're going to see him again?"

"Maybe. Just for lunch."

Beth grinned. "Not ready for the sleazy hotel yet?"

"I've got to go, get my fruit in the cooler." I pulled on my coat. "Oh, and I'm afraid I'm going to have to postpone our manicure lunch Monday."

Beth frowned. "Jonna, this is the second time in a row."

"I know, and I'm sorry. One of Rush's associates, a venture capitalist, wants to discuss a dinner party he and his wife are throwing. Of course, he had to pick that particular time." I tilted my head to show her how much I regretted doing this. "Not only is it someone important to Rush—they pitch the entrepreneur's company to him when they need the big bucks—I need the business."

"Well, you don't really. Your husband is rich, remember?"

At times I detected a hint of bitterness when she said things like that, but her smile said otherwise. "That's *his* money. I want my own career." I reached out and squeezed her shoulder. "I've lost most of my other friends, trying to build my business. I don't want to lose you."

Beth smiled wanly. "It's a good thing I love you so much." She stood and pecked me on the cheek. "Friday?"

"Definitely."

I walked out with my bags and headed toward the nearest T station. While waiting for the crosswalk light, I glanced behind me, wondering if Rush was still around. I saw Dom instead, loitering outside the shop windows on the next block. When he glanced up, I looked away. Why was he still hanging around? The Walk sign beckoned, and I joined the surge of people crossing. When I looked back again he was gone.

CHAPTER FOUR

Blog entry: November 2, 9:30 p.m.

Blog friends, yes, I know, I know, you're anxious to find out
how it went. You don't have to hound me. I had to think about
what to say. Meeting someone on this blog makes it rather, er,
awkward. I can say this: Dom was sexy and charming. Will I
see him again? Probably, but on a casual—I hesitate to use the
word *date*—basis.

Those of you who have posted about the woes of cheating . . . three words: *Oh. My. God.* The guilt is terrible, and I
haven't technically done anything yet. Some of you warned
me about regret. I can see it now, like a massive storm hovering on the horizon.

A note to Dom: I'm hoping the "gift" was a joke, in refer-
ence to the heated discussion we had a few weeks ago about
crotchless panties. A bit over-the-top, don't you think? I hope
you're teasing rather than being presumptuous. At least you
didn't slip a vibrator into my bag! My husband happened to
spot the silver bag among my produce. Natch I had to explain,
ruefully, that the outfit was for him. I'm hoping he forgets
about it. Please let him forget.

Then again, he might remember precisely because he was
so surprised to find such a thing in my possession. He doesn't

know about my reluctance to don overtly kinky wear. And, in fact, I don't know how he feels about such things, either, though he was clearly intrigued.

Good night, all.

—Montene

I reluctantly pulled my attention away from the computer and looked at the folders on my desk, which sat in the open platform of the loft. In the months since I started my blog it had become something of an obsession, at times to the detriment of my work. I focused on the notes for my next assignment, a beach-themed party for Big Brothers Big Sisters I was doing at cost. In the ten months since I'd started JEvents, I'd done two gratis events for charities. I loved the feeling of giving something back.

Beginning a new assignment, however, always made me nervous. Would it live up to my growing reputation? To their expectations? To mine?

I'd always loved organizing events and parties and, in fact, did that at the hotel. AngelForce hosted a monthly dinner meeting where angel members reviewed previous investments and entrepreneurs pitched their ideas. It was natural to take over organizing the meeting and fun to make it a real event with different themes each month. One of the members asked if I could create a dinner party for her husband's birthday. Then another phoned.

Rush encouraged me to quit my job and start my own company. I think it alleviated a lot of guilt for him. Between AngelForce, consulting with the company that bought his technology, and mentoring entrepreneurs he had funded, he usually worked late and sometimes on the weekends. Though he always called just to say hello, I needed more than that to fulfill my empty evenings. So I welcomed the opportunity to keep busy.

JEvents was building slowly but steadily. I refused to take Rush's money for my business. It was bad enough that he was paying the household expenses. I felt a need to prove myself, which brought out all those feelings from childhood when I longed for my parents' approval.

Despite my nervousness, I loved the planning stages. I loved finding the perfect vegetable for an accent table and when an idea for a prop came out just as I'd planned. I loved coming up with a drink especially for each event. For the kids I'd created a slushy drink called the Blue Whale. I still had a few other things to figure out, but my mind wouldn't focus. I sang along to an old Janet Jackson song on the stereo and wondered if I should obliterate the lingering scent of garlic from the spinach frittata I'd made for dinner. What I really wanted to do was check my e-mail.

"Weak woman," I chastised as I scanned offers to enlarge my penis, job quotes, a joke Beth had sent, and one from Dom. He'd written one sentence:

Can't wait to see you again.

I felt a tremor of excitement and guilt. Guilt won out, and I deleted it. Back to work.

I'd no more had ten minutes to sift through the quotes before the phone rang. When I heard Rush's voice, my heart tripped.

"I'll be home in fifteen minutes," he said in a deep voice. "I'm looking forward to seeing your new outfit."

Rush rarely came home this early. Though he'd never been shy about his desires, he'd never been quite so authoritative about it. Then again, maybe he was expecting me to be eager to show him my new . . . outfit.

Oh, jeez. I robotically walked into the bedroom, past the bed on the raised platform, to the sleek black dresser where I'd tucked the damned thing way in the back of my lingerie drawer. I'd nearly thrown it out but decided against it.

The *thing* was like honeymoon attire, both virginal and slutty. My heart thumped in my chest as I stripped out of my clothing. My reflection looked back at me, reminding me that I'd better pretend I was into wearing this sort of thing. Or at least that it was my idea to buy it.

Getting into the panties was a challenge. First I had them upside down and then sideways, having no material to guide me. When I thought I had both pieces on right, I looked in the mirror.

"Oh, jeez." My breasts jutted out, framed by scalloped lace and elastic that made my skin itch. My pubic hair was also framed thus, and I felt the cool air sweep up into my private parts. *Be Montene,* I told myself. *Be that flirty, audacious woman you've discovered inside yourself.*

I walked to the platform that looked over the living room and front door and leaned against the metal railing. The concrete ceilings and pipes snaking along the walls lent the loft the industrial feel of the factory the building had been before being converted into twelve lofts. Rush had it professionally decorated just before we met. I wasn't crazy about the minimalist decor, but even though he'd encouraged me to add my touch, I felt funny messing with it. I'd placed a couple of framed pictures from our honeymoon at his beach cottage in Beverly, Massachusetts, on the stainless-steel media console and a vase of silk orchids on the small coffee table.

I returned to the bedroom. When I heard the front door close a few minutes later, my heart tripped again. So much for that confident woman. I had found that part of myself, but I wasn't exactly comfortable with her yet. The vibrator episode had proven that.

The girls on my blog, my "blog friends," suggested

I get a vibrator. I gathered from their comments that it wasn't so much a way to pleasure themselves as a way of getting secret revenge on their husbands as in, *If you can't satisfy me, I'll get it elsewhere. Nyah nyah.* I caved to peer pressure and curiosity and ordered the Randy Rabbit, as Kitty128 and Beth had suggested. They even named their vibrators: "Ralph, the Rocket," and "Russell Crowe."

It took me a week to open the package. Another week to take it out, feel its texture. Gawd, it was big. I considered my husband well endowed, but the Rabbit—I hadn't named it—was huge. It had a rotating jelly tip, pearls, and a little appendage shaped like a rabbit for clitoral stimulation. It was purple. The damned thing had a microchip!

I'd only gathered the courage to run it across my legs and feet. It sounded as loud as a tractor, and I was sure the neighbors would know what I was up to. I knew these things weren't illegal or necessarily immoral, but I couldn't get past my prim, wholesome upbringing. I'd sort of fudged on my blog, telling everyone how wonderful it was. I was too embarrassed to admit that I hadn't worked up the nerve to use it as it was intended.

And there I was standing in front of the dresser mirror looking like a tart.

I turned to the door and caught Rush watching me with a smoldering fire in his eyes. "Montene, Montene," I chanted under my breath. Sexy, crazy Montene. I tilted my head and ran my finger along the stretch of lace at my breast. I saw the muscles in his jaw tighten. He approached me slowly, like a tiger, sizing me up as though I were prey. He took a handful of my hair and tilted my head back, kissing me hard. I could feel the silkiness of his black trousers against my bare legs, the crispness of his white shirt on my belly.

His hands possessed me, running roughly over my

skin, gripping my waist, pulling me hard against his erection. It was as though he were possessing me, claiming my body as his. It sparked something primal in me, and I matched his fervor, tearing at his buttons and pushing off his shirt. He twisted the lacy strings of my bra and tore them. As he flung the ruined piece on the floor and pushed me back onto the bed, I wondered: What had gotten into my husband? Did I like it . . . or was I afraid of it?

CHAPTER FIVE

Blog entry: November 6, 11:12 a.m.

VENT ALERT! Sometimes I really hate men. Not all of them. But some of them. I met with a prospective client yesterday, one who happens to be an associate of my husband's. I thought it was odd that he came without his wife. I wasted an hour going over options and variables, my pitch as it were. He tells me about all the times he'll need my services (yes, I know it sounds as though I'm a hooker, but I swear I'm not). In other words, he's dangling the carrot. Needing the business, I'm excited about that. Apparently he's excited in a different way.

He slides his hand up my thigh and says, "You're a beautiful woman." I'm not beautiful and I don't dress provocatively. I thank him and move away. His hand stays. In fact, it inches higher yet. "I'm an important asset to your husband's company. I could be important to you, too." My stomach rolls in disgust. "What is it that you're saying?" I ask outright. Maybe I'm misinterpreting the words, though the hand on my thigh is pretty damn clear. "I've got an apartment my wife doesn't know about." And to make absolutely sure I get the point, he adds, "The bed is incredibly soft."

I feel like throwing up on him. I'm so pissed my face is flushed and my fingers are chewing into my palms. "Are you saying that if I want your business—and perhaps if my husband needs your assistance in the future—I have to screw you?"

He smiles in a "smart girl, you've got it now" way. "You'll like me, honey. I promise."

I find that hard to believe. He's shaped like a green pepper with a comb-over. I stand, and he stands and smiles, obviously thinking I'm agreeing. I reach into my purse, pull out a five-dollar bill, and hand it to him. He looks at it, then at me. "What's this for?"

"The hooker you obviously want."

And I leave. Shaking, muttering, and then, in the privacy of my car, screaming. The thing is, I know his proposal wasn't about me. It was about power, about moving into my husband's territory. Like dogs peeing to mark their territory. Then it hits me: he was trying to pee on me!

I'm wondering if I should mention it to Johnny. If he knew what a letch the guy is, he might cut him loose, and unfortunately, the letch is sometimes involved in my husband's business dealings. Just because I lost a potential client doesn't mean he has to lose, too. So I think I'll keep it to myself.

On a brighter note, I had coffee with Dominic this morning. He's wonderfully romantic and a great listener. What I like about him most is that he shares with me. His childhood. His favorite book. I feel like I know him. I hadn't realized how much I needed a connection with someone. He's almost too good to be real. As I've told him, I'm still not sure how far I want to take this.

What do I want? I want a happy marriage. I do. Can someone tell me what that is?

—Montene

I walked the fine edge in what I revealed on my blog, just enough but not too much. Like the letch, many of my clients came from the dinner meetings I arranged for AngelForce; therefore, Rush knew them personally. The letch wasn't the first who had tried to get appetizers that had nothing to do with food. I'd concealed these advances from Rush. I didn't want to rock his boat, and I hated to admit it, but a small part of me was afraid he'd wonder if I'd done something to invite them.

More secrets I kept from my husband.

I sat in the lobby at AngelForce that afternoon, waiting for Rush. He'd called and said, "Have lunch with me." The directive gave me the same little shiver of pleasure his order to be waiting in my new outfit had. Not the outfit part, but the ordering part. Through my blog and subsequent discussions, I'd discovered something about myself: I kind of liked being ordered about. Not on an everyday basis, but in a sexual way. I'd object if Rush shoved me to my knees and ordered me to give him oral sex, for instance, but subtle orders did turn me on a little.

Priscilla, the demure woman at the reception desk, handed me a note he'd written that bore a sad face and read: "Babe, Sorry, hung up on a call! Be out soon. XOXO." It touched me and made me smile.

"Can I get you a water? Tonic? Coffee?" she asked

"No, thanks, I'm fine."

The lobby felt more like a living room, with warm colors, wood flooring, and even a fireplace that was roaring with a fire. Indirect lighting and rounded furniture lent the area softness, and the cushy leather sofa made waiting easier.

When Beth rounded the corner, she looked as though she'd walked into a glass window. "What are you doing here?"

"Rush and I are having lunch."

Her pale red eyebrows furrowed. "Really?"

It *was* a bit of a surprise, I supposed. I had tried not to speculate any further or I'd drive myself crazy. "Yep."

She sat next to me, looking sharp in a green suit that picked up the color of her eyes. "How did coffee with you-know-who go?" she asked in a low voice.

"Fine."

"Just . . . fine?"

I shrugged. "Yup."

She studied me, looking for the telltale signs of . . . lust, perhaps. "Mm." I sensed her disappointment in me as she stood. "Back to work," she said, setting an envelope in the outgoing-mail bin and returning to the open area behind the wall that she shared with Rush's and Hadden's secretaries. Not for the first time I noticed her rigid gait that seemed in contrast with her sensual image.

I pulled out my BlackBerry and with my thumbs added more to-dos on my list. I only heard Priscilla in the background until the name Kirsten came up.

"Kirsten Chastain," Priscilla recited. "I know he has your number, but please give it to me again so he won't have to look it up."

It felt as though someone had wrung my heart out like a wet sponge. So it was true. I believed Beth, of course; she had no reason to lie. But I realized I'd been holding out hope that there was some misunderstanding. That hope had been crushed. Kirsten was back in the picture and had obviously been for some time, since Priscilla knew he had her number.

A few minutes later Rush and Hadden emerged from the hallway on the right, and I rose. I swallowed back all of the anger and betrayal bombarding me and smiled, keeping my gaze more on Hadden than on Rush. It was easier that way.

Hadden St. Germain was JFK Junior handsome. His wavy blond hair curled perfectly under at his collar. His aristocratic features set off sky blue eyes. Where Rush was charismatic and passionate in the business world, Hadden was staid and reserved, a by-product of being a member of a wealthy, old-time Beacon Hill family. He approached and took my hands in his. "Hello, gorgeous." He kissed me on the cheek and squeezed my hands affectionately, but not for too long. He'd once kidded that if he'd seen me first he would have snapped me right up, but the truth was, classically handsome wasn't my type.

"Good to see you," I said, meaning it. At the monthly dinner meetings at Dyer House, historical home turned elegant hall, Hadden often ducked into the kitchen to chat for a few minutes. I considered him a friend, one of my few.

Rush put his arm around me and pulled me close for a quick kiss to my temple. "We spent the last hour soothing DEMCO's CEO. He's having jitters about Sturdivant Technologies' offer. They're just dancing right now, but it's a slow song." His eyebrow arched. "They want to get into bed together, but the virgin bride is nervous. He's not quite ready to roll the dice."

Rush's euphemisms about business maneuvers always amused me. Or they did when I wasn't seething about other things. "Maybe the bride's been betrayed before."

Both men looked at me, and I realized I'd said it a little too tersely. I added a smile I was sure seemed phony. "Just speculating."

Rush said to Hadden, "I don't have heartburn, but I have a feeling this is going to be a rocky road. Have John sniff around, find out what happened to the other companies Sturdivant's acquired over the years. See you in a bit."

Rush had kept his arm around my shoulder, and he turned me toward the door as he called to Priscilla, "I'll be out for an hour."

"I've got a stack of messages for you when you get back," she warned.

I tried to see if Rush tensed at that, but he didn't. If

only she'd said who the last caller was, it would be out in the open. Last time I'd overreacted, but now I couldn't bring myself to say, *Funny, Kirsten just left a message.*

The ornate brick building Rush's office was located in sat on Clarendon Street, two blocks from the John Hancock Tower, the Public Garden, and the Boston Common. The Back Bay area was trendy and fashionable, especially Newbury Street with its upscale restaurants, galleries, and shops. It wasn't where I shopped; I was a Filene's Basement kind of gal. But I loved to wander down the sidewalk and perhaps spot a famous face at one of the outside tables in the warmer months.

We walked three blocks to an Italian restaurant. I felt as though I were balancing on a razor blade's edge. I was scared and angry, and my stomach was hurting from holding it all in. *Get through lunch*, I told myself. *Find out what he wants.*

"How did your meeting with Archie go?" he asked once we sat down.

I focused on the menu. "Turns out he wants something more than I'm comfortable handling." Perfectly done, just as I'd practiced. And quite true as well.

"Too bad."

"Yes, it is," I said, hearing that it had come out a little clipped.

"There'll be other opportunities," Rush said, perhaps thinking I was upset about not getting the job. He was trying to soothe me. Comfort me. It would have been nice if I weren't so angry.

I prided myself on staying calm in any situation. I couldn't afford to allow the anger that was bubbling up inside me to burst to the surface. How could he look at me so intently when he was cheating on me? When he'd felt out my best friend, figuratively speaking? What kind of person was he?

I didn't know. He was honest about some things, like

when the cashier gave him too much change. I knew his employees adored him and he treated them beyond well with large bonuses and an extra paid day off now and then. We knew each other's bodies, but we didn't know each other's hearts.

Oh, God, we were my parents, who didn't talk much, who stayed in their marriage for reasons I didn't understand. I had become my father, who lounged in his easy chair while my mother attended her "club meetings," oblivious to the fact that she'd come home flushed and vibrant and reeking of perfume. Impotent, passive, or, perhaps even worse, ignoring what he suspected.

That was me, too.

I remembered something: Rush hadn't come home smelling like cigar smoke that day when he'd supposedly been buying cigars for a meeting.

"You all right?" he asked, and I wondered how long he'd been watching me ruminate.

"Just trying to decide between the lasagna and ravioli."

"What about that guy you met last week?"

I blinked. "Guy?"

"The one you had lunch with at Petries. Did you get the job?"

"I, uh . . . probably not. I haven't heard from him." Had I mentioned Petries specifically? I couldn't remember.

The waitress came then, and we ordered. After she left, I asked, "So what did you want to talk to me about?"

He gave me a Mona Lisa smile. "I've been jammed at work lately. And I'm afraid I won't be home tonight, either, so I wanted to see you." He tilted his head. "Do I need a reason?"

"No, of course not. I just thought . . . well, never mind." I grabbed a roll and ripped out a chunk. "So, you think this DEMCO thing is going to go through?" Yuck. Small talk.

"I'm optimistic. Speaking of, I want to have a dinner

party at Dyer House next week, bring all the players to
the table in an informal setting, ply them with good food
and wine, soften them up."

I automatically whipped out my Blackberry and
scrolled through the calendar. "What day were you
thinking?"

"Wednesday evening, but I don't want you to handle
it."

My mouth dropped open. "What?"

"I want you to be my wife for a change, not my event
planner."

I couldn't help bristling, especially in light of what I
suspected. "I'd rather be in the kitchen."

He bristled, too. "Dammit, Jonna, I—" He blinked,
biting back his words and the anger, looking away.

"What? What were you going to say?"

His fingers tightened around the handle of his butter
knife. "I don't want to argue."

"I do."

I saw his anger flare but dampen just as quickly. "I
won't fight with you." He shut me out, looking down so
his thick eyelashes obscured his eyes.

Why not? I wanted to ask but knew he wouldn't answer.

He'd suggested once before that we hire someone
else to handle his social events. His company's budget
could now afford outside help. I'd never told him that I
wasn't comfortable being out there mingling with the
moneyed guests. I felt out of my league with people dis-
cussing IPOs, stock options, and the future of this or
that kind of technology. I wanted to be in the kitchen,
busy with the details, caught up in the food prep and
presentation. That's where I felt comfortable.

Was that all he wanted: a functional wife? *Look, she
cooks, she cleans, she socializes on command!*

My blog friends would laugh at that. Montene always

came off as confident, sexy, a woman who would take guff from no one. The women on the blog who admitted to having affairs took charge of their unhappiness and changed it. I made a decision: Montene would, too.

I settled into the chaise lounge that was nestled in the bay window of our bedroom. It was where I loved to sit and read historical mysteries while looking out the window. I could see other buildings, windows, people inside moving about in their worlds.

We lived in Brighton, a neighborhood of Boston with a mix of college students, retirees, and young families. Our part of Chestnut Hill Avenue was a clean, relatively quiet, mostly residential area, though I was more than happy to have the European deli right around the corner.

Next to me sat a plate of Oreos. I opened my third one. The scrape of my teeth against the cookie, the tingle of sugar on my tongue, the childish delight of eating the icing first . . . I closed my eyes and savored. Oreos were my comfort food, and I needed comfort—and courage—before I picked up the phone and called my mom.

After I finished the fourth and last one—I would have eaten the whole bag if I'd brought it in with me—I dialed the phone, all the while tuning in to any noise in the vicinity of the front door.

"Mom. It's Jonna."

"Sweetheart, how are you?"

"Fine. Good." I usually felt like a kid when I talked to her. Maybe because I hadn't been around her much as an adult. "I need some motherly advice. Are you alone?"

A pause. "Sure. Your father's playing poker tonight. Is something wrong?"

The best way was to shove the words out, so I did. "What was it like to cheat on Dad? That first time when you were about to do it, what was it like?"

Not a pause this time, but solid silence. Of course she was surprised by my outright question. It wasn't like we'd ever talked about it before. I'd caught her with a man the only time I'd ever skipped school. I wandered with a friend in St. Louis and saw her with him: maybe of Italian heritage, handsome, a killer smile. On a blanket down by the Arch, their fingers touching, much more obvious than Dom and I had been. Much more in love. *Isn't that your mom?* my friend had asked innocently. *Wow, your dad is hot!*

I could only stare at them, my mouth agape. That's when Mom looked up at me. I knew she saw me, but she turned away without saying anything. I turned and walked away as fast as I could. I told my friend I didn't want to talk about it, and so we didn't talk about it over cookies-and-cream shakes. Mom had given me a funny look that evening, but we never spoke of our transgressions.

Until now.

"Mom?" I prompted.

"Jonna." I knew she was thinking of denying it. I pictured the classy, venerable Adele with her elegant hand to her collar. My mother, successful Mary Kay whiz, whose charity work had her gliding in the upper echelon of society.

"I need your advice and your truthfulness. Because I'm on that edge, Mom. I think Rush is cheating on me. I've met someone who makes me feel giddy and guilty. Who makes me feel like someone who's more than just a bed partner. Was it easy for you, that first time? Did it get easier after that?"

Adele took a breath. "Well." A nervous laugh. "It was a long time ago," she said at last. "No, it wasn't easy those first few times. I felt giddy and, yes, guilty. It got easier once I made rules."

"Rules?"

"You have to make rules right at the beginning of the affair, with him and yourself. How far you'll go, whether it stops at sex or if you'll get emotionally involved."

She was a damned pro.

"Why didn't you just leave Dad?"

She actually laughed. "Oh, honey. I had affairs so I could *stay* with him. Your father represents all that's good: stability, appearances, security. But I need more than he could ever give me. I realized that soon after we married. I didn't want to break his heart by leaving him. We have a . . . it's so strange talking to you like this."

"I know."

"Your father and I have an unspoken understanding."

My mouth dropped open, just like that day at the Arch. "He knows? About your affairs?"

"I think he suspects. He's never said anything, never asked questions."

That was our family, I realized. Don't ask, don't tell. We never confronted anyone, never argued.

"And he doesn't do anything about it?" I had pictured him in his easy chair, oblivious. But he hadn't been oblivious. He'd known! All those years I had closed myself off from him, afraid to reveal something, terrified my family would shatter if he found out.

"Sometimes . . . I wish he'd have an affair, too. Then it would be even." Her voice grew more sober. "Then again, he might find someone he likes better than me." She took a quick breath. "So you think your Rush is cheating. Well, that's the problem with marrying someone rich and gorgeous. Didn't I warn you about that?" Without waiting for an answer, she said, "Now you're thinking of cheating, too. Understandable." I noticed she never suggested I ask him about it. "Are you in love with this other man?"

In love. I remembered how I felt when I'd first met Rush: overwhelmed by my feelings, scared that it was all a dream, smiling all the time. "No, not in love. There's an attraction, but it's more about connecting on a deeper level. I feel a deeper connection with this man than I do with my husband. I keep thinking, 'If I can sleep with this man, won't that mean I don't love Rush enough?'"

"I love your father. It has nothing to do with him. It's me, what I need. If I'm happy, I can stay and make him happy."

"Thanks, Mom. I've . . . I've got to go."

I couldn't talk about my mother cheating on my father anymore. I couldn't believe that Rush and I could carry on with other people and have any semblance of a marriage.

I went into the office, but I didn't log onto my blog. I didn't want any feedback on what I was about to do. I sent an e-mail to Dom:

Dom,

I'm ready to take this to the next level. Not all the way, but I'd like to explore the possibilities on neutral ground. I've been trying to think of a suitable place. Unfortunately, the only safe place for intimate conversation is a hotel. How about the Marquis tomorrow at noon?

—Montene

My hands were shaking as I hit Send.

There. I'd done it. For better or for worse.

CHAPTER SIX

I checked my e-mail as soon as Rush left the next morning, half-hoping Dom hadn't read my e-mail and half-hoping he had.

He had.

> Montene, would love to meet you at the Marquis. But . . . you're serious about not going all the way?

> Sorry, not ready to go there yet.

I took a shower and dressed, ate a piece of peanut butter toast, and then returned to my computer. He'd responded:

> But doll, I was prepared for a long, leisurely afternoon pleasuring you beyond your imaginings.

Was he so sure he could seduce me? Mom had talked about making rules, and that made sense.

> Cuddling, kissing . . . nothing more.

> All right. One request, though: can you wear my gift? Just knowing you have it on would mean so much to me.

If he was willing to accede to my request, I suppose I could give him his.

Okay, but don't expect to see it.

Just a glimpse of lace on your shoulder will sate me. For now.

I wasn't sure I believed him. I'd stand firm. Only a glimpse and—

Damn. I didn't have the *thing*. Rush had torn it, leaving nothing more than scraps. I would have to go to the House of Pleasure on the way to the hotel and buy another one. I sent one last e-mail before I left:

I'll check in and e-mail you the room number. See you soon.

As I perused the racks an hour later looking for the same outfit Dom had bought, I felt quite sluttish. That had only been preparation for how I felt when I checked into the hotel without a suitcase. The clerk gave me a knowing smile, and though I ignored it, I felt my cheeks flame.

As soon as I got inside, I plugged in my laptop and sent Dom the room number. I released a long breath as I hit Send. It was done. No turning back.

My phone rang and I saw Beth's cell number on the screen. I didn't want to talk to her just then, but I felt an obligation. She knew about my rendezvous, out of the best-friend role as well as the safety of someone knowing what foolishness I was pursuing.

"How're you holding up?" she asked in a whisper, most likely calling from the restroom at work, where Rush was only a few yards away. Or maybe he was having his own liaison.

Yes, of course he was. Or least planning one. He was probably talking dirty to her right now, on one of his supposed conference calls.

"At least it's not a sleazy hotel."

The room was immaculate, understated, and elegant. A large window looked out over the city. Clear sunshine raked over the sea of redbrick buildings, burning my eyes when it reflected off a strip of metal in the distance. I was tucked into a chair that I'd pulled up to the window, my arms wrapped around myself at the cold air permeating the glass. I was on my eighth Oreo, a record at any one sitting, looking at the mismatched lines my front teeth created in the icing.

"Did you bring the lingerie?" she asked.

"Yes." I kicked the bag with my toe. I hadn't told Beth about Rush's torrid lovemaking. Too personal, for one thing. I had a hard enough time getting my feelings around that without explaining it to someone else. "He agreed to the no-sex thing, and I agreed to wear it under my clothes."

"Gawd, Jonna, you're such a prude!" she said with a laugh. "Be soft," she said, meaning "bold" in Bostonspeak. "You'll feel better afterward. You'll feel in control. Believe me. I've been cheated on, and I know how wonderful it feels to take control of the situation." Her tone changed to teasing. "And I bet Dom makes you forget all about that business for a while."

I didn't want to talk anymore. "He'll be here soon. I'm going to get ready."

"Good luck. I want a full report."

I disconnected and logged onto my blog. I could share my thoughts without being nudged, encouraged, or discouraged.

Dear blog friends,

I'm here, in a hotel room (that is not sleazy), about to do the thing I hated my mother for doing. Except that I'm not going to go all the way. (It sounds so high-schoolish, doesn't it?) We're just going to talk in a quiet, intimate setting.

I know what you're thinking, but yes, it's possible to spend time with a member of the opposite sex in an intimate setting and not have sex, as long as the boundaries are set ahead of time.

—Montene

I logged off and listened to the hum of the heater. I hadn't touched the bed, had, in fact, walked far around it. I stared at the silver bag, knowing I should get ready.

Teeth brushed: check.

No food in teeth: check.

Light spritz of perfume: check.

I stripped down in the bathroom, with the door closed even though Dom didn't have a key. The harsh fluorescent light glared off my skin, making me look sallow. I cut off the tags and slid into the *thing*, easier this time. I pulled on my clothes and had just settled back in the chair when I heard a knock.

Dom was leaning in the doorway when I opened the door. His smile had a trace of smugness, or perhaps satisfaction. He wore a knit sweater that accentuated his muscular chest and arms; his coat was slung over his shoulder. I thought again how different his physical image was from the e-mail image I had of him.

"Hello, doll," he purred, stepping inside. He took me in, maybe trying to tell whether I was wearing the *thing*. It itched beneath my clothing. He set a leather bag on the dresser, out of which he took a chilled bottle of Riesling and two plastic glasses.

He poured without asking if I wanted any and handed me a glass. Was he going to ply me with wine, hoping for more than a cuddle?

My stomach flipped at the smell of it. Still, I took a sip and set it on the dresser as he poured his glass.

He held his glass aloft. "Alone at last."

I didn't want to toast to that, but I did anyway.

He took a long drink and set his glass next to mine on the dresser, ducking his head as he looked at me. He moved closer, pulling me into his arms. "You said something about cuddling. Kissing." His blue eyes were smoky with desire. "I've been dying to touch you, to press my lips against yours. Your touch will feed my hunger for you. Your kisses will quench my thirst."

I felt a little shock as his mouth touched mine. Though I sometimes felt as though Rush and I were strangers, being with Dom made me realize that wasn't the case at all. I did know Rush, at least on a physically intimate level. Dom really was a stranger. He smelled different, felt different, and his tongue moved differently as he nudged open my mouth and probed inside.

I thought we'd talk, maybe hold hands. I would have even welcomed nervous small talk. He'd been here less than three minutes and we were already kissing.

You're thinking too much. You're with a beautiful man you feel a connection with.

Focus on man kissing me: check.

He was the longest kisser I'd ever touched lips with. Just when I thought he would finish and let me breathe, he plunged back in again. What did it mean that my mind kept wandering? That I wanted it to be over? Finally I gentled the kiss and tilted my head back.

"I need to catch my breath," I said.

His smile told me he took it as a compliment, making me breathless. "I could kiss you all day, without eating or drinking or sleeping. I could live on your kisses alone."

I smiled. What else could I do? Where was he getting this stuff? It reminded me of a Deepak Chopra CD that Beth had raved about where celebrities read lines from Rumi's love poems.

"Can we just talk for a while?"

I started to lead him to the chairs, but he sidelined me

to the bed. I sat down on the edge. He seemed so sensitive in our e-mails; couldn't he see that I was uncomfortable?

He sat so close I could feel his body heat. "Can I see my gift? Just a peek to stave my overwhelming hunger for you."

I thought about telling him that I hadn't worn it after all, but he reached out and edged off my sleeve. The sight of the lace filled his eyes with a visual heat. He leaned forward and kissed my shoulder, tugging at the lace. He growled against my skin and scraped his teeth over the bone.

I imagined explaining red marks to Rush.

Focus! This man wants me, possibly more than my husband does. I need this, to be wanted and heard and seen.

Is that what you need?

Bizarrely, my mother's words echoed in my head. *"I love your father. It has nothing to do with him. It's me, what I need."*

What did *I* need?

I didn't know. But I didn't need more sex, great or not. I didn't need to feel this repulsion at myself for being here with a man I'd only met twice. I liked the intimate connection we had online; being physically intimate was something altogether different.

"Tell me you want me as badly as I want you," he whispered against my skin. "Tell me how the want makes you ache, how it makes your sex pulse with the blood of your desire." He pressed his body against mine, leaving me no doubt that he was aroused.

"Ru—" My eyes widened as I realized what I'd been about to call him. "Yes," I hurried on to cover my gaffe. "But—"

"I don't want to hear the word *but.*" He pressed me

down onto the bedspread and looked at me. "I can see that you want me. I see it in your eyes, in the way your body tightens beneath my touch."

That was because I was tensing up. "Dominic—"

He cut me off by kissing me. His hands moved over me, grazing my throat, down the middle of my chest, never purely violating me but coming close. When I felt his hands on my bare breasts, I grabbed his arm and pushed it away. He'd slyly unbuttoned my blouse— without me even realizing it! I tried to push him back so I could see his face. That's when I saw that he'd also unzipped his pants. He obviously wore no underwear; his penis was peeking out of the gaping zipper.

The sight of it made me begin to scoot back, but he pinned me down and covered my nipple with his mouth.

"Dominic, no," I said, feeling panic grow when I couldn't budge him off me. He was sucking now, causing pinpoints of pain.

"Touch me," he said, taking my hand and pulling it between our bodies toward his crotch.

I curled my fingers into a fist. "I want you to stop. Let me up."

"You're just nervous. Let me relax you." He ground into me more, as though feeling his hard penis crushed into my pelvis would relax me.

I tried to scoot sideways, but he wouldn't let me. My heart tripped in fear. His mouth came down hard against mine. I thought about biting his tongue, but I didn't want to anger him. Instead I closed my mouth so he couldn't move.

He pulled back and stared at me. "What the fu—"

"Let me up!"

He pinned what felt like all of his weight on my shoulders, pushing me into the bed.

"Dom, please."

Fear clawed at me. Beth knew I was here, but she wouldn't know if I needed help. She knew who I was with, but not his real name.

"You prick tease," he spit out, lancing me with the sharpness of the word. He shoved up and to his feet, re-assembling his pants.

I leaped from the bed and fumbled with the buttons on my blouse. "I told you I didn't want to go this far."

"That's what you say to ease your guilt. Then I seduce you and it's not your fault. That's how it's supposed to work."

I buttoned my blouse with shaky fingers. "No, that's not how it was supposed to work. I wanted to get to know you better. Well, I have."

"You haven't even begun to know me," he said, jerking the zipper closed. "We were going to start something here."

"I thought that's what I wanted, but I realized I can't. Cheating isn't me."

And he wasn't the sensitive man he'd represented himself to be. That sent a shiver across my skin, stippling my flesh. Had he only played the man I said I wanted?

I saw something flash across his expression, determination perhaps. He pulled on his sweater. "You're the one who invited me here." He gestured to the room. "You wanted this."

"Meeting you here was an impulsive mistake. I confirmed that my husband is ch—I just wasn't thinking."

"Your husband's cheating," he said, making a tsking noise. "You got angry, wanted to get back at him, right?" He took a deep breath and huffed it out. "So we moved too fast, that's all." He stepped closer and clamped his hands on my shoulders. "We'll take it slower."

We moved too fast? I choked back my response to that. The door was only a few feet away. I gripped my purse strap and eyed my coat that was on a chair next to the door. My instincts were screaming to stay pleasant and calm and get the hell out of there. I'd seen his anger; now he was playing nice again.

"Okay. But I need to go now. Clear my head." Why had I said "okay"? I was leading him on again. I twisted toward the door, even with his hands still on my shoulders. "I'll e-mail you."

With a last squeeze he let me go. I held back the sigh of relief as I turned the knob, grabbing my coat off the chair. I slipped into the hallway and closed the door behind me. I was nearly at the elevator when I remembered my hat, which had been under my coat.

"Damn." I had to go back to get it. It was forty-two degrees out and I had a meeting in an hour—my way to keep mine and Dom's meeting short. I walked back to the room, but before I'd reached it I could hear him inside.

"Bitch!" I heard something hit the wall.

I turned and ran back to the elevator. He *had* been playing at being nice. But he wasn't nice at all. And now I'd opened a door I should have left closed.

"Bitch!"

Dom knocked the lamp from the dresser, sending it crashing to the floor. The phone followed. He banged his head against the wall. Dammit, he couldn't fail again. No, she'd be back. She would realize her mistake and beg him to make her come.

His heart pounded as seconds ticked by. Then minutes. He stared at his reflection in the mirror above the dresser, watched the rising of his sculpted chest slow along with his heartbeat. He held off the hard truth as long as possible, but it encroached: she wasn't coming back. Rage unfurled inside him like a roaring fire from a spark. He watched his jaw harden and the lines crease at the corners of his mouth. When he started to kick at the chair, he saw her hat.

If she wouldn't come back for him—his eyes narrowed—at least she'd return for that. It was cold outside, and he knew the cashmere hat would be incentive enough. He strode to the door and peered out the hole. No sign of her.

He walked to the window and looked down. Way down he saw her, standing at the curb next to the doorman, who was waving down a cab. Her luscious brown hair flew into her face. She wasn't coming back to get her hat. Why?

He turned toward the door. Hell, had she returned and heard him cussing? He'd let his temper get the best of him again. Time to face reality. She had no intention of thinking things over.

It wasn't supposed to happen this way. Jonna was right where he'd wanted her, in a hotel room, on the bed, and with heat in her eyes. Now she was gone.

He watched her get into a cab. Gone. But she wasn't going to get away.

CHAPTER SEVEN

I was shaking all the way home, scrunched in the corner of the cab's backseat. I ran inside and turned the shower on its hottest setting. I tore off my clothing and buried it at the bottom of the hamper. This time *I* tore off the *thing*, though it took me a lot longer than it had Rush. I heard plaintive sounds of frustration coming from my throat as I pulled and twisted. In the steam-mottled mirror I saw my reflection, and it startled me: my eyes filled with unshed tears, my hands grappling with the fabric. My hair was a mess, and the skin on my right breast was red.

Creep!

I shoved the *thing* into the small garbage bag, pulled it out, tied it closed, and set it in front of the door. I could smell Dom on me, saliva and wine. With another cry, I launched myself into the shower. Jets pummeled me with hot water. I scrubbed hard with the loofah, every inch, even places he hadn't touched.

I felt violated, but I had been the one to initiate the encounter. I had worn the *thing* at his request. That was the worst part: I was to blame.

I was crying, I realized. When I couldn't hold back I let it all out, my fear and regret and guilt. I sank to the marble floor, hugging myself into a ball, and wept inconsolably.

"Why can't I stop crying?" I said through my tears. It was more than fear and guilt. Much deeper than remorse. I pushed to my feet and reached for Rush's soap. It smelled manly and musky and deepened the ache at what I'd risked. My old insecurities rose up, engulfing me. I imagined Rush taking one look at me and knowing what I'd done. Ordering me to leave. I imagined losing my husband, my home.

As I curled around the pain radiating through my body, a realization hit me over the head: I didn't want to lose him. My test had worked. Almost cheating made me want to save my marriage. What I had to figure out was how.

When I finished drying my hair and getting dressed I looked like I'd fallen asleep in the steam room at the gym. My skin was bright red, my eyes nearly so. But I had a meeting. A luncheon to plan with three women I considered acquaintances. Two were wives of members of AngelForce; one was a member herself. I fixed my face, covering the blotchiness with foundation and powder. I wore a demure outfit with a high neckline.

I could still feel the itch of lace against my skin. I could still feel Dom's mouth on my breast. I shivered in disgust.

As I took the T to the restaurant, I thought about calling Beth. She'd be dying to know details. She'd probably think I was still with Dom, lazing in the afterglow. I couldn't bring myself to rehash it, not now. I had to be together, to feel confident. These women were nice, but I couldn't help feeling like an inferior. I felt outclassed and outleagued. My mother was an elegant, beautiful woman and I was always in her shadow. That's how I felt with these women. I was a successful career woman who worked *for* my peers. They were my best clients. I was stuck.

I pasted on a smile as I pulled open the restaurant door a short while later.

All three women hovered over mugs of coffee whispering and giggling.

"What's up?" I asked as I approached the table.

"Montene!" they said in unison.

I was frozen, but panicked thoughts darted around in my head. How did they know? Who else knew? How had I given it away?

"Have you read her blog?" Sasha said. "You know who Montene is, don't you?"

"She's about to have an affair," Taneka said. "We're waiting to see if she goes through with it."

I sagged into the empty chair. They didn't know my secret. Not yet.

Blog entry, November 7, 6:23 p.m.

Dear blog friends,

I have learned many things about myself during my months on this blog. I have now learned that I am not a cheat. I'm simply not cut out for it. Maybe I'm weak. Or maybe I'm more moral than I thought I was. I'm a God-fearing Lutheran girl, by heritage, but I'd managed to talk my way past that. In any case I'll leave the byplay to all of you more adventurous people out there.

My marriage isn't perfect, but before I could even consider going on to another relationship, I need to find out why this one isn't working—and what part I'm playing in that.

And to show you how conflicted and twisted I am, I actually feel a little guilty that I don't have something juicy to share with you.

—Montene

I managed not to read all the comments from the day before, but I couldn't resist checking my e-mail. One inquiry from my JEvents Web site, four spams, and one e-mail from Dominic. I was going to delete it, but I figured I should see what his frame of mind was.

Montene,

It's okay that you got a little freaked out. I understand. Let's go back to having lunch and getting to know each other. You set the pace.

Dom

"Like hell." And that wasn't the only four-letter word I wanted to use. I didn't want to incite him, though. I had to keep playing nice.

Dom,

Thank you for your understanding, but I'd rather stop this now. Until I can figure out what I want to do with my marriage, I don't want to waste your time.

—Montene

There. Nice and easy.

I had no energy to work, so I huddled into my thick maroon robe and went down the floating stairs. The floors were Brazilian cherry, stained dark as chocolate. They felt cool on my bare feet as I padded around the grouping of chairs and table to the curved aquarium that divided the living room and the dining room. Built into the dark wood cabinet was a ledge where guests could set their drinks and let the four-hundred-gallon saltwater tank crammed with colorful corals and fish mesmerize them.

I perched on one of the stools, my arms wrapped around me, and watched the fat purple starfish scramble over a piece of green brain coral. A clownfish that I had named Omen—Nemo backward—hovered over a burst of poisonous sea anemone. The spotted stingray that

Rush had dubbed Stevie Ray looked as though he were flying through the water. Rush was as excited as a kid whenever he got a new sea creature. I tried to think about that but kept sinking into my miserable self.

That's how Rush found me when he came home. He set his laptop case on the floor and walked over to me. I expected him to check on his new specimen, but he was looking at me instead.

"You all right?"

I was so not all right. I stared at Omen. "I think I'm coming down with something."

Cold air clung to Rush. He slipped his hand beneath my hair and massaged my neck. His fingers were cold, too, but my body relaxed under his touch. I closed my eyes, feeling undeserving of his comfort. I leaned back until I felt the cool of his coat and hardness of his body. Then I thought about who he might have been touching with those hands. I shifted away from him and I felt his movements slow in response to the wall between us. That was one problem with our marriage. His supposed affair. My reaction to it.

Just ask. Get it out in the open. Ask and look in those gorgeous eyes—you'll see the truth no matter what comes out of his mouth.

I turned to him, poised to ask, just as he said, "I'll make you a hot toddy," and moved away.

My body, tensed with my effort to get out the words, sagged in relief. I was too fragile to hear the truth anyway. Maybe it was safer if I didn't know, a tiny voice whispered. Maybe that was why I was comfortable not knowing Rush. If we didn't know each other, we couldn't hate each other. If we weren't close, we couldn't hurt each other, either.

The truth hit me like a cast-iron pot to the stomach. The distance between us had been my shield all this time. Could I dare to step around that and risk being hurt? I didn't know. First I had to find out for sure if he was cheating. No. First I had to make sure this thing with Dominic was finished. Only then could I focus on my marriage.

CHAPTER EIGHT

I found it odd that Rush was still around the next morning as I poured coffee into my mug at the stainless-steel kitchen counter. That meant I had to put on makeup first thing, brush my hair, and abandon my fuzzy purple slippers, all to keep that "dating" image alive.

He knew something was off. Last night he'd done small things to comfort me, like brush hair from my face and kiss me tenderly on the forehead. When I curled onto my side in bed, he pulled me into his arms and held me. I had wanted to cry, but then I'd have to explain. As we lay spoon-style, his cool exhaled air washed over my neck, and I paced my breathing to match his.

Now he was leaning against the counter, one hand loosely anchored to his other arm, watching me. Assessing me. "How do you feel? You said you felt something coming on last night."

"Oh. Yeah. I feel better. Thanks."

I busied myself fixing my coffee, raw sugar, and half-and-half, stirring and stirring, and then I turned to face him. I had the urge to run my fingers along his jawline, one of my favorite parts of his body. Then I would press my thumb into the shallow indent on his chin and then he would kiss me. His mouth was another favorite part, a little too large for his features and yet somehow perfect. He started to say something, but I quickly said, "I heard you get out of bed in the middle of the night. Couldn't sleep?"

"I had a lot on my mind."

I'd heard him walk down the hall and open a drawer at his desk. He was being quiet. Not to wake me out of politeness? Or because he didn't want me to know what he was doing?

"I thought I heard the front door close."

"I went for a walk, thought it might help me to get sleepy again."

Why would he go outside at night? I hated my suspicious mind. It was stupid to think he'd sneaked out of the house in the middle of the night to meet Kirsten. After all, my evil mind had to remind me, he had plenty of time during the days and evenings to do that.

I would ask him. Point-blank. *Are you seeing her?* I would ask as soon as my conscience was clear. "Have you given any more thought to the dinner party you want to throw next week? I need to get started on it."

I saw his expression harden; yes, I was being stubborn.

"Rush, if we hire someone else to do it, I'll still be in the kitchen supervising. No one would do a good enough job. I'd make them crazy. So I might as well do it myself."

His dark eyebrows furrowed so subtly, if I hadn't been studying his expression I might have missed it. He was still analyzing me.

Are you nervous about being around my associates? I could hear him ask in my dream conversation where he read my mind.

Yes. A bit. I don't feel like I fit in. It's not anything you do. You're very attentive. It's me, totally, completely me.

But he didn't ask, and I didn't tell. Typical of our marriage, and as much my fault as his. I remembered those times trying to talk to my dad, not meeting his eyes, not saying much, because I didn't want to give away my secret. Or, more precisely, Mom's secret. I pulled away from him instead, and I'd had trouble connecting with men since then.

I charged on toward another subject. "Thanksgiving's only a few weeks away. Why don't we get together with your family? We've been married for a year and a half and I haven't met them." I gave him a hurt look I didn't have to fake. "I'm beginning to think you're ashamed of me."

He poured the last of his coffee into the sink. "Of course I'm not ashamed of you." He walked close and pulled me over for a quick peck on my mouth. "It's not you; it's them. They're . . . well, we're just not close, that's all. We have nothing in common, nothing to talk about."

I'd heard him talk to his parents, who, like mine, were still together. It was true that their conversations were stilted. I'd talked to both of them. They seemed nice, and happy for Rush, for our marriage. They lived in a small town in South Carolina, and he sometimes sent them an envelope I suspected contained a check. His younger brother, David, was a missionary, usually living in some third-world country teaching the locals to farm and build. I could believe that he and Rush had little in common.

Rush enjoyed his wealth, but he didn't wallow in it. He wore a Swiss-made watch but nothing ostentatious. He had one custom-made suit but rather emphatically said he didn't want another one. He bought me nice gifts, like my laptop and jewelry. I suspected his most prized possession, other than his tropical fish, was an old deck of cards he kept in his desk drawer. I'd caught him rubbing his thumb over the edges at times, a wistful smile on his face.

"We'll visit them someday," he said, closing the discussion.

"How about if we do an elegant lounge decor for the dinner party?" I asked, cementing *my* position, too. "I'll see if I can find some carpet remnants. I rented dark velvet chairs for a dinner party last summer. And a grand piano. It looked like a cruise ship lounge, cozy yet conducive for mixing." I was gesturing now, indicating how the tables would be arranged, more for myself than for him. "For dinner a mixed green salad and crusty French rolls, maybe filet mignon medallions in burgundy sauce, potato puffs, green beans in garlic-infused oil."

I saw his expression soften in surrender. I even thought I saw a hint of a smile as I ran to the notepad on the counter and jotted down my thoughts. He set his coffee mug in the dishwasher drawer and said, "I'll see you tonight."

Tonight. Tonight I'd ask about Kirsten.

Once I'd dressed and bundled up in my coat, I went outside. It was overcast, with low, gray cloud masses hovering over the city. I drove to the surf shop in Quincy where I was renting five surfboards for the beach party. After loading them into my Lexus SUV, I headed to the area where JEvents operated, not far from the loft and close to 90, which led into downtown Boston. Warehouses in various stages of decay and renewal surrounded the two renovated buildings my landlord called Tristan Business Park. The Tristan buildings were divided into rows of spaces that each comprised a small office and large working area. The rudimentary space was the reason I usually met my clients at cafés or their homes.

I backed up my SUV to my shop, my mind on the shipment of candy bars and ice-cream confections that was due that day. I already had a popcorn maker and had sweet-talked the popcorn supplier into donating the kernels and butter seasoning. A local supplier was donating soft drinks.

I had two sometime employees, one a college student and the other a stay-at-home-mom, but most of the work was still mine. I hoped to grow my business so I could hire full-time help, but I couldn't justify the expense yet. Being a bit of a control freak made delegating harder.

I went through my office that was decorated in peach and earth tones and into the workspace. I hoisted up the steel door and began unloading the pink surfboard from the top of the stack.

"Let me help," I heard a voice say from beside me, nearly startling me into dropping the board.

I actually did when I turned to see who had spoken: Dominic.

He caught it, leaning close as he did so, leaving a whiff of cinnamon in the air. Once he had a handle on it, he said, "Where does it go?" just as casually as though he were one of my neighbors—*as though he were someone who should be there.*

But he shouldn't be there. Because this wasn't where Montene would be. This was where Jonna Karakosta would be, and Dominic didn't know Jonna Karakosta. He only knew Montene, who had no last name at all.

He wore a black leather jacket, brown corduroy pants, and a brown wool cap. No gloves. Misty puffs hung in the air as he waited with a patient smile, the surfboard in his arms. As though he were expected there and not a shock at all. It was such a shock I couldn't find words, much less my voice. Finally I said, "What are you doing here?"

He glanced at the surfboard. "Trying to help." He walked toward the shop.

I followed him inside, where he placed the board on one of the two large worktables. The space had enormous ceilings and no heat other than some portable units that weren't on yet. I hadn't turned the lights on, either, so it was still dim inside.

As I neared him he spun around and made to return to the car for another surfboard.

I grabbed his arm. "What . . . are . . . you . . . doing . . . here?"

He placed his hand over mine. "I thought it would be better to meet here than at your apartment."

"My . . . apartment?"

"I saw your husband leaving, but who knows, he could forget something and come back."

Fear skittered up my spine. "You were at our building this morning?"

He sauntered to the car and pulled out the blue surfboard. "I drove by, yes, but thought better of popping in. So I came here. Hey, you going to let me do all the work?" he said with a laugh.

I jerked the surfboard away from him. "How do you know where I live? And work, for that matter? How did you find out who I am?"

He took the surfboard back, kissed me on the mouth, and walked back into the shop. The moment became even more surreal when he casually said, "I looked at your wallet. That first day we had lunch."

I felt nearly as violated as I had after our meeting at the hotel. "*You looked at my wallet?* You went into my purse?"

He turned around to face me after setting that board on the table. "You can't blame me for being curious. I wanted to know who you were. Come on, Jonna; I'm mad for you. A man deserves to know the woman he's mad for, don't you think?"

I followed him to the car, where he once again hoisted another board. "Yes, I can blame you. That was completely, totally wrong. We agreed to keep our identities secret."

"That was before I saw you and knew you were the one for me."

Fear prickled my skin into goose bumps that actually hurt. He wasn't getting it. "Then who are you?"

He tilted his head as he set the third board on the table. "Ah, not yet, doll."

I had the sense to tread carefully. His logic wasn't on the same plane as mine. *You're good at staying calm. It really counts now.* "Why not?"

He cupped my face with his cold hands. "Because you're not mad for me yet. But you will be. Then we'll know each other in every way." He kissed me again and went for another board. "Besides, I know that you like a man with a mysterious aura about him. I remember you writing that there was something oddly exciting about being married to a man who seems more like a stranger, that it gave a—I think you said—one-night-stand quality to your lovemaking."

My damned blog! I raced to the car and blocked his access. "Did you get my e-mail?"

"I save each and every one."

"Did you read it?"

"You're confused about what to do with your marriage. But there's no confusion, really. I know how you feel about Johnny. Or rather, how you don't feel about him. You feel a sense of loyalty, naturally, but what you need is a shove to knock you off that fence you've been on for so long." He pulled me close. "And I'm going to be that shove, doll."

"Please don't call me that." I looked around to see if anyone was around. The building to my right was mid-renovation but work was apparently stalled. Beyond the sounds of the interstate I heard a clanging in the distance but saw no one. My heart slammed against my rib cage now. I hadn't been clear enough, firm enough. I moved out of his embrace, feeling his arms reluctantly let me go.

"Dominic, I—"

"Dom. I like when you call me Dom."

"Dominic, you're wrong about what I feel for my husband. I do love him. I'm not on the fence about staying with him. Maybe I was at one time, but the thought of losing him made me realize I want to make it work."

I saw anger flare in Dominic's eyes. "But he's cheating on you! How can you think of staying with a man who would break your heart? Disgrace you?"

He'd hit a nerve, but I kept my face passive. "Because he's my husband."

He tilted his head, studying me. "You've been hurting for a long time now. This isn't the first time he's cheated, is it?" My expression must have given me away. "That's what I thought. Once a cheat, always a cheat. You can't change him. But you *can* have me, someone devoted to your every need and desire."

He was interpreting things the way he wanted to see them, just as he had at my invitation to meet him at the hotel. He gave me a peck on the mouth as easily as Rush had done that morning and reached around me to grab another board.

"You shouldn't have to do this kind of lifting," he said, looking around at the shop as he sauntered back in.

I showed him that I didn't need help by grabbing the last board. "I have two employees." I angled my head so I could see my watch. "They should be here anytime now."

"Then why not wait until they show up? You're the boss."

I hated that he knew that much about me. He must have Googled my name. "I like doing the work." I returned to my car and closed the back door. "Dominic, I want you to leave. Don't come back. Ever."

"You're afraid you're wasting my time," he said, repeating my e-mailed words. "But I've got all the time in the world, Jonna. All the time in the world for you. You'll see that your husband is wrong for you and that I'm right. But I won't push. I'll be your friend, just kind of hanging around, and when you're ready, I'll be here with open arms."

My hands balled into fists. "You're not listening to me. I don't want to see you again. Not here, not on the blog, nowhere. Now please leave."

I pulled the metal door down and locked it, walked around to my car, and got inside. I didn't look at him as I started the engine and pulled around to the parking area. I screamed, stomped my feet on the floorboard, and tried to release my frustration at his stubbornness. I took a deep breath. I'd been clear now. He couldn't misinterpret that.

I waited a few more minutes before getting out again. I walked inside the door and locked it behind me. It felt colder than normal. I rubbed my gloved hands together and walked into the open area, flicking on the lights. It didn't occur to me until just then that Dominic could be inside. A violent chill assailed me as I looked around the space. He wouldn't be hiding, I assured myself. He was so infuriatingly obtuse about what I was trying to tell him, he would be standing right there asking what he could do with the palm-frond beach hats on the second table.

Still, I scanned the shelves that lined the two walls, checking between the props and boxes of silk flowers. I even opened the heavy steel door and looked inside the refrigerated storage area. Okay, it was really over. He got the message, finally, and had gone home. With a breath of relief, I walked over to the table with the surfboards—and stopped dead. A yellow rose sat on top of the stack.

CHAPTER NINE

"Beth, I've got a problem," I said, staring at the rose that I hadn't touched. I clutched the cell phone to my ear. "Dominic was here. At the shop."

"He couldn't have. That would mean . . ."

"He knows who I am!" I took a quick breath. "He looked at my wallet when we had lunch that first time. And now that I think about it, I remember coming back to the table and finding him in an odd position, kind of bent forward. I was too distracted by Rush being in the area to think much of it."

"So he saw your name and address, and then tracked you down," she said.

"Yes! It's beyond creepy. He thinks we have something between us—"

"Well, you did suggest the meeting at a hotel—"

"I know, but I told him it was a mistake, that I need to work on my marriage. I said it on my blog, and I e-mailed him that I wanted to stop seeing him. Just now I told him again, very clearly, that I didn't want to see him again. Ever. After all that he left a yellow rose on my table. It was like he didn't hear a thing. I don't know what to do."

"Okay, calm down. Let me think." After a pause, she said, "Well, you have to admit, in a way it's kind of romantic."

"Romantic? Are you nuts?"

"Think about the way guys pursue women in the movies. *Against All Odds. The Graduate. Endless Love,* with Brooke Shields. I must have watched that movie five times when I was a teenager," she said in a dreamy voice. "I've got it in my library if you're ever in the mood."

"Doesn't he burn down her house when he can't have her?" I shook my head. "This isn't the movies." I was pacing the concrete floor, my arm wrapped around my waist. I hadn't even bothered to turn on the heat. "This is real life. *My* life."

"Okay, okay. He's a little forward, charmingly obtuse, and maybe his behavior is a bit inappropriate."

"There was nothing charming about it, and he was way more than inappropriate."

"What I'm saying is, don't freak out. I'm sure he'll think over what he did and tone it down."

I'd walked back to the door and looked out the window, the only one in the shop. I didn't see him. I hadn't seen a car nearby when he'd been there. "I hope he does more than tone it down. I want him out of my life."

"Call me if he comes back. I'll come over. I'm in this, too, you know."

"Thanks," I said. "You're the best."

I was glad Beth knew about all this. I didn't want to post on the blog about Dominic's visit; I didn't want to humiliate or anger him. I couldn't tell Rush, of course. So Beth was my only confidante.

I tried to focus on filling the table centerpiece dishes with sand and seashells. Every time I heard a sound, I rushed to the door. He hadn't been threatening, not overtly. But he scared me anyway.

＊ ＊ ＊

I spent the rest of the day at the large warehouse that a
Big, as the volunteers of Big Brothers Big Sisters were
called, was letting us use for the event. A cleaning crew
created clouds of dust that threw me into a sneezing fit as
I laid out rolls of blue and white fabric that would cover
the brick walls. Still, I was grateful for their company. I
couldn't shake the feeling that Dominic was out there,
watching me. When I returned home, I searched the
parking lot for him. If only I knew what he drove. As I
entered our loft, I breathed a sigh of relief. Home. Safe.

Rush surprised me by coming home a few minutes
later. I found myself studying him the way he seemed to
study me lately.

"I didn't expect you home so early," I said.

"I hope it's a nice surprise," he said, giving me a
smile.

He walked over to the bar situated next to the dining
table and switched on the lights. The dining area was
darker than the rest of the space because of the platform
above, the dark floors, and the long dark table. The
rest of the loft had immense ceilings, as high as
twenty feet. I liked the coziness of the dining room with
its soft, recessed lights.

"Drink?" he asked as he dropped ice cubes into a
short glass and poured his favorite whisky, Dahlwhin-
nie. He'd been to the distillery in the Highlands of Scot-
land years ago and developed an affinity for the brand.
(Spelled, he would emphasize whisky without the *E*.)
He could talk about its smooth, heathery honey taste all
he wanted; it was *yuck* to me.

"Glass of merlot would be great, thanks." With
everything else that had gone on that day, I hadn't given
a whit of thought to what I wanted for dinner. I probably
would have gone for a can of tomato soup if Rush
hadn't come home. "Feel like some pasta primavera for

dinner?" I asked, thinking about what I had in the reefer—or reefah, as the locals called it. I joined Rush at the aquarium bar, and he handed me a glass of wine.

"Sounds great," he said with a smile, looking as mellow as his whisky. "As long as I can watch."

Had I only imagined the provocative inflection of that statement? "What?"

"I like watching you cook." He reached out and pushed a lock of hair from my face. "You talk to yourself, you know. As you're working, you're talking: 'A pinch of salt, and where's the basil? Oh, good place for it, Jonna.'" He was gesturing, pretending to be me in the kitchen looking for things, stirring, multi-tasking. "You have a glow when you're working. That's how I knew you'd be great at running your own business."

His words stirred something inside me. He meant it. I simply smiled, getting lost in his green bedroom eyes for a moment.

Then the doorbell rang. "I'll get it," he said, setting his glass of amber liquid on the bar.

I heard a man's voice say, "I have a delivery for Jonna."

I stepped around the aquarium, curious and apprehensive at once. *Not Dominic*, my first thought. The man was holding a white bag that smelled a lot like Chinese food.

"I'm Jonna."

"I have your order for General Tso's chicken, white rice, mix of egg drop and wonton soup." He handed it to me.

Rush gave me an inquisitive look before turning to the deliveryman and reaching for his wallet. "How much?"

"It's already been paid for."

Rush handed him a tip, giving me time to sort out why food had come that I hadn't ordered. Then I remembered. I'd mentioned on my blog that this was one of my favorite meals. Dominic had ordered it. Had it sent to me. It was the only explanation. Thank God he hadn't sent it under the name Montene. All my good feelings fled as Rush turned to me.

"Did you forget you'd already ordered?"

"I . . . must have. Oh yeah, I called in the order a couple of hours ago." I tapped my temple. "Too much on the brain." I forced a smile, pushing my frustration and anger at Dominic into the background. "Want to share?"

Dominic sat outside the converted warehouse cum lofts watching the deliveryman at Jonna's door. Rush wasn't supposed to be there. Jonna said he was rarely home for dinner. But he was there. Bastard.

He had to convince her that she didn't want to reconcile with her husband. It was imperative that he do so. He rubbed his hands together. He'd been parked there since she'd gotten home. Now she was in her apartment, probably sharing the dinner that he'd paid for with her husband. He gripped the steering wheel so hard his fingers ached.

"All right, Jonna, you're playing hard to get. Fine. I'll play harder." He smiled. "You're not getting rid of me that easily, doll."

This had started out as a simple seduction. It had become so much more.

CHAPTER TEN

Montene's Diary

225 Comments:

• Babz wrote:

Montene, where are you? You can't leave us hanging. What happened with Dom? And your husband? Post, girl!

• 4Star wrote:

I went through that whole conscience thing, too, after I'd slept with my lover the first time. I felt this surge of wanting to make my marriage right. I told my husband we should go to counseling, find ways to pep up our sex life. You know what he said? It was all MY problem and I should go to counseling and fix myself! So I did. I went back to my lover, and we're all very happy together.

I read through the many comments from my blog friends and stopped on Dom's post.

• Dom wrote:

Girls, I'm still very much in the picture. I think Montene feels funny posting to the blog knowing that I'm reading it, too. Yes, she's struggling with her conscience, but she's beyond

backing away from the man who gives her what she wants.
Even if she protests.

I made a noise that sounded like a garbled scream and
threw my pencil at the monitor. He'd just posted that
morning. Which meant he hadn't thought it over and
come to the sane conclusion that we weren't going to
happen. I thought he was in denial, and he thought I was.
His persistence worried me, but his delusions scared the
hell out of me.

My fingers were poised over the keyboard, ready to
write a scathing rebuttal, but they wouldn't move. What
was the worst thing that would happen if I told everyone
that Dom was off his nut and I had no intention of seeing him again? He might reveal my identity to the whole
Internet world, for one thing. Even graver, he might get
angry. Deluded was one thing. Angry was a whole different matter. When he'd called me a bitch at the hotel,
I'd heard anger. I knew provoking a stalker could spur
him to violence.

I caught my breath. *Was* Dominic a stalker? Well, he
had found out my real name and address in an under-
handed way. He'd appeared at my shop and home without invitation. And he wasn't hearing me when I said we
were over.

I closed the Web site, went downstairs, and pulled on
my coat. I was meeting Beth for our manicure lunch and
then I had to go to my shop to gather everything for the
beach party. Fortunately, my part-time helpers would be
present, helping me to load the props and food to take to
the warehouse.

When I walked out to my car, I saw a large white-
chocolate-chip cookie (my favorite) balanced on the
side mirror. No note, nothing but the cookie. I knew who
had left it. I scanned the parking lot, somehow sure he
was watching my reaction. I wanted to send the cookie

flying like a Frisbee, but that cautious voice warned me about inciting him. Besides, what if he'd poisoned it and some hapless dog or kid found it? So I tossed it on the seat to throw away later. The cookie was bad enough. Knowing he was watching me, that was the worst part.

"I dunno, I still think it's kind of romantic," Beth said, admiring her nails as she ruffled the pages of her ever-present catalog. "In an intense and, yes, crazy way. I'd love to have someone do stuff because he was madly in love with me and couldn't live without me."

I'd waited until we'd ordered our lunch to tell her everything. I didn't want to splay my personal problems out for the manicurists to hear. Besides, they might find it romantic, too. That was the odd thing, the sinister thing, really. On the surface, Dom's actions did seem wildly romantic. But not to me.

"The point is, I've already told him I don't want to see him anymore. More than once. He's not listening, and I don't find that the least bit romantic."

She ran her finger over the charm embedded in her sparkly pink nail polish. I always got clear polish, since I worked with food. Once I was horrified to discover a fleck of my polish in a crème brûlée. She obsessed over color and design choices as though they were going to be permanent.

"That's what love makes you do," she said. "Think about the way Rush courted you. He sent you four dozen roses at work. You went to Paris for the weekend with a virtual stranger. He delivered a dress via a limo that took you to a fabulous restaurant where he was waiting."

I squeezed a lemon into my glass of hot water. "But that was different. I *wanted* Rush in my life." I felt a twinge in my stomach as I remembered those wonderfully crazy days. He'd been electric with energy and enthusiasm and life. Passionate, romantic, and gorgeous. He was riding high, suddenly rich and eager to enjoy it. I had been the lucky recipient of all he had to offer.

"I think your blog friends are right," Beth said, pulling out a bejeweled pen and circling some pricey body polish she'd decided to buy. "You're just freaking out because you've taken the step of having an affair. Your conscience is throwing this stuff at you, skewing it. Deep down I think you like it."

My conscience, though bashing me for my indiscretion, wasn't just toying with me. My instincts were telling me—no, screaming—that something was seriously wrong with the guy. "I know the difference between guilt and being totally creeped out."

When my BlackBerry rang, I said, "I'm only checking this because I've got a gig tomorrow. If something's gone wrong, I need to know. Uh-oh, it's Trish, one of my part-timers." I engaged the call. "Hi, what's up?"

"I can't help with the beach party," she said, strain in her voice. "I wrenched my back big-time playing with my daughter. I can barely move."

"You take care of your back. We'll manage."

"I'm so sorry, Jonna."

"That's okay. I'll talk to you in a few days, see how you're doing." I hung up and looked at Beth. "I've lost one of my helpers. Back trouble." I gave her a hopeful look. "You wouldn't happen . . ."

She waved her hand before I'd even finished. "Nope, don't do work on the weekends, especially the labor kind. Besides, I have plans."

I sighed. "Looks like this party just got a little harder."

Beth propped her chin on her hand, studying me. "You're always so calm. So nice. I would have told her to get her ass in anyway."

"That's my philosophy: work through it. And don't waste time and energy getting upset over it."

She shook her head. "Sometimes you're just too damned perfect." She tempered the rigid words with a smile.

I walked to the parking garage feeling a vague annoyance at Beth for not supporting me in a best-friend way. She was the only person I could turn to, and she wasn't taking my concerns about Dominic seriously. I got into my car and started it, cranking up the heater even though I knew nothing would come out until the air was warm. I checked the mirrors, shifted into reverse, and backed up.

I heard a *thump*. I slammed on the brakes, looking in the rear camera screen on the dash. I saw something— or someone—back there. "Oh, God." I threw the gear into park, untangled myself from the seat belt, and launched out of the car.

I saw a man on the concrete floor trying to get up, his head bowed.

I rushed toward him. "Are you all right? I didn't see—"

He looked up and I sucked in a breath. *Dominic?* He gave me a surprised look, still struggling.

I would have punched him if he hadn't already looked like he was in pain. "What the hell are you playing at?"

"Nothing," he said in a breathless voice. "I was just walking from my car and you backed into me."

"You're following me!"

"Didn't you hear me? I was walking *from* my car. I just got here."

"So it's a total coincidence that we're both here."

"Apparently."

A car came around the corner and paused. "Is everything all right?" the man at the wheel asked Dominic. "Has there been an accident?"

"Just a bump," he said. He took hold of my arm and used it to stand straight. "But I'm fine, really. Thanks."

The man hesitated, studying us. I wanted to say something, but what? It looked as though I'd hit Dominic. The man shrugged and drove off.

Dominic still had a hold on my arm. As I was about to shrug him off, he leaned against me. "The garage is spinning."

I saw the split on his forehead, just below the edge of his wool cap. His whole weight was on me now, making us both stagger. I held him up. I had no other option besides letting him drop to the ground.

"Get in the car," I gritted out, pulling him toward the passenger door. "If this is a ruse . . ." He groaned as I opened the door and shoved him inside. "I'm taking you to the hospital."

"No, I just need a few minutes. Besides, I don't have insurance."

I studied the split; it was real. Blood trickled down the bridge of his nose.

"I didn't realize parking garages were so dangerous," he said, trying for a laugh.

If he was playing it, he was doing a good job. The hell of it was, I couldn't tell. He did look as though he was in pain. Had he thrown himself behind my car and chanced serious injury to play on my sympathy? Too risky. More likely, he'd been too busy following me and not paying attention to what my car was doing.

I pulled several tissues from a pack in the glove compartment and handed them to him. He slumped over.

"I'm taking you to the hospital."

His words were faint. "No. They'll have to take a report. You'll get a ticket."

I took the tissues, pulled off his cap, and pressed them to his forehead since he wasn't doing it. I felt torn; I didn't want to coddle him, but what if he was really hurt? He turned my other hand, braced on the center console, upright and laid his cheek into my palm with a soft sigh.

"Just . . . need to lie here . . . for a few minutes," he whispered.

I held my breath as he did just that. His breath dampened my fingertips; his stubble scratched my palm. My stomach rolled. The heat pounded out of the vents, making my skin prickle inside my coat. I said nothing.

"Don't worry, doll. I'm not going to sue you. It was just an accident. If you'd seen me, you wouldn't have backed up." He looked at me. "Right?"

I swallowed. "Of course not." What was he getting at?

I'd never been so off-balance before . . . and so pinned down. I waited anyway, hating myself for each passing second. Kelly Clarkson sang a ballad on the radio. Gwen Stefani was next and then some boy band. I looked everywhere but at Dominic throughout those songs. Finally I looked down at him. Had he fallen asleep? He wasn't moving. He was breathing, though.

"Dominic," I said, my voice hoarse. "I have to go." For a reason I couldn't name, I felt compelled to add, "I have to set up an event. One of my employees called in sick. I have a lot of work to do." I cleared my throat. "I can take you to the hospital or I can take you home."

He slowly sat up, taking my hand in his. "No, I'll be . . . I'll be all right." He looked at my hand as he rubbed his thumb over the back of it. Then he kissed it gently. "You've been kind to me, Jonna."

"Don't call me that."

He gave me a pained smile. "Can't call you doll. Can't call you Jonna. What can I call you?"

"Don't call me at all."

"Did you like the cookie I left?"

"Dominic, I—"

He put his finger over my mouth. "Shh. I can already

tell you liked it. How wonderful it must be to have a man give you everything you desire. But you can't allow yourself to give that much to me because of your guilt." He grabbed his wool cap and opened the door. "See you later."

Cold air swept in and then he closed the door. He stood there. I waited for him to walk to his car so I could take note of the model and license plate. He pressed his fingers to his mouth and sent an air kiss my way. And stayed there.

I finally relented, backing up. A horn bleated and I jerked to a stop again. I'd nearly run into a car this time. I finished backing out of my spot and, without looking at Dominic, continued out of the garage. The more I drove and the more I thought about the whole incident, the surer I became that he was playing me. Playing me well. Risking injury to do so. I wanted to know why.

What scared me most was, if he *had* orchestrated the accident, he'd taken a huge risk. If he was willing to do that, what else would he pull?

I returned home late that night, exhausted both physically and mentally. The living room was dark but for the light coming from the aquarium. The moving water sent flashes of reflected light all over the room, and the fish swooped in on the pink frozen cubes of brine Rush had recently dropped into the water. He was stretched out in one of the black leather chairs in the living room, his shirt unbuttoned, a glass of whisky in his hand. He looked relaxed in every way but his eyes that watched me intently.

"Hi," I said, setting my purse on the table near the front door. Despite everything, I felt a stir of desire at the sight of him. His maroon dress shirt framed a sculpted chest and flat stomach that I had longed to trace

with my tongue many times. I wasn't sexually adventurous and yet I'd found that a part of me was, the part I'd
discovered as Montene. The only problem was, whenever I'd thought about implementing some of that I remembered Kirsten and my desire shriveled

"A drink sounds good," I said, heading over to the bar
to pour a glass of merlot. The recessed halogens were
already on in the bar niche, so I didn't turn on any other
lights. The darkness was comforting. Camouflaging. I
was afraid Rush would see my turmoil and tension.

"Bad day?" he asked.

"Horrible." I cleared my throat. "Trish called in sick
and Carson and I only got half the prep done, which
means we'll have to hit it early tomorrow."

After a pause, he said, "Not to mention the accident."

I nearly dropped the bottle of wine. My fingers
caught it just as it was about to hit the granite counter-
top. "Why do you say that?"

"Listen to the answering machine."

Thoughts darted around my head as I walked over.
Dominic, had to be. What had he said?

I pressed the button and held my breath.

Dominic's voice in my home, more intrusion, more
violation. "Hello, I'm trying to reach Jonna Karakosta.
This is Dominic, the, uh, guy you hit today." He chuckled softly. "I know how concerned you were, so I wanted
to let you know that I'm feeling much better. Only a bit
of a headache. Okay, that's all. Oh, there's one more
thing." He paused, making my chest hurt with the breath
I was holding. "I was serious when I said I wouldn't sue
you. I wanted you to know, to be assured, just in case
your husband is worried. Have a great evening."

Son of a bitch! He was taunting me, especially by
mentioning my husband. I hit the Erase button and
turned to find Rush standing nearby.

"What happened?" he asked.

"I was backing out of my spot in a parking garage, after meeting Beth for lunch, and this guy walked out of nowhere. I bumped him. It wasn't serious."

"And you gave him our home number?"

No, I hadn't, but Dominic had found it anyway. "I wanted him to let me know how he was doing."

I was lying to cover Dominic's story. How crazy was that?

Rush tilted my chin up to force me to look at him, making me realize I hadn't been looking at him the whole time I'd talked about the accident. "You all right?"

I forced a smile. "I'm fine. It was jarring, of course. Scary."

I could see that some part of him didn't quite believe me. I wasn't sure which part of my story was suspect, though.

"There were several hang-ups on the machine, too," he added. "Blocked numbers. Maybe it was the same guy, since his number was blocked, too."

He wasn't exactly asking anything, but he was looking at me in a *Is there something you'd like to tell me?* way. Of course, it could be my paranoia. Or had he seen the cookie on my car?

I sauntered over to the aquarium, my fingers curled around the wine stem. "Where's Stevie Ray?"

"He's hiding." When I glanced over at Rush, he added, "Stingrays are good at hiding. But even so, they sometimes leave a telltale outline in the sand."

CHAPTER ELEVEN

When I pulled up to the warehouse early Saturday morning, I was relieved to see Carson's yellow truck parked outside. At least *he* hadn't let me down. He'd even shown up early.

I'd worn sweatpants for the dirty work ahead. Besides, the warehouse would take some time to heat up and it was in the forties. I pulled my coffee mug from the holder and climbed out of the car. I could see Carson in his car . . . and someone sitting in the passenger seat, too. Bless him! He'd recruited help. I had called a few people I trusted, but they'd all had plans.

Carson stepped out and waved with the enthusiasm of a child. I loved his energy and creative flair. He was studying interior decorating, and I dreaded the day when he graduated and got a full-time job with a decorating firm. His bright blond hair spiked at the tips, offset by his diamond ear studs.

"Good morning, sunshine! And how wonderful that we have help today," he said in his singsong voice.

Carson's partner? I wondered, and then the man in the passenger seat got out and my thoughts scrambled.

Dominic. No, couldn't be Dominic. Just looked like him, with the added coincidence of the guy having a bandage on his forehead. His sly smile couldn't smack of triumph, couldn't—

"Tah dah," Carson said, presenting Dominic. "You know he's a good friend when you hit him with your car and he still comes to help. He told me how you two *ran* into each other yesterday, God, how terrifying," Carson went on, oblivious to my shock.

Dominic gingerly touched his bandage. "Wish I'd been up to helping yesterday, but I was a bit dizzy most of the night."

Carson patted Dominic's arm. "What a great guy! And since he's already done some prework on the party, getting the surfboards and all, he's familiar with the theme." Carson rubbed his hands together. "Thank goodness we won't have to bust our sweet asses as much today."

I was literally speechless. Dominic was like a runaway train in my life.

Carson walked over to my SUV and opened the back gate.

Finally I uttered to Dominic, "How . . . why . . . ?"

"You said you were shorthanded yesterday."

My excuse for running out on him. "But how did you know where I was going to be?"

"I did a Web search for the date and beach party." He walked over to Carson, who was beginning to hoist boxes of candy. "Tell me what to do."

"Dominic, you shouldn't be here," I said in a firm but quivery voice.

He waved away what he interpreted as my concern. "I'm fine, really."

Carson turned around with boxes stacked in front of him. "Open the door!"

I raced to the warehouse door and unlocked it. Once Carson walked through, I saw Dominic carrying boxes on a teetering stack. He followed Carson's instructions to set them on the "bar" we'd created in the far corner.

Dominic said something about the palm fronds we'd attached to the base of the bar and Carson laughed.

I couldn't move. What was I going to do? If I ordered Dominic to leave, I'd have to explain the situation to Carson. Or worse yet, Dominic would volunteer the information. That violation of my privacy, and shattering of my respect, would be as bad as Dominic's barging into my business.

As they walked past me to the door, Dominic quipped to Carson, "Guess that's what supervisors do, huh? Supervise?"

"Oh no, Jonna's the hardest-working boss I ever had. She's probably just thinking about the layout."

I shook myself out of my dark thoughts and turned up the heat controls. Then I walked outside to help unload the rest of the stuff. Carson balanced another precarious load in front of him.

"Dominic, can I talk to you alone?"

"Now, Jonna, I don't want you to tell me to leave. I'm perfectly fine, and you need the help," he said loud enough for Carson to hear.

I wasn't good at confrontation, but Dominic was pushing me into a corner. "You have no business being here," I said under my breath. "It's not right and you know it."

He actually tweaked my nose. "It's perfectly right, darling." When he saw my anger, his pleasant expression faded. "What you are going to do, call the police and have me ejected? Make a big scene?" He pressed his hands together and affected a high-pitched voice: " 'Oh, Officer, that man is trying to help me set up this party. Please stop him!' "

When he put it like that . . . I wanted to slug him. "What do you want?"

He leaned so close I could feel the fog of his breath. "You." Then he turned to load up several more boxes.

"You can't have me," I whispered, hearing Carson returning. "I'm married."

Dominic's fake blue eyes twinkled when he faced me again. "You weren't so married when you arranged for us to meet in that hotel room."

"Damn you." I realized I'd said it loud enough for Carson to hear.

Carson gave my shoulder a squeeze. "Jonna, we'll keep an eye on him. If he looks pale, we'll send him home, okay?"

Dominic had me and he knew it. Worse, he was enjoying it. Okay, I gave up. He won this round.

Or maybe not.

When life hands you lemons . . . I make lemonade. Or rather, have Dominic make it. If he was going to use my need for help to further his agenda, I was going to use him back.

Over the next hour I had him high up on the ladder hanging yards of fabric for the blue backdrops. It was his job to string the speaker wires behind those folds of fabric and mount them high in the corners. While he was hanging the speakers I accidentally blasted the stereo, just testing, you understand.

"Sorry," I called out, hearing insincerity in my voice. He narrowed his eyes but carried on.

Give up already, dammit. But he didn't, and I felt my insides curl at his determination. How far would he take this?

Fueled by anger and fear, I assigned Dominic to cart in forty bags of sand for the sandbox. Carson and I carried in the silk palm trees while Dominic opened each bag and dumped it out, grunting and slick with sweat. When he was done, Carson and I brought in bags of brightly colored plastic shovels and buckets and arranged them into a *B* in the box.

As Dominic walked toward me, I searched for another task to assign him.

"I need you to start on the lights." I nodded toward boxes of huge lights that would give the room a sunny-day feel rather than the sterile look of the fluorescents. I saw his resolve crumble. "We're running out of time," I pushed.

But I saw him gather up again and walk toward the boxes. I'd been annoyed that my original supplier had called yesterday, stumbling over himself in apology: the lights weren't coming. The company that had last leased them wasn't able to ship them back in time. I'd had to find another supplier, paying extra because of the time element. Now that seemed trivial compared to the problem I had with Dominic.

Carson and I set up the beach bar, arranging artful stacks of bags of chips, candy bars, and other sugary snacks.

"Am I missing something?" he asked, watching Dominic wrestle one of the large aluminum lights out of the box.

I gave Carson an innocent look. "Mm?"

"The guy shows up to help, despite the fact that he's injured, and you've been giving him the ugliest jobs."

"I'm trying to discourage him. I keep hoping he'll fizzle out and go home. He needs to, ah, rest."

Carson shook his head, admiration in his expression. "He's dogged. Wish I had his stamina." He went over to hold the ladder when Dominic was ready to ascend.

My smile faded and I returned to work on the bar with furious intent. I usually loved this part of my job, when everything came together. It was the hardest part physically but the most satisfying. Not this time.

I opened a four-pack of Oreo cookies and scraped my teeth against a cookie. I bet half the kids at the party would do the same. I didn't let the fact that I wasn't a kid spoil my fun.

At nearly five o'clock, when guests were supposed to arrive, I surveyed the room. Several of the Big Brothers Big Sisters organizers were there as we did a run-through of all the effects. Sound of seashore and seagulls: check. Scent of coconut oil: check. Temperature of a warm summer day with breeze supplied by fans: check.

Stalker, dripping with sweat, coming my way: check.

I reached into my pocket and curled my hands around what was inside. "That's it," I said as he approached. "Carson and I can handle the rest from here." I handed Dominic several bills. "I'm sure you know how much your help was appreciated."

"You were a lifesaver, man," Carson said, holding out his hand and giving Dominic's an exaggerated shake. He said to me, "I'm going to fire up the grills, make sure all is well there."

I wanted to tell Carson to stay but didn't.

Dominic didn't look at the bills he'd taken but moved closer to me. As usual I could smell cinnamon on his breath. I now hated the scent. "I saw you watching me, Jonna. You can talk all you want, you can pretend to be virtuous all of a sudden, but I see everything I need to know in your eyes."

"Dom—"

He put his finger over my mouth. "I'll see you soon."

As he sauntered off, I wanted to shout, *But I don't want to see you ever, ever again!* I couldn't cause a scene. *Work through it,* I told myself. *That's what you do. Stay calm, put on a game face, and you'll manage.*

All I had to do was ignore the twist in my stomach that told me this wasn't going to be as easy as that.

I walked over to Carson, who gave a thumbs-up on the grills. "They both work."

We were going to serve hot dogs and hamburgers. I didn't have a kitchen, so I usually cooked on-site. I started setting out the packages of buns, hot dogs to the left, hamburgers to the right.

Carson said, "Interesting guy, your friend."

"He's not my friend," I said before I could play the words more casually. "Just an acquaintance."

"I think he wants to be more than that."

I looked up. "Why do you say that?"

"Did you notice the way he was watching you? It's one thing to look at a lovely person, to enjoy the way he or she moves. But to study them with open hunger in your eyes goes beyond appreciation. I thought you might want to know, just in case, well . . . in case of whatever." Carson started helping me with the packages, obviously uncomfortable advising his boss about her personal life. "Oh, one other thing: When you and Manny went to the shop for the food, he disappeared for a while. Not like he was taking a break, either. He had purpose. When I mentioned it later, he said he had to run an errand. Seemed kind of cagey about it."

I glanced toward the door and shivered. What had he been up to?

Dominic remained just outside the door, watching Jonna as she pulled herself out of her deep thoughts and returned to work. She'd freshened up and changed before everyone started arriving. He glanced down at the dust on his clothing and felt the damp circles of now cold sweat at his waistband and underarms.

She'd played him all right, and he'd had to go along. Why was she being so damned stubborn? He looked at the two one-hundred-dollar bills she'd foisted on him. He could use the money, sure. But he knew why she'd paid him, though he'd never asked for a dime: so she wouldn't owe him. Well, she did owe him. For making this so damned hard.

He'd thought of the last woman who'd messed things up. Everything about that had been screwed up, he thought, anger seething inside him. He had been betrayed. He could still feel the anger of that, the knifelike pain cutting right down to the bone. The woman . . . she was dead. She hadn't cooperated and now she was dead.

Jonna wasn't cooperating, either. Would she have to die, too? He didn't want to think of the uncontrollable fury and deadly calm that had sandwiched that terrible event. He could still see the woman's husband, his face wracked in grief.

No, it wasn't just the lingering sting of betrayal. Dominic was used to that, had lived with it like someone used to living with chronic pain. This whole thing with Jonna flared it hot and sharp again. It was probably because Jonna was playing games with him. A sense of desperation was nipping at his heels, like dogs tearing at his flesh. Their barks sounded like, *You're losing; you're losing!*

He shook his head to throw off the chant in his head. *I won't lose this time.*

He gripped the key to his plan in his hand, buried deep in his pocket. It was time to step things up. Time to take control.

CHAPTER TWELVE

Our bathroom reminded me of a spa I'd visited in Arizona, a luxury trip I'd treated myself to when I worked at the hotel. It was the only room in the loft with color, rust and earthy tones that gave me the sense of being in some desert corridor. The floors and part of the walls were stone; I liked the feel of the rough texture on my bare feet. The steam shower boasted the darkest colors, burnt umber and natural rust-colored stone. I forwent the large hot tub for the shower, wanting the body jets to knead the tension from my shoulders. The steamed glass doors obliterated everything but the soft light.

I was trying hard not to think about how Dominic had manipulated me and how his presence in my life was becoming more invasive. Maybe that chilling thought started my paranoia. I saw a shift in the light. I wiped at the steam, but it was futile.

"Rush?"

No answer. I stared through the door, seeing nothing. Then I heard the door close. Or at least I thought that I did. I slid the shower door open. Nothing. If Rush had come in, he would have said something.

From there, I kept hearing sounds and seeing shadows,

though I didn't think they were real. Not then. But in the beginning?

I cut my shower short, threw on my plush robe, and walked out and down the hallway. I leaned over the railing, listening for the slightest sound. Only accent lights that showcased the large paintings on the immense walls lit the room. I checked downstairs, hoping to find Rush sitting in the family room. No luck. As I headed back upstairs, finally convincing myself it was indeed my imagination, I glanced at the front door—and saw that it was unlocked.

It felt as though an icy finger touched the back of my neck. "I know I locked it." But did I know for sure? I was brain drained. No, I couldn't be sure.

I locked it, peered around the white blinds, and was just about to pull away when I thought I saw someone outside. I narrowed my eyes and studied the shadow at the far edge of the parking lot. I couldn't tell, but my instincts whispered that it was exactly what I thought it was: Dominic. My skin stippled and my throat went dry. No, he wouldn't be just standing out there in the cold. I refused to believe it. Couldn't believe it. The thought would freak me out.

I went upstairs and turned on my computer.

I skimmed over the comments from my previous entry, my stomach clenching when I saw that Dominic had posted.

• Dom wrote:
Don't let Montene tell you she's a good driver. She nearly ran me over! I'm sure it wasn't on purpose. She tenderly nursed me and made sure I was all right. She's a better nurse than she is a driver, that's for sure. Aside from a killer headache, I'm fine. It was worth it for those minutes spent in her arms.

I let out an agonized scream. "Okay, get a grip. Breathe. Type."

Blog entry: November 10, 7:05 p.m.

Blog friends,

I'm sorry for my absence. I've missed being here, but my world has been hectic. The two men in my life have been keeping me off-balance. I think Johnny suspects something, and that is because Dominic is around despite my having told him repeatedly that I won't go further with him. I suppose some of you would consider his persistence romantic, but what I need is to move on and figure out what I'm going to do with my marriage. Johnny's been around more lately, which is both good and bad. I mean, it's nice that he wants to be around me, but I have to wonder why. To keep tabs on me?

Men. I wish I understood them more so I knew how to handle them. Johnny is mysterious and sexy and ambitious. He's dynamic. But we have no real connection. Dominic and I had a connection, but it somehow got miswired. I can't communicate with either one of them, like we speak different languages.

I don't suppose it's any different for many of you. I've heard your stories. Why can't we communicate????

—Montene

PS: Hitting Dominic had nothing to do with my driving skills. What was he doing in the same parking garage I was in, by my car at the same minute that I was leaving? Coincidence? I think not.

I was both exhausted and wired, a frustrating condition. Rush had left a message that he'd be working late, which was good in a way. It gave me time to calm down.

I'd called Beth on the way home, telling her about Dominic's intrusion.

"It must be nice to be wanted that much," she'd said on a breathy sigh. "I know, he's going a little far, but still, to be *wanted*."

I had enjoyed that feeling early on, but not anymore. Now I only wanted to be left alone.

I sat down at Rush's desk and opened the shallow drawer where he kept pens, notes, and his deck of cards. I pulled them out and ran my fingers across the edges like he did. What did he think about when he did that? They smelled old in a pleasant way. I propped my chin on the thick edge and wondered again who my husband really was.

A few minutes later I was about to return them when I saw a stack of photos in the back of the drawer. In one a man who looked like Rush was holding a woman on his lap and she was laughing and trying to get away. Rush's parents, I guessed by the slight discoloration and clothing styles. In another, two boys fished in a river, wearing ragtag clothing. Rush had no pictures from his childhood anywhere, yet he kept some hidden in a drawer. Why?

When I heard the key in the lock I shoved everything into the drawer, my heartbeat hammering at the thought of him catching me snooping in his personal things. I threw myself into my chair as Rush stepped in and looked up at me. He was holding a yellow rose, which made my heart beat even faster than it already was. Except that he wore a questioning expression.

"This was by the door."

No rose from Rush, I thought, steeped in disappointment. Even worse, that rose meant Dominic *had* been outside. I remembered the shadows I thought I saw in the bathroom. But he couldn't get inside. We had secure dead bolts and windows. No, wait. The door had been unlocked. I refused to believe that Dominic would be bold enough to try the door and come inside. I shivered.

"I, uh, oh, must have dropped it. From the party today. One of the extra ones." I was experiencing all the anxiety and guilt of an affair without any of the pleasure.

He looked at the rose. "The *beach* party?"

"For accents," I said, knowing that roses didn't go with a beach theme. Apparently even Rush had his doubts.

I was in my robe, still damp from my shower. I toed off my fuzzy socks and padded down the cold steel steps to where Rush was lovingly dropping frozen cubes of shrimp and brine into the aquarium with silver tongs. The rose was lying on the black table.

"Were you here earlier?" I asked. "I thought I heard something when I was in the shower."

"Wasn't me." He walked to the bar and surprised me by pouring a glass of wine.

"Probably my imagination."

"You had a long day, too," he said, handing me the glass. "How did the party go?"

"Great." Usually I filled him in on the details. He seemed interested, and that felt like a tenuous connection between us. Every time I thought about the party, though, all I could see was Dominic. "The kids seemed to have fun," I added lamely.

I sipped the red liquid as Rush poured a glass of whisky, tapped it to my glass, and downed the whole thing. He set the glass on the bar and stared at it for a moment. I saw the tension in his jaw. He looked at me then, and I felt sure he was going to accuse me of something. Instead, he dipped his fingers into his glass and extracted an ice cube. He ran it along my collarbone. I shivered, from both the cold and the intense way he was looking at me. I gasped softly as cold liquid dripped between my breasts and down my belly before being absorbed by my robe.

He dropped the cube back into his glass and followed the trail of cold water with his warm mouth. The polar sensations woke my body, tightening my skin and pooling heat deep inside me. He untied my sash and parted the burgundy material without stopping his dizzying motion. He spread my legs and dipped his tongue in, teasing, waking me up. It was overwhelmingly erotic to see Rush, so powerful and larger-than-life, kneeling in front of me, pleasuring me. My legs wobbled and I flattened my hands against the wall to help hold me up. My robe slid off my shoulders and crumpled to the floor.

His hands were on my hips, pressing into my flesh. After he brought me to climax, he stood and kissed me. His hand locked around my neck, holding me close. I felt that stir inside even as I wondered what had gotten into my husband.

He was throwing me completely off-balance lately. I had to admit a warped part of me liked it. The rest didn't understand why. I wanted stability, normalcy—whatever that was. But the Montene part of me was on fire, uttering intermittent groans as his hands roamed possessively over my naked body, not skimming the surface but gripping me as though he were afraid I'd slide away. I ran my fingers through his hair and along his jawline. He hoisted me up, and I wrapped my legs around him as he carried me upstairs.

He turned on the lights beneath the floating bed, laid me down, and stripped out of his clothes. Just looking at him nearly made me climax again. The light played off the angles of his body, from his wide shoulders that tapered to his narrow hips and the hard length of him pointing toward the ceiling. When he knelt down over me I felt his penis slide across my thigh and between my legs. He shifted, and it traced circles against my skin. Except . . . it felt too smooth now. I'd no sooner had that thought when his penis vibrated to life.

I shot up, seeing my vibrator, my unnamed vibrator that I'd hidden in my lingerie drawer, in his hand. He was trailing it across my already sensitive flesh and giving me a positively naughty look.

"Where'd you get that?" I asked, the embarrassing realization washing over me.

He gently pushed me back on the bed. "I left a gift in your drawer, to replace the outfit I tore." His voice lowered even more. "And I found this. Thought we'd have some fun with it . . . together."

He thought I'd been tooling myself, because, hey, why else would a woman have one hidden in her drawer? "I haven't . . . it's not . . ."

He was moving it over me again, and words failed me. Jonna was mortified and uncomfortable. Montene, however, was reveling in the electric feeling of sexual decadence. When she came again, it was the most powerful orgasm I'd ever had.

He covered me with his body, rolling me over so I was on top and pulling me down against him when I impaled myself on him. Our lovemaking had been more intense than ever lately. Was it me, realizing how close I'd come to betraying him, to betraying my faith and my belief in our marriage? Or was it Rush, trying to make up for his own betrayal?

I didn't—couldn't—think about that, not now. I let myself go, riding the wave of an even larger climax. I felt him explode inside me as his body tensed. As he pulled me against him, our bodies still together, the words in my head pleaded, *I love you,* and, softer, *Please don't hurt me.*

He twirled his fingers through my hair, staring at the ceiling. He never looked at me when we made love. I'd never asked him why, but I sensed it went somewhere deep inside him. I wasn't even sure he knew. I could hear his heartbeat hammering in his chest. I splayed my hand over the ridges of his stomach.

I love you. I wanted to say the words, but they wouldn't come. Maybe I was afraid all the rest would come out, too. How afraid I was to love him. How afraid that I'd be hurt. And mostly, how scared I was that this was the only way we'd ever connect.

◆ ◆ ◆

Late that night, Rush watched her sleep. The accent lighting cast just enough light to see the contours of her face, the curve of her shoulder. The silk strap of her nightgown had slipped to her arm. He reached over to push it back up but stopped. He didn't want to wake her.

She always slept with her hands tucked beneath her pillow. She sometimes mumbled in her sleep, but he'd never been able to coax out any intelligible words. He took a lock of her hair and brushed the ends against her cheek. She twitched and then swiped at it. He smiled. He had dipped into her dream, though she would never know it.

He'd been surprised to find the vibrator in her drawer. Annoyed at first, because hell, wasn't he satisfying her? Ego aside, he probably hadn't been. Then he decided to have a little fun with it. He'd never seen her as the kind of woman who would own a vibrator. He rather liked that woman. Jonna, it turned out, was full of surprises. Not all of them pleasant, though.

He eased out of bed and walked down the hall to the loft. He'd told Jonna that they'd pick her out a large desk, but she insisted on a small one. His wrapped around two walls, the many drawers containing his personal documents and miscellaneous research. He sat down, naked, and turned on the computer.

Once the computer was booted up, he opened a software program and checked on a particular research project. Nothing worrisome. He closed it and pulled up the Internet. The site wasn't bookmarked, but he knew the address by heart.

He glanced toward the darkened hallway, just in case. Then he read Montene's latest post.

CHAPTER THIRTEEN

Blog entry: November 11, 4:00 p.m.

What is it with men? I'm used to my husband working all the time, being preoccupied when he is home, and great but sporadic lovemaking. Lately Johnny's been home more and, um, quite amorous. (Sorry, you know I don't kiss and tell.) What does it mean? Gifts, flowers, I could understand. I'd think he's feeling guilty. But being home? Sexing me up more? I'm totally confused. Any thoughts?

—Montene

"Filet mignon medallions in burgundy sauce, potato puffs, green beans." Monday morning I sat in my office at the shop and drew up my lists for Rush's dinner party. I calculated quantities and then moved to the dessert. "Flourless chocolate cake snuggled up with fresh raspberries and nestled in a bed of whipped cream."

However, my focus was more fragile than torched sugar on crème brûlée. Rush and I had had a leisurely Sunday morning, going over the details for the party. I'd noticed his hand on me from time to time: my shoulder, my thigh. Suggestive, slightly proprietary, possibly affectionate. The yellow rose, wilted because I hadn't put it in water, lay on the table. I caught him looking at it when we were waiting for the coffee to brew, and I'd tossed it in the trash.

Gawd, the vibrator. I'd always thought of them as self-pleasuring devices, not as toys for two. My face still warmed at the thought of Rush finding it but heated from what he'd done with it.

See, there went my focus again. I made three calls to suppliers and then gave in to what I'd been wanting to do since yesterday: check my blog.

247 Comments:

• Consuela wrote:

Montene, why are you holding out on us? I can tell you're leaving out so much. No, I'm not talking about the details of your sexcapades, but everything else. Do you think your husband is cheating? I'd say he's up to something. Haven't you ever heard of guilt sex? Keep the old lady happy so she won't suspect.

• Muffin wrote:

I think your husband thinks YOU'RE cheating. When I was having my little fling last fall, all of a sudden my husband was soooo sweet. When I stopped the affair, he stopped being sweet. Now I'm looking!

As I read through the comments, I realized everyone had a different opinion. Several took me to task for being secretive. Some urged me to have an affair. Some tried to discourage me. I had begun to close the page without adding anything new when I spotted Dominic's entry. I should have ignored it, but I couldn't.

• Dom wrote:

Things are moving along nicely. I helped Montene with her work on Saturday. I don't want to give away any details, you know, to keep her identity secret. Let's just say we went to the beach together. She told me her name, her address, and even invited me to her shop. I'm touched that she trusts me to keep her secret. But what is it you girls say all the time? Hm, let me see . . . never trust a man. Yeah, that was it. Do you trust me, Montene? As long as you're a good girl, you have nothing to worry about.

"Son of a bitch!" I slapped my hand on the desk. He was taunting me with his ability to out me! The thought stilled my fingers as I was about to type a post that would slam him. I could see it now, the *Globe* laying out my life—and Rush's—for all to read.

"Let it go. Ignore him. Don't provoke him."

He had me and he knew it. That made me madder than almost anything else.

When my phone rang, I cheered up at the sight of AngelForce's number on the screen. Either Beth or Rush.

"Hey, it's me," Beth said, and I could tell by the tone of her voice that she didn't have good news. I could also tell, by the traffic sounds in the background that she was outside. "Look, sweetie, I thought you should know, I think Rush is having lunch with you-know-who today. I don't know for sure, but I heard Priscilla take a message for Kirsten, though I couldn't see who she was calling for. Not long after that Rush asked Mona to make a reservation for two at the Plum Café. It all seems pretty odd, considering. I read your blog entry. What's going on? What's he doing?"

I felt funny divulging what Rush and I did sexually, even to my best friend. "He's been very . . . intensely . . . sexual. I thought that when men were cheating, they didn't want sex with their wives. Judging from the comments, I was wrong." I realized, in the wan way I'd said it, that I was disappointed, that I'd harbored hope that Rush wasn't cheating after all, or that he'd stopped the affair.

"Oh, sweetie. I've told you before, cut your losses and move on. He's playing you, don't you see? Keeping you happy so you'll be around when he needs you. Or even worse, he's fantasizing about her while doing his duty at home." She made a snorting noise. "Men are bastards. The weak link, I'm telling you."

Damn, that hurt. I focused on Beth's attitude instead. Maybe her sexual habits—and inflated ego—had more to do with harboring bitterness toward men than a shaky self-esteem. She talked little about her previous relationships, other than a recent inference that she'd been cheated on. I only knew about her ex stalking her because we'd seen him twice; she'd had us ducking down and sneaking out the back way. He hadn't seemed warped; in fact, he'd reminded me of my first love.

"You may be right," I acknowledged with a sigh.

"Want to have a liquid lunch at Tomatillo's Margaritas? Isn't that the most beautiful word? Mar-ga-rita!"

"No, thanks. I'll be fine."

"That's right: you have someone on the side yourself. Anything new with him?"

"He's not on the side. He's not anything to me." I pushed the anger from my voice. "He left a rose on my doorstep Saturday night. Rush found it. I told him I must have dropped it when I came in, that I'd brought it home from the party. I don't think he believed me. And it pisses me off that he seemed suspicious after what he's pulling." I reached for a pack of Oreos that was sitting on my desk and opened it. "Can a man be that much of an ass, to be jealous that his wife is having an affair when he is?"

"Oh, jeez, yes. It's the caveman thing."

I thought of the possessive way Rush held me. "Maybe you're right." I opened a cookie and skimmed the icing off the top wafer.

"I am. So what are you going to do about Dom? He's

obviously completely head over heels. He won't take no for an answer. Are you going to give in?"

"No. Mold can be pervasive, too, but I'm not about to let it grow everywhere." I was thinking of the mold I'd discovered when I moved in here. "I keep thinking he'll take the hint eventually. But he's getting more and more invasive. It's beginning to scare me."

"Honey, you've got a lot going on right now. And I'm probably not helping, but I assume you want to know what Rush is up to, right?"

"Yes. No. Oh, I don't know." I thought of my father. "Yes, I do. I just wish I could come out and ask him." The thought alone gave my stomach the twisties.

"I've got to go back in," Beth said. "I snuck out for a cig, and don't lecture me; I'm tense. For you," she added, as though her taking up her bad habit again was my fault.

After that call, I couldn't focus anymore. I kept seeing Rush and Kirsten having sex on the table at the Plum Café, him doing to her what he'd been doing to me lately.

"No, stop it. You want to save your marriage? Then be a man and find out if he's seeing her for absolutely sure. That's step one." I wasn't sure what step two was.

I locked up and drove toward Back Bay, parked in a nearby garage, and walked toward the stone building. The drab weather perfectly matched my mood.

What do I hope to accomplish here? Catch him and Kirsten leaving for lunch?

Why, yes, that's exactly what some reckless part of me wanted. Then it would be out in the open. Rush would have to explain himself, and maybe he'd say what a terrible mistake he was making and beg me to forgive him. Maybe he'd say he was glad I knew because he'd been trying to find a way to tell me he wanted a divorce.

That made me pause, and it was there, looking conflicted and God knew what else, that Hadden found me when he stepped out of the building. He looked as though he'd stepped off the pages of *GQ* with his thigh-length black leather jacket and perfectly creased pants. He fit right in to the fashionable Newbury Street atmosphere with its high-end shops and trendy restaurants.

"Jonna," he said, his smile indicating that seeing me was a pleasant surprise. It morphed to concern. "Are you all right?"

"I . . . well, I was coming to see Rush."

"He already left."

"Oh."

"Was he expecting you?"

"No, I was just . . . I don't know. I should probably go."

He took hold of my arm as I was about to turn to leave. "What's wrong?"

I wanted to ask him, was Rush seeing Kirsten, but I couldn't push out those or any words. I tried to shrug it off. "I was . . . it's not important."

Hadden was studying me, not with the intensity Rush had been lately but definitely worry. "I was on my way to lunch. By myself. Join me." Sensing that I was about to gracefully decline, he took control. "You obviously need to talk, or at least sit down for a few minutes. Come with me to Sonsie's."

He didn't give me a choice but led me down the sidewalk to the chic restaurant. Inside, women glanced his way. With his regal bearing and sculpted features, they probably wondered if he was one of the models or aspiring actors who frequented the place.

He waited until we ordered before saying, "Tell me what's going on."

I decided to start small. "Have you noticed anything . . . different about Rush lately?"

"He's been distracted. Staring off into space, going to unpleasant places if his expression is any indicator." Hadden picked up his glass of chardonnay but rolled the stem between his fingers instead of taking a sip. His nails were trimmed and buffed, no sign of a hangnail anywhere. "He won't tell me what's wrong. I thought it might be something at home."

He waited for me to affirm or deny. I honestly didn't have a straight answer. "It's complicated, but"—*push out the words, Jonna, one word at a time*—"I think . . . he's seeing someone."

Hadden arched an eyebrow. "Why?"

"All those late hours for one thing."

"He's always done that. He's driven to succeed. Lately we've both been putting in the hours on this DEMCO thing. There's a lot at stake."

He waited for more information. He was right; that hadn't changed. What *had* changed was Rush coming home more, making wild love to me. I couldn't tell Hadden that.

"I've noticed the same thing you have, that he's off somewhere a lot. Sometimes he's up in the middle of the night, too. He's acting more intense. And he . . . looks at me differently. I can't explain it."

"Is it woman's intuition?"

I was twisting my wedding ring around my finger. "Something like that."

He leaned back in his chair. "You're not telling me everything."

I took a deep breath. How much to tell? How much did I want to know? I didn't want to betray Beth's confidence, either. I fell back on my pussyfoot habit. "Last year I walked in on Kirsten and Rush in his office. They were . . ." Hadden was leaning forward now, fully engaged in what I was telling him. It made me feel both special and nervous. "They weren't kissing exactly, but there was something going on. You know, you can sense it in the air. Chemistry. Forbidden feelings."

"Oh yes, I know," he said in a soft voice that told me he did know.

"I left. I'm bad about confrontations. Rush brought it up that night and told me that they'd dated before he met me but there was nothing between them since then."

"Did you believe him?"

"Mm, sort of. I mean, I wanted to believe him, and yet, I'm not sure I did." I tore a piece of my bread and stuck it in my mouth without even buttering it. "I don't think I really let it go," I admitted. "But Rush promised that he wouldn't have any dealings with her."

"And now?"

Yes, Hadden was going to make me say it all. Looking at him, at the glint in his crisp blue eyes, I saw that he knew something. It made my heart ache.

"Kirsten's back, isn't she?"

"And you know this how?"

"Please promise not to repeat this to anyone. Beth told me. She's my best friend, only looking out for my interests. What confirmed it was hearing Priscilla take a message from Kirsten the day Rush and I had lunch."

Hadden nodded, but he wasn't looking at me. He was tearing his bread into small pieces, not even pretending to eat it. Finally he looked up at me. "I'd like to tell you, for my own selfish reasons, that Rush is a cheating son of a bitch. Honestly, I doubt he would ever cheat on you. Yes, he's keeping something from you. But it's not an affair, at least as far as I can tell.

"Kirsten approached us two months ago about a guy she knows who has a phenomenal new wireless technology. He's ripe fruit and all he needs is the right backing and mentoring. She has some of the capital—and it's going to take a lot—but she wanted us to get in on it, too. So we've been talking to her about it. I should say, *I've* been talking to her. Rush has given it completely to me. That message Kirsten left was for me, not him. He said that if things actually moved forward, he would tell you. He didn't want you worried before then."

"So you already knew about Kirsten, about me seeing them together."

He nodded. "Rush had to tell me why he didn't want to be involved in such an exciting deal. That day Kirsten came in to see him, she wanted to restart the relationship. So you were right; the air was charged. But Rush told her he was happily married, period. I believe him."

I felt something release inside me. Not completely, but a little. "So he's not . . . having lunch with her right now?"

My question clearly perplexed Hadden. "No. I was supposed to meet with her and the technology people for lunch today, but they canceled." He glanced at his watch. "Right now Rush is having lunch with Mrs. Moreland."

"Mrs. Moreland?" I asked, wondering if Hadden was leading into something else.

He gave me a smile. "She's about seventy-two."

"You don't have to patronize me. I'm not insecure in general. Just about Kirsten. Because of their history, and I'm not even sure what history they had exactly."

"Why don't you ask him?"

"I will," I said, though I couldn't imagine doing so.

Then I thought of something else and couched the question with a look of chagrin. "Have you ever noticed anything between Rush and Beth? On his part?"

Hadden laughed, which I took as a good sign. "To be honest, Rush doesn't even like her much. She does a good job, but he views her as your watchdog."

"That wasn't the intention, honestly." Could Beth have just misinterpreted the conversation in the conference room? Like, I realized, she did sometimes, seeing something that wasn't necessarily there. I hoped so.

Rush having an affair with an old girlfriend was one thing; coming on to my best friend would be despicable.

Just after our meals arrived, something Hadden said earlier struck me. "Just now, you said for your own selfish reasons you wished you could say Rush was a lothario."

He gave me a pained grimace. "I was rather hoping you missed that." He reminded me of a teenage boy caught with a dirty magazine. He rubbed his face, looking to the ceiling. Finally he met my gaze. "I sometimes wondered if you knew, but I guess you haven't noticed, which is good. When you were talking about sensing chemistry in the air, forbidden feelings . . ."

He waved that away. "I've had feelings for you since I met you. It was your second date with Rush, and the three of us went out for drinks. I remember thinking, 'Damn, I wish I'd seen her first.' " He reached over and took my hand in a casual gesture, obviously picking up on my surprise. "I'm glad I hid it well. And I intend to keep hiding it, so don't worry. I'd never come on to you. I respect you and Rush too much. He's like a brother to me. Now, let's eat."

My appetite had only just returned on the news he'd given me and now he'd dumped that on me. He was watching me pull apart my pizza, making sure I was all right with what he'd revealed. It made me feel funny, self-conscious. I was aware of him as more than a friend now. I noticed how long and curled his eyelashes were, how his mouth curved, and the patch on his cheek he'd missed with his razor. I didn't want to see him as a man, and particularly as someone who was interested in me as a woman.

Damn. *Work through it,* I told myself. I didn't want his confession to spoil our friendship.

Just as I mustered the wherewithal to take a bite, I glanced to the right—and saw Dominic two tables away

watching me like a jealous husband. At the shock of seeing him I gasped.

"What's wrong?" Hadden said, following my gaze to
Dominic, who did nothing to hide his disdain.

I quickly looked to Hadden. "He's . . . I . . ." I
couldn't tell Hadden who Dominic really was. I couldn't
involve him or anyone else. I'd done something stupid
to bring Dominic into my life, and now I had the responsibility to get him out. I'd learned that early on
when my mother made me return a candy bar I'd taken
from a store. At four years old I'd had to admit that I'd
done a bad thing and pleaded with the manager not to
call the police. "I met with him to do a job and he's been
sort of hanging around ever since. I told him I'm not interested, that I'm married, but that doesn't seem to deter
him."

I saw Hadden stiffen. "Want me to have a talk with
him?"

Refined, classy Hadden having "a talk" with Dominic
would have been laughable if I could have scrounged up
any of my humor. "No, please don't. He'll get the hint
eventually."

"Jonna, this could be serious. If he's stalking you—"

"I can handle it," I said, patting Hadden's hand to
emphasize the words and then quickly removing my
hand. "Let's eat."

I picked at my Mexican chicken pizza, spending all
my energy acting as though Dominic's venomous stare
didn't bother me in the least. Throughout the meal I
found myself rubbing the yellow diamond in my wedding set. Hadden noticed but said nothing.

When we left, Dominic left, too, but he lingered far
behind. Unfortunately, I knew that because I was looking for him.

"Can I walk you to your car or the T station?" Hadden asked, also glancing around.

"That's not necessary. I've got errands, so I'll be walking. I'll be careful," I added at his concerned look. "He hasn't done anything threatening." I wasn't going to admit that just having him around was threatening.

Hadden studied me, giving me that tilted-head gesture I was used to seeing. "If you want to talk, you know you can trust me. I'm still your friend, and nothing but."

I felt my eyes tingle, wanting badly to reach out and tell him everything, to hear supportive words and corroboration that I wasn't being silly. But I couldn't. I'd buried myself in a moral hole I wanted no one to know about. "Thanks," I managed.

He hugged me, being careful not to press me as close as he used to. Things had already changed between us and I hated that. When we parted, he got a funny expression on his face, making me turn around to see what he was looking at: Rush and, true to Hadden's word, a lady who could have been my grandmother. The woman bid him good-bye, but Rush's dark green eyes were on me. Specifically, me with Hadden. I saw the nearly imperceptible frown of Rush's eyebrows.

"Look who I ran into," Hadden said in a falsely cheerful voice. "She came to see you and since you were gone, I talked her into having lunch with me. How'd lunch with Mrs. Moreland go?"

"Fine." He let that word hang.

How could I tell Hadden that the reason Rush was probably suspicious was because of all the oddities swirling around me lately? It didn't help that Hadden looked guilty.

Hadden said, "See you at our afternoon meeting," to Rush. He gave me a smile and headed inside.

I had to admit that a naughty part of me liked the jealousy I saw in Rush's eyes. It meant he cared enough to be jealous. I tried to keep my gaze trained away from searching for Dominic and looked at Rush. "Hi."

"Why do you look so uneasy?" He arched an eyebrow. "Guilty, even. Is there something I should know?"

That was an understatement, and I could have enjoyed the irony if I weren't so worried about how guilty I looked. "We just had lunch. It's . . . it's not like that."

It struck me then that Rush had said those same words after I'd walked in on him with Kirsten. I leaned forward and kissed him, a silent reassurance. He pulled me hard against him and deepened the kiss. He'd never been one for public affection, and that alone stirred my fire. That and the fact that he was staking his claim. Me. His soft mouth devoured mine. He ran his tongue over my front teeth. He liked my slight overlap and had once begged me not to fix it when I'd mentioned getting braces.

"I'll see you tonight," he said after releasing me.

I had to lean against the stone facade for a few minutes as I watched him walk inside. My thoughts were careening into one another, creating sparks. I felt the heat from the stone emanating through my coat and warming my back.

He hadn't cheated. I took a deep breath, feeling my eyes tear up. He hadn't cheated. Knowing that was such a relief. But why was it scary, too?

Because, as insane as it was, it had been easier to think Rush was a cheat. Why?

Because suspecting him made it easier to keep the shield between us. That distance kept me from being fully involved in my marriage, which kept me from getting fully hurt. Now I knew why my father had always been emotionally distant. As much as I denigrated him, I had become him.

Roll the dice, I could hear Rush say, one of his favorite expressions. Now I had no excuse to let anything come between us. More important, I didn't want any excuses. I had to make my marriage right. That meant I had to get rid of Dominic before Rush realized he was stalking me—and why.

When I opened my eyes, I was looking right into Dominic's face.

CHAPTER FOURTEEN

"Trying to make me jealous?" Dominic whispered, an evil hiss that smelled like a combination of cinnamon and coffee. I heard the venom in his voice, saw it in his fake blue eyes.

I moved away from him, uncomfortable trapped between him and the wall. "Leave me alone." I didn't want to invoke the threat of calling the police. I felt intuitively that it would be the wrong thing to do. Maybe because I didn't want to admit who I was and how I'd met him. According to the article about Montene's Diary, men weren't exactly happy about the way we women sometimes talked about them. Not me so much, but my blog friends. I wasn't the only one who was taking steps to change her life. Then there was the whole discussion about the hidden foibles and not-so-hidden egos of our men in uniform, courtesy of their wives.

He fell into step next to me. "It won't work, you know."

"What?" I asked, kicking myself for answering him.

"You could screw him right here on the sidewalk and it won't put me off." He sounded so nasty, as though I'd betrayed him. It startled me to think he might feel that way.

"That wasn't for your benefit," I said, feeling it important to clarify that.

"Screwing his best friend isn't going to deter me, either, you cheating bitch."

I paused for a second but forced myself on. Not only because of the vehemence of his words but because he knew who Hadden was.

"I'm not screwing him," I said, continuing to look straight ahead and walk. I was sure we looked like a quarrelling couple to anyone passing by. I hated that thought.

"Did you tell him about me, about how we shared our deepest secrets in our e-mails? Did you tell him how you lured me to a hotel room and how my mouth tasted and how your nipples hardened when I sucked on them?"

I wanted to scratch him, to scream and kick and shove him to the sidewalk. I flexed my hands and swallowed back all the angry words exploding in my mouth.

"Did you tell him how much you liked it? How much you still want it? You do, Jonna. You want it bad. And you will come around again. You'll be begging me to—"

I made a quick turn into a store filled with porcelain figurines. Classical music played in the background, and a few customers milled about, talking softly. I hoped he would continue on down the sidewalk, but he stuck his head in the door and finished his sentence. "Suck your clit 'til you scream," he spit out before ducking back outside.

Everyone turned to me, as though I'd brought those filthy words into this elegant shop. I stared hard at the Lladro figurines rotating in a glass case, pretending I had nothing to do with it. Look calm and unruffled: check. Act entranced by the golfing-man figurine: check. Breathe: getting there.

I was shaking, feeling cold even though the store was warm. I heard whispers, but it all blended into the humming noise in my head.

He was gone. For now. But I had the terrible feeling he would be back again and again.

When I left Back Bay, I began looking in the rearview mirror. I saw a jumble of buildings and lots of cars. I still didn't know what Dominic drove. I didn't even know his real name. But he knew mine. My fingers tightened painfully on the steering wheel. It seemed he knew everything about me.

I drove to my shop, scanning the parking lot for anyone skulking around. My car looked terribly vulnerable sitting in the small lot, even though it wasn't the only vehicle. Several of the small businesses that operated from here were open, including the classic auto restorer at the end of my building. I should have felt safe, but I didn't.

My fingers trembled as I unlocked the door and stepped inside the cold space. I needed to focus on the dinner party in two nights. This was important to Rush, so it was important to me.

I called the art gallery where I had an ongoing arrangement to rent paintings for events. The deal was mutually beneficial, as the emerging artist got exposure to people with money.

"I've got eight paintings," Menlo, the gallery owner, said. "The artist is very excited."

"Wonderful. I am, too." The paintings were brightly colored depictions of martinis. Elegant and fun at the same time.

I was about to get to work on the centerpieces, candle lamps I'd picked up at a flea market, when my phone rang. I recognized Beth's cell number.

"Who are you seeing now?" she asked without preamble.

"What?"

"Haven't you checked your blog comments recently? Dominic just posted, accusing you of cheating on him."

I leaned against the table, pressing my forehead to the cold surface. "I don't want to read it. I don't want to think about him anymore. I don't want to see him lurking around, yelling at me in public—"

"What?"

She'd picked up on the hysteria and tears in my voice. I took a deep breath to calm myself and told her what had happened. Oddly, she didn't focus on the Dominic part at all. "Hadden was your date?"

"It wasn't a date. We just ended up having lunch. And I'm so glad I did." Mostly, anyway. "Rush isn't having an affair with Kirsten. And he wasn't having lunch with her today, either. Kirsten is setting up an investment opportunity with the company, but she's working with Hadden, not Rush."

"Thank goodness. I'm sorry I misled you, though not on purpose. I guess I'm as paranoid as a jilted woman would be. For you."

"I appreciate that." I decided not to tell her about Hadden's confession, since he was her boss. "Now, will you admit that Dominic is acting crazy?"

"Yes, definitely crazy."

"Thank you—"

"Over you," she added. "I'm sorry, Jonna, but I still think it's wildly romantic. Okay, it's a bit on the edge, sure. But it's your fault. You've done something to the man. I think you should just go with it, ride the wave, and see what happens. Probably it'll crest and then fizzle out. But how many women ever have a man that crazy for them?"

She was as stubborn as Dominic. "I've got to work on Rush's dinner party. I'll talk to you later."

Frustration swamped me. She was the one person I

could confide in and she wasn't taking me seriously. I felt very alone in my turmoil and fear.

I immersed myself in my work for the next two hours. I finished the centerpieces, double-checked the food I had stored in the cooler, and stacked the art deco silverware and black-and-white tablecloths on the table. I hummed along with the jazz station when I wasn't talking to myself.

It was nearly six when I looked at the clock. Rush would be home soon. But I couldn't hold off any longer. I logged onto my blog, scrolled through several pages of comments, and read Dominic's post.

Montene's Diary

> 625 Comments:
> • Dom wrote:
> Montene, it seems, is stepping out on the one she's stepping out with. I saw her at a restaurant all cozy with some Ken-doll guy. Has our girl gone off the deep end of slut? It broke my heart, of course. Girls, what do I do?
> • Lola wrote:
> Dom, Montene is holding out on all of us. We don't know what's going on with her lately.
> • Godz Girl wrote:
> Well, she did say she wanted to work things out with her husband. That she isn't a cheat. Leave her alone!

I skimmed the many posts after his, stunned at how most of the posters were comforting him and advising him on how to win me over. "You people are nuts!"

Many of my blog friends were all over my case about my keeping secrets from *them* of all people! I started to get a clammy, clawing feeling inside, the same one I got when I was stuck way in the back of a crowded elevator.

Unable to let it go, I posted.

Blog entry: November 12, 6:15 p.m.

Blog friends,

Thank you for the support Godz Girl and others have shown in my decision to back off from the whole affair idea. To the rest—shame on you! Buying vibrators on your advice is one thing, but cheating on my husband is another. And seriously, Dominic doesn't need your encouragement. He's been dogged in his efforts to change my mind. For the record, I was not having lunch with a paramour. He is a friend of my husband's and it was nothing more than lunch.

Dominic, it was entirely unnecessary, not to mention creepy, to have you staring at me the whole time. Please cease and desist.

—Montene

I knew I was being too soft on him, but provoking him wasn't what I wanted to accomplish. Today had shown me that.

I called and left a message at home, just in case Rush got there before I did. When I left the shop, it was nearly dark. Most of the workers had gone home. I heard my shoes scrape across the pavement as I walked to my car. The lot was well lit, but anyone could hide in the shadows. Maybe it was paranoia, but I could feel Dominic watching me. My heart thudded in my chest as I jabbed the button on my remote, which thankfully only unlocked the driver's door. I slipped in and relocked it.

As I pulled into the loft's parking lot I remembered seeing someone standing at the shadows' edge. A someone that was probably Dominic.

Rush was waiting when I got inside. Relaxed in one of the chairs in the living room, he looked alluring and sexy. But very closed. He acknowledged me with a nod and not much else.

"I ordered a pizza from Cicero's," he said.

I stood in front of Rush. "It wasn't like that," I said, kicking off my shoes. "My lunch with Hadden. I'd never have an affair with your best friend, and he wouldn't, either."

There. I'd come out and said it. Rush didn't seem moved, though, his expression remaining impassive. "Okay."

So maybe that wasn't what was bothering him. Stymied, I walked to the bar and poured a glass of Pinot Grigio. The answering machine light was blinking. I pressed the button and listened to hang-up after hang-up. Rush had obviously already checked. He was watching me.

When I picked up the phone to check the caller ID, he said, "They're all blocked. From the same number, no doubt. Maybe it was someone calling just to hear your message, since he waited until after the message before hanging up."

My face flamed; I hoped Rush didn't see it in the dim light. "Then you leave the outgoing message," I said, really wanting him to do so.

When someone knocked on the door, Rush pushed up from the chair and pulled out his wallet. I went into the kitchen and took out two plates. When I walked out to the dining table, I heard the man at the door say, "Order for Rush Karakosta?"

I nearly dropped the plates. Dominic's voice. No, it couldn't be. I couldn't see the man standing outside holding the pizza box. As I walked forward, my legs felt as though they were slogging through mud. I paused by the aquarium, peeking around the edge.

Dominic leaned in, a pleasant smile on his face. "Good evening, ma'am."

I wanted to run to the door and tell him to leave me alone, to stop invading my life. How in the hell had he managed to deliver our pizza? Probably bribed the deliveryman. I saw the yellow light on top of a car waiting outside.

Rush paid him and Dominic said, "Thank you, Mr. Karakosta. You both have a nice evening."

When Rush closed the door, he had a puzzled expression on his face. "How did he know our last name? I always give my first name."

"Maybe they have caller ID. Who cares, let's eat!" My words and expression were overly bright. I had to bury my fury and fear.

"Something wrong?" he asked, bringing the box to the table.

"No." I inspected the pizza carefully, just in case. "Everything looks great." Untampered with.

As I ate, I saw Rush in a different light. Not as a man who might break my heart. I could now look at his hands and not see them touching another woman's skin. I saw them on my skin and mine alone. I wanted to reach him, and now he was closed up, guarded. The hell of it was, he had reason to be. All the little things Dominic had been doing, and now the hang-ups, everything added up to something illicit.

I filled the silent gaps with updates on Rush's dinner party, but he was only half-listening. All of those long silences at our family dinner table, of things unsaid hanging in the air, made it hard for me to open up. So, too, did the secrets I was holding on to, then and now.

After we cleaned up, I had to fight the temptation to go to the front window and look out. Mostly I didn't want to give Dominic the satisfaction of knowing he was getting to me. What was he up to? Why go to all that trouble to deliver our pizza and do nothing?

Because he wanted to remind me that he could infiltrate my life.

"Oh, this came for you today," Rush said, handing me a package. "It was sitting on the doorstep."

I took the small square box from him. It was posted but had an obscure return address on the label.

"Aren't you going to open it?" he asked when I set it on the aquarium bar.

A challenge, maybe. If I had nothing to hide, then open it in front of him. I stared at the box. Could I hear ticking? No, surely not. What if it was from Dominic? I would have to come up with some explanation off-the-cuff. I hated that he had me in this awful place. If I had met him in the way I'd told Hadden, I could tell Rush. If Rush got involved, Dominic would tell him everything, even about the blog. Rush would see my feelings and fears and temptations splayed out like a *Playboy* centerfold.

He handed me a knife, thoughtful man. I sliced through the tape with infinite care. When I opened the box flaps, I stared at the contents. Packs of Oreo cookies. Seemingly innocuous, but not at all.

Rush pulled one out. He held up the package, studying it, and then he opened one and showed me the cookie sandwich.

The frosting was missing. In every single cookie.

I couldn't hide the way my face froze. Had I ever mentioned my silly habit on my blog? I didn't think so. How had he known? Had he been watching me in my office?

No, at the beach party.

"Who would have sent these?" Rush asked, looking for a note.

My gaze darted to the box, but there was nothing but the cookies.

I laughed then, an out-of-tune laugh that sounded more like a screech. "That Beth. She's such a jokester." At Rush's blank expression I said, "You don't know I always scrape the icing out from between my Oreos?"

He shook his head.

"Oh. Well, I do. I like to split them open and eat the icing first. And I like to read *People* magazine, too. And wear fuzzy purple slippers." He gave me a funny look, and I added, "In case you didn't know."

He was staring, not quite sure what to make of me. Well, that made two of us. I wanted him to know me, and I wanted to know him, too. Now wasn't the time. I dumped the box into the garbage. I had to give Beth a heads-up so she would cover in case Rush mentioned it to her.

That's when it hit me how whacked all this was. I was lying about things that I didn't want sent to me, hiding someone I didn't want in my life to begin with. And I had no idea how I was going to get him out of it.

CHAPTER FIFTEEN

The next morning Rush woke early, took a shower, and left before I got out of bed. I needed some quiet time to sort things out. I put on my wedding ring and the charm watch Rush had bought for me while on a business trip to Italy. It was really a bracelet with several charms, one of which was a bejeweled clock. He bought me a charm every now and then, for no reason at all. I pressed the point of the Eiffel Tower charm into the pad of my finger. For our date in Paris. A yellow flower because he saw it in the window and thought of me.

I ached for what I'd almost thrown away. Maybe that was how he reached out, by buying me things. Like the emerald—my birthstone—ring that Rush had given me on my birthday. It was delicate and fit on my pinky. Things seemed so much simpler then. Now . . .

I called Beth on the way to work.

"If Rush says anything, you sent me a joke gift of icing-less Oreo cookies, all right?" I totally expected the puzzled silence on the other end of the phone, so I launched into what had happened.

"Oh, like one of those private-joke gifts," she said.

"Yes, except that it wasn't our private joke."

Beth was quiet for a few moments. Was she finally

seeing how off-balance Dominic was? She said, "Why didn't you tell me about what Hadden told you?"

"What do you mean?"

"Read your blog! It is your blog, after all. Dom said Hadden is hot for you."

"What?"

"He overheard you. And that didn't seem an important thing to share with me?"

Instead of getting support, I was getting flack from her in the form of a wounded jab. "I just want to forget about it. The whole thing made me uncomfortable."

"Which is why you should have told me. That's what best friends are for, you know, sounding boards, shoulders, that kind of stuff."

That's what I thought they were for. "Well, I guess I was distracted by the whole Dominic stalking and yelling in public thing afterward. Hadden didn't come on to me, and he didn't even mean to tell me he had feelings for me. It kind of came out, and he promised it would never be an issue. So will you say that you sent the cookies if Rush mentions it?"

"Sure. What are *friends* for?"

I ignored her snippy tone and wished her a good day. As soon as I got to the shop I logged onto the blog.

Montene's Diary

125 Comments:
• Dom wrote:
Montene, you are such a liar. For one thing, the man wants you. Not only could I see it in the way he was looking at you, the way he held your hand, but I heard him tell you he has a hard-on for you.

See, blog friends, Montene is holding back big-time. We should punish her.

• Cathy1412 wrote:

Montene, damn, girl, you are holding back on us! Whazz up
with that? We're your friends. We've been here for you. Give
it up!

The entries went on, taking me to task for not giving
them every intimate secret I possessed. Now it seemed
I possessed none anyway.

Farther down Dominic posted again:

Montene had me over to her apartment last night. She's got a
cool fish tank right in the middle of her living room. She has
finally come to terms with the bad girl side of herself that
wants me. Oh, and I do love that bad girl. My love and passion
for her overwhelms me.

     Just One Night Now and Always . . .

I stared at that last sentence, wondering why he'd capi-
talized the first letter in every word.

Just One Night . . . J.O.N.N.A.

Stupid, stupid, stupid, choosing someone from the
blog! Someone who could out me at any time, tying my
hands on outright refuting him. Not that I'd planned on
him rifling through my wallet to find my identity. I
wanted to throw my laptop across the room. Instead, I
let out a scream that bounced off the walls. I cringed,
thinking that someone would come knocking at my door
or at least check to see who was in distress. I walked to
the glass window and looked out.

No one was curious about the scream.

Which made being here alone even scarier.

I stalked back to my desk and posted my own entry,
furious again at the line I had to walk. And annoyed that
my blog fiends—er, friends—were getting more demanding.

My husband's friend did not tell me that he had a "hard-on" for me. He inadvertently admitted to having feelings for me that he wouldn't act on. No big deal. As for Dominic's assertion that I had him to my apartment—not exactly true. I don't count bribing the deliveryman to let him bring the pizza to our door as "having him over." He's toying with you the same way he's toying with me. Things are getting better with my husband, and I'm not going to do anything to mess that up.

                                                                    —Montene

I reached for the drawer where I kept my Oreos but remembered that box of stripped cookies and pulled back. He'd even spoiled that.

I made a point to be out of the shop before it got dark. I returned a call from a woman who wanted me to orchestrate a romantic dinner at her apartment for her boyfriend, the kind of assignments I loved best. Just not today. I set up a meeting with her the next morning and gathered my things.

When I was securely locked inside my car I called Beth. "Hi. Just wondering if Rush asked about the cookies?" If he had, he'd been testing my story, which meant he was suspicious.

"Nope, but there wasn't much of a chance. The heater at work went wonky and we were roasting all day. We all left early."

We chatted for a minute and then I signed off. I wanted to go home and soak in the tub and forget about Dominic. I was surprised to see Rush's Range Rover in the parking lot. He'd left early, too.

When I walked in, I heard the shower going upstairs. Before my lunch with Hadden, I might have been suspicious about why Rush was taking a shower right after work. My suspicions would pour me into a well of despair. Now I knew he wasn't washing off the scent of another woman. He was probably washing off the sweat of a day spent in a hot office.

I set my purse and laptop in the cabinet near the door and went upstairs. I was on the way to the bedroom, but my body stopped outside the bathroom door. The sound of water changing as it hit his body stirred something deep inside me. I opened the door and walked in. The room smelled of his musky soap. He was taking a cool shower, so I could see him through unfogged glass soaping his naked body, unaware of my presence. My eyes drank him in: the contours of his muscles as he moved, the way the water sluiced down his back and over the curve of his buttocks.

A powerful need rose so quickly it took my breath away. Not sexual, though that was there, too. I needed to reach out to him. To connect with him. I was the one who had put distance between us; now I needed to close the gap. I was already stripping out of my clothes.

He braced his hands against the tile and lifted his face to the jets, his eyes closed. I opened the door, and only then did he become aware of me. Before he could turn around, I slid up behind him and wrapped my arms around him. I pressed my cheek against his back and squeezed my eyes shut. My hands flattened against his stomach and his coarse hairs pressed into the pads of my fingers. He seemed to soak in our connection the way I was, for he put his hands over mine for several minutes. Or maybe I was holding on too tight for him to turn around to face me.

I loosened my hold and kissed across his back. He turned around, cupping my face in his hands and looking at me. Maybe he could see my need; I felt it shining in my eyes, as naked as me. He kissed me gently. I was the one who deepened it. Our hands skimmed over each other's bodies, touching, exploring, all in silence. I couldn't talk to him, couldn't think of how to tell him what I was feeling, but I could express it in the one way we always knew how to connect: physically.

I had to get Dominic out of my life without Rush finding out he'd ever been there to begin with. Now, more than ever, I didn't want Rush to know what I'd done. I couldn't let my secret destroy what was growing between us.

CHAPTER SIXTEEN

I spent the following day at Dyer House preparing for Rush's dinner party. I was grateful for the diversion, though I was worried that Dominic would show up to "help" again. This time there was no event listing in the paper, so I should have felt safer. I didn't.

Once the guests started arriving—and exclaiming at the decor—I went into JEvent mode, where I was most comfortable. I noticed that Hadden didn't pop into the kitchen as he usually did, and that both saddened and relieved me. He'd given me a warm smile when he arrived, but something had changed between us. Damn him for spoiling our friendship.

Rush introduced me to the group before I had to dash back to the kitchen to prepare another batch of champagne martinis. Most of the guests brought spouses or significant others. He and Hadden were, in fact, the only two who were solo. In that moment I realized why Rush wanted me at his side. Not as an adornment, but as his wife. I felt embarrassed at my reaction to his request—and it had been a request, not a demand.

I hardly had time to fit in more than an introduction. I didn't have help, not wanting to cut into an already slim profit margin. Twelve was my max to handle alone, and I was at it. The only help I would get was a busboy who would clear the dishes. I set out fresh martini glasses and two pitchers on the bar before dashing back to the kitchen.

I laid out three rows of salads and placed toppings on each one. "Cucumbers, two on each, hey, don't you slide off there, and two and two and two. Carrot slivers, fan 'em out, oh, so pretty . . ."

When I turned, I started at the sight of someone leaning in the doorway watching me. Rush, not Dominic. His smile reminded me of his comment about watching me work.

I needed to tell him. Right now, before I chickened out. "I'm sorry I insisted on coordinating this. It's just . . ." I leaned against the stainless-steel table. "I'm more comfortable here. I don't have to be classy and knowledgeable about politics and technology. I don't have to worry about saying or doing the wrong thing. I can be me."

He furrowed his eyebrows in surprise as he came closer. "Who said you had to be knowledgeable about anything in particular? And you're classy anyway. I never wanted you to be anything more than you are."

"I know you didn't. It's the way I felt. My expectations." It felt odd, and oddly freeing, to open up to him.

He rubbed my pinky that wore his ring, looking at me. "So next time . . ."

I smiled. "I'll be your wife."

He kissed me softly. "I'd better get back. . . ."

"Yeah."

I put the finishing touches on the salads and announced that dinner would be served. After one last survey of the table, as everyone took their seats, I returned to the kitchen to prepare the main meal.

When the busboy indicated that he was about to clear the salad dishes a short while later, I readied everything and served dinner. I could take a breather before preparing the desserts. Two flourless chocolate cakes sat on the counter in their covered containers. The nice thing about small events was that they were wholly under my control. I was the only one who could screw them up.

That's when I noticed the raspberries weren't sitting next to the cakes. I checked the large reefer but only saw the homemade whipped cream. I swore I'd brought them in but must have left them in the car.

"Please let them be in the car," I prayed as I headed out the side door leading to the employees' parking lot.

Sodium lights buzzed, casting a yellow glow on everything, including swirling snow flurries. I loved the winter. I loved the way the snow caught the light, especially at night, and the way it came alive on a breeze. I loved knowing that soon I'd be inside again and appreciate being warm and safe. I loved all of that until about February, when I was sick of the cold and overcast skies, but now it was fresh and new.

I took a few seconds to watch the snow, breathing deeply and enjoying cooling off after hustling in a hot kitchen. It didn't take long for the chill to take hold, and I headed toward my vehicle. I opened the back where I had stored everything and searched for the container.

"Looking for this?" a man said from right behind me.

I spun around to find Dominic holding my container. Fear clawed up my throat. "What are you doing here?" I was surprised at how calm I sounded when that was the last thing I felt.

He shook the flurries from his hair. "I need to talk to you."

"You have to leave. I've got work to do." I left out the part about him scaring the hell out of me. I snatched the container from him while glancing around to see if anyone was nearby. "You took this from the kitchen?"

"When you were serving the salads." He dug his fingers through his hair. "I've been walking. Walking and thinking, thinking and walking." He came closer, reeking of liquor. "And I really think it's time we stopped playing this little game. Whatever it is that you want, I can give you. You want wild sex, fine. You want an emotional connection, that's fine, too. Give me a chance; I can give you everything your husband can't. I promise once you've been with me, you'll never look back."

I swallowed hard. *Breathe. Stay calm. Act as though you're talking to someone reasonable.* "This has nothing to do with you. It's me. I discovered I can't be a cheat. I need to make my marriage work. There's no game. You have to understand, Dominic. It's over."

Up to then, he'd been calm, if oblivious to the truth. As he paced in an agitated manner, he looked on the edge, disheveled. I searched for something I could use as a weapon but saw nothing within easy reach. My fingers maneuvered the container so the corner pointed out. Oh yeah, that'd be good for . . . what, a bruise?

His gaze raked over me. "I have to make *you* understand. When we started seeing each other there were certain . . . expectations. Then you invited me to the hotel, and we were supposed to be something."

"We were never supposed to be anything. We never talked about becoming something. We weren't even supposed to know each other's names."

"That's how it began. But you and I both knew it would grow into more."

I changed my tact. "In the beginning, two people have—let's not call them expectations. They have hopes. They hope the relationship will work. But a lot of times, it doesn't work. I decided to honor my wedding vows. And you should honor my decision and move on."

He shook his head as though a fly were buzzing near his ear. "I can't move on. We have to work. We already walked down the pathway. You can't just stop and"—he made a twirling gesture with his hand—"turn back now."

My heart felt like a block of ice. I could hardly breathe, knowing it was imperative that I handle this the right way. I wasn't even sure what the right way was. He was obviously off-balance and drunk. The question was, how off-balance? "Talk to me, Dominic. Why do we *have* to work?"

His eyes were wider than I'd seen them before, his face rigid with tension. "I hear it in my head all the time. 'Don't fail this time.' Putting pressure on me. I have to . . . get . . . this . . . right."

"Why is there pressure?" I asked in a whisper, hoping my fear wasn't as obvious to him as it was to me. Did he hear voices in his head? *Was* he crazy? Not totally crazy; he'd been eloquent in his e-mails and during those first meetings. Something had tipped him over the edge. That something was my rejection.

He backed away, staring into my eyes. He enunciated every word. "We have to be together, understand? Then everything will be all right. How far do I have to go to prove us? Because I'll go as far as I need to. I'll go all the way."

"There is no us. You're drunk, that's all. Go home and sleep it off."

He laughed. "I know you think I'm a little crazy. Maybe I am. But you made me that way."

A little? I wanted to scream, and took a breath to still the words. I noticed that he was trying to dump the responsibility onto me. "I think if you stop stalking me and get some perspective, you'll see how unreasonable you're being."

His smile gave me the chills. "But I enjoy it so."

"I have to go back inside. My husband's waiting for me."

"And his guests, I know. You once said that you didn't feel anything. That you were numb inside. I make you feel, don't I? At first it was desire. Now it's fear. But you feel something. I have a message for your husband." He moved so fast I couldn't begin to react. He pulled me close and sucked at my neck like a vampire. I pushed at him as I felt blood prickle to the surface. He loosened his grip and I stumbled. His expression was eerily deadpan. "You're mine, Jonna."

I ran, and only when I reached the door did I dare look back. He wasn't there. I slipped inside and searched for a way to lock the door, but it required a key. Soft laughter and conversation floated in from the dining area. I was panting, my breath raspy. I grabbed my purse and went to the restroom. Thankfully no one was in there. "Bastard." A red, mouth-shaped mark marred my neck. I dabbed concealer on the raw skin. How long did hickies last? Damn him! He was trying to make Rush think I was having an affair.

I looked horrible, especially in the harsh fluorescent lighting. My eyes were red, my skin pale. I slapped at my face to bring back the blood. Then I had to return to the kitchen. That's when I realized I'd dropped the container of raspberries. The least of my worries.

When I left the bathroom, Hadden was heading to the men's room. He paused, and I gave him a forced smile. "Enjoying dinner?"

He saw through me. "Are we all right?"

No! I wanted to say. *You ruined everything.* Instead I said, "Fine," and started to continue toward the kitchen.

"Is that guy still bothering you?" he asked, halting me again. Now I was a few feet away, and it felt less intimate. I was surprised that he brought up the guy at the restaurant. Maybe I had the same spooked look on my face.

"He's around," I said, keeping myself from touching my neck.

"Have you told Rush yet?"

I shook my head. "I'll handle him. I've got to . . ." I gestured to the kitchen and rushed off. In those dark, long moments in the night, I thought about telling Rush. Then I imagined the conversation and stopped.

I paused in the doorway of the dining room, watching Rush talking with the nervous "bride," a skinny dark-haired guy who looked sixteen. Rush looked debonair in a crisp green shirt and black trousers. He used his hands to accentuate what he was saying. He had a fire in his eyes as I heard him talk about those heady days after he'd sold his company. In mid-conversation, he sensed me there and looked up. He flashed a smile before continuing, and the warmth in my chest spread all way to the tips of my fingers and toes.

This was different from the way I'd felt about him when we first met. My insecurity and jealousy had tainted that. Now, when I looked at him, I felt more than the rush of lust. I felt the sun inside me, glowing and growing brighter. I was falling in love with him again. Real love. The more I fell, the more I didn't want him to know what I'd done. I didn't want him to know that he had good reason for suspecting me of having an affair. I didn't want him to know that I'd found reaching out to strangers easier than reaching out to him.

More than ever, I had to eradicate all evidence of Montene and her activities. I resolved that night to have my blog expunged from the Internet. Then I had to figure out how to expunge Dominic. I knew that would be the hardest task. I was only partially right.

Dominic curled up on the floor, his head on her thigh. "I messed up," he said in a whimper after telling her about his visit to Jonna.

She was stroking his back, but he knew she was mad

at him for getting drunk. Her long nails grazed his bare
back, just hard enough to go from pleasant to painful.
"You might have scared her away."

"I'll make it right."

"Do you want her?"

"Yes."

"You more than want her. You need her with every
fiber of your being. She is water to your thirst, food to
your hunger, the very air that you breathe."

"Yes."

"Then you'll do whatever you must to win her over.
And you will win her over. But you have to get hold of
yourself. You have to stay away from the edge of the
abyss. This is what happens when you fall in."

He nodded. "I know. I'm sorry, Mamu."

"I told you not to call me that anymore," she said in
her harsh voice, the one he hated. The one he remembered from so long ago. "Or Mommy. You're twenty-
seven years old, for God's sake."

She had many voices. The kind, tender one when she
was pleased with him. The seductive one when she
wanted something from him. And the harsh one that
criticized him.

She would always be Mamu to him. He'd lost her a
long time ago, but she'd come back. His father had
called her an evil bitch. He'd said, in a careful tone, that
his mother was sick in her mind. The shrinks had tried
to tell him, too, but he shut them out, and they finally
gave up. Yes, sometimes she was a bitch. She made him
hate her and she made him love her. But she had always
loved him and taken care of him. She pushed him to
succeed. When he made her happy, everything was all
right inside him and he was her good little boy.

When he made her unhappy . . .

When she'd come to his apartment, he'd been curled
up naked on the white fur rug. She'd pulled him onto her

lap and stroked his back as she'd always done. It was still dark inside, other than the three halogen pin lights dangling from long rods. The concentrated bursts of light aimed at the red pillows on his black and steel couch.

"I have to go now," she said, scooting out from beneath his head and getting to her feet.

"You're not mad at me?" he said, standing up next to her. "Please don't be mad at me."

She took his head in her soft hands. "If you can prove you're a man and not have these breakdowns, I won't be mad at you."

Always, she kept her approval at arm's length. Except for those times when she needed him. He wanted her to need him.

She kissed him, leaving traces of her lipstick on his mouth, and left him in his dark apartment.

When she was there, he felt like a boy. It wasn't a bad feeling. There was comfort in being dominated. Now that she was gone, though, he felt stronger. Capable. He sneered at the memory of his cowering self.

He walked into his second bedroom that was outfitted like a gym. His hands curled around weights, and he lifted them. He admired the way the muscles in his arms bulged. He watched his naked reflection and huffed out the count. "Forty, forty-one, forty-two . . ."

His jaw locked tight as he continued. The veins in his neck rippled his skin. "Fifty-six, fifty-seven . . ."

Inside a war raged—the needy boy versus the strong man. He gritted his teeth as his arms and shoulders burned. "One hundred, one hundred and one . . ."

He thought of Mamu. Of Jonna. "Bitch. Bitch. Bitch," he said instead of counting.

The anger swelled again, and he threw the weights at the wall of mirrors. They hit with a crash. Pieces of himself, now shattered, looked back at him. The boy. The man. Twisted into something he hardly recognized.

CHAPTER SEVENTEEN

The next afternoon I was on the phone with the person whose information was given on the blog registration form. Unfortunately, the man I imagined being a gangly college kid was reiterating his e-mail response.

"Lady, there's no way I'm removing your blog. I got *exposure* from it. Twice. Didn't you see the follow-up piece in today's *Globe*?"

"Follow-up?" Oh no.

"You betcha. That columnist, Marty McLaughlin, brings up some good blog issues, like responsibility and morals. Do you know how many people flocked to my site after the first column? My advertising's up, registrations are up, and your diary still gets more hits by far than any other blog."

"Look, I don't care how popular it is. It's my blog. I want it removed."

His voice took on a smug tone. "I'll bet you never read that agreement form you agreed to when you set up your blog. It says that it's in my sole discretion whether a blog is removed—or not. So even though it's your blog, it's really my blog."

I was furious, at him and myself. I hadn't read that stupid agreement. I'd only read the part about privacy, that my personal information would never be revealed. "Well, then I won't post anymore."

"That's your prerogative. Everyone else is having such a good time, I don't think it'll matter."

I hung up and indulged in a temper tantrum, foot stomping and all. My blog had become a beast. My blog *fiends,* as I now called them, were demanding answers, and I was afraid that Dominic would provide his fantasy version of them. Worse, that he'd reveal who I was.

I logged onto *The Boston Globe*'s Web site and found Marty's column, this time titled, "Is Montene a Tease?"

Oh, crap.

It's like when your best friend begins holding back on you. She goes to a concert and doesn't invite you. You find out about the guy she's digging only because your mutual friend mentions it. Yeah, it hurts. That's what's happening over at Montene's Diary, the blog I mentioned in a recent column where Boston girl Montene shares her secrets with her closest friends—which is anyone with a computer.

Except she's not sharing anymore. After flirting with a blog poster named Dominic, and changing her mind about cheating on her husband, Montene has become mum. In fact, it's the spurned Dominic who's been feeding the hungry mouths of Montene's blog friends. Only through him have we learned that her husband's business partner came on to her at lunch the other day. Most confusing yet is what's actually going on with Montene and Dominic. Are they, or aren't they? They're both giving different versions. This has the blog friends in an uproar.

It made me wonder, what's a blogger's obligation to his or her audience? Is it, in fact, like a real friendship that needs constant nurturing? Or, like a casual acquaintance, can it slide for days or weeks at a time? Maybe it's really an entertainment thing? Readers and blog friends come to expect a certain level of entertainment and are disappointed when they don't get it. What is Montene's obligation?

Those are questions that remain unanswered, as are the questions Montene has left us wondering about. For now, her blog friends have picked up the slack and continue to keep things lively. Ah, the speculation!

What was my obligation? I'd never asked hundreds of people to read my posts and to hang on my conflicted existence. I'd never promised to continue to expose my innards to them. Now Marty's new column would generate even more interest.

With a long sigh, I pulled out the small mirror that I checked every other minute. The hickey was still there, visible beneath the concealer, even though I'd been icing it all day. I was glad I wasn't going to see Rush much today. That would give it time to fade. I rolled up the collar of my turtleneck sweater.

Speaking of friendship obligations . . . I picked up my phone and called Beth. "Hi. Did you see the *Globe* article on Montene's Diary?"

"Another article? No, I haven't. What did it say? Oh, my gawd, they didn't find out who you are, did they?"

"No . . . thank goodness. It just talks about my obligations as the creator of the blog. And unfortunately, it's going to renew everyone's interest again."

She didn't sound particularly sympathetic when she said, "It's tough to be a celebrity. Hey, I'm glad you called. Can we grab a drink tonight?"

"Sorry, I can't. I've got a dinner to prepare."

"Oh, sure, *I'm* always here when *you* need *me,* but when I ask—"

"Of course I'm here for you. You didn't say you *needed* to talk." Not that I was up for it, but I'd manage. "Talk to me now."

"It's just that . . . well, I've fallen in love with this guy."

"That's great."

"Except he's married."

"Oh, not so great. When did this happen?"

"A couple of weeks ago. I didn't want to bring it up. I mean, you've had your own morality play going on, and then Dominic . . . my problem seemed trivial compared to yours, I guess."

I felt bad, but then again, Beth's romantic dramas were usually center stage in our relationship. "Where did you meet this guy?" I tried to give her some support.

"A bar. We hit it off immediately. Jonna, he makes me feel *alive*. We laugh, we connect, and I even respect that he's trying to be a good boy. But I know he's in love with me, too. I keep thinking about his wife. I hate her and yet I don't even know her. I feel terrible, of course. She's probably a nice girl. But I'll bet she doesn't love him the way I do. I keep telling myself to back away, but then I see him and . . . I can't." I heard the strain in her voice. "I don't know what to do."

I felt like a hypocrite when I said, "I think you should wait until he's divorced, if that's what he plans to do anyway. For your sake."

She had a funny tone in her voice when she said, "You're probably right."

Now I knew why Dominic's pursuit seemed so alluring. She obviously wanted this man to pursue her the same way.

I glanced at my watch. Damn. I had that romantic dinner for two to prepare. "I'm really sorry, Beth, but I've got to go. We can talk later, 'kay?"

"Sure. I understand," she said, when it was obvious she didn't. "Bye."

I was meeting Valerie Stevens at her apartment in less than an hour. I went into my work area and started gathering props: a rich red tablecloth, a heart-shaped crystal vase with red marbles to hold an array of dried flowers. I arranged all of the food into a large box. When I walked out to my vehicle fifteen minutes later, I found a huge red heart painted in icing on the hood. The way it dripped reminded me of blood.

I instantly searched the parking lot. Dammit, this had to stop. He wasn't in sight, but I knew he was out there watching me. What, hoping for a change of heart? Or was he content to terrorize me in a "romantic" way? I couldn't help but remember how he'd admitted that he enjoyed stalking me. Now I was going to have to factor in time to run through a car wash.

I threw everything into the back of my car and sped out of the lot, watching the traffic behind me. I actually hoped he would tail me so I could get his vehicle description. I needed to even the balance between us. I wanted to know who he was, where he lived, what his life was like. Then I could decide what to do next.

Valerie was a vivacious blonde with a sparkle in her eyes. She was surprising her boyfriend, whom she was picking up, with a special dinner where she would propose. I'd made a double chocolate layer cake covered in a smooth ganache icing with the words "Will You Marry Me?" in red icing—icing eerily similar to what Dominic had used on my car.

I tried to feel her enthusiasm, which was my job, after all. Instead I kept looking at the big picture window that faced out to the parking lot. I hoped that it was simply my paranoia that I felt someone watching me. Since it was dark out and bright inside, I couldn't see a thing. The apartment complex was partially complete, and I'd only seen a couple of units that looked occupied. The apartment next door was vacant. I'd seen drywall tools through the specked window.

Valerie had put on some romantic jazz while I set the

table and she got ready. She rushed into the dining room, where I was tucking in the red velvet seat covers.

"I've got to get going. We should be back in about twenty minutes."

I glanced at my watch. "I'll light the scented candles, make sure the food is ready, and skedaddle."

She closed the front curtains and smiled as she took in the room with a sigh. "Perfect."

"Good luck," I called as she closed the door.

The reds I'd chosen complemented the lovely apartment decorated in Moroccan colors of cumin, ginger, and clove. Valerie had chosen the candles, and their cinnamon scent fought with the garlic and Cornish hens. Unfortunately, the scent reminded me of Dominic.

I rolled red napkins into wire rings with crystal hearts and set the small table. Fluted wineglasses caught the flickering light. After a check of the hens, I sank onto the maroon couch and relaxed for the first time in what felt like days. It had been over a week since I'd made the terrible mistake of inviting Dominic to meet me at a hotel.

A bottle of Shiraz sat on the side table next to a corkscrew. The wine was so tempting I had to turn away from it. The food did nothing for my appetite, which had fled along with my peace of mind. That was probably why I jumped when I heard the noise. A *click,* faint and innocuous. This was an apartment building. It was probably the neighbors. So why had the hairs on the back of my neck perked to attention? Because it sounded like it had come from *inside* the apartment.

I got up and crept toward the darkened hallway. My curiosity—okay, and fear—warred with my sense of propriety. Both bedroom doors were closed. I glanced into the bathroom, finding it simply decorated and bare of anything personal. I remained in the hallway, holding my breath so I could pick up on any sound.

I heard it again, coming from the room on the right. More like a snapping sound. My throat grew tight. Okay, just open the door. One quick movement, see if I startle anyone lurking in there.

Dominic.

Yeah, that's who I pictured.

I closed my fingers over the doorknob. Turned it. Pushed the door in.

Huh? The room was empty but for a couple of boxes along the back wall that contained, or had contained, lighting fixtures for the bathroom. I saw what had been making the noise. The heated air, coming from a vent in the floor, was causing the loose label on one of the boxes to lift and scrape. But that didn't comfort me. Because I could see that this room was the master bedroom, the one that Valerie would—should—occupy. She said she lived alone, was in fact hoping to cohabitate with her boyfriend someday.

I opened the second bedroom door. That room was empty, too. The rest of the apartment, the public part, was decorated as though someone lived there. I looked in the master bathroom hoping to find cosmetics, deodorant, anything that indicated Valerie was sleeping on the couch. Nothing. My heart stopped beating for a moment as I tried to make sense of it.

No one slept here. Which meant no one lived here. Which meant Valerie had lied to me.

It didn't take long for my thoughts to link to Dominic. Oh, my God. It was a setup. He'd hired this woman to set me up so he could have me alone in a romantic setting.

I turned and fled down the hallway at the same time I heard a soft *pop*. I dropped to the floor with a cry, even though I felt no pain. My brain registered someone running toward me. I saw a lethal corkscrew in his hand.

Darkness flashed in and out at the edges of my vision. He said my name as he knelt down next to me.

"No," I managed as I focused in on his face.

Not Dominic's face.

Rush.

My brain synapses blew into overload and to my horror I began giggling hysterically.

"Jonna, are you okay?"

It took me a few seconds to pull myself together and wipe the tears from my eyes. He was looking at me as though he thought I'd explode. Or perhaps as though I'd deteriorate into hysterics again.

"I wanted to surprise you, not scare you."

I sucked in several breaths, forcing that phony smile I was getting so good at. "Rush! What . . . ?" I took him in, heard his words in my mind: *"surprise you."*

"I was hoping for a reaction, but I see I've thrown you completely off," he said, offering me his hands to help me to my feet.

Breathe. Think. Play it cool.

"I thought . . . discovered no one lived here and it kind of freaked me out because I realized she'd lied about living here, and then I heard a shot"—I eyed the corkscrew in his hand—"the wine cork popping, I guess."

"Valerie's the wife of one of our angels. I asked if she'd set up a romantic dinner so I could surprise you. She and her husband own this complex, and she offered me the use of one of the apartments. I hired someone to decorate it and stock the kitchen. What the heck were you doing snooping in the bedrooms?"

"I heard a noise." It was sinking in. Not a trap, not a setup. Well, sort of. A good one.

"Are you all right now?"

I nodded. My heartbeat and thoughts were settling.

He guided me to the table and began pouring a glass of wine. He looked young with his hair trimmed shorter than the last time I'd seen him and smelling of an unfamiliar shampoo, maybe fresh from the hair salon.

I lifted my eyebrow at him. "You made me fix my own romantic dinner?"

He gave me a roguish smile as he handed me a glass. "I know how you like to be in charge of these things. Now I understand why, but I already had all this in motion before you told me, so here we are." He touched his glass to mine and smiled. "To us."

I was still overwhelmed, in both a good and a bad way. I looked at the closed curtains and wondered if it had only been Rush I'd felt watching me. I still wondered if Dominic was out there, too.

As soon as Mamu had come into Dominic's apartment, she'd kicked up the heat to eighty and settled on the couch with her long legs hanging over the armrest. "I just want to be warm. It's cold outside. It's cold in here." She looked at his decor with disdain. "It's always cold in here. I hate these monochromatic colors. I hate this coffee table." She thumped the table with the palm of her hand and pulled it back with a hiss of pain. "Damned table!"

"It wasn't the table's fault," he said, kneeling down and rubbing her fingerprints off the surface. "You're just in a bitchy mood. You know I love this table. It was the biggest splurge in my life." He'd seen it in an artistic furniture shop and plunked down his credit card—three thousand dollars' worth. It looked like a can of anchovies with the lid peeled back. Inside the "can," the fish were actually oversized rolls of hundred-dollar bills in a lacquer that looked like oil.

"I'm impatient," she said, crossing her arms over her chest.

He was hot. The vent over the couch pounded out hot air. Sweat dripped down his neck and trickled down his sides. "Then you'll like my news. I didn't mess things up with Jonna after all. I know you thought the hickey was drastic—"

"It was stupid. You could have blown everything right there."

Her words, and especially her tone, made him feel like the "bad little boy" again. He tried to stamp out the feeling. "Don't you remember that she likes when men take charge? And stop talking to me like I'm ten."

She gave him a smug smile as she slipped out of everything but her bra and panties. "You'll always be that boy who crawled into my lap and begged for your mama's love. And I gave it to you, didn't I?"

He shot to his feet and jammed his hands into his jean pockets. "I'm not that boy anymore." He narrowed his eyes at her, hating her for reminding him how weak he once was. And sometimes still was. How weak *she* made him.

"Oh yes, you are. That's why you called me over and admitted what you'd done. You knew I'd be displeased and you wanted to hear me tell you. So I'm telling you: you're a naughty boy."

He stalked to the bar, pouring another glass of vodka and viciously twisting in a lime.

"Is that for me?" she cooed, sweetening her voice to the one she used when she wanted something.

He should tell her to get her own damned drink, but he pulled out another glass and filled it, too. He couldn't help notice the way the Friday afternoon light slanted in through his blinds and washed over her as he handed her the glass. Beautiful, bitchy, manipulative, and the only person in the world who meant anything to him.

Instead of saying, *Thank you,* she said, "Watch the drinking. You know how you get when you're drunk.

You're going to screw this up. I told you, this one's important."

"Why? Are we going for more money this time?"

Her mouth quirked in a smile. "Yes."

He'd been a con's cohort since he could remember. Mamu had used him as a decoy from the time he was three. He'd learned how to throw up on command in order to create a distraction so they could get away. When he was eight, she taught him the fine art of getting "hit" by a car and bilking the driver out of a settlement. He'd broken his arm the first time; he got better after that.

It's us against the world, little boy, she'd tell him over and over again. *We deserve to take what we want. We're special.* She would kiss him tenderly on the mouth and leave traces of her lipstick there.

Then she'd been taken away from him, and he'd nearly shriveled up and died. Until fate brought her back into his life again. But two jobs ago *she* had conned *him.* Betrayed him. Lied to him. He couldn't shake the anger and hurt. He had a similar bad feeling about this job. She had that same glint in her eyes. She was up to something.

That's what was making him reckless, edgy. He couldn't tell her that, though, or tell her about his fear of failing. "I've been doing this for a long time now. I think I've got a handle on things."

"Like you did the day you went to see her drunk." Her laugh was harsh. "Yeah, that was effective."

He dropped down onto the couch opposite, sending some of his drink sloshing over the edge of his glass. Defiantly he finished off his drink. "I've got it under control."

"You're getting desperate. Be a man and take responsibility for failing to woo her. A simple task, really." The edge in her voice grew with each sentence. "All you had to do was get a neglected, frustrated woman into bed. She even arranged to meet you at a hotel, for God's sake. She was right there, on the bed, and you couldn't close the deal."

It wasn't anything he hadn't told himself already, but he hated hearing it from her. "I got pictures. But you didn't like them."

"She had a pained expression, was trying to push you off of her!"

He curled his fingers around the glass until his knuckles ached. The last job hadn't gone well, either, but that wasn't his fault. He'd done his part; the mark was the problem. When he'd presented the woman with pictures of the two of them having sex, threatening to show them to her wealthy husband if she didn't cough up some money, she just laughed.

Show them to him. He couldn't care less. What are you, some sleazy con artist . . . oh, crap, you are, aren't you? Her expression had filled with disgust. *Oh, I get it. You seduce us middle-aged women who you think need an ego boost because our husbands are too busy either screwing their secretaries or working to pay us any attention. Scare us into paying so our husbands won't see the pictures and boot us out on our penniless asses.*

Yes, that's exactly what it was. He had come up with the brilliant yet simple scheme: find the right woman, seduce her, get pictures, and blackmail her. The women, humiliated when they realized that his wooing had nothing to do with their sex appeal, had never gone to the police.

Well, here's the thing, Romeo, she'd said with a sneer in her voice. *I have as much dirt on my husband as he has on me.* She'd grabbed up her purse. *You get nothing, scumbag.*

Except for the money he'd pilfered from her purse during their assignations.

Still, it had been humbling, and on top of the disastrous con just before that, he *was* beginning to feel desperate.

Mamu drained her drink, set it on the coffee table, and started grabbing up her clothing. "You said something about the plan working."

He removed the glass from the table and set it on the bar. "She sent me an e-mail, wants to meet Monday afternoon."

She didn't look as pleased as he thought she'd be. "Just like that? You scare her, give her a hickey—"

"I left the heart on her car."

She waved off that effort. "Think about this. You stalk her, attack her with a hickey. Do you really think she's going to tell you she's had a change of heart?"

Yes, he had. He wanted to believe that so much, needed to believe he'd finally won. He wanted this con to go smoothly. He didn't want to think about that other woman, her body twisted and bloody. He did dream about her—no, they were nightmares. He'd had another one last night. Except it was Jonna lying there dead.

Now that he thought about it, her invitation did seem suspect. Dammit, Mamu was probably right. He swigged the last drops of liquor in his glass, accepting the validity of her suspicions. Maybe he had gone about this the wrong way. But in the end, he would succeed. He had to show Mamu he could do this. That he could be her big man as well as her little boy.

He knew just what to do.

The surprise dinner was wonderful, and I took it as a sign that Rush wanted to bridge the gap between us. I felt as though we were trying to reach each other across it. Holding me back were the secrets that I held close and the threat I knew was closer.

It was much later that night that I felt our fingers touch across that chasm, and it only happened by accident. Actually, it was Dominic's doing.

I heard a wolf howling. My eyes snapped open—and I found Rush lying next to me, head propped up on his hand, watching me. The bright moonlight slanted in through blinds that he had obviously opened, washing us in silvery light. At first it startled me, but I could see something more open in his eyes than I'd ever seen before.

"Hi," he said in a soft voice I'd also never heard.

"What . . . are you doing?"

He reached over and stroked my cheek. "Watching you sleep. Well, I *was* watching you sleep until some drunken idiot started howling."

Dominic? I pushed the idiot out of my mind, which was amazingly easy as I looked at my husband. I felt something swell inside me. The moonlight lent a two-dimensional cast to the contours of his chest and the sheet draped over his hips.

"Why?"

He shifted his gaze to the circles he was tracing on the sheet between us. I noticed he looked somewhere else if our conversation became too personal. Which, I thought, was maybe why he looked away when we made love. "I've done it since we got married."

I sat up, even more intrigued. "Watch me sleep?"

"Maybe a couple of times a week."

I wasn't sure how I felt about that. It was a bit strange but romantic, too. What if I snored or twitched in my sleep? The question remained: "Why?"

He met my gaze. "It's my way of connecting with you."

I knew exactly what he meant. I told him so by smiling. "I wish I'd thought of that."

"It's my fault that we . . . that we're not connected. I

know that. But I don't know how to fix it." He reached over and ran his thumb over my mouth. "I always thought sex was connecting. Now I know that even great sex isn't a real connection."

"I used to think that, too, about sex." This whole thing with Dominic had made me realize it wasn't. What had illuminated Rush?

"In my family, communication was yelling and fighting. You want to know about my parents?" He knew I did. His gaze drifted down again as he spoke. "They're the most passionate people I've ever known. Passion, though, is all they have. When they talk, they fight. There was nothing between casual chat and fiery, all-out brawls that brought the police to visit on many an occasion. My mother as much as my father, maybe even worse. She burned all of his clothes on the front lawn once. Ran over his foot with the car. He was no saint, either. He tried to drown her in the kiddie pool. While my brother and I were right there."

I'd made a sound of shock, but I held back any pity. "Sounds exciting," I said simply.

He laughed softly. "That it was, but it was miserable for my brother and me. We couldn't have friends over; their families didn't want them in any fallout once they heard about the crazy Karakostas. Dad couldn't hold down a job, so we moved around a lot, sometimes even sneaking out in the dead of night. He tried to support his family, but he always had excuses. Bad back. Lousy boss. Terrible working conditions. I remember some guy saying, 'Man, can't you take care of your family?' My dad hung his head in shame, and it hurt to see him like that."

"That's why you bought the loft outright," I said. "Why you work so hard." The demons of poverty and shame nipped at his heels like junkyard dogs.

"The loft was the first thing, besides a car, that I

owned. I could actually decorate it, settle in." He tilted his head, looking at me. "You never put your touches in the loft. Like you weren't sure how long you were going to be here."

"That's not the reason. It was just that, you'd spent all that money having it professionally decorated. I didn't want to spoil it."

His mouth twisted into a crooked smile. "Spoil it. I want to get a sense that Jonna lives here, too. That it's a place she wants to be."

"I do. I will."

He twined his fingers with mine. "Because of my past I shut you out. I didn't want to communicate because all I ever knew was fighting. It was easier to close myself in."

"It's not all your fault." I should have admitted my jealousy to him, but I couldn't. I hated that it made me sound—and feel—like a shrew. "The chasm between us felt comfortable. I never tried to bridge it, either."

He pulled me close and held me spoon-style, his hand splayed on my stomach. It was the most he'd ever said about his soul, and I wanted to memorize every word. Throughout my marriage, I'd held myself at a distance in case I got hurt. I could walk away without dragging my shattered heart with me. It was different now. I couldn't imagine living without Rush.

It was only then, in that warm silence, that I heard Dominic howl again and realized he'd been doing it all through our talk. Once, on the blog, I'd said I loved the sound of howling wolves.

When I started Montene's Diary, Beth had said, "What can one little secret hurt?" Now I knew. My little secret was about to destroy my marriage—and very possibly my life.

CHAPTER EIGHTEEN

When Beth called the next morning, I could hear the petulance in her voice immediately. "It's one thing to ignore your blog; it's something else entirely when you ignore your supposed best friend."

"I know, and I'm sorry. I—"

"Good, let's go to lunch today. My treat."

I could hear the unspoken *you owe me*. "Okay. Sure, why not?" At least I could share some good news with her for a change. We made plans to meet near AngelForce's office.

Two hours later we met outside the stone building and traded hugs.

"You look great," I said, meaning it. She wore a fur-trimmed coat and matching hat that had to be new.

"Thanks." She tilted her head. "You look tired."

Dominic had howled until three o'clock. Rush called the police, but Dominic was gone by the time they arrived. Then he returned to howl again.

"Haven't been sleeping well," I said, and left it at that.

Her nails were freshly manicured again, golden flecks in red polish. She slid her arm through mine and we walked to Newbury Street together. As we walked, she glanced at her reflection in the mirror with a lift of her chin.

"You must be having a good day," I said. "Or things are going well with your guy."

She flashed me a coy smile. "He's leaving his wife."

I could only manage a weak smile. I could hardly encourage her pursuit of a married man.

Her smile melted when she saw someone up ahead. "Oh, shit." She looked away.

"Beth, honey!" A woman waved as she hurried toward us.

She had rich red hair and Beth's sea green eyes. She must be the Queen Bitch Mother, as Beth called her, though she'd never elaborated on why.

As her mother gave her a hug Beth's confidence shriveled. Her shoulders slumped, but her body went rigid.

Though in her fifties, Beth's mother wore a fur miniskirt and enough gaudy jewelry to make me think she'd recently come into money and felt a need to show it off. "Wow, imagine running into you here." She turned to me. "Hi, honey. I'm Beth's mom, Diana."

I took her proffered hand with nails as overdone as her daughter's. "I'm Jonna, Beth's friend."

She took me in with a curious smile and then said to Beth, "Wow, you've actually got a pretty friend." She confided to me, "She usually picks homely friends so she'll feel better."

"Mom," Beth growled. "We've got to go."

Diana waggled her fingers and said in a singsong voice that reminded me of a bragging child, "Look what your father bought me, just for the heck of it. Wow, huh?"

"Stepfather," Beth corrected. "Bye, Mother."

"You're just jealous, like you always were," she said as Beth shuttled me onward. "You're jealous 'cause you haven't found your sugar daddy yet!" Then in utter contrast, she called after us, "You could come by sometime, you know. Wouldn't kill you."

Beth's fingers tightened on my arm, hurting me even through my coat. She ushered us into the café and said nothing as we hung up our coats and found a table in the bright, cheery space.

"No wonder you can't stand your mother," I said, letting her know she could talk to me about it if she wanted to.

"Bitch," she muttered as the waitress appeared to take our order. "Cappuccino, please, low-fat milk . . . shot of vodka," she added under her breath.

"Vanilla frappe for me."

Once the waitress left, Beth slapped on lipstick even though she was about to drink it off. Never mind that she already had some on. Her fingers were trembling and her cheeks were flushed a bright red. "She's always been competitive. I used to think it was because she'd had me so young and we were close in age. She got preggo by a married man who wouldn't leave his wife for her. And somehow that made her superior," she bit off sarcastically.

Was that why Beth was going for her married guy?

She took out her pack of cigarettes and fiddled with the clear wrapper. "She was always crowing about what she had that I didn't. She'd come in from lying in the sun and be all 'look at my beautiful tan,' when she knew I couldn't get my skin to tan, and 'look at my big boobs.' She used to tease me when I was fifteen about my mosquito bites. Yeah, that's what she called my boobs. Sensitive mother, huh?"

"That's terrible."

"Oh, it gets worse. Whenever I had a boyfriend, she'd come on to him. Said she wanted to test his honor. Yeah, right. I stopped bringing them home, of course. Then I realized that my girlfriends would do the same thing, be all flirting and stuff. They weren't smart enough to use the testing excuse. Pretty soon I dated guys who went to other schools and dropped all my supposed girlfriends."

It was the most I'd ever heard about Beth's past, but it gave me some insight into her promiscuity and the ego she used to shield a tender psyche. She must have realized how much she'd revealed, because she stuck her cigarette pack away and smiled the phony kind of smile I'd been producing for the last week. "Enough about my shit. Tell me why you're ignoring me."

My head spun with the change of subject. Knowing it would come up, I'd rehearsed what I wanted to say, trying to be delicate. Her mother had thrown me off. "I'm not ignoring you. I'm just not telling you everything that's going on."

"No kidding," she said with a twist to her mouth. "I've got to read about Hadden's proposal in the damned blog. How good does that make me feel? Like I'm the weak link or something."

"I wasn't going to tell anyone. And I stopped telling you about Dominic because you're not taking me seriously. He's stalking me, terrorizing me, and all you can say is, 'Oh, it's so romantic!' It doesn't feel romantic to me. It feels like . . . well, stalking and terrorizing." I filled her in on the stunts he'd pulled, finishing by tugging down the collar of my turtleneck sweater. "He gave me a hickey the other night! Attacked me in the parking lot and branded me like I was some cow."

Beth looked at the mark but thankfully didn't ooh and aah over it. "He's getting . . . desperate."

"Desperate and unhinged. And what really bugs me about your thinking it's romantic is that I know your ex-husband stalked you and it freaked you out."

The waitress brought our drinks and we ordered lunch blindly since we hadn't even looked at the menu.

Beth stirred sugar into her coffee, deep in thought. "Gary did freak me out. But I guess, in a way, it excited me, too." She looked at me. "To be desired like that is a woman's fantasy. Deep down inside I liked it. Does that make me warped?"

"I guess I can understand it a little, and yet . . . not really."

She dug into her large purse. "I guess it's like the rape fantasy. Some women fantasize about that, but they don't really want to be raped. What they want is to be dominated, taken. Don't most women fantasize about being pursued in a dramatic fashion? I do."

"I'm not sure about *most* women."

"A lot of them. Remember that discussion on the blog. You said you thought it would be flattering."

"Well, I suppose."

We lapsed into silence for a few minutes and then she pulled out a magazine and shoved it in my face. A large penis floated before my eyes.

I pushed it back at her. "Would you stop doing that?"

Beth laughed her evil-girl giggle, as she did whenever she whipped out a *Playgirl* to shock and titillate me.

"I don't know how you can look at those pictures," I said, focusing on my frappe.

"That's not what Montene would say."

I thought of the vibrator. "Maybe I'm only a little bit Montene." The truth was, I wasn't as much Montene as I wanted to be. As I'd portrayed myself to be.

The waitress eyed the magazine when she brought our sandwiches, and Beth handed it to her. "Here, I'm done with it." The waitress lifted her hands surrender-style and left, and Beth laughed as she dropped it back in her bag.

Seeing that magazine in Beth's bag made me think about Rush, about the vibrator, and then about our deep discussion. As I picked at my mound of carrot salad, I started thinking about how I would tell Beth about Rush and me. My smile gave me away.

"Okay, why the cat-shit grin?"

"I'm falling in love with my husband."

Beth dropped her fork on the plate, making everyone look over at us again. "With Rush?"

"Well, he is my only husband. I'm old-fashioned that way."

"I didn't realize things were going that well."

I shook my head. "It's so weird. It's like he knows about the blog, because he's done a few things I'd talked about on there." Before she could ask what, I continued. "But he can't know because he'd be hurt, angry. He's not acting like that at all. At first he was all dark and possessive, probably because he suspected that I was seeing someone. Now he's different. Opening up to me like never before. We're beginning to connect, really connect, on an emotionally intimate level." I couldn't hide my excitement. "I feel like a schoolgirl again. Or, more precisely, like I did back when Rush and I just met. Only better. He finally told me about his childhood. I understand why he closed me out. And more important, why I closed him out, too."

"Why did he close you out?"

"It's . . . private. Nothing personal, Beth. It's just . . . we're sharing intimate details, like a couple."

"Wow," she said, echoing her mother's overuse of the word. She smiled. "That's great. Wonderful." She raised her coffee mug, and I toasted. "Here's to true love reigning victorious!" Before we even took our drink, she said, "Have you told him about Dominic?"

"No. Before Rush and I move forward, I have to take care of that problem myself. I made it. I don't want to drag him into it."

"Take care of it?" Beth repeated slowly. "How are you going to do that?"

The slight laugh in her question annoyed me, as though I were powerless. I'd felt that way too long. "I'm going to file a restraining order."

"But how? You don't even know who he is."

"I'm going to arrange a meeting with him and follow him back to his car, maybe to his home. Then I'll give the information to the police." And hope they wouldn't laugh me out the door. "I've got to do something. My sanity is on the line. So is my marriage." And possibly my safety, but I wasn't going to go there.

"That's crazy-stupid! What if he sees you?"

"Then he does. I'll tell him again that I don't want him in my life and leave. There'll be people around." Beth had grown quiet. "Okay, maybe it's a little crazy, but I'm desperate. I've got to do something."

Did she doubt my abilities? My sanity? No, the hardness in her expression didn't match concern for me at all.

"Beth?"

"What am I supposed to say? Oh, I know. Poor, poor Jonna. She has three men after her. I feel so bad for her. All because she became this famous blogger chick."

I felt as though she had slapped me. Not only the words but the sarcastic way she'd said them. I didn't want a misunderstanding to mess up our friendship again, so I tried to keep the bite out of my voice when said, "Yeah, it's a hell of a lot of fun. Three men. One a freakin' psycho, one just screwed up our friendship."

"But you still have your gorgeous, rich husband."

She'd thrown everything I'd ever confided to her my face. I wished I hadn't. Beth knew so many of my secrets. Right then she reminded me of an artichoke, prickly at the tips and difficult to enjoy.

"Look, you're obviously in a bad mood. Not that blame you after seeing your mother." I threw some money on the table despite her earlier assertion that was her treat. "I've got to get back to work."

I didn't say, *See you later.* I just left, afraid something else might come out of my mouth I'd later regret. Was she jealous of me? The thought was ludicrous. Beth seemed fine financially in her own right, and Rush's money wasn't mine. I'd never flaunted it as such. Still, as I walked to my car, I ached with a loss similar to the one I'd experienced with Hadden. I felt terribly lonely. I had no one to confide in about Dominic.

No one but the police. First I had to find out who Dominic really was.

CHAPTER NINETEEN

Blog entry: November 19, 11:15 A.M.

Blog friends,

I have been duly taken to task by many of you for not posting much anymore. The truth is, I am no longer a desperate housewife. My husband and I are beginning to bridge that chasm between us. Baby steps, to be sure, but steps in the right direction. Despite what Dominic may have posted, we are not involved in any way. He is out of my life. Since I don't feel right posting about my marriage, there really isn't much for me to say anymore. Alas, I've become boring. Egads. Honestly, it's a wonderful thing. Thanks for being here, for all of our lively discussions, and for your friendship.

—Montene

I had only skimmed over the vast number of comments. Just as I'd feared, the new column had spawned even more posts.

I checked my appearance in the community bathroom mirror at my shop's building. I'd borrowed one of Rush's business shirts and paired it with a pair of black wool pants. I'd pinned up my hair and would hide it under a hat. I slid into one of Rush's old coats.

Person who doesn't look like Jonna: check.

I headed out to an area of town I wasn't familiar with. Dominic had chosen it because of its proximity to his workplace, which he still hadn't specified. I got the impression he was playing hard to get now. My plan was to arrive early and find a place from which to observe him. If I could follow him to his car I'd write down the license plate number. If he lived in the area, I could follow him home. Or to work. With one tidbit the police could find out who he was.

No one knew I was going to be here. I'd mentioned it to Beth, but we hadn't spoken since our lunch. I needed time away from our friendship, and perhaps she did, too. Besides, she'd already told me how crazy I was to do this. What she should have then said was, *But I'm here for you. I'll even go with you.*

It wasn't all that crazy. Dominic wouldn't see me. He'd go inside, wait, give up, and leave. I'd follow him, take down whatever information I could garner, and get the heck out of there. See, no problem.

I drove around the block in an area crammed tight with buildings. At least he was probably telling the truth about working here. He'd once mentioned a favorite pizza shop with the dancing pizzas on the sign. It wasn't a chain as far as I knew. I passed the café where we were to meet and continued on. After finding a parking spot, I went into a shop next door to the café and hovered near the window. I had become the stalker, I realized. I liked the power it gave me even as I hated having to lower myself to his level.

When he showed, my heart jumped. I hadn't seen him all weekend, so the sight of him jarred me. He looked harmless, walking in the sunshine, nodding at passersby. I knew better. He walked into the café. Now I would have to wait until he gave up on me.

It took twenty minutes. His body was rigid, mouth set

in a grim line, when he walked out. With a hitch in my breath, I stepped outside and followed him down the sidewalk. At last I would have a way to know who he was. He probably had a history of stalking women he'd met on the Internet. If he had any violence in that history, the police would understand what I was dealing with. Having seen that crazy look in his eyes, I thought he probably did.

And I had let him into my life with one simple e-mail.

I remained several yards behind, though I felt pretty secure that even if he did glance back he wouldn't recognize me. I wore dark sunglasses along with the manly clothing and kept my head down. My trembling hands were buried in my pockets.

He never looked back. He walked three blocks and into a multi-level parking garage. I saw him head toward the stairs, but by the time I got there I'd lost him. I heard footsteps above me, so I ascended. I stopped at the second floor and looked. I heard a shoe scrape on the concrete and continued up another few steps. The third floor was sparsely filled with cars. I figured I'd hear a car door slam and an engine roar to life. Then I could identify the car and plate.

I heard nothing. I took another step up, putting me at visual level with the garage. No sign of life. Dammit, he'd given me the slip when I'd been so close to finding out who he was! As I began to turn around, I saw movement, heard sound, but nothing registered as I was knocked against the wall and fell on the steps. I felt someone pressing me into the sharp edges.

"Don't move, bitch," a gruff voice said as he rifled my pockets.

I was being mugged? Fear pulsed in my throat. *Or worse?* I didn't have my wallet or a purse. Was I wearing any jewelry? No, I'd removed everything—everything but my charm watch. Damn, I'd forgotten to take that off. I felt the man rip it off my wrist. I expected him to demand to know where my money was, but he didn't. I stared into the crevice between the steps, careful not to look at him. Now I hoped Dominic was somewhere nearby and that he'd come upon us.

Bizarrely, my cell phone rang with its jaunty tune.

I thought the mugger might take the phone, too, but he didn't do that, either. What did he want?

Please God, don't let him hurt me, I prayed over and over.

I'd barely gotten the prayer out the third time when he pushed away and ran down the stairs behind me. I heard his footsteps fade into the distance. I stumbled down the steps to the platform below and crumpled to the concrete. My hands were dirty, one nail broken. I rubbed at the imprint the edge of the step had left on my forehead but saw no blood on my trembling fingers. I could see where my watch had been, where he'd scratched me trying to take it off. I rubbed at that scratch, trying to erase his touch. Lying on the dirty floor was my Eiffel charm. It took me three tries to pick it up.

Adrenaline drained from my body as though someone had tipped me over and poured it out. I couldn't move. My thoughts scattered in my head. What if I'd worn my wedding ring? The thought of losing it was devastating. How would I explain the absence of my watch to Rush? And something else that had wedged in my brain when the mugger had spoken to me. The way he'd said the word *bitch*.

Finally I pushed to my feet and made my way downstairs. I replayed the word again and then from another time I'd heard it spoken so vehemently. Had I smelled cinnamon or was it my imagination?

CHAPTER TWENTY

Dominic called Mamu from his car. "It's me. You were right; she was up to something. She followed me to the parking garage. And I taught her a lesson."

"What did you do?"

"I mugged her," he said, hearing the satisfaction in his voice. As always, though, he feared what Mamu's reaction would be. "Took her watch. And yes, I'm sure she didn't know it was me." He waited through the silence. She probably did it on purpose, just to keep him guessing. Good boy or bad boy?

"I don't think that was a good idea. Someone else could have seen you."

"I hadn't planned on mugging her. She was standing in the stairwell, no one was around, her back was to me . . . it was the perfect setup. Except she didn't have her purse. And don't worry, I'm not going to pawn the watch. It's my personal trophy."

She still wasn't convinced. "Well, the plan has to change anyway, since our original one isn't working. Once again I've got to bail us out."

His fingers tightened on the steering wheel. Damn her. He could point out how she'd screwed up the last two cons, but he didn't want to get into an argument. He hated fighting with her. She always took away her affection, her approval, for so long.

She said, "I'm playing with an idea, but it's going to take some great acting ability on your part. More than just seducing some desperate housewife. And it's going to mean involving someone else."

"What is it?" he asked, keeping the anger from his voice. "Who?"

"Let me think on it, make sure there are no kinks."

He hated being left in the dark until *she* was ready to include him. He focused, instead, on the positive. "So I'm not wooing Jonna anymore?"

"No point in that," Mamu said on a sigh. "She's not buying the goods."

He winced at the barb. "Then it's okay if I scare her a little."

Her chuckle sent relief through him. "Sure, have a ball. Serves her right for not cooperating. Just don't get caught. If we want to salvage this we've got to be careful. I'll talk to you tonight."

He disconnected and picked up the watch. Several charms dangled from it. He had discovered something during this job. He enjoyed scaring Jonna. In fact, he enjoyed that more than the seduction. That part was boring anyway. There was only one woman he wanted to touch and hold. Having sex with these other women only sated a perfunctory physical need.

His desperation to snag Jonna had driven him to do things he'd never done before. Deep down he'd known that he was frightening her. Even his gifts scared her. Watching that fear *did* trigger something inside him. Something exciting and thrilling. It reminded him of the early days of their schemes, when it was new. Maybe he had failed at seducing Jonna, but he sure had succeeded in scaring her. Now he was about to step that up.

I was gathering my cool in the police parking lot when my cell phone rang. For a few seconds it brought back all the terror of those moments in the garage. I was definitely going to change the ring tone. I looked at the display. Just seeing Rush's number made my eyes tear.

"Hey, babe," he said. And then oddly, "Where are you?"

"Just shopping for props," I said, wondering if my voice sounded as shaky to him as it did to me.

"You all right?"

"Fine. Just traffic . . . you know." I cleared my throat. "What's up?"

"Your dinner party last week seemed to give my guy at DEMCO the courage to take the next step. They're moving toward an overnighter. He's going to visit Sturdivant's headquarters in New York and toy with a prenup. It might be time to finally roll the dice. He fessed up about the reason behind his cold feet: he's not ready to let go of his baby yet. The big guys were smart enough to offer him a position that puts him in charge of merging the two technologies and seeing his baby to its fruition. Thing is, he wants me with him during the negotiations, since I've been through all this with SIChipX. That means leaving tonight, possibly being gone two nights." Then he surprised me by adding, "Want to come with?"

"Oh . . . I'd love to, except that I've got the Women's Club of Boston awards dinner tomorrow."

I could hear his disappointment. "Well, can't change that, I suppose."

I hoped he could hear mine, too. "I wish I could. I'm not comfortable putting either of my part-timers in

charge of an event. Not with my reputation on the line."
I sighed. "So I probably won't see you tonight."

"I doubt it."

Being alone would give me some time to think about
what I wanted to tell him. That was good. Being alone in
general wasn't so good. We signed off, and I remembered the call I'd received while I was being mugged. I
checked my voice mail and heard Beth say, "I've made a
manicure appointment for both of us this Friday. Let me
know if that doesn't work for you. Our usual time and
place. Bye!"

Like nothing had happened. I'd hoped for an apology
or at least a bit of contriteness in her voice, but no, her
usual cheery self. I turned off the phone. Step one
hadn't worked out so well. Time for step two: involve
the police.

I got out of the car and scanned the parking lot. If it
was Dominic who had mugged me and if he'd followed
me, he wouldn't be around anymore. I went inside and
waited before being taken into a large room filled with
desks and noise and people. I'd hoped to talk to a
woman, but I mostly saw men.

Officer Pat Barker looked as though he should be in
the Army, with his lean, sharp features and bristle hair-
cut. I guessed him to be about my age. He seemed sympathetic and pleasant, offering me a drink and making
sure I was comfortable.

I declined the drink and I wasn't comfortable, but I
settled into the hard chair next to his desk while he readied himself to take notes.

"You're being stalked?" he said, referring to the note
he'd been given by the receptionist.

"Yes. I made a list of everything I could remember." I
held up a page from my notebook. "Unfortunately, I
don't know his real name. When I tried to find out today,
I was mugged."

His eyebrows raised on that. "Are you all right?"

"Shaky more than anything. All he got was my watch. I'm not sure if it was my stalker or not."

"Okay, we'll deal with that part separately. Now tell me everything from the beginning."

I wished I had Beth with me. She would have held my hand and helped me explain why I'd become Montene. But I was alone and so I began. I'd only gotten as far as being Montene when his eyes narrowed.

"Wait a minute. You're the chick with the blog that everyone's talking about." He said it loud enough that those nearby tuned in.

"Yes, you see—"

"I don't believe it." I saw a mixture of both surprise and derision in his face. "You're the one calling us cops a bunch of macho meatheads—"

"I never said that." I held out my hand. "I never even participated in that discussion."

He narrowed his eyes. "Someone printed it out and stuck it on the break room wall. Yeah, we all had a big laugh about that," he said without a bit of humor. "You all like to dis men, too, saying what pigs we are."

"Some of the gals on the blog are pretty harsh, I'll give you that, but—"

The guy at the next desk made a motion with his hand. "My wife is always yammering about that stupid blog. 'The girls said this and the girls said that.'" He sat back and narrowed his eyes at me. "So you're Montene."

I wanted to shrink into my chair. "I never meant it to be a big deal. It was like having my diary online, that's all."

"Sure, and you hate all the attention, don't you?" Barker said, leaning back in his chair. "My wife got a freakin' vibrator because of that blog. She calls it Arriba, as in 'Arriba, arriba, andale, andale,' or whatever that cartoon mouse used to say. She won't let me play, either. All she wants is that damned thing."

A couple of the guys burst out in laughter, and one guy said, "It's better than her calling *you* Speedy Gonzales!"

Everyone was listening in. I shrank farther down. "Can we . . . get back to my stalker?"

His eyes widened. "Wait a minute. You met this stalker through your blog?"

I knew where this was going: nowhere. It would only get worse from there. I was going to cheat on my husband, I put myself in a dangerous situation by meeting a stranger at a hotel, and on and on. Worse, it was true.

I stood. "I've made a mistake."

"No, wait. I'll take your report, Ms. Montene!" he called after me. "Come back."

I heard several men laugh. I hadn't realized how threatened men were by our discussions on the blog. It wasn't necessarily my comments that spurred so much interest but the comments from others.

The receptionist gave me an odd look as I shrugged into my coat and barreled out the door, my face suffused with heat. For a few minutes helplessness and frustration swamped me. I'd only felt good and in control when I had a plan. With that plan gone, I needed a new one or I'd shatter.

I decided on one before I'd even left the parking lot. If I couldn't document the stalking with the police, I'd do the next best thing: I'd do it on my blog.

Blog entry: November 19, 7:00 p.m.

Dear blog friends,

I know you're disappointed that I withheld information from you. You're mad because I haven't been blogging recently and probably annoyed that I bid you all good-bye. Now I'm going to tell you why. Dominic has been stalking me. I was afraid to post because I knew he was reading this. I didn't want to incite him any further. But I can see that it doesn't matter. More important now is to let you know what's going on. I haven't told my husband about any of this, and I don't want him to know. So you will be my witnesses.

It began the day I met Dominic for lunch. . . .

I was exhausted by the time I was done. Now, at least, someone would know what was going on. I turned off my computer and sagged in my chair. That's when I heard the knock on the door.

CHAPTER TWENTY-ONE

Dominic sat in his car that was parked at the far end of the small lot designated for visitors. From there he could see the light inside her loft, though not much more with the blinds drawn. She was alone in there. He'd taken the night off from his bartending job to pay her a visit. He'd told her the truth about that part, anyway, though it wasn't at a private club. Now he wished he'd lied about that, too. This had escalated to war. She wanted to find out who he was, probably so she could go to the police. He couldn't let her find out.

He didn't see the deliveryman until he went up the ramp and approached Jonna's door. He had a bouquet of yellow roses. She peered out the blinds before opening the door, no doubt checking to see if it was him. Then she accepted the flowers.

Dominic got out of his car once the deliveryman left. He could howl again, but it was a bit of a pain. He had to keep leaving, especially when he saw a cop car coming down the street. He wasn't even sure Jonna had heard him, so there wasn't much satisfaction in it. He had a far better way to satisfy himself. He'd kept something secret from even Mamu. If she'd known, she probably would have forbade him from continuing to torment Jonna.

Because he had special plans for Jonna tonight.

I stared at the bouquet of yellow roses after I'd read the note: "Miss you . . . Rush." He had sent flowers before, but not yellow roses.

Was this a trick? The card wouldn't be in his handwriting, because he would have called it in. Did Dominic want me to thank my husband for flowers he hadn't sent and restart his suspicions? It was like receiving the box all over again, not knowing how to handle this. I left them on the dining table and went upstairs. I was exhausted, from the mugging, the ordeal at the police station, and re-living everything on the blog. I needed sleep.

I wore my thin silk pajamas and a thick robe over them. My fuzzy footies kept the cold metal stairs from chilling my feet as I went upstairs. After one last look at the bouquet I flicked off the lights. I'd taken a long, hot shower to wash away the violation of the mugging. I checked the mirror one last time in the bathroom. The red line across my forehead was nearly faded now. So was the hickey. I'd trimmed all my nails and removed the polish. The only thing I couldn't fix was the missing watch, other than buying a new one.

I had to tell Rush about Dominic. My stomach tightened at the mere thought of that conversation. I wasn't sure how Rush would react, which made it all the worse, but he needed to know what was going on.

I was spared more ruminating by the ringing of the phone. I smiled when I saw Rush's cell number. "Hi, honey," I answered.

"Hey, babe. I'm in New York."

I liked when he called me babe. I rubbed the smooth surface on the back of the phone and stared at the flowers.

"How was the flight?"

"Non-eventful, which is the best you can hope for. We're heading into Manhattan right now. I'll let you know tomorrow what the return plans are."

"Hopefully you'll be back tomorrow." Two nights alone didn't thrill me. I missed him. And I was eager to get my confession over with.

After a pause, he asked in a playful voice, "Did you get any deliveries tonight?"

I smiled, feeling relieved. "Mm, like Chinese food maybe?"

"Or something a little less edible."

We were playing a game, and I liked it. I slipped out of the robe and dropped onto the bed. "I love them," I said. "They brightened a crappy day."

"What happened?" he asked, taking me off-guard.

"Oh, you know, this and that." Not the time to unload. "But why *yellow* roses?"

"That rose you brought home from the beach party got me thinking that you'd once mentioned yellow roses were your favorite."

I forced a laugh. "The way you were staring at it that night . . . well, I kind of thought you suspected someone had left it on the doorstep." There, I'd flirted with the truth.

"I may lose you. We're about to go in a tunnel. If we do, I'll call you tomorrow. I knew someone hadn't left it. I was staring at it because I felt bad that I'd forgotten that."

"Oh. But . . . how did you know someone hadn't left it outside?"

"Because it was inside the house," he said just before I lost the connection.

Inside the house. Fear gripped my throat. No, he couldn't have been right about that. We don't have a mail slot, so there wasn't any way for the rose to get in.

Unless . . .

I shot out of bed and ran to the railing at the upstairs loft. My heart was pounding as I stared at the front door. It was locked now. I remembered the time the door wasn't locked when I was pretty sure I'd locked it. God, had he tried the door, found it unlocked? Come inside and into my bathroom? Now that seemed entirely and chillingly probable.

I heard the murmur of noise. Maybe the neighbors' television, though I'd never heard it before. They'd done a great job insulating the walls between units.

Was Dominic out there blaring his radio? With that thought I descended the steps and crept to the front window. I was only halfway there before I saw the play of lights in the family room. The sound was coming from there.

As I walked down the long hall I remembered the time an electrical burp had tripped the television/stereo equipment and turned it on. That time it was just the CD player, not the television. Another time the volume went up by itself. We laughed about having ghosts in the loft.

As I reached the room, I saw that a movie was playing on the wall that we used as a theater screen: *Batman*. It was a dark movie, sending shadows undulating through the room. I saw the lights on the DVD player. Somehow it had come on, too.

I took in the black leather couch, silk palm in the corner, and modern fireplace. My body was in a heightened state of alert. Did I really think Dominic had somehow gotten in and turned on the television? Wouldn't he have crept up the stairs and attacked me in my sleep?

Oddly enough, the creepy thought relaxed me. I could almost laugh as I walked to the cabinet that housed the equipment. As I knelt down to try to make sense of the buttons, I heard a noise. Like the sound of a knee popping. Not my knee.

Before I could even begin to turn, arms clamped around me and jerked me off my feet. A hand slapped across my mouth as a frightened gasp escaped. I fought, but he—the monster behind me—was larger and stronger. I kicked his shins. I stretched my fingers to see if I could make any contact, but my arms were pinned to my sides. He carried me around the couch and threw me down, keeping his hand over my mouth.

I saw him hovering over me, the big screen behind him throwing his features into shadow. But I knew who he was, who he had to be. I felt my eyes bulging with fear and the pain of my nose being crushed beneath his hand. My heart beat madly in my chest.

"Montene," he whispered, erasing all doubt. He knelt over me, pinning me with his legs on either side of my body. "You know, you should have given in that day at the hotel. It would have been so much easier."

Oh, God, he was going to rape me. Or worse, rape me and kill me. The reality of it soaked me in cold fear and sweat. I heard whimpering sounds coming from my throat. *No, don't give up! Didn't you always say you'd fight?* I had imagined some anonymous thug, not two hundred pounds of rebuffed male.

"Are you afraid, Jonna?" he whispered, close to my face. "Yes, I can see that you are." He licked my face, running his tongue from my temple down to my neck. I gagged. He touched my breasts with his free hand, rubbing across the silk fabric of my pajamas. He jammed his hand down the front of my pajama bottoms, but because he had me pinned he couldn't get between my legs. He dug his fingers into my pubic hair instead.

"Nice flowers," he said with a tilt to his head. "From your hubby, huh?"

He loosened the pressure of his hand just enough that I could talk, but I knew if I screamed he'd jam it down again. So I tried another strategy.

"He'll be home any minute, you son of a bitch."

The "son of a bitch" part I hadn't planned; that had just come out.

He laughed.

"Ooh, I'm scared," he said in a high-pitched voice. "What do you think he'd say if he walked in and found us here like this? 'Oh, excuse me. Didn't meant to bother you.' Maybe he'd join us. D'ya think? I'll bet he's always fantasized about a threesome."

"You're disgusting."

"Come on, Montene, you know us men are pigs. 'Course, I'd rather have two women and not have to share. And since this is my fantasy, I say he just sits there and watches me stick it to you, maybe even gets off himself."

"He'll kill you." I didn't know what Rush would do, but I had to think he would hammer Dominic.

"Yeah, well, I know he's not coming home tonight. I saw him leave with an overnight bag. And here you are, all by yourself. Thought I'd keep you company."

I tried to struggle free, knowing full well that I wouldn't be able to throw him off me. I started imagining how Rush would find my body and even about what the Women's Club ladies would think when I didn't show.

Fight, I told myself. *Don't let him do this to you.*

"You didn't show up for our date today," he said as parents would say to their naughty child.

"I got hung up."

He crushed my mouth with his hand, pushing my head into the couch and my lips into my teeth. "Don't lie. You were setting me up so you could follow me."

When he leaned his weight forward, he freed up my legs. I pulled my knee up and rammed it as hard as I could, having no idea where I was hitting. I was hoping for his balls.

He let out a grunt of pain but didn't curl up in agony. He clamped his thighs on either side of my legs to immobilize me. "Come on, Jonna. I can call you Jonna, can't I? Sure, I can." He leaned closer. "Let me see you cry. Show me some tears. And fear. I remember how you looked when I had you pinned on that hotel bed. After you teased me. At least I got the satisfaction of seeing you afraid. That and my hand after you ran off and left me with an unresolved hard-on."

He had one now. I could feel the rigid length of him as he pressed down on me and did the hip grind. He stopped at the sound that I recognized as the doorbell. My eyes widened. Hope.

"Who's that?"

I couldn't answer, so he lifted his hand slightly and I said, "I don't know. M-maybe Rush didn't make his flight."

"Nice try. He wouldn't use the doorbell." His hand pressed down even harder.

The doorbell rang again as we waited, hope draining out of me with every passing second. Finally it went silent.

He laughed softly. "Now, where were we?"

CHAPTER TWENTY-TWO

Nearly midnight. Hadden rubbed his eyes and stared at the monitor in front of him. His focus strayed again to the picture on the desk: Jonna. Smiling, sitting on a sailboat, her brown hair flying in the wind, cheeks dimpled. A woman in love. Probably taken on their honeymoon.

Rush had another picture of her on the credenza, this one more formal. She didn't have that same glow in her eyes. Hadden hadn't seen that glow in a while.

He closed his eyes and leaned back in the chair. "Is that why you opened your mouth?" he said, pinching the bridge of his nose. Had he been hoping that she was on the verge of leaving Rush and knowing he was interested might push her to make a move?

Maybe some part of him had. The idiotic part. He could never have Jonna Karakosta, simply because she was Jonna Karakosta. Even if she divorced Rush, getting involved with his friend/business partner's wife was out of the question. Knowing that only made it worse.

Seeing the distance in her eyes since his admission hurt even more. Would she ever feel comfortable around him again? She obviously needed someone to confide in, and he'd blown it.

He wondered if Rush was acting as cool to her as he

was to him. It didn't seem to be just the fact that they'd had lunch together. After that Rush was as distracted as he'd been. It was a few days later that Rush had turned arctic. Hadden had tried to talk, but Rush had blown him off. It worried him that two friendships were deteriorating.

Now he was on Rush's computer. It had started out innocently enough; Hadden had needed a file. Since a virus destroyed the whole network, Rush kept the computer containing all of his files separate and off-network.

Hadden felt like a traitor as he turned on the other computer and opened Rush's in-box. It was his job to find out what was behind Rush's odd behavior. AngelForce and all its members and entrepreneurs depended on it. Hadden skimmed the e-mails after stopping before it downloaded anything new. He didn't want Rush to suspect anything.

Hadden considered Rush a close friend. They often had lunch, shared some of the same political and business views and morals. They'd met at MIT, where Rush had been on scholarship. Hadden had helped Rush acclimatize to society. Rush had helped him kick a growing coke addiction no one else knew about. Lately Rush had sunk into some dark place. He'd rebuffed Hadden's attempts to find out what was going on and help. Now Rush was treating Hadden like the enemy.

Hadden didn't know enough about Rush's family to suspect something was going on there. In fact, Hadden didn't think Rush had much to do with them. He'd always been vague about his background, but Hadden guessed a poor childhood was behind Rush's hunger for success. He had a drive that he insisted their entrepreneurs possess as well, and he fought for them if the angels were dithering over an investment. People were drawn to him, and Hadden sometimes envied Rush's charisma. Though they were cofounders of AngelForce, it was generally acknowledged that Rush was the true leader—the archangel.

Hadden knew very little about who Rush was lately. Looking around at his office, Hadden couldn't see that much had changed. Rush still had the pictures of Jonna and the model of a 1967 Mustang on one shelf. He had the pair of dice he flipped from hand to hand whenever they were in deep discussion about a potential investment. He liked fine things—mahogany furniture, artwork—but he didn't live ostentatiously.

Hadden doubted Rush would cheat on Jonna. He demanded loyalty from his friends and employees and gave the same in return. So Hadden had gone to the next type of stressor—business trouble. Large sums of money sometimes corrupted innocent and desperate people. He was the devil's advocate, the cynic on the lookout for signs of embezzlement. Though he doubted Rush would embezzle money from his beloved company, Hadden wondered if something else was going on. Compulsive gambling? Involvement with shady business partners? Nothing looked out of sorts, however.

He saw the icon as he was about to close down the computer. Recognizing the logo, he clicked on it. He remembered Rush showing him the software and also remembered the log-in he'd used.

"What the . . . ?" Hadden scrolled down the list, more puzzled, and angrier, with every passing second.

"Rush . . . we've got to talk."

He printed several sheets of paper and closed everything down. He looked at the clock. It was too late to call Jonna. His loyalty should have been to Rush, but Jonna was his friend, too. She had to know. First, though, he'd confront Rush and, he hoped, find out what was going on.

It wasn't a conversation he was looking forward to.

• • •

Dominic hovered over me, his warm breath huffing over my face. It smelled of cinnamon and liquor. The hairs at his neck were damp. He smelled like sweat. My heartbeat hammered throughout my body, making my chest hurt, pulsing at my temples and throat and even my fingertips. *Fight or flight, fight or flight,* each throb seemed to say.

I couldn't flee, not pinned like this.

Breathe. Think. Fight, fight, fight.

If I couldn't fight him physically, I could try to mess with his mind. "Okay, you want sex. Fine. I'll give you sex."

He blinked in disbelief, but instead of looking satisfied, he looked annoyed. "Just like that?"

I nodded, probably too vigorously.

"Uh-uh. You're playing me. I don't buy it."

I had felt some give in my left hand. I needed to distract him some more. "No, I want it. Really."

My assurance only seemed to annoy him more. He didn't want me to offer myself. He wanted to take me against my will. Either way, I was throwing him off, making him think, and if he was thinking, he wasn't paying attention to holding me down as hard. Before he could refocus, I cried, "Just don't hurt me. Please." I didn't have to fake my fear.

I saw the spark of cruel pleasure in his blue eyes. That's when I jerked my hand free and reached between his legs. This time I hit my mark. I crushed his balls as hard as I could. When he contorted, I shoved him with my feet. He landed on the coffee table. I launched off the couch but didn't get far. He grabbed my ankle. I went down hard, hitting my side on the corner of the table and losing my breath with the pain.

That's when I heard a knocking on the rear window and a woman's voice. "Jonna? You in there? It's Beth."

Dominic sprinted for the door, pushing me down just as I'd started to get up. I heard his footsteps pounding on the wood floor, heard the door fly open. I rolled over and saw Beth's silhouette.

"Beth," I called in a hoarse voice. "Come around to the front!"

By the time she'd gotten to the open door, a puzzled look on her face at that, I had managed to reach it myself. She was holding a bottle of something. Her expression transformed to concern when she took me in, holding my side and limping toward the door.

"What the hell is going on here?"

"Close the door," I managed. "Lock it."

She did as I said. I'd gotten to the chairs in the living room and collapsed into one. "He was in here. Dominic." I was still breathing hard.

She knelt down beside me. "Inside? Just now?"

I nodded. "I don't . . . know how. He was . . . was . . . was going to rape me."

"My God, Jonna." She looked around. "He's gone?"

I nodded again. "When you came around to the back. You . . . saved me."

"I knew Rush was out of town so I brought some schnapps and a dirty movie. When you didn't answer I went around back, saw the lights, and figured you hadn't heard the doorbell. I never imagined . . ." She hugged me. When she backed away, she said, "I'll get a paper towel. You've got blood on your lip."

The inside of my lower lip felt raw as I ran my tongue over it. The blood tasted coppery.

She grabbed the bottle and went into the kitchen. She returned a minute later with a glass and a damp towel. "I put ice in it." After I'd gotten it pressed gently against my inner lip, she handed me the glass. "And something to calm your nerves."

I nearly threw up at the smell of peppermint schnapps. I pushed it back at her, shaking my head. "That's how *he* always smells, at least close to it. Please, take it away."

She downed it herself and set the glass on the aquarium shelf. I pushed to my feet, my arms wrapped around my waist. "I'm moving the couch in front of the door. Then I've got to take a shower."

"Here, let me help you." After helping me with the couch, she led me toward the stairs and we walked up side by side. She stood in the bathroom doorway as I began to undress. I hoped she would step out, but she didn't. How could I ask her to give me privacy when she had saved me? I took off my pajamas, pushed them into the trash, and stepped into the shower even though it wasn't hot yet.

"How did he get in?" she asked. I could see her walk to the sink and open my medicine cabinet.

"I don't know. But he knew Rush was out of town."

"How?" She was washing her face.

The water turned hot, and I let it scald my skin. "He saw Rush leave with an overnight bag. I don't even know how long he was inside. I came home, got online . . . he could have been down there the whole time." I shuddered and leaned against the wall. The adrenaline was draining, taking my bones with it. "I've never felt so helpless. You think you'll fight, that you'll somehow manage to get out of the situation. But pinned beneath him, listening to him taunt me, for a few minutes I couldn't do anything."

If she heard the tears in my voice, she didn't comment. "Men are weak sons of bitches inside, but outside they're strong as hell. It's all testosterone. That's what rape is about, you know. Power. Control."

"I know. All this time he's been trying to get me to date him. Now he's furious because I rejected him."

"You were right about him," Beth said, rubbing a wash-cloth over her face and hanging it up on the towel bar. She was nearly obliterated by the steam. "I'm sorry I didn't see that. He's sick." Her support now was little consolation. "What are you going to do? Go to the police?"

When my skin felt as though it might peel off, I turned the water to cold. "I've already tried them."

"You have?"

I turned off the water and slid the door open. She at least made herself useful and handed me a towel. I wrapped myself in it before stepping out and then snagged my robe from the hook.

"Earlier today, after he mugged me."

"*Mugged* you?"

Seeing her pale, nearly invisible eyelashes and eye-brows startled me. She looked so different without makeup.

"After I tried to follow him." My legs felt weak. I didn't want to try the stairs, so I went into my bedroom. "I'm pretty sure it was him, anyway."

Beth followed, perching on the bed next to me. "Are you all right?"

I shrugged. "He took my charm watch. But that wasn't as bad as going to the police."

"What happened?"

I pulled up my legs and wrapped my arms around them. "The officer I spoke with didn't appreciate Mon-tene's Diary or the discussions his wife was participat-ing in. She bought a vibrator and won't share. And remember that anti-cop discussion? The gals talking about their cop husbands, the whole penis compensation thing, how they think they're God's gift? That happened just after the article ran, so a lot of people read it. Ap-parently, the cops did, too.

"I think they were actually amused by my situation. And dammit, I did bring it on myself. Who I am and what

I've done makes me a less than sympathetic victim." I pounded on the bed. "Dammit, I hate being a victim!"

Beth rubbed my arm.

"And even though he's gone much farther now, I can't get past the memory of my earlier visit to the police station. Besides, I still don't know Dominic's true identity. I'm not sure how much they could do except file a report. So I did that myself."

"How?"

"I put everything on my blog. I'm going to post this, too." Beth's breath smelled like mint, turning my stomach again. I focused on the drops of water swirling down the wet locks of my hair and soaking into my robe. "And I'm going to tell Rush everything when he gets home. It's going to be awful, but I hope he'll understand."

Beth pulled me close for a hug. "I'm so sorry, honey. I'm staying here tonight. Everything will seem better in the morning."

I couldn't imagine that it would. We checked all the windows; none were unlocked. I even checked the door to the roof deck. "How did he get in?" I told her about the rose being inside. "Maybe twice." That scared me more than anything.

Though I had planned to pull out the sofa bed downstairs, she walked into the bedroom. "This bed looks so comfy. What side do you sleep on?" When I gestured to my side, she walked over to the other side. Then she slipped out of her clothes and into bed, wearing nothing but pink socks. At my surprised look she said, "I can't stand to wear anything to sleep. You don't mind, do you? I mean, we're just girls. Like a slumber party!" she added with a grin.

What could I say? She was here for me. I just shrugged, put on my silk pajamas, and got into the king-size bed beside her.

Beth took a deep breath as she settled in. She re-
garded me for a moment. "Are you all right, sweetie?"

I shrugged again, feeling my mouth curl in a frown.

She reached over and rubbed my shoulder.

"Thanks for staying."

"That's what friends are for," she said, a soft smile on
her face.

Within minutes she was asleep, snoring softly. The
rest of the night I lay awake and listened to the sounds
outside the loft. Mostly I listened for sounds *inside* the
loft. I needed to figure out how he'd gotten in so he
couldn't do it again.

Dominic read the latest post on Montene's Diary. She'd
spelled out everything, and in those words he looked
like a deranged, psychotic, dangerous stalker. He liked
it. And he liked the fear he read in her words. What
would she say about tonight?

He'd gone too far. He hadn't gone far enough. He
cupped his hands over his still-aching balls. If her husband didn't return the next night . . .

The blinking light on his answering machine kept
catching his eye. He'd been ignoring it since he got
home. After sucking down two vodka and tonics he had
the nerve to press the button.

"It's me," she said in her deadpan voice, the one that
said she was in control and he was to do as she said.
"Did you read the latest post on her blog? At first I
thought it would complicate things. But lucky for you
the whole stalking thing fits right into the plan I've been
formulating. Let's meet at our usual place for lunch and
I'll outline it for you. It's your chance to redeem yourself. Don't blow it."

He fixed another drink. He bet she'd left a similar
message on his cell phone, which he'd turned off before

he'd gone to Jonna's. He was torn between making Mamu happy and making Jonna scared. The former made him feel submissive. The latter, powerful. He needed to feel powerful.

He sat down at the computer and composed a post:

> Montene, why are you toying with me? You invite me over, grab my crotch, and then send me away! You've got to get a grip (no pun intended) on your guilt. You're a bad girl. Go with it. But stop playing me. A man can only take so much. Remember that.

CHAPTER TWENTY-THREE

Sometime during the night it came to me, how Dominic might have gotten in. The day he'd "helped" at the Big Brothers Big Sisters party Carson said Dominic had gone off on an errand and had acted odd about it. I had put my purse in the little office at the warehouse, and at times I was nowhere near it. Maybe Dominic had taken my keys, had duplicates made, and returned them before I even knew they were missing. Manny had driven his truck when we went to get the food, and I'd left my purse at the warehouse.

It explained how the rose had gotten inside the loft, too, though that thought made me nauseated. Worse was thinking about seeing movement when I was in the shower.

I finished getting ready and headed down the stairs. Beth had already gone, and I welcomed the chance to be alone. I was grateful for her comfort and especially for saving me last night, but I couldn't rely on her support.

With hardly any sleep at all and a bruise on my side from where I'd hit the coffee table, I had to put on my game face and organize the dinner for fifty women. Fortunately, I was working with the Beaumont Hotel, where

I'd been employed when I met Rush. They were doing the cooking and serving; I was organizing everything else.

I'd coordinated with the building manager to meet the locksmith who would be due that day to change the locks as well as install extra security on the windows. That would be my opening for telling Rush the truth. I pushed the couch from in front of the door and left.

As I neared my shop, a realization sickened my stomach: Dominic had had access to the key here, too. As I pulled up to the building I stared at my door. It looked safe, normal. So had my loft.

The sky was low and gray and it leached the color from everything. It also made the air seem even colder. I got out of my vehicle and wrapped my arms around myself. My fingers gripped the key as though it were a weapon as I marched toward the door.

I peered inside the window. I saw my office but not much beyond that. He could be waiting in the dark for me. The thought sent chills prickling down my neck. I stepped back, fear keeping me from walking into what might be a trap. I went around the building and found a man I'd met before. He was a metal sculptor, and I'd admired his works and once asked if he'd be willing to rent them out for the right event.

"Hi, Sergei," I said.

"Ah, hello, Miss . . ."

"Jonna," I supplied, shaking his gloved hand. "Can you do me a favor, please, and come into my shop with me? My keys were stolen, and I'm just . . . well, a little afraid to go in by myself."

Sergei was a huge, Slavic-boned man. I wasn't sure how capable he was, but he looked intimidating. "Yes, of course."

He accompanied me back, where I pushed open the door and started to walk in. He held out an arm and walked in first. I turned on the lights, illuminating the large space.

"Don't look!" he shouted, turning me away and blocking my view. "We must call police."

"What is it?"

"Women's bodies . . . in pieces."

My stomach rolled as he pushed me to the entrance. Then I remembered something. "Wait. Let me see."

"No, you don't want to."

I managed to peer around him and saw what had frightened him: arms, legs, headless torsos covering the tabletop. "It's okay, Sergei. They're only mannequins. Like dolls."

His face was still pale and he wouldn't look, so I walked over and lifted an arm. "See, not real."

His eyes were closed. When I touched him with the hand, he let out a squeal. Only then did he look at what I was holding.

I tried to hide my smile. So much for my strong protector. "I'm hosting a dinner, and the guest speaker is an expert on the history of fashion. I borrowed these from a friend who works at a discount clothing store. We're going to put historical clothing on them."

He ran his thick fingers along the smooth surface of a stomach, and then his face reddened and he pulled his hand away.

"You should have seen them when I organized a vampire ball. There was blood and torture devices. . . ." I waved that off. "Anyway, no one was harmed in the making of these mannequins."

He nodded and then continued to look around. Everything looked eerily . . . normal. I'd expected something. Yet it felt off somehow.

On the other table sat small gold bags filled with goodies and rows of table centerpieces, waiting for the flower arrangements that were in the reefer. I walked to the large steel unit, taking a breath, and opened the door. Again, it looked normal.

"Everything is okay?" he asked.

"I . . . think so. Thank you for coming with me."

"Let me know if you need something."

My body remained tense even after I locked the door behind Sergei. I had also arranged for the locksmith to come here, but for now Dominic could come in anytime.

I kept looking toward the door as I piled the creamy silk tablecloths the ladies preferred next to the bags. The historian giving the presentation was bringing accessories to use for displays, too. I pulled out boxes from the reefer filled with the prearranged flowers and set them on the table. Two of the boxes contained flowers that were for the buffet tables. I set those aside and started pulling out the smaller arrangements I'd made the other day.

And nearly threw up.

Mixed among the flowers were dead rats. I screamed and backed up, my body hunching over. "Oh . . . oh, gawd. O-o-o-o-h." I took several deep breaths before inching forward again. They were all stiff, their limbs sticking up, eyes dry. Some were grimacing as if in pain, though I saw no wounds. Had he bought them at a pet store and poisoned them? It was an awful thought. I was terrified of rats and mice, but having them killed on my behalf was revolting on so many levels.

I had mentioned my fear on my blog, hadn't I? Yes. Dominic was using my fears now, instead of my desires.

I didn't want to think about it. I took the box, flowers and all, and put it into the Dumpster. Outside, I put on a stoic face just in case he was watching. I treated it as nothing more than normal garbage. Back inside, I gagged at the scent of dead animal lingering in the air.

I quickly arranged everything into one grouping so loading it would take minimal time. I went to my desk to grab the paperwork and came to a stop. I hadn't checked my office carefully when Sergei was here, only gave it a cursory looking over. On my desk were several Oreo cookies arranged in a heart shape. They were all licked free of icing.

I shuddered again, sure I would never eat another Oreo in my life. I scraped them into the garbage can with a notepad and took that out to the Dumpster, too. Then I started loading everything into my car, keeping an eye all around me.

What scared me the most about Dominic was his inconsistency. I'd seen the lovesick Dominic, the drunk and desperate Dominic, and the angry, vindictive one. I didn't know what to expect. All I did know was to expect something. That frightened me more than anything.

I managed to get through the dinner, though the ladies kept asking if I was feeling all right. One asked if I was pregnant. I nearly laughed hysterically; that's how close to the edge I was. I took a deep breath and assured them I wasn't. I wanted to say, *If I can get rid of my vicious stalker, maybe I'll start working on that.*

Rush and I had talked about children once on a late flight back from New York City during our whirlwind courtship. I wanted one or two, and he was fine with that. That's about as far as we'd gotten.

Faced with telling Rush everything, I wasn't sure if my marriage would even be intact. The possibility crushed me when I thought about how close we were to connecting . . . and how much I loved him.

During a break I checked my cell phone and got a disappointing message from him. He wasn't going to be home that night. Everyone was "warming to" the marriage now, and the "engagement ring was on the finger." He'd be on the morning flight but had to go right to the office.

By the time the ladies filed out, I was near exhaustion. I went to the conference concierge's office where I'd stored my purse and an overnight bag I'd brought just in case. I was getting a room at the hotel tonight. Even with new locks, I couldn't sleep at the loft alone.

Beth had left a message, too, offering to stay with me. That didn't appeal, either, but I phoned her back and thanked her. After I checked in, I wandered into the sports bar that attracted area residents as much as visitors. Tonight it was relatively empty, other than a group of guys playing darts. Two televisions blared, one with a game and one with ESPN. I walked up to the bar to order a glass of merlot to take up to my room.

The hotel was decorated for Christmas even though it wasn't Thanksgiving yet. I had always marveled at how early everyone got the holidays into gear. This time I was too distracted by work, my marriage, and Dominic . . . not necessarily in that order.

I vaguely remembered the bartender, whose tag read "Tony," from the times Beth and I used to come in after work. I hadn't seen anyone else I recognized other than in passing. That was good. I didn't want to answer the question "How are you doing?" As he poured my wine, he said, "Hey, you used to work here, didn't you?"

"Yeah. I was conference concierge." I rustled up a tired smile. "Nice to see you again."

As I waited for him to bring my bill, I watched the dart-playing group in the back. They'd obviously had a few drinks, judging by their loud voices and the crowd of beer bottles on the table. One of the men looked familiar, and when he turned and saw me he seemed to recognize me, too. Except, as he came over, he eyed me as though I'd kicked his dog and called his mother ugly.

He had a square build that went with a square face, and he parted his dirty-blond hair on the far left side. His skin had the pallor of a man who didn't eat well.

He sidled up next to me and ordered a pitcher of beer, but I knew he'd turn to me. "You're a friend of Beth's, aren't you?" he asked, a slur in his voice.

That's when it hit me. He was Gary, her ex-husband. God, another stalker. We had seen him in here once, and Beth had freaked.

"Yes," I said, and left it at that, turning to see if Tony was back with my bill.

"How's that crazy bitch doing?" Gary steadied himself against the bar, though his body seemed boneless.

"Now that you're not stalking her, fine."

"Me?" he said, splaying his hand at his chest. "Stalking *her*?" His raspy laugh sent spittle flying. "Oh, that's priceless." His humorous expression fled as he pointed at me. "Now you listen up. She was the one stalking me. After I told her I was going back to my wife, she begged me to stay with her. Then she got pissed, called me forty times a day, and followed me everywhere. She'd just sit there staring at me. Creepy. I started coming here because of her. It was six months before I could come back, when I knew she wasn't working here anymore."

The bartender set my change on the counter, but he was looking at Gary. "Hey, Gar, chill out. You giving this lady a hard time?"

"Nah," he said with an exaggerated wave.

I signed for the wine, making sure I kept my room number from his sight. "But you were at Stephano's. And we saw you here, too."

"Stephano's used to be my hangout. She went there because of me. Then I saw you and I thought, 'God, she's got a stalking buddy'!" He leaned against the bar again. "I guess I deserved it. Screwing around with my wife's best friend." His face seemed to melt into grief. "I deserved everything."

He went back to his table without his pitcher, and I

fled before he decided to tell me more. I nervously waited at the bank of elevators and breathed a sigh of relief when I stepped on and the door closed.

Should I tell Beth that her ex was bad-mouthing her, drunk enough to accuse *her* of being the stalker? No, why get her riled up over nothing? I stepped off on the fifth floor and, balancing my wine and bag, unlocked my door.

I checked my cell phone again and found two messages. The televisions in the bar had been too loud to hear my phone ring, I guess. One was Rush, hoping to catch me before I went to bed. That made me feel good, but I wasn't up to talking to him. I sipped my glass of wine, feeling fragile and very, very alone.

The other message was my mother. She was in New York City attending a Mary Kay function for the week. She wondered how I was doing, subtle language for wanting to know if I'd gone through with my affair. I wasn't up to that, either. We'd taken a step forward when I'd confronted her about her affairs, but spilling about everything else would be too much.

I would, however, update my blog. I logged on and fought the temptation to read the comments posted since my last entry. I didn't want to know if they believed me, if they blamed me, or if Dominic had posted something contrary to what I'd said. I simply documented his assault.

They read Montene's latest post together. Mamu stood just behind him, where he was seated at the computer. He could hear her breathing grow more erratic.

"That was stupid," she said, smacking him in the head. "What the hell is wrong with you?"

He turned, feeling that same anger that Jonna fired up aimed at Mamu. "I get to play in this game, too. And you said it would be all right to scare her," he felt compelled to add, hating himself for doing so.

"Scare her, not rape her!" She paced, her fist pressed to her stomach.

Turning his self-hatred into strength, he said, "I wasn't going to rape her. But I liked scaring her. It's the first time I've felt . . . excited . . . in a long time." He wouldn't tell her just how excited he'd been. How close he'd come to actually tearing off Jonna's clothes. The beast had been building inside him as he'd had her pinned beneath him. Powerful. Masterful. For a few minutes he wasn't sure he could—or wanted to—push it back down inside him. If he hadn't been interrupted . . .

"We've got a bigger plan than getting you off." She was studying him, and for a second he saw something flash in her eyes that excited him even more. She feared him. Not fear of rape, of course. Fear that he would edge from under her control.

Confirming that, she stepped up behind him and pulled his head against her stomach, tilting it so she could look down on him. "We've been a team for a long time now. We need each other, sweetheart." Her fingers trailed over his face, lovingly, sensually, just the way she knew he liked. Her voice took on that sweet, lulling quality. "You're very good at what you do. But I'm good at what I do, too, and that's running the show. I may be in the background, planning, investigating, finding the perfect mark, but don't forget that I'm in charge."

He felt himself being drawn back in, felt his strength and anger waning. Her fingers stroked his neck, his ears, his shoulders. He felt the struggle to break free of her. She always sensed it. Maybe it was her maternal instinct. Or her animal instinct.

"When we've got what we want, you can terrorize her to your heart's content," she continued. She chuckled softly. "Rush sure won't be protecting her."

"Is he going to be a problem?"

"Are you kidding? He's going to solve our problem. If we can't make money the old-fashioned way, we'll make it a new way. You'll like this part. You can keep stalking; it fits in the new plan. But subtly. No physical attacks. Be very, very careful. Don't do something stupid and get caught."

His eyes opened at those last words, spoken more sternly. Mamu had walked around to stand in front of him, her hands still massaging his shoulders. She slid down onto his lap, her long legs straddling him, her face close enough that he could feel her breath.

She kissed his nose, his cheeks, his forehead. "I'll let you call me Mamu," she whispered between kisses. "Anytime you want."

She *was* afraid he'd slip away from her. She was using her sensuality the way she'd always done, but now she was offering much more. "My special boy," she whispered, pulling him close against her. He could hear her heartbeat next to his ear. "I'm the one who loved you. I'm the one who protected you, who held you when you cried in the night. I'm the only one, my love. Always remember, the only one."

Though he felt his resolve crumble, he still held on to one shard of it. He also remembered when she'd betrayed him.

He couldn't forget that. He'd grown stronger. Angrier. She'd broken one of the crystal strands that held them together. Maybe it would be enough to allow him to break free of her emotional hold over him one day. Maybe he could let the monster out without fearing repercussions.

And Jonna would be the one he would unleash it on.

CHAPTER TWENTY-FOUR

My stomach knotted up when Rush called the next morning. I was still at the hotel, getting ready to leave my safe cocoon and head out into the cold, cruel world.

"Hi, babe. I just landed." I could hear airport noise in the background when he paused. "Is everything all right?"

"Fine," I said on a breath, as though forcefully pushing out the word. "You'll be home tonight?" I let him hear the relief in my voice.

"Miss me?"

"Definitely."

Another pause. "Let's have a quiet dinner at home tonight."

There was something ominous about that request. Or maybe I was only hearing the *we have to talk* in his voice. We would talk. Tonight our marriage could end.

"Okay, I'll see you then."

"Are you sure you're all right?"

I didn't want him coming into the conversation expecting something, so I forced cheer into my voice. "I just missed you. See you tonight."

I'd gone over every scenario all night. Rush would be disgusted and ask me to leave. He'd leave. He'd admit he was having an affair—and leave. Or he would step into the male role and become my protector. Get to the bottom of all this, as it were. Take me to the police station and force them to take action.

I both welcomed and dreaded that last scenario. This was my problem. I hated dragging him into it. I'd failed at following Dominic to find out who he was. Maybe the police, if they were suitably alarmed, would be able to trace his posts to his computer.

I desperately needed to take charge of my situation. Finding out who he was would help a great deal. He had obviously been suspicious of the meeting I'd set up, especially when I hadn't shown. I knew he was familiar with that area of town, so it was likely that he lived or worked nearby. What if I staked it out? Became a private investigator of sorts? I knew their job wasn't like the television shows that portrayed them. Private investigators spent much of their time sitting around waiting to catch someone doing something wrong.

I felt a spurt of strength at the idea and threw my toiletries into my bag. I'd start today. Maybe I would have at least that much information by the time I spilled everything to Rush.

The last thing Rush felt like doing was going to the office. He'd heard something in Jonna's voice that concerned him. More concerning, she wasn't where she was supposed to be. Unfortunately, he had to update Hadden on his trip, which had gone very well, and he had two other urgent business matters to attend to. Tonight he'd get Jonna to tell him what was going on—and he'd tell her what he knew.

When he walked into his office, he was surprised to find Hadden sitting at his desk. He was annoyed to discover that Hadden had pulled up SIChipX on his computer. That was his baby, the technology that he'd sold.

It allowed users to attach a transmitter to a vehicle or other item and track its position using GPS as well as gather other valuable data like miles per gallon and speed. It was simple, inexpensive, and easily tailored to suit any corporation's needs, from a small company to fleet services and rental car companies. It also tracked one's wife, and since he still consulted with the company, he had access to the software and transmitters.

"You're spying on your wife?" Hadden said.

"How did you get onto my account?"

"I'll tell you when you tell me why you're tracking Jonna."

Rush set his laptop case on the corner of his desk, trying to stay calm. "I'm not going there with you."

"Just what do you think Jonna's up to?"

"It's not your business."

"You're tracking your wife's movements. You've been acting strange lately. You helped me through my addiction. It's my obligation as your friend and Jonna's friend—"

Rush laughed, though without a trace of humor. "Jonna's friend. You mean the one who wants to screw her?"

That stopped Hadden cold. "She told you?"

"Doesn't matter how I found out. What pisses me off is that my business partner and supposed friend came on to my wife."

He held up his hands. "I didn't come on to her. She thought you were cheating on her. I assured her you weren't, but I accidentally let out that I . . . well, that I have feelings for her. Ones I never intend to act on."

"Swell," Rush said, tossing his keys on the desk.

"Are you having Jonna followed by a private investigator?"

"No, why?"

He hesitated. "Never mind. Look, I feel terrible about

my slip. But it's behind us. I thought maybe that was why you're tracking her movements, but you were doing that before she and I had lunch."

Rush pinched the bridge of his nose. "I don't want to talk about this right now," he said just as Mona, his secretary, knocked on the door.

"Sorry to interrupt. I sent your earlier messages through electronically, but this one just came in and the system's down. It sounded important."

She handed him the slip, and he set it aside without looking at it. "Thanks." Rush didn't even look at Hadden. "Are we going to talk about my meeting in New York? If not, I've got a lot of work to do."

"I want to hear how it went, but now's not the time." Hadden walked toward the door. "We need to talk about this. I don't want it standing between us. And I don't want you continuing to shut me out. Whatever you've got going on is interfering with your work. We've got a great business relationship. Let's not jeopardize that."

Rush let him leave without responding. He sat down at his desk and kneaded his temples. He didn't want to mess up AngelForce, either, but he wasn't sure whom he could trust, and he hated feeling that way.

He glanced at the message slip marked "URGENT" but stopped at the name scrawled at the top: Dominic.

I was at the market that afternoon shopping for our Thanksgiving dinner as well as the one I'd be creating for one of my clients when my BlackBerry rang. I didn't recognize the number, which made me tense. This was my business line, though, so I often received calls from people I didn't know. So far Dominic hadn't called me on it, but he had been leaving hang-ups on the home answering machine all week.

I heard the tentativeness in my voice when I answered, "JEvents, Jonna speaking."

"Jonna, it's Hadden." He paused to let the fact that he was calling sink in, I guessed. The origination number must be one of the secondary lines at the office. "Is everything all right?"

I thought that was a strange question, just as I thought it had been strange coming from Rush that morning. Did my voice give everything away?

"At the moment, yes. Why do you ask?"

Another pause. "Jonna, there's something you should know."

The seriousness of his voice made me lean against a nearby crate, sending three grapefruits to the floor. "Okay." I braced myself, spiritually and physically.

"Can you meet me for lunch? Or coffee?"

"I can't." I'd spent an hour and a half watching for Dominic. Now I was running late. "Just tell me."

"Have you done anything to make Rush suspicious of you?"

I'd done *everything* to pique his suspicions, but I didn't want to get into that with Hadden. "Why do you ask? What's going on?"

"He's tracking your movements. I was looking for a file on his PC last night and found his software installed on his machine. He must have a GPS device on your car. Last night you were at the Beaumont Hotel. You were there all night."

I had trouble assimilating everything. Rush was tracking me. Spying on me. Hadden was wondering why I'd been at a hotel all night. That was why Rush had asked if everything was all right. He'd known I'd been at the hotel, too, but couldn't ask.

"How . . . how long has he been tracking me?"

"About two weeks."

What else had Rush seen? He'd called me Monday,

after I'd gotten mugged, and asked where I was. Maybe he'd known but wanted to hear *why* I was in that part of town. He may have seen that I'd gone to the police, too. Well, I'd be explaining all that to him tonight.

"I had a dinner event at the Beaumont," I said, feeling obligated to explain. "And I spent the night there afterward. I . . . do you remember that man who was following me the day we had lunch? He came by the loft Monday night. I didn't want to be there alone."

"Jonna. You could have—"

"Called you. Stayed with you? I don't think so." I heard him sigh, and it was filled with regret and frustration. "It wouldn't have looked right, in any case."

"You're right. Look, I have to go; I've got an international call coming in. There's more. I really want to talk to you in person."

More? That tightened my stomach. "Okay. I'll call you later."

"Call me on my cell phone if you need me. You have the number?"

"Yes, in my book."

I continued shopping after we hung up, but my mind was nowhere near fruits and vegetables. Why was Rush keeping tabs on me? Maybe because he suspected I was having an affair. Two weeks ago I'd just met Dominic. Had Rush been suspicious after seeing me with him after all? Or was that why Rush had been in the area that day? I couldn't imagine what I'd done to pique his suspicions before that. I felt violated that he'd been spying on me all this time. What I really wanted to know was, what was the *more*?

By the time I struggled to get the bags out to my car, it had started snowing, the pretty kind of snow I enjoyed when I wasn't driving. I'd just gotten into the car when my BlackBerry rang again. Beth's cell phone number appeared on the screen.

"Thank gawd!" she said when I answered, her voice on the edge of hysterical. "Where are you?"

I gave her an approximate location. "Why?"

"Jonna, I . . . oh, sweetie, it's not good. I've got something you need to see. Pictures."

"Send them to my e-mail address," I said, feeling even tenser than when Hadden had called. "I can retrieve them on my BlackBerry."

"I can't believe it. I'm seeing it, but I can't believe it." Had she seen Rush with Kirsten? It had to be even worse than that; I'd never heard this level of shock in Beth's voice before. "I'll send them now. Call me when you get it."

I hung up and retrieved my e-mail. I stamped my foot on the floor. "Come on; come on."

Finally it popped into my mailbox. It took me a few seconds to get my mind around what I was looking at once I'd opened it. They were two pictures of the same scene: two men sitting in a booth at a restaurant. One of the men was Dominic. The other . . . oh, God. Rush. Dominic. Together.

My thumbs felt numb as I dialed her back.

"Did you get them?" Beth answered. "Jonna, can you believe it?"

"No," I said, the word sounding far away from me.

"I was walking past O'Malley's Pub, the one around the corner from the office on Boylston, and I looked in the front window. You know how I like to do that." I knew she liked to look at her reflection. "I, of course, thought I was seeing things. So I stepped inside, keeping out of sight. But it was real. I thought, 'She won't believe me.' *I* wouldn't believe me. Then I realized I could send you proof."

I felt my stomach turn over and clutched it. "Could you . . . hear what they were saying?"

"No, I didn't want to get that close, didn't want them

to see me. Jonna, what the hell? Why would Rush and Dominic be having a drink together?"

My mind had been hammering away on that. "Maybe . . . maybe Rush saw Dominic and . . . no, Rush has only seen Dominic once, as our pizza deliveryman. I doubt he would have remembered him at all. Maybe . . ." But I couldn't think of one good reason they'd be together.

Beth supplied the one bad reason I'd been avoiding. "Maybe Rush found out about your blog—"

"He knows about my blog!" That just hit me. "If he knows Dominic, he knows about the blog." I groaned, pressing my face into the seat, breathing in the scent of leather.

"Do you think . . . Jonna, I hate to even say this, but could Rush have put Dominic up to this whole stalking thing? He found out and then hired Dominic to seduce you?"

"No." That was my automatic response. It was too heinous, too evil. Then it started to make sense. "Maybe to test me. When I didn't have sex with Dominic, Rush started becoming more loving."

"Then why is Dominic still bothering you? Damn, Jonna, I have another theory, and I really hate to say it."

"Just say it," I said, impatient and ragged, watching snow accumulate on my windshield. I hadn't even turned on the car.

"If he only meant to teach you a lesson—or test you—he wouldn't have had Dominic attack you. What if . . . if Rush found out about the blog and became furious. So he hired Dominic. Not to test you, but to . . . kill you. Maybe it started out as a way for Rush to punish you for the blog."

"But Rush has changed in the last week. He arranged a romantic dinner for us. He's finally opening up about his childhood."

"Jonna, don't be naive. It could all be part of the plan. Romance you so it'll look better when you end up dead. He knows they always look at the husband. So you tell everyone on the blog—and me—that he's been so sweet lately, that things are looking up. Takes the suspicion off him."

I was glad I was sitting down. I felt as though my insides had imploded. My brain felt dull, achy, and my throat dried up. I kept swallowing and swallowing, trying in vain to moisten it. "Hadden just told me that Rush has been tracking my movements."

"Aha. That's how Dominic knew where you were. And think about it: that's how he knew Rush was out of town. Maybe even how he was able to get in. I'll bet Rush purposely went out of town to give him the opportunity—God, Jonna, he was probably supposed to kill you that night. If I hadn't shown up . . ."

I would have been dead. I shuddered, wrapping my arm around me and leaning forward until my forehead touched the steering wheel.

"I'm sorry," she said. "So, so sorry. Look, if you need somewhere to stay tonight . . ."

Her words became a buzz. Tonight. Rush and I were supposed to have a quiet night together. How was I going to talk, to make love with him, knowing what I knew? Somewhere deep inside me, I couldn't believe it. Even seeing the picture on my Blackberry's screen, I still couldn't believe it. "No, I'll be all right."

"Jonna, you have to get out of there."

"He's not going to kill me. He's hired Dominic to do that, if your theory is right. Dominic will need to get me alone and Rush would be somewhere else for his alibi." I couldn't believe I was even saying those words.

"Maybe I'm being paranoid. All I know is that the man who's been stalking and terrorizing you is having a drink with your husband."

So she finally admitted Dominic's behavior was criminal. Now wasn't the time to point that out, though. It didn't even matter anymore.

Beth said, "I have to go. Call me. You can always stay with me if you need to. Bye, honey."

I started the car, switched on the wipers, and watched the snow fall. It was supposed to be a stormy, cold holiday weekend. I had looked forward to enjoying it in the warm confines of my home once Thanksgiving dinner was over. Now I dreaded it. If I were closer to Rush's office, I'd walk into O'Malley's. But I could do the next best thing.

I called Hadden on his cell phone. When he answered, I could tell he was outside by the sounds of traffic in the background.

"It's Jonna," I said, hearing the breathlessness in my voice. "I need to know . . . what was the more you wanted to tell me. I need to know now."

He paused, and I knew he could hear my tremulous voice. "He knows about my inadvertent confession to you. I wasn't sure if you'd told him; he wouldn't say how he knew. That's why he's been so cool lately."

"I didn't tell him. It's a long story, but basically he read my diary. Hadden, I need you to do me a favor."

"Sure, anything."

"Take a walk to O'Malley's Pub. Beth just told me she saw Rush and the man who's been stalking me sitting together. Could you go in, like you didn't know they were there, and see what Rush says about his companion?"

I was still hoping Rush had another reason for meeting Dominic. Maybe Rush knew about Dominic from my blog and was threatening him not to go near me again. I knew it was a crazy hope. I knew it was probably denial.

"Sure. I'm heading there right now. I'll leave the phone on so you can hear, too. Jonna, are you all right? You sound scared."

"I'm just confused. I don't know why Rush would be talking to this person, other than warning him off." I didn't want to get into Beth's theory. I could hear Hadden's shoes crunching in the snow. "I'm sorry to send you walking in the snow."

"Don't be. I think there may be something else going on. I don't want to say anything until I know for sure, though. It could confuse you even more."

"Hadden, please don't hold back."

"I'm at O'Malley's." I heard a bell ring as it hit the glass door and then the din of voices. After a few seconds: "I don't see him."

I sagged. I wanted some kind of explanation, and I'd loved that Hadden would leave his phone on.

"Are you home?" he asked.

"No, but I'm headed there in about thirty minutes."

"I'll try to stop by before Rush gets there. When he comes home, we can talk to him together."

"That sounds"—I let out a long breath—"good. Thanks."

"I'll see you there."

I squeezed my eyes shut and curled up in my seat. At last I had an ally.

Hadden stepped outside and had taken three steps before he decided to go back and get an Irish coffee to go. He had one more call to make before he could break away and see Jonna. Hearing her fear scared him, too. He had a bad feeling about all of this.

As he stood at the bar waiting for his coffee, he turned and saw a man coming out of the restroom who made his stomach clench. He'd seen the guy before, when he and Jonna had had lunch. Tall, good-looking, wearing blue contacts that made his eyes look phony: the man Jonna was afraid of.

He returned to a booth off to the side, talking to someone Hadden couldn't see because of the panels. He took the Styrofoam cup the bartender handed him and edged toward the rear of the bar, pretending to look for sugar packets. He could hear just enough of the conversation to confirm what he'd only suspected—and worse.

He set his cup on the bar and walked out. After digging through his deep coat pockets, he found his cell phone and flipped it open. He needed to tell Jonna what was going on. He needed to warn her.

The snow was getting heavier. Clumps landed on his eyelashes and distorted his vision. He could hardly see up ahead. Even the headlights of the traffic passing by looked blurred. People ducked their heads, hurrying to get to wherever they needed to go. He felt cold deep inside but not on the outside. Fat snowflakes landed on the pad of his phone as he removed his glove to dial the number.

When someone stepped near him, he glanced up— and into a familiar face just as he felt his feet go out from beneath him. His phone went flying as he wheeled his arms to save his balance. Because of the snow, his feet had no purchase. He fell onto the ice-covered asphalt and slid a couple of feet.

Traffic moved past. But he'd stopped in time, just short of sliding into the busy road. Then he looked up and saw the bus bearing down on him. He heard the squeal of brakes and the wail of the horn. It all seemed to happen in slow motion. He saw the terrified look on the driver's face because the bus couldn't slow down fast enough.

The grille coming closer.

Tires.

Then nothing at all.

CHAPTER TWENTY-FIVE

I was making dinner, pushing myself through the process. Turn the chicken cutlets. Stir the sauce. Touch side of hot pan. Hold burnt finger under water. Steam billowed from a pot of boiling water, dampening my face every time I went near it. The table was set. Not because I felt obligated or because I was hungry . . . gawd, no. I needed something familiar and comforting to do, so I fixed chicken and fettuccine. My hands trembled throughout the process. I tried to sip chardonnay, but my stomach rebelled at the smell of it. All the while I listened for the sound of the door. Rush would put his key into the lock. It wouldn't turn. I would unlock it and tell him someone had stolen my keys, so I'd had the locks rekeyed. True. What I told him from there depended on what he told me.

I wanted to hear everything spill out of him, how he'd found out I was Montene and how he'd come to be meeting Dominic. How he'd threatened him if he ever went near me again. Yes, I was still holding out for some plausible explanation. I kept hopping from scenario to scenario. He was innocent. He was trying to kill me. He was only trying to scare me. I wanted to hear him burst in and say, *You wouldn't believe what happened today!*

When I did hear the key in the lock, I froze for a moment, all those thoughts jumbling inside my brain. I dried my hands on a towel and went to the door. Rush had a puzzled look on his face when I opened it. Behind him snow was falling steadily, covering everything like a white cashmere shawl.

I gave him the story of my missing keys as I returned to the kitchen. He shrugged out of his coat and hung it up.

"Fettuccine . . . dash of oil, pinch of pepper flakes . . ." I stirred the pasta in the pot and looked up to find him leaning in the opening as he usually did when I cooked, watching me. This time his expression wasn't soft and amused. It was cool, discerning. I shivered. Was he annoyed that Dominic hadn't done his job while he was out of town, spoiling a perfect alibi?

"How was your day?" I asked, wondering if he could hear how tinny the words sounded. So many other questions crowded into my mouth ready to burst out. I wanted the right answer.

"Fine," he said, never taking his eyes from me. "Yours?"

I drooped. He wasn't going to tell me about Dominic. He waited for my answer as intently as I'd waited for his. Of course, he knew I'd spent the night at the hotel, and he knew why. He knew where I'd been, what I'd been doing, thinking, feeling, and considering for some time now. I felt violated, angry, as though he'd found my diary beneath my mattress and read it. But I had put it out there for all to see, robbing me of my right to be angry. Yet I still was.

I turned back to the meal. "Same."

If he wasn't involved with Dominic and he'd been reading my blog, he would have been concerned about everything I'd written there. He wouldn't have been able to ask me about it without giving away his knowledge, but he would have tried to get it out of me. The stolen-keys story was a perfect opening. He hadn't asked any further about it.

He took the pot of water out of my hands as I began to lift it from the stove to pour out the water. He did that, completely focused on his task. I removed the cutlets and set them on the plates, then drizzled sauce over them. We worked together in silence, both of us seemingly lost in our thoughts.

As we took our places at the table I couldn't help but think what this night was supposed to be—spilling everything, including how much I loved him and didn't want to lose him. Had the hunger I'd seen in his eyes, the need for connection that night I'd woken to find him watching me sleep . . . had it all been a ruse? So that Beth and my blog friends would be able to say how wonderful things had been between us right before it had happened? Whatever *it* was.

I ached at the thought. I wanted to be back in those moments when he was opening up to me about his past and his family. I knew how stupid it was to be reminiscing, to want something I probably never had to begin with.

Melted snow glistened on hair the color of burned caramel and made his thick eyelashes gleam. "I brought you something from New York," he said, breaking into the silence and my thoughts. He pulled out a small velvet box and pushed it toward me. A faint smile flickered across his mouth, as though he couldn't muster the energy to even fake it.

I opened it, finding a gold Statue of Liberty charm with my name etched across the bottom.

"For your watch," he said, looking at my wrist.

My fingers automatically went to my bare wrist that sported nothing but a scratch. I couldn't believe it! Bastard. He was taunting me. Testing me! I hadn't posted about my watch being taken. Which meant the only way he would know about it being missing was through Dominic.

Dominic's words about wanting to see me afraid rang in my mind. Did Rush want to watch me squirm? Or maybe even confess the mugging? I would have told him everything if Beth hadn't spotted him with Dominic. Would he have enjoyed my fear as I recounted what my stalker had done?

"I . . . I lost the watch. The clasp must have broken, because it slipped off."

He watched me, as though waiting for more. "That's too bad."

He cut his chicken and took a bite. I did the same. Our eyes met, and we each kept our expressions passive.

"Tomorrow is Thanksgiving," he said.

"I've got a dinner to prepare," I said too quickly. "Mid-afternoon. I have a duck in the reefer for us."

I saw a glimmer of regret on his face, too, or maybe I was imagining it. His gaze shifted to the yellow roses he'd sent me. That's how he'd known about my love for yellow roses, I realized. My blog. If his goal was to get me to tell witnesses that things were going well in our marriage, he'd succeeded. And he knew it.

Would he push Dominic to finish the job? Then why was he acting so cold and distant now if he wanted to convince me everything was wonderful between us? Maybe he wasn't trying to have me killed. Somewhat less devious, maybe he was only having Dominic scare me. Or, better yet, what if Dominic had approached Rush trying to convince him we were involved—

The phone rang, startling us both. He got out of his chair and answered it. "Yes, this is he. . . . What?" I saw his body tense; his fingers tightened on the phone. "Okay, thank you for letting me know." His arm dropped to his side. The phone slipped from his hand and fell to the wood floor.

I was already out of my chair. "What is it?" I felt as tense as he looked, without even knowing what was wrong. I knew it was bad.

"That was Hadden's father. Hadden's in the hospital. In a coma." He finally looked at me. "He was hit by a bus."

I followed as he walked to the coat closet, grabbing my coat as he put on his. We left everything on the table and walked out into a white night.

When we arrived at the hospital, Hadden's parents were there. We had met on occasion, though I hardly knew them beyond polite conversation. They were moneyed, classy, and dignified, even now while their son lay in a coma. We greeted them, and I was surprised to see Rush give Hadden's mother a hug.

"You said he was hit by a *bus*?" Rush asked, rubbing his fingers through his mussed hair. "H . . . how does something like that happen?"

Hadden's father, Winston, answered. "Apparently he slipped and fell into the path of the bus. It was snowing hard. The driver didn't see him in time. The officer who notified us . . . he said that someone standing nearby tried to keep him from falling. Then people started running over, so he or she got lost in the crowd."

Winston's wife said, "The police are investigating. They treat accidents like this as . . . as . . ."

"As a traffic homicide until they can rule out foul play," Winston finished for her.

Horrified, I said, "Do you mean they think someone pushed him?"

Winston said, "I think their focus is on the bus driver. I overheard the officers saying that two passengers on the bus reported he was getting agitated over a radio talk show he was listening to, muttering and gesturing. Someone else smelled liquor on his breath. They're looking for the person who tried to help to see if they can get more details."

"How is he?" I asked, feeling guilt wash over me that the last few times I'd seen him I hadn't been friendly. At least I'd turned to him that day, so he'd known I still trusted him. "He'll be okay, right?"

The way Winston looked away said it all. "He's been in surgery since they brought him in. It's been hours now. He sustained massive head and chest injuries." He fought tears. His wife pressed her face against his arm and let them out.

After the St. Germains had composed themselves, I asked, "You said he's been in surgery for hours. When did this happen?"

"Around three o'clock."

I stifled my own sob. He'd been on that sidewalk because of me. Because I'd asked him to check O'Malley's Pub.

Candace, Hadden's secretary, rushed in, already crying. Rush had called and asked her to alert the other employees. A lovely young woman with three children, she adored her boss. "How is he?" she asked in a thick voice.

My throat was so tight with grief I couldn't answer. I could see the shock and disbelief on Rush's face as he filled her in.

He offered to get coffee for everyone and left us in the waiting room. Though Candace offered to go instead, he said, "I need to do something." I watched him leave, fighting the pull to go with him. The St. Germains remained standing, their hope for news so plain in that. Candace and I sat at the end of a row of chairs.

"Do you know where Hadden was going?" I asked, remembering that he had been outside when I'd called him.

"To get a cappuccino," she said in a broken voice, and then in something close to a wail, "He might die because of a cup of coffee!"

No, he might die because I had asked him to check on Rush.

CHAPTER TWENTY-SIX

Rush woke early the next morning, sitting on the edge of the bed for a few minutes. His shoulders were hunched forward, and I watched his bare back move with his deep breaths. When he began to twist around toward me, I snapped my eyes closed. I felt him watch me as I willed my eyes not to wiggle under my closed lids. Finally I felt him stand and heard him step off the platform and open a drawer.

I couldn't keep my eyes closed anymore. In the dim light I saw him, naked and beautiful, standing near the open drawer seemingly lost in thought, faced away from me.

Then I saw his face in the mirror—he was looking at me. I hadn't thought about the reflection. Caught, I quickly rolled over and buried myself in the blanket. He closed the drawer, and after he ran water in the bathroom for a few minutes he went downstairs. I dozed fitfully as I'd done all night. As Rush had done, too. When I heard his voice floating up, I wondered if he was talking to Hadden's parents. That propelled me out of bed, where I grabbed the robe and covered my naked self as I went to the bathroom. I had slept in the nude since Rush and I had married, but I now felt self-conscious.

A short while later I found him sitting at the aquarium watching the fish, his finger tracing the rim of his mug. I'd sat there many a time when I felt confused and sad. What was he thinking about as he watched Stevie Ray glide through the water? I envied those fish their simple, safe lives.

"Any word on Hadden?"

Rush didn't turn around as I walked up behind him. "I called his parents. No change." He bowed his head and pressed his fingers against his closed eyes. I could see agony etched on his face. "How does someone just fall in front of a damned bus?"

I saw the muscles of his back move beneath the waffle fabric of his long-john shirt. Despite everything, I felt an urge to reach out and place my hand there. To touch, to comfort, to be comforted. *I must be crazy,* I thought, curling my fingers into my palm.

He turned around to face me, his green eyes filled with pain. I'd never seen him look so torn. Was it an act? If it was, he was damned good.

Just as he was about to say something, I said, "I've got to go." I walked into the kitchen and took the duck out of the reefer and set it in the oven. "I'll be back about five. The duck will be in the oven, chilling until the timer kicks in. I'll get everything else sorted out then."

I wished I could get everything sorted. I grabbed my briefcase and headed to the door without looking at him. "Call me if you hear anything." I needed time to think.

I chose to do that thinking at the café where Dominic hung out. Once I'd gotten my frappe, I returned my mother's call.

"Hi, honey," she said. "I've got a flight home in about forty minutes, but I've got time to talk. I wanted to check in on you. Wish you a happy Thanksgiving."

She wasn't asking. Typical. And I wasn't going to tell. Typical, too. Neither would I ask what kind of organization would host a convention during Thanksgiving week. "Thanks, Mom. I've got a dinner to organize for a client and then Rush and I are going to eat later."

"Things are going well there, then?"

I choked on the sip I'd been taking. "Sorry, inhaled when I should have swallowed," I explained between gulping breaths. "Mom, do you think it'd be all right if I came to visit? Maybe soon?"

"We'd love that." She took that as my answer. "They're wrong about that, you know. You *can* always go home again."

Tears sprang to my eyes. Home had never been more than a facade of a happy middle-class family. Right then it was a hell of a lot more than I had. "I may do that." I swallowed hard. "I'd better let you go, get to your flight. Tell Dad happy turkey day for me."

I had been watching the sidewalk the whole time. The snow had stopped during the night, leaving the sidewalks slushy and dirty. The sun was watery through a layer of clouds. I was thinking that I had better get going pretty soon. That's when I saw Dominic.

Rush sat at his desk at work staring at the computer. He thought about Hadden, about their last conversation. He thought about Jonna and rolled a pair of dice around the palm of his hand. Like his card deck at home, these reminded him of good times when life was stable and, for a few hours, happy. Like the cards, they served as a worry stone. He couldn't stop the thoughts careening around in his head and giving him a headache.

A soft tap on the door brought him out of them. Beth walked in. "Everyone's gone."

He'd told the staff to take the day off. No one was getting anything done, not with Hadden consuming their thoughts. "Fine."

She walked closer. "What about you?"

Being at the office was better than being at home. "I've got a few things to wrap up."

"Anything new on Hadden?"

"No."

"It's hard to believe. One minute he's fine, healthy. The next, hanging on by a thread. Life's so unfair."

He could only nod. He wanted her to leave.

His lights were off. Only the feeble light coming in through the window lit the office. Beth stood at the corner of his desk with the window behind her, throwing her features into shadow. "Rush." She cleared her throat. "I saw you with Dominic yesterday."

He leaned back in his chair and looked at her. "Okay."

"*Okay?* Jonna's being stalked by this guy, and then I see you having a drink with him. What's the story?"

"Have you told her?"

"I wanted to get your side first."

Interesting, considering she was Jonna's best friend. He walked to the window, looking out onto the street below. People hurried to wherever they were going. In the distance, the Hancock Tower nearly blended into the sky with its mirrored surface. How much should he tell her? He wasn't sure about her loyalty, though the fact that she was asking him before telling Jonna meant she was willing to give him a chance.

"Dominic called me yesterday, said we had to meet. Since I knew he was the one Jonna had met, I was curious as to what he had to say."

"And?" She was leaning against the glass next to him, waiting for his next words.

"He told me that he and Jonna started out having an affair and then she asked him to kill me for twenty-five thousand dollars. But he had second thoughts and decided to give me a chance to up the offer. For twice that he'll stall until I can file for a divorce, taking away her monetary motivation."

He remembered Dominic sitting across from him coldly telling him about the affair and their deal:

"The plan is for me to act like a stalker who's so obsessed he kills her husband. Double her money in two days, and I'll stall long enough for you to get divorce papers ready. Once you've filed, if something happens to you it's going to bring a lot more heat down on her. I'll talk her out of it, tell her to cut her losses." He tilted his head at Rush's disbelieving expression. *"Look, I don't have to do this, you know. Twenty-five thousand's a decent chunk of change, but I figured, us guys gotta stick together. My ex stuck me, that's for sure."*

Rush knew the guy wasn't doing him any favors. Greed sparkled in his fake blue eyes. "Plus you double your take."

"Yeah, that, too."

"How do I know you're for real?"

He held up Jonna's charm watch. "She gave this to me as a token of good faith. She's getting antsy, wanting me to get you gone. The other night I had to break in and pretend to attack her."

"Why hasn't she told me about the attack then? Or her stalker, period?"

"She will, when the time is right. That's her part of the plan. Maybe she'll say we met at a function or I was a potential client."

"I know how you met. I've been reading her blog."

He smiled. "Ah, so you know everything."

"You delivered our pizza once."

His smile grew bigger. "So I could get a close look at my target."

"And if I don't pay you and file for a divorce?"

"Then I do my original job and let her handle the fallout. I'm way out of here after that."

"I need to think about it."

"Sure, fifty thousand's a lot of money. You'll probably have to cash out some stocks and stuff. I'll be in touch on Friday for your answer. You seem like a nice guy. I hope I don't have to kill you."

Rush's mother had hired some mechanic to off his father once. Rush had intervened, meeting with the guy and finding him to be someone his mother had railroaded into agreeing to do the deed for her. The guy was relieved when Rush canceled it.

Did he believe it? He wasn't sure. Just when they'd seemed to reconnect, Jonna had become even more distant, and she'd been nervous.

Beth had come closer when he'd given her the gist of the conversation. "Oh, my God, Rush." She put her arms around him. He didn't hug her back, and after a moment she stepped away. "I can't believe it. And yet, in a way . . . well, maybe I can. She's been acting so strange lately. I'm her best friend, but she's shut me out. A couple of times she's taken a call and told whoever was on the other end she'd call them back later, you know, kind of furtively. She told me Dominic was stalking her, too. I didn't believe it at first. She was making a big deal out of nothing. Then it became more elaborate. Dead rats in her work reefah. He broke in. I told her to go to the police, but she refused. Now it all makes sense. She needed to convince me. She . . . she even lied to me."

Her eyes widened. "You don't think I knew about this, I hope. I may be her best friend . . . well, I was her best friend, but I would have nothing to do with anything like this. I'm your friend, too. And if this is what she's going to pull, my loyalty is firmly with you." She tilted her head and looked at him. "God, what you must be going through. Hadden, and now this." She put her hands on either side of his face and gave him a quick, soft kiss. "I'm here for you. As a friend."

He should have appreciated her support and comfort, but he moved out of her space and leaned against the glass, his fingers pressed against the cool surface.

She moved up beside him. "What are you going to do?"

"Figure out if it's true."

"You know she's not going to tell you the truth. She's got too much at stake. Money," Beth said when he looked at her questioningly.

"That's what doesn't make sense. Money's never mattered to her."

"How well do you really know her?"

He didn't, and his non-answer seemed to confirm Beth's suspicions.

"I say pay the guy and get the hell out of the marriage. You'll have to give her some of your money, but it's better than dying."

He was never quite comfortable with Beth, even beyond his feeling that she was Jonna's spy. She was always encroaching on his personal space, though never by much. He supposed she was just one of those touchy-feely people. Then she'd become his spy. He'd inadvertently started this whole confidante thing two weeks earlier when he'd asked her to come into the conference room. He'd sensed Jonna moving further and further away and didn't know how to pull her back. His only relationship role models were two people who communicated by running each other down with motorized vehicles. He was getting desperate. Asking Beth had been a spur-of-the-moment act that, in retrospect, was a bad idea.

"You're my wife's best friend. I know it makes it sticky that I'm your boss, but forget that for a minute. Tell me what's going on with her."

She'd put her hand on his. "Do you really want to know?"

He'd looked at her hand, the gesture out of place. She removed it . . . and told him about the blog and Dominic.

She touched him now, her hand lightly on his shoulder. "I'm here if you ever want to talk, Rush. And if I learn something, I'll let you know."

She left, but he remained at the window. He tried to picture Jonna as a scheming bitch, but it wasn't easy. He watched one car pull out in front of another. The thwarted driver honked his horn.

Rush had an idea.

CHAPTER TWENTY-SEVEN

Frozen, I watched Dominic walk toward the café, his shoulders hunched against the cold. If he looked to the right he'd see me. Yet I couldn't pull my gaze away from him, like that deer in the headlights I'd heard so much about. He didn't look my way, though. I left my table and stepped outside once he'd passed by. He had purpose in his walk. I followed to see where he was going.

My disguise, such as it was, hadn't worked last time. Then again, he'd been expecting to see me. This time he wasn't. I wore a red wool coat and matching hat pulled low over my forehead and a blond wig I'd purchased for a Marilyn Monroe–themed party I'd organized three months ago.

Dominic paused at the corner, and I slowed, too. I needed to make the crosswalk light but remain some distance behind him. I looked down at my watch, which kept my face hidden. It also reminded me that I was running late for my dinner. This was more important.

The light turned and people surged across. I was at the tail end of the crowd that made it across before traffic began to move again. Dominic, tall and easy to find, was up ahead. I heard Kanye West and Jamie Foxx's "Gold Digger" burst from his pocket. He stopped in front of a storefront and took out his cell phone. I pretended to try to read the price of a flower urn in a store window and strained to hear him.

"You accused *me* of almost screwing things up. What the hell were *you* thinking? Good God, are you crazy?"

His agitated tone made me instinctively look his way. He was ramming his fingers through his hair, looking down. As he began to look up, I averted my gaze.

"Yes, I do know who I'm talking to," he parroted back. "No, I won't calm down. You're the one who's out of control. Don't hang up on me! Dammit!" He jammed the phone back into his pocket and huffed off.

Who was he talking to? I hated thinking it could be Rush. Maybe Dominic had other things going on besides terrorizing me.

I continued to follow him, seeing his temper in his jerky movements and hunched shoulders. It made me think again how on the edge he was. I'd seen his volatility when he'd had me pinned on the couch. It gave me the shivers.

He turned the corner, and by the time I peered round it, he was gone.

I walked slowly down the sidewalk but didn't see him. He'd given me the slip again, whether intentional or not. Now I had to go.

I came home in time to start the sides for our dinner—green beans, whipped sweet potatoes, and cranberry pie. I wasn't sure how I was going to endure the evening. Rush came home, mumbling a greeting that I couldn't interpret, and poured a glass of whisky. His expression was dark, his jaw tense. I thought about the argument Dominic had had with someone.

"How's Hadden?" I asked when Rush came into the kitchen. "Any word?"

He shook his head. "But the police determined that the bus driver was intoxicated. He's been arrested."

We fell back into our own silent worlds, suffering alone. I could see it in his eyes. I felt it in my soul.

He started working on the salad, cutting up the vegetables I'd already laid out. We were about to take dinner to the table when the doorbell rang. I stiffened, picturing Dominic standing on the other side of the door. Or some gruesome delivery.

Rush was already striding toward the door; I followed in his wake, feeling both relieved and surprised to find Beth in her fox-fur coat. Especially since she had an odd combination of chagrin and fear on her face. Rush stepped back to let her in.

She looked at us as she walked inside, carrying an overnight bag. "I'm so sorry to barge in like this. I . . . I couldn't think of anywhere else to go. Someone was in my apartment when I got home tonight."

"What?" I said, reliving the terror of Dominic's trespass.

"I walked in and sensed something different. When I went into my bedroom to change, I saw a shadow move. And then he . . . he burst out of my closet. Knocked me down. I fought him off, and he ran. But I don't know how he got in, and I'm afraid he's going to come back."

As I rushed over to put my arms around her, Rush asked, "Did you call the police?"

She nodded. "They said I should find someplace to stay for a few days." She gave me a beseeching look. "You know I couldn't bear to stay with my mother and her husband. So I came here."

"Absolutely," I said. "Stay as long as you need to." I took her bag and set it by the hallway. "You can stay in the family room; the sofa pulls out."

She looked apprehensive at that, and then I realized why. That's where I had been attacked.

She looked at Rush. "I hope it's all right with you."

"Of course," he said. "We were just about to eat. You're welcome to join us."

"I'm not the least bit hungry, but I'll have a glass of that scotch, maybe a nibble."

She followed me into the kitchen after shrugging out of her coat and draping it over one of the chairs. As Rush got out another place setting from the china hutch, she leaned closer and whispered, "It was Dominic!"

I spun around, feeling horror fill my chest. "What?"

She nodded. "I think I'm paying the price for thwarting him that night. Maybe he came back in the morning, saw me leave, and followed. I think he wants to punish me. Or scare me."

I felt horrible. She'd saved me and was now included in my terror. "I'm so sorry, Beth."

"If we're together, here, he can't hurt us. Right?" She gave my arm a squeeze.

Rush walked into the kitchen to get an extra set of silverware out of the drawer. In a way I was glad she was there. It broke up the tension between Rush and me.

Dinner was polite but strained. Apparently Beth's appetite wasn't in the least bit bothered by the break-in. She wolfed down two helpings of food. Afterward I excused myself to go to the bathroom. When I returned, I could hear them talking in the kitchen as they put the dishes in the dishwasher drawer.

When I walked in, Beth said, "I told Rush I'd handle the cleanup, but he wouldn't let me."

I helped, too, and after everything was cleaned, Rush went upstairs to his desk. Beth and I went back into the family room, where we put on the television to mask our conversation.

I tucked myself into the corner of the leather couch. "Did you really call the police?"

Beth sat down next to me. "No. I just said that because Rush would think it odd that I didn't."

"Why didn't you?"

"Because then I'd have to tell them everything. After the way the police treated you . . ."

I nodded in understanding. "I followed him today."

Her eyes widened. "Jonna, look what happened the last time you tried that."

"I know, but I've got to do something. This has to stop."

"The best way to get this to stop is to divorce Rush. Let him have his money, get out of here, and start over. Maybe then he'll let this go."

What she was saying made sense, but it still made my stomach clench. "You're probably right."

"I'm definitely right. Did you find out anything about Dominic?"

"I heard him arguing with someone on the phone. Then he gave me the slip."

Her body brushed mine as she pulled her legs up and hugged her knees. "I don't want to sleep down here alone."

"I had extra locks put on the windows."

"I know, but it's a"—she looked around—"vibe thing. Put some blankets in the loft. I won't feel so vulnerable there. And if anything should happen to you . . . well, I'll be close by."

It wouldn't have surprised me for her to suggest we all sleep together. "All right."

"You haven't told him about the break-in here, have you?"

"I was going to tell him everything last night. Then you saw him with Dominic."

Beth squeezed my hand. "Make an appointment with a lawyer. The sooner, the better. I'll go with you if you'd like."

I could only nod. She was right. And yet something felt wrong about actually going through with it. Was some part of me clinging to the thin chance of a misunderstanding? I knew that could be a deadly mistake.

Rush was shaving at the sink the next morning when he heard a soft tap on the door. He grunted in answer, and Beth opened the door. She didn't back away when she saw him, wearing only a towel in the steamy bathroom, but walked right in. Her light red hair was tousled, cheeks flushed with sleep. She wore the pajama top someone had given him for Christmas years ago that he'd loaned her when she realized she hadn't packed anything to sleep in. Because she wore nothing to sleep, she'd admitted coyly. The top, unbuttoned halfway down, had fallen off her shoulder, showing white skin sprinkled with pale freckles. He could see the white skin between her breasts. She closed the door behind her.

"Good morning," she said in a husky voice. "Wow, never thought I'd see my boss looking quite like . . . this."

"Never thought my employee would just walk into my bathroom."

She laughed softly but didn't get the hint. "God, I love this room. It's like a spa. And this bathtub!" She leaned in to take a closer look. In the mirror's reflection he saw a hint of her bare derriere when she bent over.

Even though he averted his gaze he still cut himself. She sidled up to the sink next to his, frowning at the blood he was trying to stanch with a tissue. "Ouch, here, let me—"

"I've got it."

Her arms fell to her sides. After a moment of awkward silence, she said, "You're meeting him today?"

"Yes," he said, now understanding why she'd closed the door.

"What are you going to do?"

"I don't know." But he did know.

"It's a good thing I'm here, despite the circumstances. To give you moral support. At the least, someone who knows what you're going through, someone to bounce ideas off of."

"I can handle this on my own," he said, rinsing off the last traces of cream.

She looked hurt by his blunt rejection. She traced her finger along the edge of the square porcelain sink. "Sure you can. I didn't mean . . ."

He didn't look at her when he said, "Sorry, but I don't want anyone involved." He turned just as Jonna opened the door, wearing the long johns she'd worn to bed last night.

She took Rush and Beth in, puzzlement in her sleepy eyes. "Good morning," she said, not meaning it.

An odd tension charged the air. He dried his face and walked out.

I closed the door behind Rush, trying to forget the blank look on his face when he'd seen me. "What are you doing in here?" I asked Beth, who was going through my medicine cabinet again.

"Looking for your face cleanser. I was in such a hurry to get out of there I forgot that, too."

"No, I mean in here . . . with Rush."

She flashed me a clever smile. "Keep your friends close, your enemies closer. I'm going to be on him like white on snow, seeing what he's up to. Here and at work."

It made sense, but something still bothered me. I merely nodded and then thought to add, "I appreciate it."

She moved to Rush's sink, squirted out some cleanser, and started rubbing it on her face. "Anything for a friend. You'll learn I'm like that: loyal to a fault."

I smiled, walking woodenly to my sink.

"It's important that you not be alone with Rush," she said. "Keep me with you at all times. I don't think either one of them will try something if we're together. I'm going to keep you safe, sweetie."

I didn't know what else to say, so I gave her a wan smile. I felt so damned numb inside, and my mind seemed incapable of thought.

"You have to do your part, though. What about the lawyer?"

"I'm going to make an appointment."

"Good. And don't let on to Rush. You need to get the papers ready and then spring it on him at the same time that you're packed and ready to leave. We need to find you someplace to stay. Since Dominic knows where I live, it can't be there. Maybe someplace out of town."

"I can't go too far. I've got clients." When this was over, all I would have was my career.

"Clients or your safety? Come on, Jonna, where are your priorities? You can always start over, build your clientele again." She lowered her voice. "You can't get a new life if you're dead."

CHAPTER TWENTY-EIGHT

At noon, Rush walked into O'Malley's Pub and spotted Dominic sitting in the back booth. He was obviously looking for a briefcase, anything that might hold fifty thousand dollars. Rush slid into the booth, where the waitress descended almost immediately to take their orders.

Rush ordered a beer he had no intention of drinking. Dominic, antsy to get rid of the waitress, ordered the same. As soon as she left, he said, "So?"

"I wouldn't give an entrepreneur money without proof that he has a viable product. I'm not paying you unless I have proof that she hired you."

Frustration tinted Dominic's cheeks. "The bracelet—"

"Isn't enough. Get her on tape talking about offing me."

Dominic was agitated, his fingers tapping on the table's scarred surface. "Are you trying to set me up? For the cops?"

"No, I just want proof. When you bring it to me, I have another deal for you to consider: I'll pay you a hundred thousand if you kill her."

Dominic's body tensed; his eyes bulged. "You want

me to, uh . . . I mean—" He wiped sweat from his upper lip. "Yeah, sure. Yeah. I'll do it."

Rush felt peace steal over him. He could breathe deeper now. In contrast, he could see the gears going in Dominic's brain. The waitress brought their mugs, and Rush got to his feet. "Call me when you've got it. We'll proceed from there."

He walked out, his feet crunching on the dirty ice. Somewhere around here Hadden had fallen. In one second, everything had changed. In just those few seconds back in O'Malley's, everything had changed for him, too. Now he had to figure out what to do about it.

"He got away," Beth told me after we'd had our manicure that afternoon. She picked at her chicken Caesar salad. "I'm sorry. One minute he was in his office, I had to take a call, and then he was gone."

"Did you check O'Malley's?" I asked.

She shook her head. "I couldn't get out of the office. My boss needed me to join him in a meeting with one of the entrepreneurs to brainstorm some advertising ideas. Which were brilliant, if I don't say so myself. By the time I got out, Rush was back. But don't worry, I'm going to stick by you whenever I can."

I wasn't worried about being alone with him, other than the awkwardness and tension. If he'd hired Dominic to hurt me, he wouldn't do so himself. Having to keep up the facade of happy couple would be hell. "I made an appointment with Kurt Samper for next Tuesday. He's an attorney one of my clients used."

"Good," she said, relief in her voice. "Don't you feel better already?"

"No," I said honestly. "Any word on Hadden?"

"Mona said he had a heart attack, but they revived him. We still haven't heard whether he has any brain activity. It's like a morgue at work. Everyone's a zombie, waiting for news, still absorbing what happened. But at least they nailed the drunk son of a bitch who hit him."

My heart ached for Hadden. I knew his skull had been crushed. If he came out of the coma, he could have brain damage. I brushed away a tear, staring into my bowl of tomato basil soup, no appetite.

Beth changed the subject. "I'd planned to go out tonight, hit the clubs. I need to release some of this pent-up tension. Why don't you come along? It'll take your mind off everything for a while. And who knows, you might even get laid."

I stared at her in disbelief. "Beth, that's disgusting." I pushed away my soup. "I've got to go. I'll be at the shop tonight, getting ready for a birthday bash I'm hosting tomorrow."

She shrugged. "Montene would have mind-blowing sex all night long."

"Yeah, well, I'm not Montene," I said, grabbing my purse and standing. I was ashamed to admit that I even let Beth think I was as adventurous as Montene was on her blog.

Beth's cell phone rang. She glanced at the screen and dropped it back in her bag.

"I heard it ring in the middle of the night," I said.

She waved it away. "Some guy I met a few weeks ago. I almost gagged when he laid the ugliest prick I've ever seen on my leg. I pretended I was sick and had to leave. He keeps calling me."

I couldn't imagine why she put herself in those situations. "What's going on with the married guy?"

Her face glowed. "He's definitely getting a divorce. We're laying low until it's finalized. I'm finally going to get my happy ending." She tamed her smile. "I'm just sorry it's at the same time that yours is falling apart."

I put money on the table. "Yeah, life happens like that. Be careful tonight, 'kay?"

"You, too."

I hadn't seen Dominic since Monday night when he'd broken into the loft, other than when I'd spied on him. His absence didn't comfort me, though. I knew the other shoe would drop eventually.

Beth said, "Call me when you're heading home so I can be there." She tilted her head. "That's how good a friend I am. I'll leave just to be with you."

"Thank you." I bussed her cheek and left, glad I'd be busy all weekend. Away from Rush. And in a way, glad I'd be away from Beth, too.

I pushed myself late into the night. It was a relief to think about something other than Dominic and Rush. I felt a trill of anxiety with the former and an ache at the latter. It was as though I were being forced to walk the plank—talking to a lawyer, planning an escape. Why did the open ocean look so wrong to me?

I arranged the last of the floating floral arrangements for the birthday party. I worked to the piercing sounds of opera, not because I liked it but because the birthday girl was an opera singer and that's what would be playing at the party. The candles would be lit and all twelve of the arrangements would float in the indoor pool at the mansion. I looked at the profusion of ruby red flowers and imagined the sounds of laughter and music and joy. I couldn't help but think back to that romantic dinner Rush had orchestrated. I had seen something in his eyes then, something real and warm. It was gone now. The question kept nagging me: why?

I set the arrangements in the cooler, my thoughts turning to those dead rats. Knowing that Dominic had had the keys to my home and shop still tore me up.

Every time I went to the shop I looked everywhere to make sure he wasn't there. I looked out the glass window in the door, seeing my car parked right outside, the passenger door only two feet away.

I thought again of how Dominic had used my desires to rattle me. With the rats, he'd used my fears. What else had I revealed? Some of the blog gals read erotica and one woman admitted to writing to men in prison. And . . . I got a chill. The rape fantasy debate. It was one of the threads the journalist had jumped all over. It had started with the discussion of alpha males. Strong, take-charge men. I admitted to finding that arousing. When Rush took me the way he had a couple of weeks ago, it had been ultra-arousing.

Others confessed their excitement about being taken by a man who ignored their weak protests. Then one blog friend admitted to a rape fantasy, and a few others (including Beth) had chimed in about their secret, dark desires. I had pointed out that in the fantasy you were in control, but rape wasn't about being in control; it was about being controlled.

I remembered the discussion that came out of the rape one—being tied up. What had I said? *Please, please don't let me have fudged the truth by saying that I fantasized about being tied up.*

I pulled out my laptop computer and logged onto my blog. It had been a while since I'd posted, and I was sure that there would be many comments about my last post. I didn't want to read those, though. When had we talked about the tying-up thing? After a couple of guesses, I found it.

483 Comments:

• Molly Girl wrote:

Montene, you obviously don't go in for the rape fantasy, but what about being in the submissive role? In particular, being

tied up? With someone you trust, of course. Giving yourself
up like that is a totally erotic experience. Especially when
you're blindfolded <evil grin>

I scrolled down to my next entry and cringed.

Mm, no, Molly Girl, never thought about that particular scenario. I can see the erotic overtones, though. He's in complete
control. He can do anything he wants. And you don't see it
coming. I get a shiver just thinking about it. Even more so
when I think about tying the guy up!

—Montene

I *had* gotten a shiver . . . of unease. But I'd let them
think I was sexy and adventurous and would consider it.
He had no doubt read this same entry.

I looked out the window again. It was snizzling, a
combination of snow and drizzle. Tiny specks flew at an
angle in the wind. I should go. I didn't want to go. Even
those couple of feet to my vehicle seemed like a mile. It
was well lit, though. If he was lying in wait beneath my
car, I would see him. I would have parked in my shop if
I could have. I wondered about just staying there tonight, but because of the high ceilings it was cold despite the heaters. No bed, either. Even sleeping on the
table would have been better than my soft bed with a
man I wasn't sure I could trust lying next to me.

I heard a *clunk* somewhere. There were twelve units
in my building, six on each side connected by a hallway
in the middle where the bathrooms were located. It was
comforting to know someone else was there.

I counted out the deep red tablecloths and fine silver
service, setting everything out for easy loading tomorrow. The table centerpieces were sitting on the other
table, artful arrangements of dried flowers and pieces

of bamboo. My two part-time employees and I would prepare the food in the mansion's gourmet kitchen.

Speaking of bathrooms, the coffee I'd been drinking to keep warm had now worked its way through. I unlocked the door to the hallway and turned on the light. My sneakers squeaked on the concrete floor as I made the trek all the way down to the end. I stared at my reflection while I washed my hands a few minutes later. I looked horrible under the fluorescent lights, shadows under my eyes from lack of sleep and from stress. I returned to my shop, locking the door once again.

I rubbed my hands together—the hallway and bathroom were arctic—and took one last look at everything. My breath caught in my throat. A coil of ribbon sat on the edge of one of the tables, looking like a snake.

A coil of ribbon that I had not put there.

My heart jumped into my throat as I spun around. Dominic stood just behind me with a smile that spoke of anticipation and smug pleasure. In his hand was a pair of my scissors with knifelike points.

"Hello, Jonna. Oh, that's right, you want me to call you Montene. But Montene hasn't been around much lately." He nodded toward the computer where my blog was still on the screen. "I see you've been reliving your fantasies. Well, I'm about to make them come true."

CHAPTER TWENTY-NINE

Rush was on the phone with Mike Patterson, DEMCO's jittery CEO, when Beth returned to the loft. He'd been happy to see her go out for the night so he could have the place to himself. He needed time to think, but he'd gotten little of that. Mike had called soon after, and Rush had been on the phone with him ever since. At least it looked like Mike was going to roll the dice.

"Of course, I'll be there until the last signature and handshake," Rush told Mike, nodding to Beth as she shed her coat, revealing a slinky black dress.

Rush leaned against the bar, staring at the gold and blue-tipped queen angelfish grazing on the algae on a rock. He only had one; two would fight until death.

Beth took his glass and went to the bar to fill his and get one for herself.

"The travel agent's working on flights for Monday afternoon. That'll give us a chance to talk on the plane. We'll have dinner with Sturdivant's guys that night and make things official over the next day or so. . . . I think you're making the right move, but you've got to be comfortable with it. . . . Okay, I'll let you know what the schedule is. Later."

She handed his glass to him as he wrapped up the call and settled on a stool next to him. It bugged him how she'd made herself so at home.

She gave him a frown. "You're leaving?"

"DEMCO and Sturdivant might be coming together finally." He felt like a traitor, carrying on while Hadden languished in a coma, but he knew Hadden wanted this deal to go through as much as he did. It was a hell of a time to have to leave.

"Oh." She took a long drink, crossing one leg over the other, her foot brushing his leg. She smelled like smoke and liquor.

"Where's Jonna? I thought she was going with you."

Beth waved that away. "She was too wrapped up in her work."

"She's still at the shop?" He looked at the clock and then stood. "I'm going to drive up and check on her."

"She's not there. I just did that on the way back. I thought she'd be home, actually." She gave him a look that reeked of sympathy. "She must be somewhere else."

He tried her cell phone. No answer.

Beth said, "Did you meet with Dominic today?"

He kept his gaze on the aquarium. Usually watching the graceful movements of his sea creatures relaxed him. Nothing could relax him now. "I told him I needed proof before I'd give him any money." He didn't tell her about his counteroffer.

"Well, sure, that makes sense. Though I imagine getting it might be tricky."

"That's his problem."

"I can work on my end, too, try to get her to tell me what's going on."

He only nodded. When her cell phone rang, she looked at the display and then dropped the phone back into her little gold purse. "Some guy I went out with," she said when Rush glanced her way. "Keeps bugging me. I swear I don't do anything to lead them on, but they hound me like dogs in heat."

He looked at the way she was draped against the bar, her long, pale legs provocatively angled toward him. Sure, she didn't lead them on.

She got to her stiletto-heeled feet and put her hands on his back. "I didn't feel right being out with all of this going on. I wanted to be here . . . for you." She started rubbing his back. "You're tense. And no wonder."

Despite himself, his muscles relaxed beneath her kneading fingers. She positioned herself directly behind him for a better angle, working across his shoulders. He felt her breasts graze his back as she leaned closer.

"Feel good?" she asked.

"Mm-hm."

She made a sound like a purr. "I give great massages. You can have one anytime."

As her fingers moved down his back, he watched the blue-eyed anthia hovering near the bottom of the sand he'd had brought in from the Keys. Anthias could change their sex depending on what the "harem" needed. It seemed to be looking right at him, as though it were asking, *Hm, what's going on out there?* He wasn't exactly sure. As good as her hands felt, that it was Beth standing behind him seemed disconcerting. She was right, though. His muscles melted beneath her skilled fingers. After a few minutes, she laid her cheek against his back and wrapped her arms around his waist.

He turned around. "What are you doing?"

Her cheeks flushed red, matching her lipstick. "Sorry. It's just that, I feel awful about what's going on. I'm a part of it, like we're in it together. Just knowing what you must be going through . . ." She shook her head. "I just wanted to give you some comfort, that's all."

"Thanks, but—"

"I know." She looked him right in the eyes. "You have a hard time letting people in. But Rush, if you let me in, you won't be so alone. And you must feel terribly alone right now."

She was right on both accounts. He backed away, running his hand through his hair. "I've got to check on something." He went upstairs, turned on his PC, and logged onto SIChipX. Jonna was at her shop, or at least her car was. "I'll be back in a few minutes," he told Beth as he went down the stairs and pulled his coat out of the closet.

"Where are you going?"

"I have an uneasy feeling. I'm going to check on Jonna."

"Jonna? Why? She's probably with . . . well, you know." When he opened the front door, she said, "Wait; I'll come with you."

"No point in both of us going."

He left before she could get her coat and join him. If Jonna was scheming with Dominic, then he'd catch them in the act. But that's not the image that was in his mind as he pulled out of the parking lot. He remembered when Jonna had come in while he was taking a shower, how the wall he'd always kept up had crumbled as she'd touched him with such beautiful earnestness.

Now he had one goal: get Jonna alone.

CHAPTER THIRTY

I couldn't believe what I saw. But Dominic was real. I could hear his light, shallow breaths. I screamed as I darted to his left. He jabbed with the scissors, backing me away. I kept screaming, remembering the sound I'd heard, someone else in the building.

Or had it been him?

He was still smiling. "No one's around, doll, but go ahead and yell all you want. I like it."

My scream faltered in my tight throat. I glanced at the door. "How did you get in here?"

"When I had the run of this place—before you changed the locks on me—I discovered that hallway. I inquired about the empty unit on the other side yesterday and made sure the door wasn't locked."

"How did you know I'd be here?"

He merely shrugged, as though keeping the answer to that was quite pleasurable.

I wanted to ask if Rush had told him but didn't want to give away that I knew about their alliance. If they had one.

He walked closer, scissors pointed at me. I eyed the door, calculating how long it would take to unbolt it and get to my car. Too long.

He picked up the coil as he approached me, waving the length of dark blue ribbon back and forth. By the smile on his face, I could see that he was enjoying my fear. Dammit, I couldn't hide it, either.

"What do you want, Dominic?"

He chuckled. "That's for me to know and you to find out."

My jaw tightened so hard it hurt. "Leave Beth out of this."

"What?"

"My friend. She has nothing to do with this. You broke into her apartment."

He said nothing for a few seconds. "Is that why she's staying with you?" His eyes narrowed. "Oh yeah, big, bad Beth. Protecting you from me, just like she did when I paid you a visit Monday. But she can't protect you now. She's at your place."

She was? Of course, he had gone there looking for me. Beth must have gone back early.

He lunged without warning, locking his fingers around my wrist as I tried to move out of his way. I dropped to my knees, but he dragged me toward him. He pinned me against him with one arm and cleared the table of the tablecloths and silverware with the other as I struggled. Forks and knives clattered to the floor.

"You're a fighter," he said in my ear, breathless. "The beast likes that, too."

"The b-beast?"

"The one inside me. The one who wants to come out and play."

He held the scissors to my throat. I could barely feel the point. I couldn't afford to move. He knew that. It's why he loosened his hold enough to run his hand down the front of my body. Behind me, I felt the heat radiating from him. I felt his chest move with his breaths, out of sync with my own hard breathing. I felt his erection pressed into my lower back as he rocked back and forth against me. I also felt something hard in his jacket pocket. A gun? The thought spiked my pulse. But if he had a gun, why was he using scissors?

"Montene, I can feel your body trembling," he whispered. "Do you know how excited that makes me? I'm glad you didn't surrender to me that day at the hotel. This is so much better."

I tried to still my body, but I couldn't control the trembles that wracked it even more at his words. Worse, I felt his hand slowly traveling from one breast to another. I tried to separate myself from my body. Not *my* breasts. Not *my* stomach. Not *my* . . . *my* . . . Revulsion shot through me as he headed toward my pubic area. As soon as I felt his fingers slide between my thighs, I jerked my leg up and rammed it down on top of his foot.

Spewing out expletives, he threw me onto the table, pinning me with his body, one of my hands trapped beneath me. He tied the ribbon around my wrist even though I tried to move it so he couldn't. I felt his body jerk as he tied the ribbon around the leg of the table with quick movements. He reached for the scissors that he'd set on the next table and cut the ribbon. I pulled my hand, but it didn't have much give. The ribbon was stronger than I thought.

Panic washed over me. I let out another scream as he repositioned himself to tie one of my feet down.

My arm ached as the weight of my body and his crushed it. Still, I tried to squirm as he tied first one ankle and then the other down. He slammed the scissors down on the next table and hovered over me, a wild light in his eyes. When I expected him to start taunting me, threatening me, or worse, he said, "Tell me about your husband."

I wasn't sure I heard him right. "What?"

"Tell me about your husband."

A sob escaped my throat. Why was he doing this? "What do you want to know?"

"Tell me about your marriage."

Another sob. Would Rush hear what I'd said? "I love my husband," I managed to say.

"Don't lie, bitch. Maybe you do love him . . . for his money."

"No. He's good to me. He let me start my business, encouraged me."

Impatience reeked in Dominic's voice. "Come on, Jonna, tell the truth. You hate him. He cheated on you. Humiliated you. And you wanted to hurt him back by cheating . . with me."

"He never cheated." I could hardly breathe with the pressure in my chest. I couldn't say that I now suspected him of something even worse.

"You hate him."

"No."

"You hate him!" Dominic screamed in my face.

"I don't hate him!" I screamed back, feeling as though I'd used my last breath.

His mouth relaxed, as though I'd given him the answer he wanted. "Do you wish he were dead?"

"Of course not!"

"You wouldn't admit it. But deep inside, you wish he were dead, don't you?"

Dominic was up to something. I remembered the conversation I'd overheard. He'd told the person he or she was crazy. That person had obviously told Dominic he'd almost screwed up. There was a plan here, and this nonsensical questioning was part of it. I wasn't going to play his game anymore. I didn't answer.

He gave me a shove. "Come on, admit it!"

I shook my head.

He slapped me. I could feel the sting of his handprint on my cheek as he stared at me. He was losing control, just as he had that day he'd come to Dyer House. I could see him thinking, though, desperately trying to figure out something.

My arm was nearly numb now. If I told him that, he'd tie it, too. Then I'd have no chance of grabbing the scissors. But if my arm stayed beneath me much longer, it would be useless.

"He wants me to kill you," he blurted out. "He hired me, all the way from the beginning. He's in love with someone else. He wanted you to sleep with me so he'd have proof of your unfaithfulness and leave you with nothing. When you wouldn't comply"—his mouth tightened so hard I could hardly see his lips—"he told me to get rid of you."

I started crying. Bawling. It was easy. I let everything that had been pent up these last few weeks explode out of me, most of all my confusion.

"Stop crying!" he said, gripping my face with his hand. "Now tell me you hate him. That you want him dead."

I said, "You son of a bitch," purposely garbling my words—and releasing my arm. He was too impatient and angry that I wasn't cooperating. That made me cooperate less, wailing like a banshee, rocking back and forth, curling myself up as much as I could.

"Stop crying and talk to me."

While he was trying to calm me down, I grabbed for the scissors. The points bit into my palm as I blindly reached for them. My fingers were tingling and hurt like hell, but I forced them to curl around the blades as I jabbed Dominic. I didn't know where I'd hit him, only that I had. He screamed and fell back.

Still holding on to the scissors, I cut the ribbons. He was crouched on the floor clutching his thigh. Blood soaked into his jeans and through his fingers.

I stumbled as I came off the table, using the other

table to launch me back to balance and toward my office. The scissors clattered to the floor. I hesitated only a second, deciding not to take the time to get them. I grabbed my purse and fumbled with my keys as I unlocked the door. I dared a glance at him. He was trying to get to his feet, his face contorted in pain as he reached for the scissors. I slammed the door closed and ran to my vehicle.

When I pulled away, I saw him running out the door into the night. Despite the wound, he could run. I hadn't hurt him enough.

As I drove home in automatic mode, wiping my eyes, I couldn't help thinking that something was very, very wrong. Dominic had been lying. But I wasn't sure exactly what part was false.

I knew I should go to the police. I still had no proof. I looked at the stinging hole in my palm—self-inflicted. The ribbons would be tied to the table, but they might think it was part of some kinky act. Especially once they knew who I was. I suspected most of them did, thanks to the wives on the blog.

I managed to clean up at a convenience store before getting home. Beth was waiting up, wearing Rush's pajama top and sitting in one of the living room chairs reading a magazine.

She looked up. "Rush went looking for you. Didn't you see him?"

"No. Why was he looking for me?"

"He said he had an uneasy feeling. Then he went upstairs, checked something on his computer, and left. I think he's up to something. And something did happen, didn't it?"

I guess I still looked spooked, and I was trembling. "Dominic." I dropped down into the other chair and took a ragged breath. "He got into my shop. He tried to . . . tie me down to one of my tables."

"My God. Did he . . . ?"

"No, he didn't rape me." I opened my hand. The cut wasn't bleeding, but it was an angry red. "I stabbed him, and he ran off."

She covered her mouth, probably imagining the horrible scene. "Oh, Jonna . . ." She took my hand in hers, inspecting the wound. "I don't think you'll need stitches." She looked up at me. "Did you hurt him bad?"

I leaned forward, rubbing my temples. "I got him in the thigh. He ran off, so it couldn't have been that bad. The really weird part was, he kept asking me to tell him how much I hated Rush. How I wanted him dead. He . . . he told me Rush hired him to kill me."

"Oh, honey." Beth put her hand on my arm. "But it shouldn't have come as a big surprise."

"I didn't believe it, not really. Not the killing part."

"How can you not believe it? It makes sense. How Dominic got in, how he knew where you were. You saw the two of them together."

"I know. I know. It's probably some desperate part of me that can't believe it."

"That's the dumb part of you."

"Don't worry; I'm going to disappear for a bit. Stay at a hotel, begin divorce proceedings from a distance. I'll be busy all weekend with events, but after that I'm going to let my employees handle things. I've got to do something."

"That's a relief. And you've got the perfect opportunity. Rush is going out of town on Monday. I overheard him talking to the DEMCO guy about wrapping up the deal. That'll give you a chance to pack and get out of here, which is a good idea anyway, considering . . ."

"What?" I prodded.

"That Dominic probably plans to kill you while Rush is away."

"What about you? What are you going to do when I leave?"

"Stay here, keep an eye on Rush. I'm going to play dumb about your leaving . . . and try to become his best friend and find out what's going on in that head of his."

I shivered. Foreboding?

I heard the key in the front door lock, and we both turned to see Rush walk in. He took me in, as though looking for evidence that I'd been traumatized. I wasn't going to give him the satisfaction.

"Beth said you were looking for me," I said. He'd probably seen that my car was at the shop on his tracking software.

"I must have missed you."

"She said you had an uneasy feeling?"

He shrugged. "Guess I was wrong."

"I'm fine." I stood. "I'm going to take a shower." I didn't look at him as I passed by on the way to the stairs. "Good night, everyone."

Was I making the wrong decision? No, Beth was right. My home and my shop had been tainted. My marriage shattered. I had to start over, piece my life back together again. That was if I could manage to stay in one piece myself.

CHAPTER THIRTY-ONE

Saturday morning Dominic waited in a parking lot across the street from the loft. He watched Rush leave, looking lost in dark thoughts. Then Jonna left, looking haggard and afraid as she searched for Dominic. He hoped she'd stayed up all night thinking about him and about the man lying next to her who wanted her dead. He'd certainly spent most of the night awake, nursing his throbbing thigh.

Finally, Beth headed to her green VW Bug with the bearing of a queen in her fox-fur coat, her milky red hair curling out from under the matching hat. It was her that he followed through town to her apartment building, waiting until she'd gone up in the elevator before going up to the fourth floor. He knocked on her door and didn't answer when she asked who it was. When she opened the door, he pushed her back inside and slammed the door shut.

She let out a scream and kicked at him when he pinned her against the wall. "Let me go!"

A picture crashed to the floor, glass shattering. His body mashed hers as she tried to squirm out of his hold. She tried to pull up her knee, and when he twisted, she was able to slide out from between him and the wall. He was on her, though, grabbing her. With a grunt, she went down, and he fell with her, finally pinning her to the floor just as he had done to Jonna the night before. At least Beth hadn't kept screaming. Her face was suffused with red anger, her eyes with surprise.

"Stop it! Stop fighting me," he said.

She was panting, glaring at him.

"You're going to listen to me. What the fu—"

She shoved at his mouth, knocking his head to the side. "I told you not to use that kind of language around me. Now, get off of me." She pushed him to the side.

His laugh was rough and gritty. He stood, running his hand back through his hair. "Oh, that's priceless! I can't cuss, but you can push someone in front of a frickin' bus."

She crossed her arms in front of her chest, looking every bit the petulant child. "He was sabotaging me. He told her that Rush wasn't cheating, which nearly screwed up everything. Jonna and Rush almost got back together because of him."

"And you tried to kill him because of that?" Dominic screamed.

She pressed her hand over his mouth. "Stop telling all the neighbors, you idiot. That's not why I pushed him."

He pulled her hand away. "Well, why don't you enlighten me?"

She was giving him that *I don't have to explain myself to you* look. Now in her gym clothes, without her high heels, she had to look way up to him. "You didn't have to sneak over and grab me."

"Yes, I did. You've been avoiding me since the bus thing. Not taking my calls or hanging up on me, hiding out at Rush and Jonna's loft, of all places. You said you wouldn't do it again. At least without telling me first."

"All right, all right," she said, and for a second he saw apprehension flicker in her eyes. It amazed him how seeing that made his groin tighten. "I hadn't planned to do it. But he saw us together. He must have followed me from the office. I don't know why. I glanced up and saw him looking right at us. And he knew what was going on. I could tell that he knew who you were. From when you were spying on them as they were having lunch. He walked away and I followed him. He pulled out his cell phone. He was about to call Jonna. I had to preserve the plan."

"What if the police investigate?"

"They have their guy—the bus driver. And no one saw me push him. Didn't you see that on the news? They were looking for the person who was trying to help him. They don't even know if it was a man or woman. I grabbed someone else's coat in my hurry to get outside, so they couldn't tell." She reached out and squeezed his arm. "You won't freak out on me and do something stupid, will you? You've been acting so strange on this job." She was worried. Then she straightened and he saw the powerful expression he was used to seeing. "You're the one who created the problem by letting Hadden see you. You have to take some of the responsibility. You put me in that situation."

Typical Beth, trying to lay the blame elsewhere.

"What if he recovers and remembers what happened?"

"He won't recover; it was pretty bad. But even if he did, he wouldn't remember those last few minutes before the accident. People never do."

"Accident," Dominic said with a sneer. "We could have just cut and run."

"No way. We've invested too much." Her face was flushed again, her hands fisted. "We can't just walk away, not now." She calmed herself down, tempering her voice. "You won't let me down, right, Peter?"

"Don't call me Peter anymore. I like the name Dominic. I'm going to keep it."

She rolled her eyes. "All right, *Dominic*. Don't worry about Hadden."

"That's what you said last time, about the wife."

"And nothing came of it. She was about to mess everything up, too."

He pointed at her, raising his voice. "No, she was about to screw *you* up! We had the money. But you wanted *him*, too. You lied to me. You betrayed me."

She was stroking his arm. "I know. I'm sorry. I got a little crazy."

"*Obsessed*, Beth! You were over-the-top, frickin' obsessed." He angled his face in front of hers. "It's not like that with Rush, is it?"

She met his gaze straight on. "No, not at all." But he knew she was a good liar.

She pulled him toward the couch. "Come on, I'll give you a back rub, calm you down."

It was like her obsession for buying things and doing her nails, spending money she didn't have. Like her obsession over sex. He gave in, lying with his head on her thighs, and she stroked his back. "You hurt me," he said, the words slurred because his mouth was pressed against her leg.

"I know. I didn't mean to, you know that. I . . . I couldn't help myself."

He turned so that he could see her. "Why are you living with them?"

"Because I want to make sure they don't reconcile again. We're too close. And there's a lot more money at stake this time. Trust me, Pe—Dominic."

She was using her soothing, persuasive voice. He knew it well. She ran her fingers through his hair, tracing his ear and making goose bumps rise on his neck and arms.

She said, "One of your messages said you met with Rush. He told me that he asked you for proof."

"Yeah. That's why I was trying to get Jonna to talk about him last night." He lifted his head and narrowed his eyes at her. "I wasn't being an idiot. I had a tape recorder on me. But I'm not sure I got enough. We may have to play with it. What else did Rush say?"

"That was all. I still haven't gotten him to trust me enough to really open up. Jonna couldn't do that in a year and a half of marriage. But I will." He heard her determination. "He's going out of town, though, so let's wrap this up before he leaves."

Funny that Rush hadn't told her about the one-hundred-thousand-dollar offer. He had planned to tell her. He had. But he decided not to. For her betrayal. And because it gave him a sense of power that he rarely got in their relationship. He rolled over so that he looked up at her.

"What did it feel like? To kill someone? I feel electricity when I see fear in Jonna's eyes. The power, the excitement . . . it's overwhelming. Seducing them is easy. At least it usually is. I've never scared someone before. Now that I have, I think about it all the time."

Her green eyes widened. "Stop thinking about it. This isn't about getting you off. It's about the money."

"Is it? Only about the money?"

She met his gaze. "Don't you trust me?"

"Yes. No. Not anymore." He wasn't sure he believed her. "So what did it feel like? Did you feel a thrill when you saw Hadden bleeding in the slush? Did you feel a sense of power when you pushed him?"

"It was out of necessity, not for a thrill. The only thing I felt was . . . well, yes, a sense of power at taking care of a problem that threatened our plan. But that's all."

"And the wife? You pushed her out of anger, too."

"No." She studied him, her face bent over his. "Dominic . . . I don't like that light in your eyes. It scares me. You've been on the edge this time, veering out of control. I need you to focus on the plan. He's going to pay you the money, we'll split it, and then I'll find the next lonely housewife who's married to some rich guy." She leaned over and kissed his forehead. "Okay, my sweet little boy?" She kissed his eyebrows, his nose, his chin. Then his mouth. She did that so rarely, just enough to make him crave it. Most of the time she held back, like that carrot on a stick.

"Okay, Mamu," he said, and she didn't tell him to stop calling her that.

She was pulling out all the stops to keep him in control. He planned to take advantage of it, getting to his knees and kissing her back. Sometimes she wouldn't open her mouth to him, but this morning she did. She let him into all of her, murmuring, "My sweet little boy," and, "We need each other," stroking his hair as he lost himself in her body.

Afterward they lay together on the couch, his head on her chest. During those times when she let him screw her, he never heard her heart racing afterward. He never heard her breath coming quickly, and he doubted she ever had an orgasm. She didn't even bother to fake one. Cold bitch.

"If you love me," she said in her lulling voice, "you'll forget about wanting to scare people. That's not in our plans. That will mess things up. Okay?"

He nodded, looking at the fine pale red hairs on her stomach. "I'll be your good little boy," he said in a sleepy whisper. "I promise."

But he wasn't sleepy. And he wasn't going to be her good little boy, not completely. Because while Beth complained that he had all the fun during their schemes, he didn't enjoy that sex. He used to fantasize about Beth so he'd have a hard-on. After her betrayal, though, that fantasy stopped working. What *had* gotten him hard with Jonna was the power he felt as he'd pinned her to that hotel bed and seen her fear. He wasn't about to let that go. Not for the sake of the plan and not for Mamu, either.

Beth watched Peter sleep. She had an extremely uneasy feeling about what he'd said, especially when he asked about killing someone. He'd been out of control this time, and she didn't want him to be out of her control.

He'd been hers since the day he'd come to live with them. Gus, his father, had married Diana, her mother, and a year later she was pregnant with their perfect wonder child. Beth hadn't even known that Gus had a son, but suddenly there was a lot of talk about Peter and, in particular, his mother, Paloma. Or that's what she called herself at the time. Beth had heard just enough about Paloma to be intrigued. She was a sexy outlaw, a clever con artist, with a love of glamour and luxuries. She was exotic, of mysterious heritage, and she'd died a fantastic, blazing death, crashing her car after a long police chase.

She had an eleven-year-old son named Peter, who was now coming to live with them. Gus was an absent father, just like Beth's father. Unlike Diana, Paloma probably hadn't been trying to snag a rich man to support her; she had more fun conniving them out of their money and flying as free as the wind.

Beth brushed a lock of Peter's hair from his forehead, remembering the sulky boy who'd inherited his mother's looks. She knew he felt unwanted in their home, just as she felt. The coming baby was all their parents talked about.

When Gus told Diana what he'd learned from the police and psychologist about Peter's background, Beth had listened in. She liked knowing other people's secrets. She was good at keeping them.

"His mother used her body, her sensuality, to win people over," Gus had said in a quiet voice. "To get her way. It worked, obviously. The police found furs, jewelry, and cash stashed all over her apartment. Worse, she had a warped relationship with my son. He's slept in her bed his whole life. She called him her little boy and treated him like a baby. She would manipulate him if he dared separate from her, as boys naturally do. She'd criticize him and tell him he was nothing without her. Like in emotionally abusive relationships. When he did what she wanted, she lavished him with praise, affection, and expensive gifts. He was, in effect, her personal little slave. And he adores her."

To be adored, to have power over someone . . . the thought was seductive for a gawky fourteen-year-old with red hair and freckles. Especially when her own mother put Beth down and told her she'd never amount to anything. Diana wore sexy things and told Beth she'd never look as good as she did, that she'd never be able to snag someone as handsome and rich as Gus.

Paloma was everything Beth wanted to be . . . except dead, of course. She stepped into the role with Peter first.

"You miss your mama, don't you?" Beth asked when they were alone on the front porch swing.

"I called her Mamu," he said on a whisper, his body drawn in on itself.

"Would you like me to be your mamu?"

He looked at her with pitiful eyes, his need so transparent. He nodded.

"Come here." She patted the spot next to her and he

scooted over. "Tell me everything about her. Tell me what she said, what she did. I'll be her. And you'll be mine."

While their parents doted on the baby, Beth doted on Peter. Using her powers on him boosted her sexual assuredness. To make sure of his devotion, she poisoned him against Diana. In fact, Beth poisoned him against all women. She acted hurt when he became interested in girls in high school, so he stopped. Though she had become his mother figure, she realized that he was a growing boy with sexual needs. So she gave him just enough to sate him, but never more. She wanted to keep him wanting her, needing her.

He held her spellbound when he talked about Paloma's schemes. Her shoplifting; dating wealthy men and then charging outrageous items to their accounts; the personal injury schemes. The way she changed her name and personality like a chameleon. The way she hated men, hated their weakness even while she exploited it. That was something Beth could understand.

She convinced Peter to show her how Paloma stole things. The rush from thievery was exhilarating. The power, the joy of getting away with it. Beth wanted more. She wanted all of the beautiful things Gus bought for her mother that Diana flashed in front of her face. So she began to get them for herself.

Shoes were her first obsession. Every color, every style, the more expensive the better. Then it was sunglasses, and then purses. Jewelry was harder, but she and Peter had managed a few pieces.

Later, it was her disdain for women that put an idea into her head. She worked in a hotel where the wives of rich men would go to meet their young lovers. Beth watched the men slobber all over women who were sometimes twice their age, most probably going along for what they could get. She struck upon an idea. What if a man who knew just where to touch and what to say seduced a lonely, neglected wife? What if he got pictures of them having sex and blackmailed her?

Peter had gone along immediately, once again seeing Paloma in Beth and sensing the excitement of the con. That's what they both craved, what they got high from, and what sometimes drew them into frenzied sex amid a shower of one-hundred-dollar bills.

It had worked a dozen times. Beth would target a likely mark and befriend her. Then Peter moved in. One hit, one payoff, and the woman got the pictures. They never hit the same mark again, and the pictures never resurfaced. Not so much out of honor, but because repeat blackmailers sometimes got killed.

It had gone so well until the last two schemes. The previous con had been a matter of bad judgment. The one before that . . . Beth didn't want to think about that one. Peter still hadn't forgiven her, but he didn't understand. She'd probably never get him to understand, either. Just as she couldn't get him to lay off of her sex life. With most of those other men, it was only that— sex. She craved it, craved the way their desire made her feel. She rarely saw them a second time.

Then there were others. . . .

Peter opened his eyes, and she pretended she hadn't been sitting there watching him. She inspected her nails, frowning at a chip in her polish. He sat up and scratched his head.

The gleam wasn't in his eyes anymore. She hoped she'd only imagined it. She smiled. "Rise and shine, sleepyhead." He always fell asleep after they had sex. She had come to expect it. "Where's that tape?"

He walked over to his jacket and pulled out the digital recorder. They sat down at the table and he pressed the Play button. Jonna's scream filled the air.

That's when Beth saw the sadistic gleam again. His

mouth twisted into a smile, his eyes glazed as he sank back into the moment. She hardly recognized him.

She felt that anxious flutter in her stomach again. She couldn't afford to lose control of him. Especially not now, when he would soon find out what she'd been hiding from him.

CHAPTER THIRTY-TWO

Saturday afternoon I was already on edge when I heard a knock on the shop door. I was in the work area, so anyone standing at the door couldn't see in. The only thing that didn't send me through the ceiling was the fact that Dominic had never knocked.

I wasn't expecting any deliveries or my helpers yet. I stood rigidly still and waited until whoever was knocking gave up.

Then I heard: "Jonna? Are you in there? It's Rush."

That didn't reassure me in the least. I could hear Beth's warning about not being alone with him. Made sense to me. We had nothing to talk about anyway. So why was he here?

I waited another few minutes while he continued to knock and call out to me. My vehicle was parked out front, of course. He might think I was in the restroom.

It seemed like hours before he gave up. After several minutes of silence, I crept into the office area and peered around the edge of the window. Rush was standing by his Range Rover but still looking at my door. He couldn't see in because of the reflection, but even so, I shrank back.

What was he thinking as he contemplated my shop?

How to break in? Where I could be? He pulled out his cell phone, and a moment later mine rang. It stopped four rings later. I saw his mouth move as he left a message.

He looked so handsome with the sun shining on his hair, his eyes camouflaged by sunglasses, and wearing his long, black coat. I had to remind myself that in nature some of the most dangerous animals were the most beautiful. Tigers. Coral snakes. Lionfish.

Dominic. And very possibly Rush, too.

That night, as the birthday party was winding down, I felt emotionally and physically exhausted. I'd been pushing myself too hard, trying to drive away my fear by cramming work into every thought. Now, as I stood alone at the bar and watched the Skeevers say good-bye to the departing guests, I felt fear encroaching again.

Trish and Carson were cleaning up. I hadn't yet told them that they'd be handling some of the upcoming events by themselves. I dreaded telling them why, lie or not. Fortunately, the monthly AngelForce dinner meetings weren't scheduled in November or December because of the holidays. Rush would have canceled them in light of Hadden's condition anyway.

Rush's message had given me some good news. "Jonna, I'm at your shop. If you're in there, come to the door. I want to talk to you." A pause. "We got some encouraging news. Hadden's parents saw some brain activity on the monitor. It was just a flicker, but . . . it's something, anyway. Okay, I guess you're not there. But we need to talk, Jonna. Alone."

About what?

Waldo Skeever, who had orchestrated the party for his wife, wandered over for another Operatini, the pear and grenadine concoction I'd created just for her birthday. He was a tall, sturdy man with a handlebar mustache.

He let out a long breath as he took a seat. "Too bad Rush couldn't make it," he said.

I stopped pouring his drink midway. "Rush?"

Waldo was an angel, but I had no idea they socialized or that Rush had been invited. "I figured, with everything he did, he would have come. Pesky business deals," he said with a shake of his head.

" 'Everything he did'?"

Waldo's mouth, framed by his mustache, formed an *O*. "Oops. I wasn't supposed to tell. Well, it's probably all right to let the cat out of the bag now. Rush paid for this." He gestured to include, I assumed, the party.

"He did?" I said, feeling like a parrot.

"I told him it wasn't necessary, not at all, but he insisted. When Rush first came to Boston, Marnie took him under her wing." I knew about Waldo's involvement in Rush's company, but not about her role. "When you mentioned that you were organizing her sixtieth birthday party, Rush wanted to give it to her as his way of thanking her."

"Why didn't he want me to know about it?" More secrets?

"He was afraid you'd cut your profit margin, and he didn't want you to do that. He's quite proud of your success, you know. But I sensed . . ."

"What?" I prodded.

"Maybe I shouldn't say this. It's only speculation, after all."

Did you sense that he was trying to have me killed? I wanted to ask. My hands were frozen on the pitcher of Operatinis. "Please, tell me."

"He admitted to working too much, and at first, he was glad you had a career you were passionate about, too. He talked about the glow you have when you're organizing or cooking. Said he wished he could put it there instead. I sensed that he missed having you around."

My lips trembled. When had I started working on this event? Two months ago. Before Dominic, but after the blog. Had Rush been laying the groundwork for his plan back then? Even down to wanting to preserve my profit margins? Doubtful. Or had everything changed in between?

"Cheer up," Waldo said, pushing to his feet. "It's not too late. Marnie and I went through the same thing. Look at us now."

I nodded, forcing myself to finish pouring his drink and nudging a pear slice onto the sugared rim of the glass.

Carson and Trish carted trays past me to the kitchen, and I followed them to help with the cleanup.

"You don't look well, darling," Carson said, tilting his head as he took me in.

"I'm not well," I admitted. My stomach was a knot and my heart ached. I'd told Rush that I thought I was coming down with something, my reason for wearing long johns to bed. Now I felt as though I really was coming down with the flu.

He put his arm around my shoulders. "Let us finish up here. You go home." He turned to Trish. "I'm going to walk her out to her car. Be right back."

The Skeevers lived in an exclusive, gated community; still, it was nice to have Carson accompany me.

"Please tell the Skeevers good-bye for me," I said when Carson and I reached my car.

I surreptitiously looked in the backseat and beneath the car, realizing I didn't feel safe anywhere. Once I was locked inside, I waved good-bye to Carson and started the engine. As I pulled away, I saw a vehicle do the same behind me. I couldn't see it clearly, since it remained several car lengths behind me, but I thought it might be a dark green Range Rover . . . like Rush's. It followed me for several miles before veering off just as I reached home.

As I unlocked the front door Rush pulled into the parking lot. I doubted it was a coincidence. If not, then why had he been following me?

CHAPTER THIRTY-THREE

Sunday afternoon Rush packed his overnight bag, preparing for his evening flight to New York. He didn't want to go, but Mike Patterson would fall apart without Rush to hold his hand during these final negotiations. Sturdivant's people were getting impatient with all the delays. Rush didn't want to screw up Mike's future because of his problems. He'd be back by tomorrow night, though, no matter what.

He could hear Jonna and Beth downstairs, their voices intermittently floating up. He hadn't gotten a chance to talk to Jonna alone, not with Beth hovering around and sleeping just down the hall from their bedroom. Not with Jonna working so much and avoiding him when she was around. That Beth was there for moral support made it harder to ask her to return to her apartment. So did the intruder who had scared her enough to make her move in with them.

Jonna had come home late the night before looking pale and complaining of being achy. Coming down with the flu, she'd said, using that as an excuse to sleep downstairs. He'd cut out of his meeting early enough to head to the Skeevers' party . . . just in time to see Jonna getting ready to leave and follow her home. She'd looked tired and ragged but didn't want to talk to him about it.

While they'd had breakfast that morning, he'd caught her watching him. She always quickly averted her gaze. He watched her, too, trying to figure out what was going on. Beth kept interjecting useless small talk, valiantly trying to cheer the somber mood.

"Maybe I shouldn't go," he'd said, surprising Jonna. "With you being, ah, sick. The flu." He gave her a meaningful look. "Should I stay?"

She quickly shook her head. "No, go. I'll be fine."

Beth said, "I'll stick close by, keep an eye on her."

Jonna said, "This deal's important. Don't cancel it for me."

"You could come with."

"No." Last time he'd offered that, he could tell she wanted to go. Not this time. She clearly wanted him to leave. Why?

It hit him then. She wasn't afraid of Dominic. She was afraid of *him*.

He stiffened when the phone rang. His first thought was always Hadden. He'd gone down the night before and stood outside the ICU room, staring in through the glass. Hadden was hooked up to machines that kept him alive. He didn't look anything like the vibrant man Rush considered a surrogate brother. If only he'd told Hadden what was going on. They wouldn't have had that last conversation that haunted him.

He was simply too conditioned, from his earliest memories, to keeping his business to himself. Innocuous questions like *So, what'd you do over the weekend?* usually invoked memories of the violence between two people who supposedly loved each other. *Well, on Saturday my mom tried to set my dad's NASCAR collection on fire and then he flushed her jewelry down the toilet, and then they spent all day Sunday moaning and groaning in the bedroom making up.*

He reached for the bedroom phone and without thinking answered it as he did at the office. "Rush."

"Can you talk?"

Dominic.

"Sure."

"I have a recording. It's hard to hear; we met at a bar last night, before her birthday gig. But you can tell what she's saying. When can we meet?"

"Not until I get back from a business trip."

"When do you leave?"

"Tonight."

"Let's meet before that. Then you can start the arrangements to get the money and I can proceed with my part of things. Timing could work well if you're out of town."

"I can't."

"Dammit, man, this is your life we're talking about!"

"Call me later in the week," he said, and hung up. Nothing would happen while he hung Dominic up. He zipped his luggage closed and walked to the stairs.

Jonna and Beth sat at the aquarium bar, Jonna staring at the reef. Beth looked up and winked, as though he and she were coconspirators. He descended the stairs and set his bag near the door.

When Beth saw that she said, "You're leaving already?" while Jonna just looked at him with eyes filled with angst and confusion. If only Beth weren't there . . . frustration swamped him. He couldn't get Jonna alone. Worse, she didn't want to be alone with him.

"Yeah." He wanted to stop at the hospital again, when Hadden's parents would likely be there. He watched the blue-and-yellow-striped clown tang dart between the brown "fingers" of a devil's hand coral and then turned to Jonna. "You'll feed the sunset anthiases? Remember, they have to be fed twice a day. All the fish need to be fed tonight."

She nodded, her gaze going to the bright pink fish.

He turned to Beth. "I'm sure you're tired of living out of your suitcase. When I get back, I'll see what I can do about getting your apartment safeguarded."

Her face flushed. "I hope I'm not imposing."

"Not at all," he lied. "But I'm sure you want to get back to your life."

Jonna's voice was dull when she said, "We were just talking about going over so she could get some of her things. Maybe we can talk to the building manager while we're there."

He hesitated at the door. Would it seem unusual for a husband not to kiss his wife good-bye when he was leaving town? He walked over and stood in front of her. "I'll be back tomorrow evening."

She nodded, a jerky movement, her eyes on him. When she realized he meant to hug her good-bye, she awkwardly got to her feet. "Have a good trip."

He pulled her against him, feeling her body tense. Was his wife a cold-blooded gold digger? She wasn't acting like a woman who was about to come into a lot of money due to her husband's premature death. She *did* look like a woman who was jumpy and nervous and lying about the reason why.

He leaned down and kissed her. Not a gentle kiss but a deep, probing one that snapped her eyes open. He probed with his eyes, too, searching for traces of cunning . . . or the woman he'd fallen in love with. He felt his chest tighten. He backed away, almost certain he had it figured out.

"When I get back, we will talk. Alone." Without giving her a chance to respond, he left.

CHAPTER THIRTY-FOUR

"What was *that* all about?" Beth asked after Rush left, her eyebrows furrowed in suspicion.

I put my fingers to my lips, still feeling his mouth there. "I . . . don't know."

"Maybe it was like a Mafia kiss—the kiss good-bye. Maybe it was for my benefit, too. I'll bet Dominic's supposed to kill you while he's gone. Jonna, I've got a bad feeling about it. See, he was even trying to get rid of me." She rubbed my arm. "Thank goodness you're leaving. I couldn't bear knowing you were here or at your shop."

What Beth said made sense. He had been trying to get rid of her. The kiss, that bothered me. He hadn't kissed me since he'd left for his trip last week. And the way he'd looked at me, searching my eyes for something . . .

"But why does he want to talk to me alone?"

"It's probably better if you don't find out. Come on, let's get you packed."

As she led me up the stairs, I said, "What about you? You can't stay here alone. Or at your place."

"I know, but I can't afford a room at that hotel."

"You could stay with me."

"Thanks, sweetie, but that would be way too cramped.

Maybe I'll suck it up and stay with my parents." She made a face at that. "It's just for a few days, until Rush gets back."

"Do you really think it's a good idea to stay here with him?" That bothered me for some reason. I remembered the uncomfortable feeling I'd had seeing them in the bathroom together.

"He's not going to do anything to me, and Dominic won't try anything while he's here. It'll keep me safe. And it's important that I keep tabs on him." She paused. "I'll just have to convince him to let me stay."

She helped me pack, because I couldn't seem to make my body move. I put my clothes and personal things into two suitcases and all of my business papers into another one. She helped me carry my computer and luggage to the car.

I scanned the parking lot, wondering if Dominic was watching us. I would have to make sure he didn't know where I was going. At least I'd feel safe in the hotel with its security and lots of people around.

"The fish!" I said, stopping at my car. "The anthiases need to be fed tonight and tomorrow morning."

"I'll take care of it. But I'll need a key."

"I'll give you my spare when we get to your place. To get what you need," I clarified when she looked at me questioningly. "I don't want you going there alone."

She hesitated, then smiled. "Good idea."

I followed her VW Bug across town to her apartment building. Despite the fact that we were best friends, I'd only been to her apartment a couple of times. She'd had Rush and me over for dinner twice.

She pushed her door open and stepped inside. The decor was teenybopper: bright pink accents, paintings with huge polka dots, pink vinyl curtains, and bead chains that separated the kitchen from the living room. I smelled the cloying scent of jasmine.

Beth had stopped, and I did, too, taking in a small room that looked as though someone had shaken the building. Lamps were knocked to the floor, the paintings I'd remembered lying at odd angles across the furniture. Her face paled, and she put her hand to her mouth.

"I'm hoping you had a wild party," I said.

She shook her head. Then she ran to the bedroom. Before I could reach the door, she ran back out and closed the door behind her. "He's been here."

"Dominic?" I asked, strain in my voice.

She nodded. Her face was frozen in fright and her hands trembled as she seemed to be trying to decide what to do.

"We should go to the police. It's gone too far," I said.

"No. He's only trying to scare me. Probably because I'm staying with you now, protecting you." She wrapped her arms around herself. "Let's get out of here. I'll buy what I need."

We left, with me feeling terrible that I'd brought this on her. As we reached the cars, though, I had a thought. "Beth, would Gary know where you live?"

"My ex? No, I doubt it. Why would you even mention him?"

"I saw him last week, at the hotel. He was drunk, and obviously still bitter about your breakup."

"Creep." She looked up at the building. "I don't think this is him."

"The only reason I brought it up was because he was so angry. He even said it was you who was stalking him."

She gave a high-pitched laugh. "He's crazy. But I still don't think he did this. I'm almost sure it was Dominic in here last week." She searched the parking lot. "He's probably watching right now, getting off on our reaction."

That made me shiver. "Please promise you'll go to your parents' house."

"I will. And I'll be in touch with you."

We hugged, and I left in one direction, Beth in the other. I took a circuitous route to the hotel and left instructions that no one tell any caller I was staying there. When I unpacked, I realized I hadn't left a note for Rush when he returned. I hadn't thought about what I would tell him about my absence. That I knew about his plan? Some other story? I decided I wouldn't answer his calls, wouldn't talk to him at all while he was gone. I did call the loft and left a message that could be interpreted any way he wanted:

"Rush, I've gone away for a while. I'll . . . see you later."

I curled up on the bed in the darkened room and stared at nothing for a long time.

Dominic watched Beth turn back into the parking lot. She got out of her car and ran to the building. He followed her, taking his time. He quietly opened her door and stepped inside. Seeing the devastation he'd wrought renewed his fury. Mouth set in a hard line, he stalked toward her bedroom.

She was crouched on the floor trying to piece together the pictures he'd shredded. She jumped when he said, "You did it again."

Still she kept trying to put the picture of Rush back together even as she stood to face him. Her expression was wracked with angst and regret—but only because he'd found out. "Peter, listen—"

"No, you listen to me. You said you wouldn't do this again. You promised!" He grabbed her arm, tore the pieces from her hand, and flung them away. "I *knew* it! I knew something was wrong. It all reminded me of the last time. Gary," he bit out the word. "And because of your obsession with him, that woman died. You jeopardized everything for your obsession—again."

He started to walk away, and she pulled at him. "No, it's different this time. I saw Rush first! I didn't fall in love with him because of the con. He walked into that bar and I saw him, and gawd, I felt a zing. I said something to Jonna about him, and then he came over to talk to us. To me. She came on to him, flirting and standing close to him. She stole him from me. I was supposed to have her life. Don't you see? I was supposed to be his wife, living in that loft, sleeping in his bed." She was breathless, her eyes red and wet, trying to convince him. "So you set this up because you wanted him."

"Yes. No. I wanted their marriage to disintegrate. I thought it would, since they'd gotten married so fast. Then I got a job at Rush's company so I could be close to him, knowing he'd finally see me."

"But he didn't," Dominic said with a sneer.

The agony of that was clear in her expression. "Then I saw that working with AngelForce would help us." She stroked his arm. "I could meet marks there. And that's all I was thinking, until . . . until Jonna started the blog. It meant there was a weak link in her marriage, so I thought I could make this work for both of us. You could seduce Jonna, blackmail her, and we'd get money, just like always. And I'd get Rush."

"You told him about the blog."

"So he'd know she was cheating. See, it was supposed to work out beautifully. She'd pay us, but he'd find out anyway and divorce her."

He pulled away from her and walked into the living room. "But it didn't work. She wouldn't cheat, and then they got closer."

She followed him. "You failed at seducing her."

She was trying to push blame onto him, even now. "Because she loves her husband." He spun around. "You failed, too. You failed at making him love you."

He might as well have stabbed her. She slapped her

hand over her stomach and winced. "He does love me; he just doesn't know it yet. Peter—Dominic, you have to understand. I love him. It's not just a sex thing; it's not like going to bed with some guy I hardly know. He's beautiful and sexy and mysterious—"

"And rich."

"I don't even care about that. See, that's how bad it is. Or how good it is. I want him so bad it aches everywhere." She ran her hands over her shoulders and down her arms. "It hurts all the time. Seeing him every day, only being able to touch him casually . . . just a graze of fabric, an 'accidental' brush." She was staring at her hand, imagining just such a touch. Her voice dropped to a whisper. "The way he smells . . . I bought his cologne so I could smell him all night. I dream about him. I dream that he's touching me, that we're making love on his desk. He tells me he never loved Jonna, that he wanted me, but she cast some sort of spell on him. Now it's broken, and he sees that I was the one he wanted all along."

She looked up at him finally. "I know you don't understand what I feel for him. You're mad because I didn't tell you. But I wanted the con to go through. Even afterward, when Rush and I are together, we can still do our cons. We'll still be a team."

Dominic knew better. Beth would have to cut him out of her life; she couldn't afford for Rush to ever see him. She had already chosen Rush over him. He watched her sink to the arm of the couch, holding on to his hand, pleading with him.

She was wrong. He did understand that kind of obsession. As pitiful as she looked to him now, groveling, all of her power melted, he saw himself, too. But his devotion had been stretched by her affair with Gary. Now it was broken. Watching her cling to her illusions about how Rush felt about her, Dominic saw her as weak. She would never hold sway over him again. He was the powerful one. He would conclude his own deal, giving Beth half of the fifty thousand. And he would do as he pleased without worrying about her criticizing him. He could do whatever he wanted with Jonna. Make her afraid. Make her dead.

"Dom," she whined, snapping him out of his thoughts. "We're still together. We're still a team, right?"

He smiled. He'd mastered every kind of smile during his cons. This one would fool even a pro. Even Beth. "Yeah. Sure."

With a breath of relief, she kissed him. He let her seduce him, knowing that it was another man she wanted. He took of her just as she'd been taking of him all these years. She gave him her body as a token, a carrot to keep him going. Now he would do the same. Someday he would hurt her as she had hurt him.

A thought came to him. He smiled. He knew just how he could do it.

Beth watched as Peter got dressed and left instead of snoozing. Okay, he was angry. She'd tried to keep the truth from him as long as possible, but she knew he'd find out eventually. It would have been better if she could have played it that Rush had turned to her in his time of need and things had progressed from there. This had been so much uglier.

But it was over. Peter had accepted it, if reluctantly. It was a relief.

She went into her bedroom and whimpered at the sight of the torn pictures. Some of them were on her digital camera, taken during dinners and parties over the past two years. The picture she'd tried to put back together was one of her and Rush, taken by Jonna. Beth didn't have the image anywhere else. When she looked at that picture, she imagined that she and Rush were the couple and that Jonna was the third wheel.

All those agonizing months, Beth had waited patiently, then fed Jonna suspicions based on truths. Kirsten, after all, *was* in contact with the company. Rush *had* looked at Beth in that certain way while they were in the conference room. She had seen the promise of their future in his eyes, felt it when their hands touched.

She packed some of her things and walked to the door. The place was a mess. Peter had had a temper tantrum. She was glad she hadn't been here. His violent streak was a weak link that worried her. So was his fascination with scaring Jonna. Beth looked at her arm, where he'd put a mark on her. A shiver traveled across her skin. She'd lost control of him. Even when she'd let him have sex with her, he hadn't looked grateful and sated.

Right now he was a wild card who could screw up everything. She wouldn't need him anymore when she and Rush were together. He would take care of her, buy her beautiful things. They would work together, and everyone would respect and envy her. She would get him to open up as Jonna never did. That was the most tantalizing thing: Jonna never really had him. Where she had failed, Beth would not.

She drove back to the loft, intending to shed her coat and luxuriate in the home that would someday be hers. She would strip out of her clothes and snuggle into Rush's bed. That night she'd spent with Jonna had been an unexpected treat, thanks to Peter. Beth had breathed Rush's scent on his pillow all night, which made it easy to dream about him being there, holding her. She'd had to sleep naked, to get as close as possible to the sheets his body had slept on. She'd worn his robe for the same reason. Soon she would be lying next to him every night. She'd be brushing her teeth at the adjacent sink every morning. She would make love with him in that big, jetted tub.

That Jonna had had that pleasure for the last year and a half tore at Beth. It had been hell pretending to be Jonna's friend, listening to her talk about her marriage. Though she rarely mentioned her and Rush's love life, Beth tortured herself by imagining it. When Jonna told Beth that Rush had become more amorous, rather than drifting further away, Beth had been incensed. She'd relived the rage that had consumed her when Gary had told her, at a ritzy restaurant no less, that he wanted to try to get back together with his wife.

Beth had felt the sting of betrayal that went all the way back to her birth father's abandonment. She'd stalked Gary. Everywhere he went, there she was. If he saw her enough, he'd realize it was her that he wanted. It hadn't worked. He became angry, threatening to get a restraining order. And every night she imagined him making love to his wife, a woman who had to be gloating that she'd won.

As if that weren't bad enough, several months later his wife spotted Beth with Peter. She had no business being in that part of town, but there she'd been, gaping at them, her mind putting the pieces together: Beth, her former friend and then husband's lover, with the man who had seduced and blackmailed her. She'd turned and walked in the other direction, eager to tell Gary everything. They probably would have gone to the police. Beth had followed her.

Large vehicles were the perfect weapon. It had been raining, a cold, miserable day. They'd been standing at a street crossing, waiting for the light. The moment she turned to check on the light, Beth tripped her, sending hcr careening into the path of a truck. In the confusion and ensuing horror, Beth had disappeared.

Problem solved. Revenge served.

Soon her problem here would be solved, too. As Beth began to get out of the car, a terrible realization hit her: Jonna hadn't given her the spare key. She couldn't get into the loft. After allowing herself a small temper tantrum, she called Jonna's cell phone. No answer. Then she called the hotel, but the desk clerk said he had no record of Jonna being there. Had she changed her mind and stayed elsewhere?

"Dammit, Jonna! If it takes me until my last breath, you're going to pay for messing everything up."

Beth had lied to Peter. Watching her adversary lying in a puddle of blood and mud while people frantically tried to help her *had* given Beth satisfaction. She'd bested her enemy. Jonna had become Beth's enemy, too, first by stealing her chance at Rush and then by not co-operating. With Jonna gone and Beth in a position to continue playing her and Rush until they got divorced, her dream should come true this time.

And if it didn't? Then Beth would kill Jonna, too. Successful, beautiful Jonna who had stolen Beth's happiness . . . yes, she would enjoy watching Jonna take her last breath.

CHAPTER THIRTY-FIVE

Late in the hours of Monday night, a dreadful realization wrenched me from sleep: I hadn't given Beth the key to the loft so she could feed the fish. We'd gotten distracted by the break-in. I pulled myself from bed and dressed, visions of Stevie Ray floating at the water's surface. Though they were Rush's fish, I still couldn't let them die. None of this was their fault.

I looked out the window. It was dark, but the emerging full moon brightened the clear sky. Dominic would have no reason to be hanging around the loft at this hour. He would have already surmised that I wasn't there. I'd made so many turns and side trips getting here, I couldn't imagine that he'd been able to follow me.

I still looked around as a valet retrieved my car, and I watched the traffic behind me as I drove to the loft. I parked directly in front of our door. I wouldn't be more than a few minutes. I slid my key into the lock and stepped inside. The light was on in the aquarium, illuminating the otherwise dark room. I could see the fish moving around. I let out a breath of relief. Took it back.

I hadn't turned on the aquarium light.

I heard a sound, like someone sucking in a gasp of air. I saw movement from the kitchen. I looked up, my heart beating in my throat. Rush stood in the dimly lit kitchen looking at me. His black shirt was unbuttoned and hanging loose over his waistband. His face was shadowed by stubble. Even in the shadows I noticed something different about his face, but before I could try to figure it out, he turned back into the kitchen.

Turn. Run to the door. Leave. These were the words of logic. But I didn't. Couldn't. It wasn't logic but instinct that drove me toward him. He was standing at the sink, his hands braced on the counter, facing the stone backsplash.

"What are you doing back so soon?" I asked, trying to sound casual, as though coming home at four in the morning was normal.

He bowed his head, and his voice was tight when he said, "Hadden died."

His words hit me in the chest like bags of flour. Hope gone. A life gone. I felt tears well up, but I pushed them back. I had to set what that did to me aside. I had to push the pain way down inside me. "That's why you came back?"

He nodded, still facing away from me. His wide shoulders were hunched, his fingers tensed on the steel counter.

He'd cut his important trip short, risking his deal, because of Hadden's death. Possibly cut his alibi trip short. No, he wouldn't have done that. He couldn't have afforded to come back and find me dead too soon. Unless he'd called Dominic off. Would a man in the process of having his wife killed hurry home because a friend died? I stepped closer, my body tense, my heart racing. His shoulders trembled.

I stepped closer still and then beside him. "Rush?"

He turned his head away, but the light on the hood caught a trace of moisture on his lower lashes. My throat tightened.

I pulled at his arm to get him to look at me. When he wouldn't, I heard tears in my own voice when I said, "No, don't hide. Look at me. Please," I added hoarsely.

With a deep breath, he turned. The moisture and agony in his eyes twisted my stomach.

"You're crying," I whispered.

"He was . . . like a brother." Rush wiped his eyes with the back of his hand. "You're crying, too."

I was. Hot tears dripped down my cheeks. I sniffed and wiped them with my fingers.

To see Rush—strong, closed—with tears in his eyes shattered the hardness around my heart. His chest swelled as he took a deep, halting breath—the sound I'd heard when I'd come in. He wasn't trying to hide his grief from me anymore. I saw it on his face. I'd never seen him so open, except for that night I woke and found him watching me.

Stop! I couldn't believe I was feeling drawn—no, sucked—into the promise of what we could have. Not now. Not after everything I knew. I took the same kind of halting breath and walked out of the kitchen.

I paused near the aquarium. What did I do now?

"You're leaving me?" he asked from the kitchen doorway. When I turned my head, he said, "Is that what your message meant?"

"I want"—another breath—"a divorce."

His shoulders slackened. I expected anger. Surprise. I swore I saw relief before he rubbed his hand over his face. His fingers circled his eyes and remained on the bridge of his nose. After a moment he dropped his arm and slid his hands into his pockets. "Why did you come back?"

I nodded toward the aquarium. "To feed the fish."

His mouth quirked in what looked like a smile in the light from the aquarium. Had to be a trick of the light. He walked closer and leaned against the bar. Yes, he was smiling. Watching the fish and faintly *smiling.* Then he shifted his gaze to me again, and I felt as though he'd pulled out the rug from beneath me and sent me tumbling.

"You packed all your clothes," he said. "Your computer, files." He tilted his head. "But you didn't take the artwork. Electronics. Or any money from our accounts."

"Why would I? I don't care about any of that." I swallowed hard. "I leave you and that's what you're concerned about—your valuables?" Of course, that was why he'd wanted me dead instead of divorcing me. "I don't want anything, Rush. You can have it all."

His smile was beautiful and so damned odd and inappropriate. Okay, he's gone mad. I should get the hell out of there. *Go, go, go!* My body tensed but wouldn't move. Something held me there and forced images of those days when we'd been so close to connecting into my brain: the shower, the romantic dinner he'd had me make, and what Waldo Skeever had told me. My heart told me that was real. It had been telling me that all along. So I didn't run. I shored my shoulders and asked, "What's so damned funny?"

"I'm not laughing." He moved closer. "I'm relieved."

I was confused. "That I didn't take your things? Or that I asked for a divorce and don't want anything from you?"

He reached out and touched a tendril of hair near my cheek. "I'm relieved that the wife who was supposedly trying to kill me for my money took nothing. That she came back so our fish wouldn't starve." He put his palm to my cheek, touching me as though it were the first time, with a sense of awe. "That she proved my instincts were right."

I stepped back but had to hold on to the ledge for balance. My brain was spinning, trying to make sense of his words. "What are you talking about? *Me?* Trying to . . . kill *you?*"

"Dominic contacted me last week, told me that you two were having an affair. That you hired him to kill me. He even had your charm watch, something you'd supposedly given him."

I stumbled back, coming to sit on the back of one of the chairs. "Oh . . . my . . . God."

"He was supposed to play at being your stalker, so obsessed with you that he would kill me. And you *were* acting spooked. Except that you hadn't told me about a stalker. For double what you were supposedly paying him, he offered to stall so I could file for a divorce. There was no reason to have me killed unless you wanted the money. Except you've never been interested in money. Then you started acting strange, shutting me out. Soon after that Hadden was in the hospital, Beth moved in, and everything went to hell." I could see that hell on his face. "But I still couldn't believe you were that kind of person. In fact, I was so sure I tested Dominic when we met Friday, when I was supposed to give him a decision. I told him I'd double his price if he'd kill you."

That sent me spinning again.

He continued before I could manage to say something. "Because he was completely flustered I knew he had no intention of murdering anyone. What I didn't know was exactly how you were connected to him. I knew you had met him a couple of times. How much was true? I needed to talk to you alone, but between Beth's presence and you avoiding me, I couldn't manage it." His voice grew softer, along with his expression. "Then I come home early from my trip and find your things cleared out. Now here you are, asking for a divorce. Not the actions of a woman who wants her husband killed."

I was blind with my tears. He'd talked about trusting his instincts. Now I had to trust mine—what I suspected to be true versus what I felt. What I felt was the same relief he'd spoken of. What I needed was to trust him as I'd never trusted him before. Throughout our marriage we'd only communicated with our bodies, mistaking sex for intimacy. Now it was time to use our mouths.

"I did flirt with Dominic," I began with a hoarse whisper. "But we never had an affair. After I broke off our communication, he stalked me." I stifled a sob. "And then Beth saw you with him at O'Malley's. She sent me a picture from her cell phone. I . . . I didn't know what to make of it. Beth said, suggested, that you had hired him to punish me for the blog. Maybe even have me killed. Then he came out and said you hired him to kill me."

"Hell." Rush pulled me hard against him, kissing the top of my head.

The feeling of being in his arms overwhelmed me. I had to swim to the surface to sort through my thoughts. "He was playing both of us. But why?"

"The money. He wanted fifty thousand dollars to stall me."

"If that's all it's about, why stalk me?" But I already knew the answer. "Because he likes it."

Rush tilted my face up to him. The water's reflection played off his features. "When I read that . . ." He shook his head, his eyes closed. "I didn't see your post about the stalking until I came back from the first trip to New York. Right before Dominic called. It made me crazy, Jonna, reading that and not being able to do anything. Then after what Dominic told me, I wasn't sure if it was true."

"I was going to tell you everything that night. Then Beth sent me that picture, and I couldn't trust you, either. And . . . Hadden had called me earlier, telling me that you were tracking my movements. It made sense, in a way, that you were telling Dominic where to find me. He always seemed to know where I was, when you were out of town. He had keys to the loft and my shop."

"Hadden." He took a deep breath, watching the red and white Sexy Shrimp picking its way across the coral, holding its tail straight up in the way that gave it its name. "He found the software on my computer and figured out I was tracking you. That was the last time we spoke. I told him to mind his own damned business."

I could see that wracked him. "Because you knew he'd admitted having feelings for me. Because you read my blog." That washed over me. He'd read my private thoughts, my deepest desires, and the false facade of Montene. He'd known everything.

"It threw me, knowing my business partner, my best friend, wanted my wife. Especially after having seen you with him at lunch. I didn't know who to trust after that."

"He never meant to tell me. He—well, you already know what I said about that. How did you find out about the blog?"

"Beth told me."

If he'd slapped me I couldn't have been more surprised. I would have called him a liar, but I saw the truth of it in his eyes. Even so, I still uttered, "I can't believe it."

"I felt you slipping away from me, and I didn't know how to bring you back. So I asked her what was going on with you. It was a bad idea all the way around. She insinuated herself into my life after that, treating me as though we were confidants. She told me about your blog and that you were . . . flirting with a man. With Dominic. That's why I put the tracker on your car. If you wanted to see this guy . . ." He banged his palm on the bar, anger on his face. "If that's what you wanted, I couldn't stop you. But I could make sure you were safe. You don't know what crazies are out there. Forget I said that. You sure as hell do."

I once again felt as though I'd been sucker punched. I had to lean against the bar stool. "Beth told you," I repeated.

"She acted like she was trying to help."

She had seized on two things to open a wedge between Rush and me, two things that created, as she liked to say, a weak link: my insecurity in my marriage and my blog.

"It was in the conference room, right? That you talked to her?"

"Yeah, why?"

When Rush had supposedly felt her out, figuratively speaking. I shook my head. My head hurt thinking about it. I slumped onto the stool.

He leaned against the ledge next to me, his head tilted in thought. "Beth suggested I might have hired Dominic to kill you?" I nodded. "Funny, she asked about my meeting with Dominic, the same one she told you about. When I told her what Dominic had said, she was afraid for me. Told me how you'd shut her out and been acting strange. How you were really into money. She urged me to file for divorce."

"She told me to get out of here, that you were probably going to have Dominic kill me while you were out of town so you'd have an alibi."

We stared at each other for a few moments, pieces clicking. Suspicions lining up. Beth playing us against each other. She'd told me she was sticking close to Rush to keep an eye on him, all the while going along with his belief that I was plotting to have him killed.

"Did you start to file for a divorce?" I asked in a quivery voice.

He shook his head. "Did you?"

"No." I had been duped. "But why?" I said. "That's what I don't understand. Why?"

"Because she's involved in this. With Dominic."

"I heard him on the phone accusing someone of being out of control." I came to my feet. "I thought it might be you. I'm sorry."

He pulled me close, his hand rubbing the back of my head. "It's okay. We didn't know each other. That was my fault."

"It was my fault, too." Someday I would tell him about the secrets I'd had to hold, how I'd protected myself from getting hurt by believing the worst. But not now. I just wanted him to hold me. I needed to feel his strength, the solidity of his body against mine.

He moved back, searching my face. This time not for the truth, as I realized he'd done when he'd kissed me good-bye. "Did he hurt you?"

I hadn't posted about his last assault. I still felt the sting of the cut on my palm. "No," I lied.

"He won't hurt you again."

I felt a little sob at those words, at feeling safe. "I'm sorry that I hurt you. That you had to read about my feelings on some Web site."

I could tell that it *had* hurt him. "You told strangers things you never told me."

"I know. The blog was a way to safely connect to other people." I reached out to him now, running the back of my hand across the stubble on his cheek. "I'd wondered if you'd read it . . . when you were acting so possessive. When you seduced me by the bar. But I thought you'd be angry and hurt, and you never acted that way."

"At first I was both. But the more I read, the more I got to know you. I got to know who you really were, what you wanted. All the things you never told me. You were funny and sweet and warm. I fell in love with you all over again."

I kissed him the same hard, possessive way he'd kissed me. "So did I. Catching you watching me sleep. The dinner."

"And all that time this son of a bitch was stalking you." His fingers tightened on my back. "Now we have to figure out how to handle him. And Beth."

We. The word was comforting. Yet it also heaped guilt onto my shoulders. "It's my problem. I did this. I agreed to meet Dominic. Now I've got to fix it."

Rush took my chin in his hands, making me look at him. "It's our problem. We're in this together now."

I wasn't exactly comforted. I remembered what happened the last time I thought I had an ally—Hadden had been killed. Still, I nodded.

"But no more secrets."

"No," I readily agreed. "Never."

"Good. Because I'll be meeting Dominic soon. He's got proof that you hired him to kill me. I can't wait."

CHAPTER THIRTY-SIX

Everyone was surprised when Rush arrived at the office Tuesday morning.

"Did the deal go through that fast?" his marketing director asked.

"I need to talk to everyone." He waited until they gathered in the open area where the three secretarial desks sat. He made a point not to look at Beth. He was tired, punch-drunk, and he didn't think he could hide his rage at her. "Hadden died yesterday. That's why I came back early."

Several employees acted shocked, as though they hadn't been expecting it at all. He had been dreading it since he'd first gotten the news, though the reality still rocked him.

"The memorial service is tomorrow. The details haven't been ironed out yet, but I'll make sure Mona gets the word to all of you as soon as possible. The offices will be closed today and tomorrow."

He couldn't bear to hear the crying, so he went back to his office. On his way, he paused near Beth. "See me when everyone's gone."

Twenty minutes passed before she was able to come. He was staring at his computer screen, not having to fake the agony on his face. "I should have asked Mona to stay. Sending out these notices is hell."

"I'll do it," Beth said, closing the door behind her. "I'll take care of anything you want." She took a ragged breath. "Oh, Rush. It's just awful." He stayed behind his desk, but she came over and hugged him anyway. He heard her sobs, but when she looked at him, her eyes were dry. Her arms encircled him, and he fought the clawing urge to shove her away.

He set his elbow on his desk, kneading the bridge of his nose. The movement forced her to back away. "This, on top of everything else . . . it's too much."

She knelt down next to him and took the opportunity to rub his arm. "I'm so sorry, sweetheart."

"I'm meeting with Dominic this afternoon. He says he has a recording of Jonna talking about having me killed. If it sounds real, I'm going to give him the money." He nodded toward a black duffel bag next to his chair. "And file for a divorce. The odd thing is, Jonna's gone. She left a message about going away for a while."

"She's up to something. We've still got to be careful."

We. Such a different meaning from the *we* they'd talked about last night. "But that's the thing I never understood. If she was concocting this whole stalker thing, why did she never tell me? Why did she leave? It would have worked better if she'd stuck around playing the perfect wife."

It was the flaw in Beth's plan, one that Dominic couldn't explain away, either. Rush let her sweat it out. "I don't know, Rush. I don't know what she's thinking. Maybe she'll blame it on her stalker, saying she left to protect you and then it ended up badly anyway."

Oh, Beth was good at coming up with an answer. She was good at acting, too, everything but producing real tears. It made him wary. He stood and took his coat off the rack in the corner.

She hugged him again. "I'm so glad you're going to take care of this. That you'll be safe."

Just as he'd studied Jonna, at first trying to figure out if she was having an affair and then if she was trying to have him killed, he studied Beth. Her face had a glow. Her green eyes sparkled. She was happy that her plan was moving forward. It seemed to be all she cared about.

"Thanks for taking care of those e-mails. There's a list next to the computer. Just eight or so. You can cut and paste the letter."

"Anything, Rush."

He ducked his head, grabbed the bag, and walked out. Downstairs, he stepped into the conference room he'd asked to borrow from the company that occupied the space. Jonna sat near a cell phone that was sitting on the table, her face taut with anger. She'd heard everything. He took a chair next to her, squeezing her hand. They listened to shuffling noises, keys tapping. He'd left a cell phone on the bookshelf with the line open to Jonna's phone.

A few minutes later Beth's voice: "Peter . . . sorry, *Dominic*. Good news. He's going to pay!" Silence as Dominic obviously spoke. "Yes, and I get what I want, too. He's going to file for divorce." Her voice grew farther away, perhaps as she checked to make sure no one had come back into the office. "Look, you're going to have to get over that attitude of yours."

She walked closer to the cell phone. "I'll always love you. We're family, for God's sake. But the way I feel about Rush . . . it's different. It's overpowering. I want to breathe him, eat him up, become part of him. I can't even explain it. Maybe it's like . . . what you said about making Jonna afraid. Maybe it's like that feeling, if that makes it clearer for you. Except that this is pure. It's right." Her voice grew harsher. "It doesn't matter how it came to be. It's going to work. He loves me. He just needed the opportunity. And now I've made that opportunity. Look, we'll talk after your meeting. Call me."

Rush had been looking at Jonna through the whole call. Her mouth had slowly opened as the truth—and more—hit home. She disconnected the call. "She's obsessed . . . with you."

He'd felt his stomach twist as Beth had talked about him. "She thinks I love her." It explained the uncomfortable feeling he'd always had when she was around. It explained why she touched him and moved into his space.

"She sometimes kidded that she saw you first. That night at the hotel bar."

"I only saw you."

Her smile was brief. "A week or so ago when we had lunch, she got . . . ugly. Like she was jealous of all the attention I was getting. Like I wanted a stalker! Like I wanted my husband's best friend to admit he had feelings for me. Like I wanted my blog to become so damned popular. I could hear her bitterness when she said I still had my gorgeous, rich husband."

Her phone chirped. Jonna looked at the display. Beth was calling.

Rush nodded.

"I don't think I can talk to her." Jonna took a deep breath and did it anyway. "Hey."

"Rush is back," Beth said over the speaker. "He came back early because Hadden died. . . . Jonna, are you there?" she asked as Jonna stared at the phone.

"Yes, sorry. I'm just . . . trying to take it all in."

"Don't go near the loft. And it's probably better if you don't go to Hadden's memorial service. I'll make an excuse for you. Stay safe. I'll let you know what's going on. I've got to go, honey."

Jonna's face reddened. Now there was no doubt. After

she disconnected, Jonna said, "I trusted her. All this time, I trusted her, and she was just playing the part of best friend to get to you. To con us."

He pulled her against him, where her cheek rested against his chest. "Don't blame yourself for not seeing through her. She was good. You're not cynical enough to have even considered the truth."

"And now she wants me to miss Hadden's service. Well, I'm not." She put her hand against his shoulder. "Not even if my evil husband's going to be there."

"As long as we make sure Dominic isn't around."

"She called him Peter. Said they were family."

"Yeah. Have you ever heard her mention him?"

"No. She only mentioned her half sister and her parents." She looked up at him. "How am I going to face her, knowing what I know? How did you do it?"

"It wasn't easy. I wanted to throttle her. I couldn't let myself think about what she'd done to you. What she tried to do to us." He kissed Jonna's temple, remembering again how close he'd come to losing her.

"When are you meeting Dominic?"

He looked at his watch. "I have to go."

"Don't forget to leave your cell phone on."

That part of the plan had been her idea. Hadden's idea, actually. Even though Hadden had revealed his feelings for Jonna, he'd at least assured her that Rush hadn't been cheating. Hadden had tried to help Jonna. Rush was grateful for that.

Rush walked out of the building and headed to O'Malley's. Though only a block south, Boylston was a street that catered more to the working class. Dominic was waiting, looking a little too eager. Rush's fingers curled into fists. He knew Jonna was downplaying what Dominic had done to her. He had to keep his cool and not choke the guy right there at the pub.

Beth had tried to drive a wedge between Rush and

Jonna. Now they would drive a wedge between Dominic and Beth. From what Jonna had overheard of his phone conversation and what they'd just heard, there was already tension in Dominic and Beth's relationship. Rush was going to compound it.

Dominic's gaze was on the duffel bag that Rush set on the bench seat next to him. "Let's hear it," he said as soon as he sat down.

The pub was noisy enough to drown out the sound of the recording, but it also made it hard to hear what the woman—supposedly Jonna—was saying.

"I hate him!" That sounded like Jonna's voice, though the first two words were a millisecond too close together. Rush knew what Jonna had said when the son of a bitch had pinned her to the table. Damn, he wanted to hurt Dominic. He had to take several deep breaths to calm himself.

"I want him dead," the woman said, though she sounded different now. "Get it over with already. Then the loft, the money, everything will be mine."

"You're sure?" Dominic's voice said.

"Positive. Make it happen and make it quick."

Dominic stopped the recording and waited.

"I want the recording. I need to study it."

"No way. You'll take it to the police, and I'll get busted for agreeing to a murder for hire. I'll play it again."

Rush figured that would be his answer.

Dominic held it up to Rush's ear. The woman saying the last part did sound a bit like Jonna, but he knew it wasn't. He suspected it was Beth. After he listened for a third time, Dominic pulled the recorder away and tucked it into his pocket. "Well?"

"I don't think so." Rush grabbed the bag and scooted out of the booth.

"What?" Dominic followed him out of the restaurant. "She's trying to kill you. Don't you get that, man?"

"I'll take my chances."

On the way to the garage, where Jonna would be waiting in the car for him, he pitched the duffel bag filled with stacks of paper. Beth and Dominic weren't the only ones who could play.

CHAPTER THIRTY-SEVEN

Beth only had to wait twenty minutes before Peter rang in. As soon as she answered, he said, "No deal."

"What do you mean, 'no deal'?"

"He didn't pay. I don't know if he didn't buy the recording or what. All he said was, 'I don't think so,' and left."

"Don't lie to me. I saw Rush walk out of here with a duffel bag full of money. The recording was good. Not the best, granted, but good enough to convince him. He said he was going to pay."

"Beth, I'm telling you, he walked."

"Okay." She took a deep breath to catch her balance. "I'll talk to him."

When Rush answered his cell phone, she said, "It's Beth. I was worried about you. How did it go?"

He let out an agonized breath. "I'm fifty thousand dollars poorer, but I don't have to worry about this schmuck offing me."

"I'm sorry," she said, and meaning it. But not only for Rush. "Are you all right?"

"Fine." He didn't sound fine. He sounded tense and edgy. "Considering."

"I'll talk to you soon." Then she dialed Peter again,

anger and confusion building inside her. "He said he paid you."

"He's lying."

"Someone's lying."

"Oh, sure, you're going to believe lover boy over me?"

"Why would he lie, Peter? What reason could he possibly have?"

"Why would I lie?"

"Because you want to punish me for loving Rush."

"Oh, that's priceless. You lie to me and then accuse me of lying. Well, think what you want. I don't care. You'd better get down on your hands and knees and beg him to marry you. We're over."

She hung up, her jaw rigid with anger. It wasn't the money, not really. Once she and Rush were married, she wouldn't have to worry about money again. It was the principle.

She felt an odd emptiness at losing Peter. *Forget about him,* she told herself. Now Rush would be the most important person in her life. He would be everything. He already was.

"Red peppers: check. Garlic: check. Maybe a pinch more, pinch, pinch, pinch."

Rush watched Jonna fix dinner, lost in a moment from the past. For now he could forget what Beth and Dominic had done to them, forget the way his chest had ached when Jonna told him she wanted a divorce. Those words, though, had been his ultimate confirmation of everything he'd believed.

She couldn't seem to stop looking at him, either. He felt the same electricity between them that had always been there, but now there was so much more. They had almost lost each other, and now they were closer than ever. As she stirred the tortellinis around in the sauté pan, she said, "So what do we do next?"

"We need to find proof that Beth and Dominic are working together. Maybe Dominic will get in touch with me again. He's not going to let fifty thousand go that easily."

"Gary! Beth's ex-husband. I ran into him when I was catering the Women's Club dinner last week. He recognized me from a couple of times when I was with Beth and he was stalking her. Except, according to him, he wasn't stalking her; she was stalking him. I thought he was just being surly, drunk, and bitter. Maybe there's more to it. He said something about deserving it for messing with his wife's friend. We're not the first ones they've done this to, I bet. I know he hangs around the sports bar at the hotel. We'll track him down."

"Good idea."

Rush walked up behind her, sliding his arms around her waist and nuzzling her neck. "How hungry are you . . . exactly?"

She closed her eyes and leaned back against him. "Maybe not so much. What do you have in mind?"

"I recall reading that you were intrigued by the thought of bondage. I've got some silk ties we could use."

Her body stiffened, and she turned to face him. Her cheeks were stained pink. "We agreed not to keep secrets from each other, right?"

"Right."

"Well, here's one. I'm not really Montene. I mean, I am. But I'm not. Some of that stuff I kind of went along with, because I didn't want to seem prudish. I liked seeming adventurous online, but in real life . . ." She shook her head. "The *thing,* for instance."

"The thing?"

"That getup from House of Pleasure. Well, you probably know that Dominic bought it." He nodded. "That's why you tore it off me, isn't it?" He nodded again, not looking in the least bit sheepish. "So you also know that I never—he never saw it on me. And the vibrator. I'd never used it."

That made him smile, despite himself. "Really?"

"Really. I'd only worked up the nerve to use it on my feet. I don't know, maybe it's the midwestern upbringing. It just wasn't me."

He pulled her hips against his. "*I* thought it was."

She ducked her head, but he could see her shy smile. God, he loved this woman.

"It was much more fun with you."

"But being tied up . . ."

She shook her head, and he thought he saw a shadow cross her expression. "Something else I didn't tell you, but only because I didn't want you to get too upset. The night Dominic broke into my shop and tried to get me to say how much I hated you . . . he didn't just pin me to the table. He tied me up. He was using everything from my blog, things I said I liked and things I admitted I was afraid of."

"Son of a bitch." He held her so tight he was probably squishing her.

She leaned back and looked up at him. "But if you want to give it a try . . ."

"Why don't you tie me up instead?"

She smiled and was just about to say something when the doorbell rang. "Who could that be?"

He stalked toward the door, his hands fisted. "I hope it's Dominic."

She remained behind while he peered out the front window. "Beth," he whispered.

"Damn. What's she doing here?"

Jonna ran up the stairs as he called, "Hold on a minute!"

As far as Beth knew, Jonna was still at the hotel. They needed to keep up the charade. He opened the door, finding Beth wearing a mink fur coat and a smile. On the stoop were two bags. His chest sank; he knew what was coming.

She picked up her bags and walked in as though she'd been invited. "While you were gone I stayed with my parents. But that guy, he's still out there. And . . . and I didn't tell you before, but I'm pretty sure it was Dominic who broke into my apartment. When Jonna and I went over on Sunday he'd broken in again and trashed the place." She put an Oscar-quality tremble in her voice. "I can't stay there."

"Let me get you a hotel room, then. I just want to be alone right now. I've got a lot on my mind."

"That's the other reason I came back." She shrugged out of her coat and tossed it onto the back of a chair. "I know you think you want to be alone, but you don't. You need someone who can feel the pain with you. Someone who knows what you're going through. With Jonna and with Hadden." She put her arms around him. "Let me comfort you."

He stepped out of her embrace. "Beth, I really—"

She grabbed his arms. "I know how you shut Jonna out, but I'm not going to let you shut me out. You need me. You may not know it, but you do." She lifted her chin, sniffing the air. "I was going to cook you dinner, but I see you've already started." She walked to the kitchen. "Let me help. I'm famished."

He glanced upstairs, where Jonna was pressed against the wall peering down. She gave him a helpless shrug. If he forced Beth to leave—and he could see it would have to be forceful—she'd wonder why. Her reasons for being there would ring true if he didn't know the truth.

"See," she said, lifting the wine- and highball glasses. "Mixing alcohols. Drinking isn't going to solve your problems. Only a good meal and company will." She took the pan that Jonna had set aside when the doorbell rang and put it back on the cooktop. "You sit. I'll take care of everything."

He mentally uttered every curse word he could think of while he relented to Beth's persistence. At least she hadn't been suspicious about why he'd had two different types of drinks going. But now Jonna was trapped upstairs. He had to get food up to her without Beth noticing. He had to play tonight very carefully. Making her pay for what she'd done would depend on his playing it cool and not letting his anger show.

And he had every intention of making her pay.

CHAPTER THIRTY-EIGHT

The previous evening had been hell. I'd had to listen as Beth laughed and soothed and played the caring friend. As if that weren't bad enough, I had to smell the dinner I'd been cooking. Rush had managed to bring some up while Beth settled into the downstairs bathroom; he'd insisted that she stay in the family room. Then he'd retired early, citing a headache. We'd had to whisper and hold down the sounds of our lovemaking. Beth had spoiled our original plans, but she wasn't about to spoil all of our plans.

Now we had the tricky task of getting out of the loft. Once again I was subjected to the scent of food cooking downstairs. Beth, the sweet little homemaker, was making waffles in our waffle maker. I heard Rush say, "I appreciate you making breakfast, but I'm not hungry. I can't warm to the idea of food when Hadden's memorial service is today."

I couldn't imagine how hard it was for him, knowing what she was up to in addition to her obsession with him.

"You really should eat, sweetheart," she said, sounding infuriatingly like his wife.

"Just coffee. I've got a few things to take care of today."

"I can go with you. For moral support," she added.

We'd talked about the possibility of her offering that, and he was prepared. "I'm meeting with Hadden's parents, to talk about his share of AngelForce. It's something I have to do alone. What I need you to do is go into the office and check the messages. I'm sure there are people who haven't been able to find out where the service is being held. Let them know."

I heard the reluctance in her voice when she said, "Sure. Of course."

"As soon as possible," he added.

"Sure. Rush . . . could you please give me a key to the door? Jonna was going to, but she forgot."

"Uh, sure. I'll get one made today."

I knew that wasn't going to happen.

I remained in the bedroom and he worked at his computer while Beth seemed to take forever getting ready. As soon as we saw her car leave the parking lot, we headed out, too.

"This must be what it's like when a man has an affair," he said, furtively leading me to the car.

I smiled, because it was further confirmation, had I needed it, that he'd never cheated on me. I pulled him close for a quick kiss. It was more sobering to think that I did know what it was like to hide things from my spouse. I was thankful I hadn't gone any further with Dominic, for more than one reason.

Once Rush and I settled into the car, my thoughts turned even darker. We were saying good-bye to Hadden today.

"If it weren't for Beth's scheme, Hadden wouldn't have died," I said, staring out the window. "If I hadn't asked him to check on you—"

"Don't go there, babe." He placed his hand over mine. "You couldn't have known what would happen."

But I did blame myself.

We walked into the hotel bar a short time later, and I was disappointed to see someone other than Tony. "Is Tony around?" I asked.

The older man, who was concentrating on taking inventory, didn't even look at us. "Yeah, he's here somewhere."

"Can you find him for us, please?" Rush asked, his polite request tinged with force.

He looked now. "Sure. Hold on a minute."

A few minutes later Tony emerged from the back room, smiling when he saw me and yet puzzled, too. "Hey, how're you doing?"

"I wanted to ask you about the guy who was talking to me that night. You called him Gar. He was drunk and—"

"Hassling you a little, yeah. I gave him a hard time about it when he came in last night."

"Do you know him?"

"Just from his coming in here regular-like. Don't even know his last name."

My shoulders sagged. Rush and I didn't have time to come back night after night in hopes of catching Gary. Beth had kept her last name when they'd married.

"I know he works for a stock brokerage firm," Tony said. "LaSalle, something like that. I've heard the guys he's here with, his coworkers, talking about stock tips and stuff. He gave me a card once, if I was ever interested." He laughed. "Yeah, right. I threw it away."

"That's a big help, Tony. Thanks."

It was noon when Rush and I found LaSalle's office. We decided to get a hot dog at the cart on the corner and watch for Gary to leave for lunch.

Just as we finished our hot dogs, I spotted him stepping outside with two other guys. He looked haggard, dull blond hair mussed, eyes bloodhound droopy and red. Rush and I walked over, catching his attention with our purposeful movements.

He pointed at me, his eyes narrowed. "You *are* her stalking buddy!"

"Gary, I need to talk to you. I'm not stalking you. I'm with my husband, for Pete's sake. We need to talk . . . about Beth."

That made him pause. The two men with him obviously didn't know who Beth was. He told them to go on without him.

"We'll buy you lunch," Rush said, nodding toward a deli. "We can talk while you eat."

I liked the way he gently but definitively led people where he wanted them to go. The confidence he exuded had been one of the strongest attractions when I first saw him. That and the way he moved, his long-legged stride, and the set of his shoulders. Oh, and his bedroom eyes. And his smile . . . yeah, I was in love.

Gary eyed us speculatively as we all stood in line and Rush bought him lunch. We found a table in the back corner. Gary unwrapped his sandwich but didn't attempt to take a bite. "Okay, what's this about?"

I said, "We need to know what happened between you and Beth."

"Why?"

"Tell us and we'll tell you why we want to know," Rush said.

When Gary hesitated, I started. "Beth was friends with your wife. You mentioned that when you saw me in the bar last week."

"Yeah." He was still wary. "For a while. She started going out with us and stuff. And then . . . we got involved. She was very seductive," he quickly added, as though that excused his behavior. "She would tell me things about my wife, Cammie . . . like she was spending a lot of money. Hinted that she was seeing someone. And she was right. I found a withdrawal for fifteen thousand dollars. Cammie had no explanation for that."

Rush and I exchanged a look. Money. "Were you ever approached by a man claiming to be your wife's lover?"

"No. But Beth kept telling me about this guy my wife was seeing. We were having problems, anyway, so that and the money were the final straw. I filed for divorce."

So Dominic hadn't tried to get money out of Gary. He'd gotten money from Gary's wife instead. What was his and Beth's game, and why was it different with us?

"And you married Beth?" I asked when Gary seemed to drift into his thoughts.

"No. Hell, no, though she was pushing for that."

"That's strange. She always implied that you two had gotten married." An ego thing?

"No, we were only dating. After a while I started feeling smothered by her. And the guilt . . ." He rubbed his hand over his face. "The guilt over what I'd done was tremendous. I mean, I'd screwed around with my wife's friend. A guy could go to hell for that. And I did." He tapped the point of his pickle spear against the paper. "I broke it off with Beth and told her I was going back to my wife if she'd have me. Luckily, she did. But that's when the stalking started. Everywhere I went, Beth was there. Leaving cookies on my car. Red roses. She'd send food to my house, my favorites like mushroom and anchovy pizza. It was creepy, like she was insinuating herself into my life. Into our lives."

I went cold all over. The same things Dominic had done. God, Beth had been driving him all along.

"It put a strain on our floundering marriage, but we were determined to make it. We'd both made a mistake, both screwed up. Beth had been right about Cammie having an affair, too. But all that was over."

"The man she'd seen . . . was his name Dominic?"

"No. Sebastian. She never told me his last name. I didn't want to know."

"What about the money that went missing from your

account? Did you ever find out what had happened to it?"

"Yeah. The son of a bitch blackmailed her. Said he'd show me pictures of the two of them if she didn't pay up. He knew that our money was mine, not hers. Figured I'd leave her if I knew about the affair. She paid." His voice went low. "And I left her anyway."

I looked at Rush. Now we knew what Beth and Dominic were up to.

Gary went on. "And you know, I didn't even care about the money. What caused us grief was Beth, always there, haunting us. I changed jobs, and we moved. After about six months we seemed to have lost her, and we were able to work on our relationship. We'd even talked about starting a family." I saw his expression break for a moment. "Only we didn't get a chance to do that."

"What happened?" I asked after a moment.

"She was hit by a truck. She fell into traffic on a rainy day. The driver didn't see her in time. He couldn't stop." Gary sucked in a deep, sudden breath. "She died before I could get to the hospital to say good-bye. Even worse, she was four weeks pregnant. Probably didn't even know it yet."

I grabbed Rush's hand and squeezed it hard. Blood rushed to my face and made my heart beat hard and fast. It was the same way Hadden had died. I didn't want to think it, to consider it, but my mind kept pushing: Could it be a coincidence? Two deaths by vehicle, one woman connecting them?

"Gary"—I could hardly nudge the words out of my tight throat—"we think Beth was in on the con. That maybe she targets women who have wealthy husbands, befriends them. Then she has her partner, Dominic, seduce them. He gets pictures and blackmails them: 'Pay up or I'll show your hubby the pictures. You'll lose everything.' They pay." That explained why Dominic had been so angry when I wouldn't go through with the tryst at the hotel. Why he'd said we *had* to work, that he was feeling pressure. It wasn't his ego at stake, or at least only his ego; it was money. And Beth was undoubtedly pushing him to succeed. When I wouldn't be seduced, she kept driving him to woo me. I remembered how she thought his actions were romantic. They were—to her. That was how her mind worked. She must have taken it as personally as Dominic had when I didn't respond.

When Gary leaned forward, pinching the bridge of his nose, I continued, "Beth has an obsessive personality. She likes to buy things, to spend money, have her nails done. I think she pulled the con on Cammie and then became obsessed with you."

"Oh, God," he said, pushing his sandwich away.

I looked at Rush. Somehow, with just our eyes, we agreed not to take the conjecture to the next step: that Beth might have killed Cammie. Not yet.

"Gary, I think you should be very careful. Beth may be a dangerous person. Before I realized what she was, I mentioned seeing you at the bar. I told her what you said."

He looked up at us. "You think she'd do something to me? Just for saying something to you?"

We both nodded.

"Might be a good time to take a vacation," Rush suggested.

"What about going to the police? They did this to you, too?"

"They tried," I said. "Unfortunately, we need evidence. Did you ever file a restraining order against Beth for stalking you?"

He shook his head. "I figured they'd think I deserved it." Oh yeah, I could understand that.

Rush gave him his card after he'd written his cell

number on it. "We'll be in touch when we know more. Or when we need you to go to the police."

Rush and I said good-bye and returned to my hotel room. Only in the quiet privacy of that elegant room did I allow myself to fall into his arms.

"She killed Hadden," I whispered.

"We don't know that." The way he held me tight, I knew he suspected the same.

"And she's in our home. Obsessed with you. What if she hurts you?"

"I'm not worried about me; I'm worried about you."

"Should we go to the police?"

"I thought about it all the way here. Right now the police don't consider Hadden's death suspicious. If they do"—his expression darkened—"I'll be the prime suspect. The police would know about the blog, so they'd know Hadden had feelings for you. That, as jealous husband, gives me major motive."

"Even without that, how would all this sound?" I dropped down to the bed and lowered my voice, role-playing the detective. " 'And, Mr. Karakosta, where is this supposedly violent, twisted person now?' "

"Living as a guest in my home, sir," he answered, seeing where I was going.

" 'Ah, yeah. Have a nice day. And please check your-self into a mental hospital.' "

He sat down beside me. "We need proof."

"I can't prove that Dominic is stalking me. You can't prove Dominic tried to blackmail you. We can't prove that Beth and Dominic are in this together. We could tie them together, especially if they're related, but what does that prove?"

"If we go to the police and Beth is questioned, she'll know that we know. She'll disappear and never pay for what she's done."

"Even with the connection to the two vehicular deaths, she had no apparent motive to kill Hadden. And it had been six months since she'd stopped stalking Gary, which we can't prove, either."

We both let out a long sigh as we sat in silence for a few minutes. He fell back onto the bed, staring at the ceiling.

"I have an idea," I said as a plan started forming in my head. "What does Beth want?"

"Money."

"That's only a part of it. What she wants is you. So what if we give her what she wants?"

His eyebrows arched up. "What *I* want is to hurt her . . . bad."

"I know, and that's what is going to take some supreme acting on your part. Hear me out. You realize that she is the one for you. She's been your loyal friend through all of this, and maybe you should have seen her rather than me from the beginning. And in fact, you've come to harbor some pretty vile feelings for me since learning about my plot to have you killed. But you couldn't possibly hurt me. That kind of thing isn't in your blood. You do, however, fantasize about it a lot."

"Jonna, I don't like where this is going."

I held up my hand to halt his protests. "So she offers to do your bidding. We think she *does* have that in her blood." I shivered. "She'll be so happy, so grateful that you love her back, I think she'll do it. I'm going to give her some additional incentive. I'll confess that, despite everything, I still hopelessly love you. I want to work things out."

Despite his misgivings, he could see the logic. "But what's the goal? Get her on tape saying she wants to kill you? Thing is, I'll be on tape collaborating with her."

"I thought about that, too. No, we need something

stronger than that so she can't cry entrapment. She's going to have to try to kill me."

He shot up off the bed, driving his hand into his hair. "No way. I'm not putting you in danger."

"We'll figure a way to keep out the danger element. Say you give her a gun with blanks in it. And we tape it. Either I get away or you come onto the scene and we subdue her, depending on how it goes. Then we have our statements and the tape to corroborate our claims."

He frowned. "I don't like it. What if she hurts you?"

"She won't. What else can we do? We've got to get this woman put away, Rush. Once she's arrested, we can go after Dominic, too. I bet he'll turn on her when the heat's on. Maybe we can get them both put away."

I could see how much he wanted that. I could also see the glint of revenge in his eyes. Not the legal kind, either. "There may be another way to take care of them."

"No, doing it ourselves isn't going to work. You could get hurt or put in prison. Try it my way. Please."

He knelt on the bed and took my hands in his. "All right. As long as I'm only yards away from you. And armed. Which means I'll need two guns. If we buy them, there will probably be a waiting period."

I pulled out my BlackBerry and logged onto the Internet. After doing a search, I said, "We'd have to get a permit first, which could take up to forty days."

He shook his head. "I want this over long before that."

"Where are you going to get them from? Some shifty character in the wrong side of town?"

"How about some shifty characters in a small South Carolina town?" He gave me a lopsided grin. "You always wanted to meet my parents. Now's your chance." That grin faded. "They have plenty of weapons. I'll call Steve Kantor, one of our angel members. He's got a twin engine and a son who craves any chance to fly it. He lives in a private airpark on Cape Cod. We won't have to clear any security screenings. Ideally we leave tomorrow morning, return that night. Then you're moving back home. I don't want you staying here alone."

I had to admit that I wanted to be close to him, too. I didn't want him alone with Beth, and not because I was worried about anything happening between them. Or her hurting him. I just didn't like the idea. Now I realized why I'd been uncomfortable when she had moved in the first time. My instincts knew something wasn't right.

"How are you going to explain that without piquing her suspicions?" I pulled up my knee and rested my chin on it, then snapped my fingers. "I know. Because of something she said to me recently: 'Keep your friends close, your enemies closer.'"

"You're in love with me, remember?"

"Right! I'm going to win you back."

He pulled out his cell phone. "I'm going to call Steve."

I listened as he told Steve he had a personal issue he needed to address. I breathed out in relief when I could tell from his side of the conversation that Steve was agreeable.

"That's great, thanks . . . tell Arny we'll see him in the morning." When he hung up, he smiled. "Arny is available and more than willing. I'm going to call our travel agent and book us a room on the Cape for tonight. We'll pack your things and put them in the car." He glanced at his watch. "The service starts in an hour. Do you have something here you can change into?"

I opened the armoire and pulled out a black pantsuit. "This should do."

He sat back on the bed and watched me undress. I felt self-conscious, as though we'd just started dating. Which was silly, I decided. Rush knew everything about me now. I would never hide anything from him again. So I let my pants and panties slide to the floor.

I felt a sudden need for him. Not sexual hunger; our moods were far too somber for that. Just a need to be held, to feel his body against mine. I crept onto the bed and cuddled into his arms. I couldn't let on that I was afraid of my plan. If he saw my fear, he'd nix it immediately. Okay, so I was still hiding something from him. But soon, I had to believe, this would all be over. The truth would come out.

Uh-oh. It would come out everywhere. In the newspapers, on television. Everything, including the blog, I realized.

I looked at Rush, who was holding me tight against him. "If Beth and Dominic get arrested, the press is going to have a field day. Montene's Diary, you, me. I understand if you want to distance yourself from me afterward. File for divorce, even. I know how important AngelForce is to you. I don't want it tainted by all of this."

"I thought AngelForce was the most important thing in the world." He stroked my cheek. "I was wrong. You are. I'm not going to step away from you to protect the company. But I will step away from the company. I'll talk to Waldo Skeever and Archie Thornton, two of my most active angels, see if they can step in. They're both retired. Strike that. Not Thornton. He's the son of a bitch who came on to you, isn't he?"

I gave a sheepish nod, thinking how Rush had read that, too. "Do what you need to do for the company."

"I don't want someone like that in a position of authority. Bob Traxton could do a good job, too. I'll call a meeting, give them a heads-up."

"I'm sorry," I whispered, feeling responsible for everything. Rush thrived on dreams. He lived for finding the entrepreneur with hunger in his soul. Now I was taking that away from him. I tried to bury my head against his chest, but his finger on my chin kept me from hiding.

"This wasn't you. Beth and Dominic did this. They played the game. And soon they're going to pay for what they did. To you. Me. And especially Hadden."

CHAPTER THIRTY-NINE

When I saw Beth at the service, held at the Romanesque Trinity Church, I wanted to go for her throat. An awful thought to have in a church, I knew, but that she was here when she might have caused Hadden's death . . . it was blasphemous. Heinous. Worse, she was crying, or pretending to, anyway. She dabbed at her eyes as she talked to Mona and Candace, though I didn't see any actual tears. I remained near the doors for a few minutes. Rush had made sure I'd gotten safely inside before he walked in.

This would be the first test of my acting ability. I had to hide the fact that I knew what kind of monster Beth was. And I had to hide that I wanted to hold on to Rush, to comfort him and be comforted. We had agreed that we would be no farther than a few yards away from each other, always within sight.

It was hard to appreciate the immense space, the incredible stained-glass windows, and the architecture that reminded me of the grand churches in Europe. The closed coffin in the front dwarfed all of that.

AngelForce employees and angels drew me into one conversation after another. I saw the question on some of their faces: why weren't Rush and I standing together? If anyone were to press, we would admit we were having trouble.

Such an understatement.

Speaking of . . . I spotted Kirsten in the distance. I felt silly now for being so insecure about her. Her threat was nothing compared to that of the woman I had considered my friend. I remembered how Beth had fed my suspicions about Rush seeing Kirsten. I'd gobbled them right up, feeling safe in keeping distance between Rush and me when the last thing I'd been was safe.

Kirsten approached Rush, and they hugged briefly. She left her hand on his arm, probably asking how he was holding up. She seemed to search for me. Then he moved away to talk to someone else. There were no lingering traces of attraction, at least on his side. I saw a trace of longing on her face, though, as she watched him.

I'd been there for nearly thirty minutes before Beth saw me. Surprise and irritation crossed her face as she made her way over. "Jonna, what are you doing here?"

"I couldn't miss this," I said, wiping real tears from my eyes, having just talked to Hadden's parents. "Besides, I told Rush I wanted a divorce. That I wanted nothing from him. Why should he hurt me now?"

"It's not Rush I'm worried about; it's Dominic." She glanced around, as though she expected him to be lurking nearby. "Who knows what that crazy idiot will do?"

The first bit of truth I'd probably heard come out of her mouth. "I'll take my chances." I looked up to see Rush approach. He nodded, good at keeping emotion from his face.

"Jonna," he said simply.

"Rush."

Two people who had once loved each other, and now one didn't. At least, I hoped that's what it looked like. I could at least let my feelings show plainly.

We stood in silence for a few moments. Then he said, "Look, if you want to move back home, at least until you find someplace else to live . . . you can have the bedroom." He glanced at Beth. "Beth's there, too."

I saw her surprise and more of that irritation, though she was amazingly adept at masking it. How much of that had I missed simply because I wasn't looking for it? Only that one time at the café when she'd let the ugly part show.

I nodded. "All right. I can't afford to stay in a hotel for long."

He walked away, and she moved closer. "What was that about?"

"I don't know."

"I don't like it. He's up to something, Jonna." She looked at me. "You can't possibly be thinking of moving back."

"I know this is going to sound crazy, but . . . I still love him, Beth. I canceled my appointment with the attorney. I don't want a divorce, but if that's what he wants, I'll play along. I know you're going to say it's like women who stay in abusive relationships." With doe eyes I watched Rush, who was trying not to look our way. "I can change his mind . . . about everything. I can make him love me again."

I saw her expression harden. "Jonna, it's suicide!" She lowered her voice. "Don't you see that it's over for him? If you try to renew your relationship, he might get suspicious. You know what he wants: out. With his money intact. Just give him that and you'll be safe."

Oh, how I hated her. Pretending to care about me, to be my friend. I shook my head, my mouth set in a line. "I love him too much to do that. Don't you see, I'm nothing without him? I'm going to move back and work on him."

The volume of organ music grew louder, signaling

that the service was about to begin. I waved Beth to go on. "I'm going to sit in the back. By myself."

She nodded, happy, I was sure, to take a place near Rush. I saw, though, that he was surrounded by angels who were walking with him toward one of the pews. All the people who were assembling thwarted Beth in her attempts to get to him. With slumped shoulders, she took a seat next to Candace and Mona.

The priest talked about the joy of death, quoting Romans 8 that "neither death, nor life, nor angels, nor principalities, nor things present, nor things to come, nor powers, nor height, nor depth, nor anything else in all creation, will be able to separate us from the love of God in Christ Jesus our Lord."

I kept my eyes on Rush, watching him rub at his eyes once or twice. I held in my sobs, but tears streamed down my face. Despite my resolve, my gaze kept returning to Beth. She put on a good show, rubbing her nose with a tissue, hugging Mona at times. And through the entire service, Beth watched Rush with a hunger that shook me to my core.

It was all Rush could do not to turn and look at Jonna. He had seen her in the rear of the church and ached to be sitting next to her. Mourning with her. At least she had people around her. Hundreds had packed into the church to say good-bye to Hadden St. Germain. Bursts of weeping erupted periodically, especially as the slide show flashed pictures of a young, handsome man with promise, from his birth to recent photos of a sailing regatta.

Once it was over, Rush quickly made his way toward the church's exit. He wasn't surprised to find Beth wending her way to him.

She put her arms around him and made sounds of grief. "Oh, it was so sad and wonderful all at once!"

"Yeah," he said, feeling the weight of the service in his chest. "Mostly sad. A good man died for no reason."

She didn't even wince, which told Rush how cold she was. He tried to spot Jonna in the mass of people, but she'd disappeared from view. She was supposed to merge with the crowd and find the limo parked along the curb. It would roll away, circle the block, and return for him. With all the limos, no one would even notice they were the same. Behind the shield of dark windows he and Jonna would head to the Cape.

"Let's get something to eat," Beth said, looping her arm around his. "It'll do you some good. You look gaunt. Tired."

"I've got to go."

She blinked in surprise. "Go? Where?"

"This whole thing with Hadden . . . it made me realize I need to mend my relationship with my parents. I'm flying out tonight."

Her cheeks flushed. She'd probably planned to comfort him. "Oh. When are you coming back?"

"Soon." Family business was personal. He didn't want to leave her with any opening to invite herself in the name of moral support. He handed her a key to the loft, the only part of the plan he didn't like. "Here's a key to let yourself in."

She clutched it in her hand. "Thank you. But this means . . . you're going right to the airport?"

"Yes. My plane leaves soon."

"Rush, I have to ask. Why did you invite Jonna to move back in?"

He gave her a solemn look and delivered the line that she had only recently used with Jonna. "There's an old saying: keep your friends close, your enemies closer. I don't trust her, but I'd rather not trust her under my roof."

Beth nodded. "For how long?"

"Until the divorce papers go through. Since she's so agreeable, it shouldn't take long."

As they emerged through the doors into the clear, cold night, he paused and forced himself to hug her. "Thank you for being there. You don't know how much it means to me."

Her face lit up. "*You* mean a lot to me, Rush. I want to do what I can. Anything."

"Thank you. We'll talk when I get back."

He walked through the crowd, glad to see that she hadn't followed. He glanced back once, gave her a smile. Just to open that door a little wider. When he got back, he had to tackle the hardest part of the plan: pretending to fall in love with her.

He spotted the limo and got in quickly so no one could spot Jonna tucked in the corner. She looked small there, and as soon as the limo pulled away from the curb, he pulled her into his arms. He felt her body shake with her sobs, everything she'd held in during the service. He felt grief erupt inside him, too, and he held her as he'd wanted to do every second he'd been in that church.

The limousine took them back to Jonna's hotel, where they got into her car to head to Cape Cod. Steve's son would fly them out at six the following morning, landing in Greenville, South Carolina, sometime later that morning, where the next part of their plan would unfold.

CHAPTER FORTY

We arrived in the small, hilly South Carolina town just before lunchtime. Rush had grown quiet as we drove into a rural area. I wondered what he was thinking, if he was remembering things. Then I decided to ask instead of just wondering.

"Did you spend a lot of time here?"

"No. We moved around a lot, but this was typical of the towns we lived in." His gaze followed a boy walking barefoot by the side of the road, carrying a fishing pole. Barefoot in winter, his coat riding up his arms, maybe trying to catch dinner.

Rush pulled onto a dirt road that wound past cow pastures and dilapidated barns. He had rented a regular car, nothing fancy. He wore jeans. He didn't need to prove anything, and that made me smile.

Chickens scattered when he turned into a driveway cut into a yard full of weeds. The house was in decent shape, though it needed a paint job.

"I wanted to buy them something nice," he said, taking it in. "They wouldn't hear of it. So I bought this. They don't know it, but they're paying rent into their retirement account." He looked over at me. "I know you think I'm ashamed of my past and that's why I haven't brought you here or talked about it. The truth is, I don't belong to this life. I never did."

"Rush!" A woman burst out of the front door and ran toward us. She looked young, with long blond hair and a thin but muscular figure.

As soon as he got out of the car, she slammed into him and gave him a bear hug. "I just can't believe it! You're here! You're really here."

I walked over, not wanting to interrupt the moment. He reached out, drawing me closer.

"This is my wife: Jonna. Jonna, this is my mom: Jolene."

To my surprise, she hugged me, too. Then she leaned over and hollered, "Nick! Rush is here! Get your ass over here!"

Nick walked out from a barn behind the house, a rag hanging out of his jean pocket. He gave Rush a hug, pounding him on the back. I could see where Rush got his good looks.

"Good to see you, Son."

I got introduced to him, and he shook my hand. "Nice to finally meet you." He looked at Rush, his expression sobering. "You in some kind of trouble?"

"Let's have lunch first," he said, an affectionate look on his face as he took them in. "And you can tell me what you've been up to."

We walked into the small house, filled with the kind of furniture I saw on my flea market forays searching for props. Still, it was homey . . . except for the hole in the wall. Rush paused, touching the frayed edges of broken drywall. Then he looked at his parents. Shame tinted their faces.

Jolene slapped her hands together. "Lunch is ready."

Now I knew why Rush shied away from arguments.

We continued on into a country French kitchen that smelled of fried chicken and sawmill gravy. During our meal, I began to see why Rush didn't visit much. Small bursts of conversation were followed by awkward silences. They didn't understand what Rush did. He didn't have much to offer in response to the fox getting into the chicken coops other than a sympathetic shrug. All through lunch Nick and Jolene held hands, kissed each other, and occasionally each slugged the other on the shoulder. Their passion and love were evident. I could see why Rush kept his feelings in check, but I wasn't going to allow him to do that anymore.

As long as he didn't slug me.

"I'll help clean up," I said, his opening to talk to his father alone.

Jolene watched the two of them walk outside. "Is everything all right?"

"Someone's stalking us," I said, sticking to the simplified version. "We want to get some protection without waiting for over a month." I could see her concern, so I said, "It'll be okay," even though I didn't know if it would be okay.

As we washed the dishes, she said, "I bct your family's rich, huh? Came over on the *Mayflower* or something? Isn't that what people in Boston are like?"

I couldn't help but laugh. "I'm from St. Louis. My mom sells Mary Kay products."

Jolene gave a relieved smile and patted my hand with her soapy one. "I like you. You seem sweet and calm, and Rush looks happy. Thanks for making him happy."

After cleaning up, I wandered the living room and looked at the numerous family photos displayed. "I've always wondered how you came up with the name Rush. It's not short for anything, like Rushton."

She grinned. "We named him after our favorite rock group. Nick and I fell in love at a Rush concert. He was conceived one night when we was playing their albums and laying naked up on the roof." She blushed. "Well, you didn't want to know all that."

Actually, I wanted to know everything about Rush. I spotted a deck of cards on the coffee table, old and tattered like the ones he had in his drawer. "Who plays cards?"

"Nick and his buddies. Poker," she added, rolling her eyes. "The smoke—cigars!—and the swearing, it's awful." She led me to a collage on the hall wall and pointed to one of the pictures.

"See, there's Nick and the boys playing poker. They used to do it every Wednesday night. The boys weren't allowed to play with the menfolk, see, but they loved playing with their dad."

The picture showed Rush and David holding unlit cigars and mugging for the picture. Rush had been cute, even skinny and wearing ratty clothing. Even then, he'd had the regal bearing I knew so well, as though he'd innately known he was made for something better.

"Rush has an old deck of cards at home," I said. "He just holds them sometimes, and I can tell he's far away, thinking of something pleasant." I nodded toward the picture. "I think that's it."

When she smiled, her mouth trembled. "Thanks for telling me that. Sometimes I think Rush is happier just forgetting where he came from."

"No, he's not. The problem is you don't have much to talk about. Your lives are so different. Maybe we can remedy that."

"I'd like that," she said on a whisper, her finger rubbing that picture.

My heart warmed that I could give her that small gift. I wanted to do more.

We were still looking at pictures when the two men returned. I didn't see any guns in Rush's hands, but he looked resolved and ready to take on any sort of evil.

We visited for a while before Rush said, "Mom, we have to get going."

She gave him a fierce hug, and then she hugged me, too. "Be careful."

Nick said, "You sure I can't help?"

"I'm sure, thanks. We've got a plan."

"We'll be in touch," I said to Jolene. "We'd love to have you up for Christmas."

Rush gave away his surprise at my spontaneous invitation but smiled. "We've got a place on the coast with plenty of room."

We headed out soon after that, the warmth of the visit fading as we thought of what waited for us at the end of the trip—Beth.

CHAPTER FORTY-ONE

Rush had meetings all day Friday with the angels who would continue to steer the company. All current business dealings would proceed, but they wouldn't pursue anything further for the time being. They would formalize the arrangement the following week, and Rush would step down and simply become one of the angels.

If things got ugly, he'd back down from even that.

Beth hovered like a dragonfly, waiting for an opportunity to talk to him alone. She finally snagged him on the way to the restroom.

"Rush, I've been so worried about you."

He took a ragged breath. "I'm coping. Right now I've got to figure out what's going on with the company now that Hadden's gone."

Again, he saw no remorse, no real grief, in her green eyes. "You'll make it all right again. I know it."

"I appreciate your confidence, but . . . things are going to change. I'm bringing other angels onboard."

"Are you saying that people may be let go?"

"Possibly. The two men I'm talking to don't think we should be providing marketing assistance. That department may go. I'm giving you warning now in case—"

"I want to find another job? No way. You'll find some-place else for me, right?"

He rubbed his face, not answering. "I'm tired and I'm hungry; I didn't have time for lunch. Let's grab some-thing to eat after work."

"Sounds great."

"I'll meet you at O'Malley's in an hour."

"O'Malley's?" She shrugged. "Okay."

By the time she arrived, he'd ordered—and dumped out—two pints of ale, leaving the empty mugs on the table. She slid into the booth with him, and he gave her a loopy smile. "It's good to see you."

"You, too. I've been dying to talk to you all day. How was your trip?" Her hair was brushed and curled under at the ends, makeup refreshed, lips glistening a frosty pink.

"Good."

She eyed the mugs on the table. "You started with-out me."

"Yeah, well, I had to get out of there."

He drank three more through the course of their meal, pouring some into her mug whenever she went to the bathroom. He reminisced about Hadden the entire time, and he could tell that she was getting on edge.

"I guess it's good that I didn't drive to work," he said, nodding toward the last empty mug. "I needed to drown myself for a bit."

She gave him a sympathetic smile. "I'll drive us home." Her smile faded, though. "I suppose Jonna will be there."

"It'll be hard having her around, but I feel better keep-ing tabs on her." That last bit was true. "Maybe you can sniff around, see what's she's thinking. Shall we go?"

It was dark by the time they pulled into his building's parking lot. He acted off-balance as he got out of the car. "Guess I should have eaten more, not drank on an empty stomach." He leaned against the car. "My head's spinning."

She came around to his side. "You've been under a lot of stress lately." She glanced at the building. "And you'll be under more once we go in there. It's good for you to let off some steam."

"Maybe you can help me in," he said, leaning into her.

She put her arms around him, and they fell against the car, her pinned in front of him. Her eyes were wide and full of anticipation as he remained so close their mouths were nearly touching. Then he kissed her. He had to push back his gag reflex as his tongue touched hers. She let out a sound of pleasure and pulled him closer.

She continued the kiss long past when he wanted to finish it, but he eventually pulled back. "You don't know how long I've wanted to do that."

Her laugh sounded like a cry. "Me, too. I've felt awful, having these feelings for you. Working with you made it so hard to suppress them. I wondered if you had feelings for me, too. That's why you always seemed so uncomfortable around me," she said, eating up his charade.

He nodded. "I tried to tell myself that they weren't there."

He was glad they weren't having this conversation in the light, where his hatred might show. They were parked at the edge of the lot where the lights weren't as bright. Keeping her between him and the car, he tilted his head and looked at her. "I wish I'd seen you . . . really seen you that night." He touched her lower lip with his thumb. "But I see you now."

She let out a joyous whimper and kissed him again. He had to kiss her like a man who had just found his salvation. Agonizing seconds crept by as he went through the motions.

He finished the kiss and looked up to the sky. "It's just so complicated."

"It doesn't have to be. Soon you'll get a divorce. I couldn't be friends with Jonna now, not knowing what she tried to do."

He watched a couple of moths dive at the light. "Whenever I think about that . . . it's like her treachery opened up some dark place inside me."

She leaned toward him, her eyes wide. "Tell me, Rush."

"Maybe I shouldn't. I just found you. I don't want to scare you away."

"You can tell me anything."

He turned away, as though this were difficult to admit. "I could divorce her, and even if I walked away with everything, she's already cost me fifty thousand dollars. But it's more than the money. She wanted me dead. Dead. I can't get past that. Because some part of me wants her dead back. I'd even thought about hiring Dominic to do it. Crazy, huh? But I can't trust him. He could do the same thing with her that he did with me." He dared a look at her.

She was frozen, her mouth open. Had he not played it well enough? When he saw tears glittering in her eyes, he was confused. "Did I just ruin everything?" he asked in a quiet voice.

"No," she said on a fierce whisper. "I feel the same way about her."

He took a mental breath of relief. She had bought it. In fact, she was ecstatic.

"Don't worry. I couldn't actually kill someone. It's just a fantasy."

"I want to make all of your fantasies come true, Rush." Now she was searching his face, gauging his reaction.

He hid the horror at how easily she'd offered and at the fear that the plan would go wrong.

"You'd kill Jonna?"

"Shhhh." She looked around. "You never know who might be listening." She was probably thinking of Dominic. She gave Rush a pointed look. "I would do *anything* for you."

"I couldn't let you do that. You might get caught."

She relaxed, probably thinking, *He isn't worried about the actual murder, only me getting caught.* "With me, you'll never have to want for anything. All I ask is that you keep yourself open to me. Like you did just now, admitting how you felt about Jonna."

"I will." He took a breath, watching the moths again. "We need to think about this."

"I don't need to think about it. Do you?"

After a pause, he shook his head. "You know, if we go through with this, it will bind us together forever."

"I know."

"We need to come up with a plan."

"There's something you should know. She told me that she wants to get back together with you. See, I knew she was up to something. Don't be fooled by her. We need to beat her at her own game."

Beth was convincing. He could see how she'd manipulated Gary into a relationship. Remembering how she'd given him a back rub and posed against the bar, he could understand how she'd seduced Gary.

Rush gave her a conspiratorial smile. "We can use her plan against her. I could set up a romantic weekend, a chance to start over. I've got a gun. It's my father's, and it's not registered."

Beth was nodding even as she glanced around. "And all of a sudden, it's not so complicated anymore." She pulled him close for another hard kiss.

"Let me think about the logistics. How it'll look to the police. Let me worry about the details. But no one can know about us, Beth. The oldest motive in the book besides money. Both play here. You've got to move out, and we can't be seen together. We can't take any chances." That was the one part of the plan he did like.

She, however, didn't like that part. "You're right. But dammit, we just started something wonderful."

"We'll have plenty of time together." He forced himself to kiss her again. "The sooner you can move out, the better. We'll meet, talk. And pretty soon, we'll be together."

"Forever," she added with another kiss.

Dominic watched Beth and Rush kissing in the parking lot. Slimy bitch got what she wanted. Except he was going to make sure she didn't enjoy it.

He'd gone into his apartment yesterday and found the pictures of Mamu that Beth had shredded in retaliation. The only pictures he had of his mother. Now that he was out from under Beth's influence, he could see how she'd manipulated him over the years. How she'd used him. Now she was dumping him for Rush. Damn, he thought Rush would have told her to go screw herself. Apparently not.

Where did that leave Jonna? Dominic hadn't been able to find her for the last few days, but she was home tonight. He'd called and smiled when she'd picked up.

"Hello, doll. Miss me?"

She'd hung up.

Just as he'd been trying to figure out how to get into the loft, Beth had pulled up—and, surprise, surprise, with Rush in her passenger seat. And now this public display of affection. What puzzled Dominic was Beth's believing Rush had paid him. Either she was stoking him or Rush had lied. Knowing Beth, Dominic thought she was playing him like she played everyone else. She didn't need him now that she had Rush.

Dominic had dumped her and she didn't even care.

She looked happy, excited. Hatred welled inside him. It was time to make her pay for her treachery. He wanted to hurt her in the deepest way possible. He wanted to take away what mattered most to her. Not those pictures of her and Rush . . . but Rush himself.

I was sitting at the aquarium with a glass of wine when they came in. I didn't have to fake the surly tone in my voice when I said, "I was wondering where you two were." I'd seen them out in the parking lot. Just shadows at the edge, but two very close shadows. I knew it was part of the plan—*my* plan, no less—but I didn't have to like it.

Rush said, "It was a rough day at the office. We stopped for a couple of beers."

He went upstairs, and I watched him prepare a bed in the loft. When he went into the bathroom and I heard the shower start, I turned to Beth, who was pouring herself a drink. "Was that part of your plan, having drinks with him?"

"He asked. And yes, I was hoping he'd get a little drunk and tell me what's going on. But he didn't." She took the stool next to me and her voice had a snippy tone when she said, "Sorry, did I spoil your plans for seduction?"

"A little. It's not easy when your best friend is living with you."

"Then you'll be glad to know I'm moving out tonight. I spoke with my building's manager, and he installed new locks and extra security. Since you're obviously not afraid of being alone with Rush, I figured you'd want me out." She finished off her drink the same way he sometimes did when he was tense, in one gulp, bottoms up.

"Don't take it personally, but you're in the way."

She pulled a face. "Gee, thanks."

She set her glass on the table and sauntered to the family room. A few minutes later she returned, carrying two bags and her fur coat. Now I knew how she had the money to buy all her luxuries.

"Look, I don't want you to think I'm ungrateful."

"No, you're just crazy." She glanced upstairs to indicate exactly why. "But I can see you won't be dissuaded, so I'll buy something nice to wear at your memorial service."

Those words jabbed down my spine like jagged pieces of ice. She had every intention of doing that, I bet.

She pulled on her coat, hoisted her bags, and left. I went to the door and locked it behind her. I hated that she had a key now. We couldn't change it in case she returned. Rush would have no reason to change the lock without telling her, now that they were "involved."

I moved one of the chairs in front of the door and balanced a round Christmas bell I'd dug out of storage on the arm. If someone tried to get in, the bell would jangle to the floor. It wasn't just Beth I was afraid of. Dominic was still out there. I could almost feel his presence outside. So much so that I didn't dare join Rush in the shower as I longed to do. We wouldn't hear the bell. I would never forget that day I thought I saw shadows moving in the bathroom—and later when I discovered Dominic had a key to my home.

CHAPTER FORTY-TWO

Sunday afternoon Rush and I met with Arthur Winthrop, criminal defense attorney . . . and angel and mentor. We sat in his formal living room, and after his wife had brought us coffee and left us alone, Rush said, "I think I'm going to need your services on an official basis. I'm plotting to have my wife killed."

Arthur's thick gray eyebrows shot up as he looked at me. "But isn't . . . Jonna—"

"Yes, I'm talking about Jonna. Arthur, we've got a situation that's going to sound bizarre because it *is* bizarre. We're talking seduction, blackmail, murder for hire, and obsession. And, we're pretty sure, murder."

Arthur was about to take a sip of his coffee. He set the cup down and leaned forward. "You'd better start at the beginning."

So we did. I watched his face morph from shock, to confusion, to outrage when we told him about Gary's wife and our suspicions about Hadden's death.

"You haven't gone to the police, I take it."

"I tried, early on, when I thought this was just about Dominic stalking me. They weren't too keen on helping me because of the diary. There's a contingent of cop wives on the blog who've been having fun trashing their husbands."

Rush said, "You've heard everything. Do we have enough proof to make a case? Or would they give us the toss?"

"It's all circumstantial, but we're talking about possible murder here."

I could see that he was uncomfortable. "We don't even know which one of them killed Hadden. Or that he was murdered."

"We can't take the chance of Beth getting questioned and released. We know she's vindictive, and she's no doubt capable of murder. We need to get solid proof," Rush said.

Arthur nodded in agreement. "No, you don't want this woman feeling betrayed by Rush. I had a client like that. If she's obsessed and a sociopath, she's very dangerous. So what is your plan, and where do I fit in?"

Rush said, "Beth and I are plotting to murder Jonna. Beth has generously offered to take care of the dirty work." His jaw tightened. "I'm arranging for a romantic getaway with Jonna at our cottage in Beverly. She's going first, while I'm supposedly flying to New York on business. I'll fly back late that night to join her, giving me an alibi. Beth will head up that morning to shoot Jonna. Only the gun will be loaded with blanks."

I added, "We're going to set up video cameras to capture everything. Knowing Beth as I do, she'll enlighten me about snagging Rush and their plan. She'll gloat."

"Then I'll make my appearance and subdue her. I bought handcuffs at a pawnshop yesterday. Realizing Jonna and I are working together will knock her so off-balance, I think she'll freak—hopefully tell us everything. But if she doesn't, we'll still have her on tape trying to kill Jonna. We'll have attempted murder as a start.

"I'm recording my conversations with Beth, but, of course, I'll sound like a husband who wants to have his wife killed. I've already got the conversation where I confess to having dark feelings toward Jonna, wanting her dead, and Beth offers to take care of it. If she's trapped in a corner, she might try to implicate me. You, my friend, are witness to the fact that Jonna and I are working this together. In fact, I'm going to ask you to arrange to have the house readied; we haven't been there in over a year. I couldn't possibly be plotting to kill my wife if I'm running everything through my attorney."

Arthur seemed to digest this. "As your attorney, I have to tell you, it's risky."

I was relieved that he wasn't telling us to find a psychiatrist. "We'll have everything covered," I said. "If Beth tries to kill me some other way when she realizes the gun isn't working, Rush will be on the scene. As soon as I call the police from the cottage, we'll call you, too."

"Well, you seem to have covered your bases. I'll accept the case."

Rush pulled out his checkbook. "I'll give you a retainer—"

Arthur pressed his hand on the checkbook. "If this woman killed Hadden, it's on me. He was a good man, and his family and mine go back a long way."

"Thank you," Rush said. "Here's the conversation Beth and I had about killing Jonna." He gave Arthur the first recording he'd made in the parking lot, burned to a CD. I hadn't heard it and wasn't sure I wanted to. Even knowing that Rush was only pretending would make it too creepy to contemplate.

"Does she actually say she's going to commit murder?" Arthur asked.

"No. She was very careful. She might have been afraid her former cohort was around."

We gave him the specifics on the cottage so he could make arrangements and bid him farewell. The next step in the plan was in place.

Sunday night I was cuddled up next to Rush in bed when he called Beth. His voice was low, furtive. "It's me. Jonna's in the shower, so I have a few minutes to talk."

"I've been going crazy, wondering if you'd changed your mind. And thinking of you and her together."

"I'm going crazy, too. I want this to happen. It's been hell pretending," he said, pressing his forehead to mine. I knew he meant pretending to be in love with her. "But it didn't take long to get things moving in the right direction. We're going away for a few days, starting Wednesday. I've got a cottage on the beach, nice and secluded. Meet me in the parking garage early, say seven. Look for my car. We'll talk then."

"Can we put this together that fast? Don't get me wrong; I'm glad you're in a hurry. But—"

"Babe, I've got it all figured out. It's a simple plan. Trust me."

She didn't hesitate. "All right."

"Are you sure about this?"

"Yes. I told you I'd do anything for you. I meant it."

"Okay, I've got to go. We'll talk soon."

He turned off the recorder he'd been holding to the phone. His body went limp after he hung up. "I hate this."

"I know. It's scary even though I know it's not real."

"But it is real, to her."

I nodded. The woman I'd considered my best friend was eager to kill me. It still seemed surreal. I ran my hand over Rush's bare chest, tracing my fingers around the sprinkling of dark hair—and pulled one.

"Ouch."

"Don't call her 'babe.' That's what you call me."

"Sorry."

Tomorrow afternoon we would head out to the cottage where we'd spent our honeymoon. For a little while our lives would be normal, like any couple enjoying a vacation. Except we would be figuring out how to trap a killer.

Rush tensed when he saw Beth pull into the parking garage. He waved as she passed. Within a few seconds she was dropping into the car, pulling her door closed, and falling against him.

"God, I missed you," she said, kissing him like a woman starved. In between kisses, she said, "I know we've got to pull this plan off, but I can't stop thinking about what you have to do to convince her that you're open to reconciliation."

He couldn't help but think of the irony; Jonna would say the same thing. "I close my eyes and imagine it's you," he said, though that wasn't true when he was kissing Beth. He shut down his mind as soon as their mouths connected.

"Oh, baby," she said, plunging her tongue into his mouth.

He gently pushed her back. "We have to be careful."

She glanced around the garage. "Even with the dark windows?"

"Taking chances is how people get caught."

"You're right." She smoothed her shirt. "I can't wait until it's over. I just want to be with you."

"Me, too. That's why I want this over as soon as possible. I've got a flight out of here in two hours so I can wrap up the DEMCO deal. I have a cottage on the beach, up in Beverly. It's about an hour from here. That's where

Jonna and I are going to see if we can salvage our marriage, where we had our honeymoon."

He leaned into the backseat and pulled out a small black bag that had been wedged between his overnight bag and laptop and handed it to her. She obviously didn't expect it to be as heavy as it was. "What's in here, a gun?"

"Exactly. And a sketch of the cottage inside and out, as well as a map and key." He pulled out the layout and pointed to the site plan. "The cottage is on two private acres. It's the beginning of December. Most residents aren't there right now. Even if they are, with the distance between properties and the sound of the ocean, no one should hear a gunshot. Jonna is going up tomorrow to spend some time alone. I'm supposed to join her Wednesday morning. You'll go tomorrow night, when it's dark." He pointed to the site plan. "You'll park here, where she can't see you from the house and where no one can see the vehicle from the road. She'll probably be in the chair in front of the fireplace. That's where she likes to sit. You'll see her through the window if she hasn't drawn the curtains, but she won't see you because it'll be dark."

Beth was following his finger and nodding.

"You'll come in the back door here, where the laundry room is. Be careful at this spot; the wood flooring creaks. If she's positioned the right way, she won't see you until you're right on top of her."

He hated imagining the scenario. He and Jonna had worked out all the details last night. Afterward, he almost felt too dirty to touch her, even though she was an active participant. Even though it was a fake plan. "This needs to look like a robbery gone bad. That's important. You broke in, hoping to score, and someone's there. She catches you. You have to kill her. That means you can't shoot her while she's sitting in the chair. Get her to stand up. This room is the best as far as sound, too. It's buffered on both sides by the kitchen and a bedroom. The sound should be muffled." He looked at her. "Do you know how to shoot a gun?"

"I bought a little one a while back for protection. I've practiced a few times, but it's been a long time. It's short-range; I'll manage."

That startled him. He hadn't thought about her owning a gun. "This one has a kick, but it'll get the job done in one shot." He felt that twist in his gut again. "It's loaded. And more important, it's untraceable. Use this one."

"Okay, so I ransack the place? Take her wallet, jewelry . . . wedding ring," she added in a low voice, obviously looking forward to that part. "And wear gloves, of course."

"Pin your hair up, too. The police are going to scour the place. You've never been there, so we don't want them finding your hair."

She stared at the layout, pulling her hair back. "Should I go early? Get a feel for the place?"

"No, I've got people going in to ready the place for me and Jonna."

"All right. I'll study this, make sure I've got it down." She looked at him. "I'll get it done. You can trust me, too."

He kissed her quick, and she opened the door. "See you on the other side," she whispered, and got out.

He watched her go to her car and tuck the bag beneath her seat, then walk toward the stairs. She touched her lips with the tips of her fingers and disappeared down the stairs. Only then did he listen to their conversation. She still didn't outright say she would kill Jonna. "See you on the other side," Beth's voice said.

He'd get this to Arthur and then pick up Jonna. They were heading out to Beverly mid-day.

• • •

Beth watched Rush pull out of the garage, her chest tight. She'd never planned a murder before. Both Hadden and Cammie had been of-the-moment and necessary. Jonna's death was necessary, too. And Beth would enjoy it. She would think of all those nights Jonna shared a bed—and her body—with Rush. All those nights that should have been hers.

Despite her joy at vengeance and the anticipation of a life with Rush, she had an uneasy feeling. This was moving too fast. Yeah, that's all it was. Too fast and too easy.

But they'd carefully planned everything out. She'd go over it again that night to make sure Rush hadn't missed something. She couldn't believe that she hadn't picked up on the dark streak that apparently ran through him. Or maybe she had, subconsciously, and that's what drew her to him. She couldn't believe they shared something so uncommon. Dominic could eat her dust. Who needed him?

She didn't need him, but she feared him. He had no doubt found his precious pictures by now. He would be furious. It served him right after what he'd done. Shredded her pictures. Lied to her about the money. She patted her purse, where her pearl-handled gun resided. That was the only deviation from Rush's plan that she could foresee so far. Her gun wasn't registered, either. Dominic had scored it for her from some backroom scuzzbag. She liked the feel of it and knew what it fired like.

She had another plan that she hadn't run past Rush. Who was the logical person to kill Jonna? Why, Dominic, of course. She would hide the gun and let him know that if he ever tried to mess with her again, she'd plant it on him and finger him for the murder. That should take care of him.

She walked into the offices, smiling as she headed for her desk. Her gaze went to Rush's office, dark and empty. Soon she would have the life she deserved. The one her mother said she'd never have.

CHAPTER FORTY-THREE

Dominic drove by the loft to see if Jonna was there alone. Though he had plans for Rush, Dominic still wanted her. She would be his ultimate reward. Hurting Rush, as Beth would say, was a necessary act.

Jonna was just leaving, hauling an overnight bag to the car. Dominic knew she'd been hiding somewhere, and though he'd enjoyed the fact that he'd sent her into hiding, he was anxious to move things along again. Now it looked as though he could.

He followed her to a hotel, probably where she'd been staying before moving back to the loft. It was damned curious, her moving out and back in again. Especially in light of what he'd seen in the parking lot. If Beth and Rush were getting it on, why had Jonna moved in and Beth out?

He would figure it out. And if he could, he'd use it to his advantage.

Jonna pulled into the parking garage and drove around to the back before taking a spot. A man got out of a dark green Range Rover next to her, pulled out a box and a duffel bag, and got into her car. Rush.

"What the hell?" This was getting interesting.

She pulled back out again and headed north. Dominic

followed them for some time, weaving in and out of traffic to keep up with them. Damn, he wished he knew what they were saying.

They turned off the highway and drove into a seaside town called Beverly, where he had to hang farther back since the roads weren't crowded. It wasn't a resort town, as he'd expect for a place right on the ocean, just nice and clean, with glimpses of open water. His targets stopped at a small grocery store and emerged a few minutes later with a couple of bags. Their journey terminated at a house at the end of a long driveway sitting out on a point. He couldn't get close or even pause without attracting attention. He turned around and doubled back, finding a parking lot for a restaurant that was closed for the season. He burrowed into his coat and hiked back. Damn ocean breeze. The wind kicked his ass and froze his ears and hands, even through his hat and gloves.

A stand of trees bordered the property line. Short evergreens and the netting of naked branches camouflaged him as he walked down to the cove and scoped out the rear of the house. Hunkered down against the wind, he settled in for a while to try to figure out the situation. It was too light to approach the house, so he'd come back after dark.

As he was about to walk back, he heard a noise. The back door opened, and Rush and Jonna stepped outside, still wearing their coats. She seemed to take a deep breath as she looked at the ocean. Rush came up behind her, sliding his arms around her shoulders and pulling her close.

What the bloody hell? He'd looked pretty chummy with Beth only days ago, and here he was even cozier with Jonna. Was Rush playing them? Maybe it had something to do with why he'd lied to Beth about paying him. Or maybe Rush had teamed up with Beth to off the wife he thought was planning to off him? Dominic didn't know, but he was starting to get very interested. He would keep close tabs on this joint for a while. He'd figure it out. It was just a matter of time.

"Why haven't we come here more often?" I asked, my gaze continually going to the picture window that faced the ocean. "I love it here."

"Too busy." Upstairs in the sitting area, he paused while adjusting the angle on the video camera. "We won't make that mistake again."

I smiled up at him. "Even in the winter, it's beautiful. Think of those cozy nights we could spend here by this huge fireplace."

Rush's idea of a "seaside cottage" was far different from mine. I'd pictured a one-room cabin. This place had four bedrooms, an upstairs loft, and a large living room with a stone fireplace. The fire was roaring now, and I felt the heat licking at my legs.

"We'll come here once a month for a long weekend from now on. You know, I almost sold it. It needs some work, and then never having time to use it . . . I'm glad I didn't."

He sat at the computer that was up in the loft. He had bought a surveillance camera setup at an electronics store before we got together that morning. We attached two cameras to the upstairs banister and hid one in a silk plant and another in the bric-a-brac above the kitchen shelves.

"Okay," he called down to me, "step to the far side of the window . . . good. Now over to the fireplace. Good. Now back to the other side of the room. We have a blind spot behind the couch, so remember that. Now walk to the kitchen, and . . . there you are. You're covered as long as you stay in the center of the room. All right, we're in good shape. We'll get into position as soon as it gets dark and wait. If I see her outside, I'll let out a low whistle, but don't count on that. Be ready. Keep her in this room."

"What if she wants me to go somewhere else? She's got a gun, even if it's not loaded."

"Then she'll have to shoot you for not cooperating, and it'll be over."

I nodded, my throat as dry as gauze. "The cameras turn on automatically when they sense motion, right?"

"Yep. And they're infrared, so we'll still get video even if she turns off the lights for some reason. I'm going to turn off the computer monitor, just in case."

"And you'll be in the bedroom up there."

He ducked into the doorway. "Can you see me if I'm here?"

"You'll need to go farther in. Yeah, right there is fine. When she shoots me, I'll gasp and fall toward her, sending us both to the floor. By the time she realizes I'm not bleeding, you'll be here."

He slid down the staircase banister, landing with a thud, his arms wide. "To the rescue."

"With cuffs and loaded gun."

We'd gone over it several times. It reminded me of a fourth-grade play I was in. I kept rehearsing the lines until I thought I knew them, but then during practice I'd flub them. I almost backed out of the role. Mom told me to stick with it, and I did. I still flubbed my lines onstage, but I got a laugh.

A lot more than my ego was at stake this time. Thinking about it made me nervous. At least I didn't have any lines to memorize. I would look shocked, confused, and then terrified when I saw the gun in Beth's hand. Simple. She would gloat and, I hoped, confess everything.

He pulled me close, touching his nose to mine. "You all right?"

"Absolutely. I just want it to be over."

"By tomorrow night. Then we'll come back for a vacation. Just you and me and that randy vibrator of yours."

I nudged him, still embarrassed about the blog. Though it was the least of my worries, I dreaded when it became public. When everyone I knew would be reading it, trying to figure out who I was talking about. I knew a few women who might be asking their husbands if they were the ones who'd come on to me.

"When everything comes out . . . with the blog and all, I might have trouble getting clients for a while."

"We'll both take some time off, do some traveling. Paris. Rome. London."

I smiled despite my dark thoughts. "Thanks for not really having me killed."

"Anytime," he said, kissing me.

"I love you," I said.

"I love you, too."

"Now you look at me when you say that. You used to glance away."

He wasn't glancing away now. "It used to feel uncomfortable. Not saying the words, but meeting your eyes when I did." He held my face tenderly in his hands. "I'm sorry I did that."

I pulled him close, squeezing my eyes shut. I loved this man. God, did I love him.

We cooked dinner and then bundled up and walked out to the shore. The moon was fat and bright, leaving a shower of glitter on the choppy surface of the water. The cold breeze sent waves swirling around the rocks that lined the shore. I leaned back against Rush's hard body, feeling safe with his arms in front of me.

We both heard the snap of a twig and turned toward the trees. Though the moonlight silvered the trees on the outside of the stand, beyond that was dark. I shivered, imagining Beth standing there watching us. We'd taken a chance coming outside, but with her thinking that the cleaning people were due to arrive, it was risky for her to come any earlier than planned.

"I'm cold," I said, moving out of his arms.

He was watching the trees, too, as we walked back to the house. Our gloved hands were linked, but we didn't talk until we got back inside.

"It was probably an animal," he said, though he looked out from the side of the curtains.

"Yeah, probably."

I hoped that my sense of foreboding came from what would happen tomorrow. Fear would make us careful, right? Even as I settled in front of the fireplace, fear settled into my heart like a cold fog. By tomorrow it would be over.

One way or the other.

CHAPTER FORTY-FOUR

The next night I'd baked maple-glazed pork chops, rosemary potatoes, and peas with lemon dressing, but I hardly ate a thing. My stomach was knotted too tight. Rush didn't eat much, either. The cooking process kept my mind on the present, though, and not the upcoming evening, so it had been worth the effort.

He rubbed my shoulders and kissed my neck as I rinsed the last of the pans we'd washed. "You all right?"

"Fine. Great." I took a deep breath and turned toward him, my cheek grazing his. "Better now. Well, we'll just roll with the dice, won't we?"

He smiled at my use of his favorite expression. "We've gone over everything ten times today. The cameras are hidden, everything's covered in the viewfinders, and I have my gun loaded and ready upstairs. The police station's number is programmed into the phone. Nothing can go wrong."

"Nothing," I repeated.

We left one plate and wineglass on the table. The sun was setting, which meant he would have to disappear.

He pulled me close and kissed me with his eyes open. "You can do this. I love you, Jonna."

"I love you, too."

He went upstairs and sat just inside the balcony doors to watch for Beth. I took a seat in front of the crackling fire and picked up a book. I could see a faint reflection of what was behind me in the picture frame on the mantel. I'd turned it so it would show movement in the hallway.

Minutes stretched painfully past. I turned pages to give the appearance of reading the book. I sometimes glanced out the window beside me, though I could only see the moon and its silvery trail on the water. If she was out there, she could see me; but I couldn't see her.

My skin broke out in goose bumps. Someone stepped on my grave, wasn't that the old saying? Someone *wanted* to step on my grave, that was for sure.

I heard a *thump* upstairs. At least I thought it had come from there. I wanted to tell Rush that he couldn't do whatever it was he'd just done in case Beth heard him, but I was stilled by another sound . . . the faint *click* of a door closing behind me.

The laundry room.

She must have come in from another way. Or Rush hadn't seen her in time to whistle, so he'd made that sound instead. Either way, I knew she was coming. I took a deep breath to calm my jittery heartbeat. *Act surprised. Shocked. Scared.* No, didn't have to fake that one.

I could hear soft footsteps over the sound of the crackling fire. When should I turn around to investigate? God, I couldn't bear it anymore. I had to turn. Had to—

"Hi, Jonna," she said, and I felt the cold, hard barrel of a gun pressed against the side of my head. "Fancy meeting you here."

I slowly turned, and I didn't have to fake the shock, either. She wasn't holding the gun Rush had given her. This one was smaller, with a pearl handle.

Which meant it had real bullets in it.

"Beth? What—"

"Get up. Stand right there. Yeah, that's perfect. A

good place to die, don't you think?" She wore a thick cable sweater and jeans and thin gloves on her hands. Her hair was slicked back with gel and tied in a ponytail.

I had to keep my gaze from slipping toward the upstairs bedroom. "Where'd you get that *gun*?" I said, emphasizing the word to alert Rush. That wasn't what I was supposed to say. "What are you doing here?"

"I'm here to kill you. Finally."

"But . . . why?"

"Because Rush wants me, Jonna. Me. And now that we're together, we're going to get rid of you. This was his idea, luring you here. But he didn't have the stomach to do you in himself, so I offered. It's what I'm good at, after all." Her eyes glittered with menace and her smile was feral. "Poor Hadden, who loved you. Gone. And Rush, now gone, too. You've been abandoned."

"You killed Hadden?" Somehow I had the wherewithal to get her to say more about that, though my voice quivered.

"He saw me with Dominic and must have figured out we were working together. Yeah, that's right, sweetie. Dom and I are stepsiblings. And so just as Hadden was about to call and tell you what a naughty girl I was, he slipped." She made a flipping motion with the hand that wasn't holding the gun. "Crunch. Now you'll be together in eternity."

She lifted the gun. She would shoot me. Rush would slide down. And I would be dead.

I nearly sagged in relief when I heard a male voice coming from upstairs—except it wasn't Rush's voice.

"Is that all we were, doll? *Stepsiblings?*"

We both looked up to see Dominic standing at the railing, a mock hurt look on his face. "Come on, Beth dear, tell her how much more we were. How we worked together all those years until you became obsessed with Rush and betrayed me."

Fury blotched her face. "Get out of here."

"Oh, but don't you want to know the rest?" I felt my insides shrivel. He'd been in the house. He'd heard us talking, rehearsing. "You did this all for nothing. I stabbed Rush." He opened his jacket, revealing a knife covered in blood.

The *thump* I'd heard. I sank to my knees as Beth made a keening sound. "No!"

"Oh yes."

While I couldn't cry, couldn't breathe, she screamed, "You . . . you . . . I'll kill you!" She pointed the gun at him.

He shook his head, laughing. "Go ahead and shoot me. The gun isn't loaded."

She pulled the gun back and looked at the chamber. "It is too loaded. What are you trying to pull?"

"Okay, it's loaded; you're right. With blanks." He looked at me, and he was having as much fun with the unveiling as Beth had had telling me about her and Rush. "Tell her, Jonna. Tell her how you and Rush planned all of this, how he gave her a gun with blanks and then planned to bring her down after she *shot* you. How it's all being taped for the benefit of the police."

Beth's cheeks now flamed red. "I don't believe you!"

"Then why is Rush in the room behind me, bleeding to death, when he's supposed to be in New York?" He pulled out his cell phone and tossed it down to her. "Why do I have pictures of Rush and Jonna here, making dinner tonight?"

Beth fumbled and missed the phone. It fell to the floor, where she grabbed it up with her free hand and looked at the picture. Dominic must have followed me and Rush from Boston.

No, no, no . . .

With a scream Beth threw the phone. It ricocheted off a chair and skidded across the floor. "Damn you!"

She kicked me in the side, and I curled up, still more in pain about Rush than anything she could inflict on me. "You *tricked* me? *Rush* tricked me? Tell me!" She kicked me again.

I could hardly breathe for the pain. "Our . . . attorney knows . . . everything. We already gave him tapes of your conversations with Rush."

She kicked me again, this time in the stomach. "You bitch!"

From upstairs Dominic said in an amused voice, "Don't like the feeling of being betrayed, do you?"

"You're enjoying this, aren't you?" she snarled, baring her teeth.

"Hell, yes. And while you're on the news in handcuffs—" he held up a pair—"like the ones Rush intended to subdue you with, I'll be living it up in Mexico on our money. Oh, come on, don't point that thing at me. This one's got real bullets in it."

"So does mine."

She pulled the trigger. The sound exploded in the room. I saw his expression change as the bullet hit. In shock, he looked down where his hand had instinctively clutched his chest, and he slumped to his knees.

I tried to get to my feet. I needed to get upstairs, get the gun from Dominic. To see Rush. She pressed her gun to my back. "Oh no, you don't. First you're going to tell me where the camera is."

Camera. She thought there was only one. I nodded, leading the way upstairs. I could hardly stand as I clutched the railing. I couldn't tell where my physical pain ended and my emotional pain began. My gaze fixed on the gun still in Dominic's hand. He was gasping, wheezing, his eyes wide open. I tried not to feel anything at the sight of him, only focusing on that gun. I lunged for it as soon as I got close enough, but Beth threw herself on top of me and grabbed it before I could.

"I'm not that dumb. Now show me the camera."

"After I see Rush," I said, stumbling into the bedroom. He was lying on the floor, blood seeping onto the Berber carpet. I couldn't tell where it was coming from. "Oh, God," I whimpered. As I started to fall down toward him, she grabbed me by the back of my shirt.

"He's dead." She was staring at him, too. "Bastard." But I saw the pain in her eyes at his betrayal. Even murderous sociopaths could be hurt—or at least their egos could. She turned to me. "The camera."

I led her to the one that covered the far angle of the living room. It was the last confirmation for her that Rush had indeed set her up. She tore it from the banister and hurled it from the balcony to where it smashed to pieces on the floor.

Then she stared at it. "That thing transmits to somewhere." She turned to me. "Where?" She found the computer before I could answer. When she turned the monitor on, she could see the three remaining camera frames. Only two were activated. She scanned the loft and found the other camera. "One's downstairs. Where's the fourth one?"

When I hesitated, she hit me in the chest with the side of her gun. "Where?"

"The kitchen."

"They're taping, I presume. Which means I have to take this thing. Unplug everything."

I took my time, squeezing precious moments out of unscrewing the monitor's plug.

"Carry it downstairs." She held the gun on me as we returned to the living room. "Where are the other cameras?"

I pointed each one out and she tore it down. "Get a garbage bag and put all the cameras in it. Including that one," she said, pointing to the broken one in the living room. Once I did, she said, "Let's go. Carry the computer." She picked up the bag.

"What? Where?"

"I don't know if the neighbors heard the shot. Obviously Rush wasn't worried about that because he *wanted* the police to come. Good thing I decided to use my own gun."

She pushed me toward the door, jabbing the gun into my back as I went.

"In your car," she said. "I parked all the way down by the theater. No one will notice it until the last movie is out. By then I'll be back."

"What are you going to do to me?"

She motioned for me to drive. "Make you suffer like you made me suffer."

"Beth, you can't get away with this. Our attorney knows everything. He knows about our plan, about you and Dominic working together, and about our suspicions that you killed Hadden and Cammie, too."

That surprised her, probably the part about Cammie.

"He's expecting our call tonight. If he doesn't hear from us, he'll call the police."

Her mouth tightened into a grimace. "Nobody can prove anything. I didn't kill Rush. And as far as anyone knows, you killed Dominic. Then you ran and, in your grief, killed yourself. Now, get in."

I did, but I couldn't see through my tears. I was the one who was supposed to be in danger, not Rush. No matter what he said, I still felt responsible for bringing this onto us.

"Drive!" she commanded, hitting me in the shoulder.

I did, blinking furiously. "Where are we going?"

"Just drive north. I . . . I've got to think. You could be lying about the attorney," she said, more to herself.

"But you can't take that chance. If something happens to me, you'll be suspect one. It's over, Beth. Give yourself up now. If Rush and Dominic survive, you won't be charged for their . . . their murders."

I wasn't sure which was worse, a killer who had a plan or one who was desperate and had no hope. I didn't even care what she did to me. All I could see was Rush lying in his blood. I started crying as we drove through town, huge, breathtaking sobs, and I couldn't stop.

Through my sobs I could hear Beth talking to herself. "Dominic may have had an idea, but Mexico's too far away. They'll have found the bodies by then. I could get into Canada. That's not far from here. But I'd have to kill you now. Can't cross with you or this gun, probably." She rubbed the gun that was lying in her lap pointed toward me. "The question is, where? And how do I get rid of your body? And more important, how do I make you suffer so terribly your guts will feel as though they've been wrenched out?"

"I already do!" I yelled, and the car swerved.

"Do that again and you'll die right now."

That was preferable to dying in some suffering way, but I stayed on the road.

"I've heard of biker gangs who kidnap women and keep them drugged, use them as sex slaves, sell them to other gangs." She looked at me. "They'd even pay me for you. Then you'd disappear." I saw her smile from the corner of my eye, and it sent chills through me.

As I drove, I sank into a deep, dark place, resigned to die. I wasn't sure how long we'd been driving when she screamed, "Pull over there! Look! Bikers."

My heart skipped as I saw at least twenty bikers and their bikes at a truck stop. They wore black leather jackets and smoked and stomped their feet to stay warm. I pulled in slowly, hoping that if she were to actually try to make some transaction, I'd have a chance to bolt. I wasn't sure if she really meant to sell me into slavery, but the prospect did just as she'd hoped—it scared the hell out of me.

"You have got to be kidding," she said, and I looked

at the group more closely. On their jackets was "God's Angels." "Keep going."

I whispered a thank-you to God and pulled back out of the parking lot. It started to snow as we crossed into Maine. Flurries filled my headlights like a snow globe all shaken up. Beth was chewing on her fingernails. She kept fiddling with the radio, searching for news, I guessed, about a bizarre double murder. I had barely been able to contain my grief, but hearing that would shatter me. So far, nothing more than a report forecasting snow.

"I screwed up," she muttered. "I should have killed you at the house."

"Then let's go back." I wanted to return to Rush. I hoped the police would be swarming the place by the time we returned.

"It's too late."

I felt the venom of her stare, but I kept my eyes on the road, the darkness surrounding us.

"Do you know how hard it was to be your friend?" she said. "I hated you for stealing Rush that first night we all met. You put yourself between us. He smiled at me, and then you got in the way."

I remembered it very differently. She probably believed it had happened in the way that justified her actions. Just as she'd believed that he had "felt her out" in the conference room when he really only wanted to know how to reach me.

Rush.

I choked back a sob, which she obviously interpreted as grief over how she felt about me.

"Yeah, I hated you. But I pretended, so when you and Rush broke up, I'd be there. Not for you, for him."

"He was never attracted to you," I said.

"Yes, he was. I could see it. I could feel it. But he felt obligated to you, so he fought it."

"Then why did he set you up?"

She backhanded me, and I felt the metal of the gun cut my cheek. "Because you convinced him to! Somehow. Someway. You manipulated him into it. Just like you slimed your way in that first night we met him."

She wouldn't believe anything else, so I stopped arguing.

"Everyone betrayed me," she continued. "My mother, Gary, Dominic. Rush."

"I was the only one who didn't," I said quietly.

"Shut up."

The station announced a caller with road news, and a woman said, "Just wanted to let your listeners know that there's a roadblock on Interstate Two going over the New Hampshire border. Traffic's not backed up too bad; they know what they're looking for. But it's a slowdown."

"Thanks for letting us know. We'll try to find out what's going on."

Beth turned it up, hunching over as though that could help her hear better. A few minutes later: "We checked with the authorities about that roadblock. Details are sketchy, but what we did find out is that a Boston woman has been kidnapped. Police are tracking the vehicle's movements and roadblocks are being set up, but we can't say where those roadblocks are. We'll update you further as the story develops."

They knew. *They knew.*

"Dammit!" she screamed, pounding the window with her fist. "How did they find out? The police went to the house on the beach, found Rush and Dominic, you're missing, but—"

"Rush," I said, feeling hope and joy gush through me. "He's alive."

"How do you know that?"

Way up ahead I saw brakes light up the night. Blue police lights pulsed. A roadblock. Or perhaps the police coming our way.

"The man said the police are tracking our movements." I wanted to laugh, to scream even. "Remember when Hadden told me that Rush was using his SIChipX to track me? He put a GPS tracking device on my car. And the only way the police could know where we are is because Rush told them. He would have had to turn on his laptop and pull up the software. He's alive; he's alive."

"Oh no, you don't get your happy ending," she said. She shoved the gun into my side. "Turn around. Go down that road we just passed."

"The police know where we are. It doesn't matter where we go. It's over."

Except now she had more reason than ever to kill me. And I had more reason than ever to live. "You know how you're always talking about weak links. Well, you're the weak link in your life, Beth." As I made the U-turn, I stomped on the gas pedal.

"What are you—"

The car flew off the road and down a steep embankment into the woods. All I saw was a murky, flooded area coming at me fast. The air bags exploded when the front of the car hit the ground, and mine punched me in the face like a super-sized boxing glove. I heard Beth hit the door and slump to the floorboard. After pulling my dazed thoughts together, I wrestled the air bag aside and tried to open my door. It wouldn't budge.

I heard Beth groaning, trying to get up. I pulled harder, grunting with the effort. Finally the handle gave. The car was at an angle, which required more effort to open the door. It took every bit of strength I had left to push it open enough to slide out. I fell into cold water that sucked my breath away. I thrashed through water and vegetation as I scrabbled up the incline to the highway.

I felt something clawing at my ankle. At first I thought it was the tangle of brush. Then I heard a frustrated grunt. Beth! I'd thought she'd be knocked unconscious for longer. I kicked, trying to dislodge her. My feet slid, and we both tumbled down. The car was out of sight from the road. Beyond I could hear the occasional vehicle fly past. And sirens wailing, passing us by. The police knew we were somewhere on this road, but not that we'd gone off it.

"Bitch!" she said, pushing me down into the water by my shoulders. "You've screwed everything up."

I kicked her off, not wasting my breath by saying anything back. She fell backward with a splash, and I tried to make it up the swale again. I could barely breathe. The cold sucked my energy away, too. It felt like one of those nightmares where you can't move. I heard her breathing hoarsely behind me. The snow swirled down faster and faster. I breathed in a snowflake and started coughing.

She pulled on me. I looked back but could barely see her in the darkness. With my other foot, I reared back and kicked hard. She let out an *oof*, and I heard her tumble down and splash into the water. My fingers slipped on the dormant grass. I dug in, feeling dirt wedge beneath my nails. I finally got enough of a grasp to pull myself up.

Behind me I heard her panting as she climbed up. I staggered toward the highway, waving my arms. This stretch had no lights, no nearby businesses. The cars were coming too fast and couldn't see me in the dark. I couldn't risk jumping in front of them. I had to get their attention. How—

Beth tackled me, and we both went down on the shoulder of the highway. "You won't win!" she screamed. "I won't let you!"

"Is that what you want? For us both to die?" I yelled as a car passed so close its tires spit gravel at us.

"You're the only one who's going to die."

She was trying to roll me onto the road. I heard sirens again. They'd tracked us down. They were coming!

She heard it, too. She lifted her head and looked for the flashing lights. The police car was behind a semi that was heading our way. "No," she said. "No."

I had barely gotten to my feet when she said, "The next ride's yours," and pushed me into the road.

I staggered, trying to gain my balance as an oncoming car blinded me with its headlights. He blasted the horn. I dove into the northbound lane and hit the asphalt, skinning my hands. When I looked up, she was standing in the road waving at me. Waving good-bye. I turned and saw the semi coming right at me.

Everything seemed to slow down, each second dragging, each image stamping itself on my brain. The flashing lights behind the semi. The blinking light on the truck's grille. The tires turning. The truck pulling into the other lane so the cop could pass. The screech of the brakes when the driver saw me. Tires trying to grab asphalt, skidding. The smell of burning rubber.

And Beth, still looking at me with a strange smile on her face. Her face lit by the headlights. Waiting for the truck to hit me. Not realizing the truck was aimed at her. Then turning. Seeing the semi bearing down on her.

I saw the flurries in the headlights. I saw the terror on her face. Then I squeezed my eyes shut at the horrible sound of metal hitting flesh. Of something dragging along the asphalt as the truck ground to a stop.

Poetic justice, some part of my brain whispered. Then I collapsed.

EPILOGUE

Two weeks later . . .

Rush and I sat in my favorite overstuffed chair and watched the foamy waves wash up on the rocks. The morning light shone through the window, spilling over the newspaper in our laps and lighting up my purple fuzzy slippers. The fit was tight, and I had to be careful about not pressing against the knife wound in his chest. But sitting close was more important.

"It's the first day there hasn't been something in the paper," he said. "The scandal has finally died down."

I pressed my cheek against his arm. "Maybe we can resume our lives again."

He tilted my chin up so that I was looking at him. "I was serious about taking some time off. You don't have any upcoming engagements." He kindly didn't mention that was because of all the publicity. "And I've already stepped away from AngelForce for the time being. I was thinking about a couple of months abroad. All those places we talked about before . . ."

Before he was stabbed and nearly died. The knife had just missed his heart and lungs. He'd lost pints of blood but somehow managed to get to the phone and then to his computer. "A sheer act of will and desperation," he'd told me after he'd come out of surgery. Fading in and out of consciousness, he tried to guide the police to my location.

"That sounds wonderful. It'd be great to be anonymous for a while."

Everything had exploded. My secret identity. The blog. Beth, Dominic, and their possible connections to Cammie's and Hadden's deaths. Beth's and Dominic's deaths had cheated us out of seeing them tried for their crimes. I'd told Hadden's parents that justice had been served, in its way. No, Beth hadn't stood trial. She wasn't sitting in prison. I told them what her last moments had been like—the same as Hadden's.

Our only saving grace was that the blog was gone. Arthur had used a bit of legal coercion to force the Web site owner to remove all traces of my personal ramblings and confessions. Now my so-called blog friends were coming out of Internet anonymity, claiming their spots of fame as participants in the most intriguing crime to hit Boston in years.

Rush and I, we were enjoying the first real sense of peace and connection we'd ever felt in our marriage. Like his wound, our souls were healing, too. We'd come back here once the police had finished picking over every inch of the crime scene and the blood had been cleaned. We wouldn't let Beth spoil this place or what we'd found together.

Instead we focused on the good that came out of it. We would never again take each other for granted. We would never take life for granted, either.

In two days his family was due to arrive. David was flying in on Christmas Eve. My parents would come soon thereafter, and we would all spend Christmas together on the ocean.

I closed the paper and let it drop to the floor. "Montene is dead at last."

"Mm, that's too bad. I rather liked her." He gave me an impish grin.

"I'm not Montene," I reminded him. "I was pretending."

He stared into my eyes as though he were looking into a crystal ball. "I don't know about that. I see her in there. What's she doing? Ah, she's drawing a silk tie between her fingers. And giving me a sultry come-hither look." His mouth touched mine so softly and briefly it left me wanting more. And that was his intent, as he moved back when I leaned forward.

"She's a figment of my imagination."

"Are you sure?" he whispered, so close that I felt his mouth brush mine as he spoke.

I felt a stirring deep inside, that same flicker of heat as when Rush had acted on my supposed fantasies. "Yes," I said. "No." I kissed him, and this time he didn't move away. "Maybe there's a little of her in there."

I felt him smile as we kissed. "I say we find her."

He stood, reaching out his hand to me. Maybe we couldn't put all the ugliness behind us, I thought, as he pulled me toward the bedroom. But we could paint it beautiful colors. And that's what we did.

ACKNOWLEDGMENTS

Many thanks go out to those who took the time to help me with my research!

John May, co-author of *Every Business Needs an Angel* and managing partner of New Vantage Group, who graciously answered my many questions about the fascinating world of angel investing.

Antonio "Tony" Sanchez, MSM CLET, CFS Captain, Biscayne Park Police Department, who has kindly answered questions for three books now.

Carlos Vasallo, Jr., of Ocean Environments, who answered my many "fishy" questions.